Dusk
Deepens

J. E. Kestner

Dusk Deepens

Cover design by Henry Hyde

Map design by Jensine Williams

ISBN 978-1984094582

Printed in the United States of America

To my readers.

I had my expectations and you blew every single one of them out of the water. Thank you for allowing me to share my words with you.

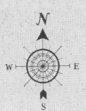

CEJ

STAVEEN

ROLOSA

KIRAT

DETDA

TRIYER

THE MAINLAND

TELYON

CORDAVI

MICOO

SAMEW

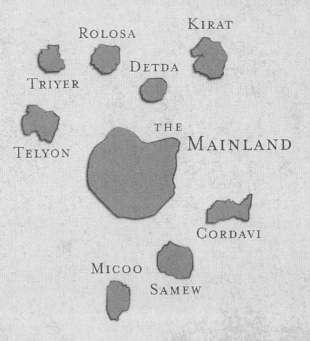

One

*S*HE HUNKERED AS CLOSE TO THE WET EARTH AS SHE could stand. The rain, which had fallen for the better part of a week, had seeped through each layer of her clothing until her base layer clung to her skin. As she loosened a button near her collar, she imagined she could see a line of steam rising as her body, hot from running, tried to dry her wet garments. She supposed she should be thankful for the muggy heat. It was hard when the rain fell as if its sole purpose was to drag her body heat to the puddles at her feet. Though exertion had reduced her breathing to short gasps, she wished their captain would order them forward again, knowing the movement would create warmth her body could horde against the inevitability of the cold.

Without a sound, the patrol's healer slipped beside her. As a child, she had grown accustomed to his wraith-like movements, thus she did not react when most others would have been startled. He was on the young side of middle-aged, but his hair had already converted to a steel gray. No one remembered his premature gray once they saw his eyes. Though they were plain gray, what they lacked in color they made up for in intensity. She had once feared those eyes. Then she had hated them. Now she loved them, finding in them all the paternal care she had been denied by her absentee father. He nudged her playfully with his elbow.

"How are you managing, Vircel?" he asked.

"Apparently poorly if you have been reduced to using my last name," she said.

"If you prefer, I could call you Anney banney. That always cheered you up when you were little."

"Who says I need cheering up?" she asked, playfully shoving him back.

"In this rain? We could all stand for some cheering."

"You could suggest to Ridge that we find a place to sleep tonight with enough cover for us to build a fire. That would cheer all of us enormously. Not that I need cheering, mind you," she said sarcastically. She had barely said the words when their captain materialized behind them.

"Aiden. Anne. Need I remind you of our policy concerning talking whilst on patrol?" he asked seriously.

"If you could, *Captain,*" Aiden said, a smile in his voice.

"That isn't funny, Aiden," their captain said frowning.

"Easy, Ridge," Aiden said, wrapping an arm around his companion. "We were partners far before this promotion. You know you have my full support, even on a pointless scout in this beastly rain."

"The council believes there are pockets of remaining Gruilitians hiding in the Hytines. They want to eradicate the barbarians before they can gather again."

"A commendable project if there ever was one! But we haven't seen a trace of a raiding party in three days. They have returned to their cursed woods with their tails tucked between their legs. We would be better used helping the Deteenians route the main body of Gruilitians to end these raids for good."

"But we have been assigned here, friend. Take heart. If there are no sightings by tomorrow, our orders are to return to the main body," Ridge said, almost apologetic. Aiden squeezed his friend's shoulder again before releasing him.

"You're a good captain, Ridge. I'm sorry if I make your job harder. You know I would follow you into the maw of death if you asked me. I simply reserve the right to jibe you when I can, *Captain.*"

Anne had always loved listening to their banter. Even Ridge's wife good-naturedly likened the pair to an old married couple. It comforted her now as other thoughts crept into her mind. It was hard to imagine the raids coming to an end. They had begun just prior to her permanent assignment to a patrol two years earlier. Since then, her days had been filled with guerilla warfare and a constant need to look over her shoulder for a Gruilitian raiding party. She would be eighteen in two months, yet she felt that an old woman's cynicism had etched itself into her spirit after witnessing all the savage images only a war could produce. That cynicism uncovered the anger she and Aiden had fought against for years. That fight was not nearly as bitter as it had once been thanks to the efforts of her mentor, whose joking exterior was a clever cover for his profound and patient soul. Regardless, she was ready to see the end of these raids for good.

Suddenly the trio heard a movement in the woods ahead of them, and they all froze in diligent watchfulness. At first, they only saw mist curling around the trees. When a flash of red appeared and floated briefly in the undergrowth, they all breathed a sigh of relief.

"That boy needs to shave his beard," Ridge muttered. "It is almost unnatural how red his hair is, and it is more noticeable on these gray days."

"If he shaved, we would never find him. I have never seen a man more adept at staying undercover than him," Aiden said.

The red-bearded man they were discussing was walking toward them, cutting short their discussion. Scaina was a handful of years older than Anne, but he was already broader than many of the older men. Up close, his hood couldn't hide his shock of red hair that matched his beard. Its fire stood in stark contrast to his by-the-book personality, much like the paradox of his size and gift for stealth. Though it seemed impossible, his normally serious features appeared even more solemn as he looked to Ridge, who, along with his companions, matched Scaina's gravity in an instant.

"What is it, Scaina?" Ridge asked.

"There is something you need to see," Scaina said in response.

Ridge asked no more questions. He gave a staccato bird call and pointed in the direction from which Scaina had come. Anne found her partner, a well-built man in his mid-twenties named Criheast. There was a question in his eyes that Anne answered with a shrug. Answers for both of them would come as they followed the scout. The rain forgotten, the pair followed Aiden and Ridge.

Anne's gut clenched when she saw what Scaina showed them. She had seen decimated villages before. Aiden had found her in one when she was only a child. Yet, no matter how many times she had seen them, she couldn't get used to seeing the skeletons of homes which had once housed families. The carnage was recent. Some of the puddles were still tinged with the dusky red of blood. No one said a word as each set of partners scattered throughout the village to look for survivors. Because Anne and Criheast started near the center of town, they found the atrocity first.

The villagers were piled high in a revolting heap, their lifeless bodies contorted in grotesque angles, as if to mock the idea of survivors. Staring at the abomination, Anne was thankful for the rain. It didn't wash away the blood seeping out of the horror before them, nor mask the atrocious smell of death, but it softened both. The partners stood staring in silence. The others soon joined them in a gathering around the heap. Though she was young, Anne had seen a great many terrible things, yet none of them drew tears from her. Not even this, though it was among the worst she had ever witnessed. Instead, the longer she looked at the pile, the harder the cold, furious ball in her chest became.

"How did we miss this?" Criheast whispered.

"The fog covered the smoke. The rain covered the rest of the evidence. There was no way we could have seen it was happening," Aiden said, curtailing his words into short bursts.

"We may not have seen them coming, but we know where they are going," Scaina said, pointing to a line of tracks that led through the mud and into the mysterious Hytines toward Gruilit. The group looked to Ridge in silence. They knew the order he would give, but waited for his formal, spoken affirmation. Ridge turned his burning eyes a final time to the sham of a mass grave.

"You know what to do," he whispered. He drew a shuddering breath before pursuing their quarry. The patrol, needing no other words, followed their captain, righteous indignation in their wake.

Night was only a few hours away when they began their search. As best as Anne could tell, the carnage had happened within the last day, which meant the Gruilitians would be camping relatively near the village. The trail of footprints was narrow, making it impossible to tell how many enemies they pursued. Anne knew their small group of eight had no hope of annihilating the Gruilitians, but, with surprise on their side, they could inflict a fair amount of damage before a forced retreat. Then they would melt into the woods to bide their time for another attack. This type of warfare was exhausting, but Anne didn't waver. She was determined to chase down this evil and stop its advance.

The day was fading into the tricky shades of twilight when Ridge held up his hand, signaling the patrol to stop. The eight of them caught their breath in silent gasps as Ridge motioned for Scaina and his partner to proceed forward. The pair disappeared into the rain. Anne strung her bow and Criheast checked his sword. When the time came, she would fire into the enemy camp while he moved forward to take advantage of the confusion. Then she would join him in fighting with their swords until their advantage was lost.

Scaina returned and signed his report. The Gruilitians were camping a quarter of a mile ahead of them. There was a score and a half of them, but they were settling in for the night without fear of attack. Only two guards were posted, and there were hidden inroads. In response to the report, Ridge signaled orders to the scouts. The partners would position themselves with one set of partners at each of the camps four corners. At Ridge's signal, they would rush forward, and inflict as much damage as possible before retreating. After acknowledging the command, the group split into their partner sets. Anne and Criheast found a spot on the southeast side of the camp where they could clearly see the enemy. The Gruilitians themselves were as barbarous as their customs. Their bodies were covered in dark paint that etched the horrid faces of their gods into their skin. Stark against the paint were long gashes running down their arms and chests — gashes that were self-inflicted during the bloodletting ceremonies they performed as worship. If this was not vile enough, Anne could make out jewelry made of the fingers of their enemies. Anne grew hot to think how many of those fingers had belonged to the innocent villagers murdered that morning. The trill of a bird broke the silence. A few of the Gruilitians noticed, but paid it only a passing notice. Anne nocked an arrow while Criheast drew his sword and pulled a knife from his boot. With baited breath, they awaited the second signal.

When the bird call rang out again, Anne took a steadying breath and fired at the nearest guard. He fell with a scream as an arrow sprouted from his chest. His companions turned to see what had happened, giving Criheast time to speed forward into their ranks. He threw his knife into the nearest soldier and, while running, deftly switched his sword to his strong hand. He cut into a man who stood fumbling with his weapon without pausing to make sure if it had been a fatal strike. A wounded man could be taken care of in a second attack while an uninjured man still posed a threat. The next man Criheast met had managed to unsheathe his sword and the two met in battle. Anne saw one of the Gruilitians rushing to attack Criheast and she felled him with her second arrow. Firing once more, she drew her sword now that she was close enough for it to be the deadlier option. Upon drawing it, she saw their advantage had been spent. The Gruilitians were grotesque in their practices, but they were disciplined and not easily shaken.

All the partners heard Ridge's retreat signal simultaneously. The Gruilitians were dividing their forces into four groups to defend themselves. Anne looked for Criheast and found him locked in battle with an able foe. She could tell Criheast would best the man, but she also saw another large man approaching him from behind. Without thinking, though the man was a full head taller than her, she jumped in the path of the charging man and locked swords with him. Her arms jarred under the strength of his blow, yet they held. The man's face twisted into surprise before snarling at her. He was so close she could feel his hot breath. She snarled back even as she felt her knees buckling beneath his superior strength.

"This is a fight you cannot win," he said with a growl.

Her defiance sparked, she pushed up against him until she once again stood at her full height. He leered at her, already eyeing her fingers as potential jewelry. She stretched herself a little taller then ducked down and to the right. He stumbled forward, but still had the presence of mind to strike out at her. She felt the sharp bite of his sword as it grazed her side, but she was already dealing a far more serious blow of her own. In one, lightning movement, she had planted her feet and used the strength of her stance to drive her sword into the side of his chest. She could see the tip of her sword exiting near his opposite collarbone. The sword stayed lodged in his chest cavity, and, as she maintained her grip, it pulled her forward with him. She landed on top of him and saw a look of sheer disbelief in his eyes as they faded into death. She only saw his gaze for a moment before Criheast pulled her to her feet, wrenching her sword from the body, and pushed her back toward the woods.

"Go! Go!" he yelled, already following her as she ran into the woods. They ran blindly. They would regroup with the others once they were sure they were not being followed. After being on the move for only a minute, Criheast grabbed her elbow and pulled her to a stop.

"Wait. Listen!" he said.

When she obeyed, she heard the wailing the Gruilitians reserved for the death of a chieftain. She grinned a little at the sound. The attack had lasted three, maybe four, minutes, but it had been long enough to drive a thorn into the enemy's heart. Cautious relief flooded Anne and Criheast. For the Gruilitians, the death of a chieftain called for prescribed ritualistic mourning. Perhaps they wouldn't pursue their attackers.

"Anne, that man you killed, did he have a sun tattooed on his cheek?" Criheast asked.

Anne closed her eyes to remember. She saw his furious eyes first, so sure of themselves, and mocking her supposed weakness. She forced herself to look wider in her mind's eye. There, beneath his left eye, was the tattoo of a sun. She nodded to answer Criheast's question.

"I thought so. I recognized him from an earlier raid. That wailing you hear? You caused it."

She began to grin again, but this grin was swallowed in a spasm of pain. The adrenaline of the moment had caused her to forget her wounded side. It would not be ignored now.

Clutching at her side, she felt the sticky blood on her fingers. Suddenly, she was lightheaded. Criheast quickly assessed the situation before supporting her in his arms. He lowered her to the ground, giving some relief to her swimming head. She felt him loosen her leather jerkin so he could look at the wound. Her hiss of pain matched his grunt of disapproval as he pulled the last piece of fabric free. Immediately, he pressed a wad of her torn jerkin against the wound, worry etched in his face. In vain, she waited for him to give a report.

"How bad is it?" she asked, breaking the silence.

"I've seen worse," he said, giving her a wry smile. She tried to match his grin, but shuddered in pain instead.

"Let me see," she said once the spasm was past. Though they both knew it was unwise to remove the dressing, since doing so destroyed any newly formed clots, he acquiesced her request, as she would have done for him. At first it was difficult to make out the extent of the wound due to the dying light of the day, but she finally managed. It started a few inches below her left armpit, traveled down her ribs, then snaked toward her navel, etching a crass smile into her now avulsed skin. Criheast was right though. The wound was grotesque and bled freely, but it wasn't deep. The width of the cut was worrisome, but Aiden had patched together worse. She could count herself fortunate.

"Your ribs did their job," Criheast said, applying pressure again. "I can see them now that the bleeding has slowed. If his blow had begun in your abdomen, we would be having a much more serious conversation. It looks like his swing became wilder the farther it went, which is why the wound becomes so jagged on your stomach. You should be fine for now, but there will be issues if we don't get you to Aiden soon."

She didn't try to respond. She was concentrating on slowing her breathing to manage the pain. Pinpricks of fire were igniting into raging conflagrations around the wound, and if she allowed herself to dwell on it, she wouldn't be able to move. Criheast understood. He was already tearing long strips of cloth to make field dressing. She listened to the tearing fabric as it intermingled with her own ragged breathing. She wanted Aiden. He would know how to make everything better.

As Criheast began to wrap her side, she noticed a subtle, but significant change in the noises around her. She strained her ears into the fast approaching night, trying to make sure she wasn't mistaken. And she wasn't. The sounds of the woods had faded to an unsettling nothing.

"Criheast. Listen."

He paused his work and strained his ears. The longer he strained to hear, the more the intensity of his demeanor increased. Only deep and utter silence filled the woods. That could mean one thing. For some reason the Gruilitians had ended their mourning prematurely, which meant they could have left their camp. She and Criheast were no longer safe. They needed to move. *Now.*

Criheast tied off the hasty bandage with concise movements. Anne, biting down hard as she sat up, pushed back the pain and prepared to flee through the woods in hopes of regrouping with her comrades. Criheast gave her an apologetic look before tossing her uninjured arm around his shoulder and standing her on her feet. The edges of her vision gave way to a white that began encroaching toward the middle. It cleared in half a second, but she begrudged losing even so short a time.

Criheast was already on the move. She struggled to match his long strides her best days, but now it was a necessary agony. They moved southeast, away from the Gruilitian camp. To distract herself, Anne scouted possible hiding places along the way. Neither endeavor was successful. Criheast tried hard to retain an element of stealth, but it was nearly impossible to do and still support her. She cringed at the sounds of breaking twigs and crunching brush they were making. Hopefully, the cover of night could be trusted to protect them from malevolent eyes.

Such trust soon proved futile. Over her ragged breathing, Criheast's grunts of exertion, and the ringing in her ears, she could hear their pursuers crashing recklessly through the underbrush at an incredible rate. Even if she hadn't been wounded, the pair would have been hard pressed to elude discovery. When she looked at Criheast, she could see the same understanding etched in his face. She bit her lip in determination to continue forward as doggedly as possible until their inevitable apprehension. She tried not to think of the terrible things she had heard from the few who had escaped Gruilitian captivity.

While she was in the middle of such musings, Criheast stopped in a clearing. She sucked in a sharp breath as new pain coursed down her side. She thought she knew why he had stopped. If they couldn't outrun their foes, then it was better to make a last, desperate stand.

"I can still draw a bow," she said, trying to keep her voice from shaking.

Criheast nodded. He didn't look at her, though. His eyes were flitting around the perimeter searching for something. He spotted a small outcropping of rock to their right and, leaving her standing on her own, went to investigate. Upon pulling several piles of dead leaves out of it, he discovered it was a small cave. Rushing back to her, he roughly pulled her toward it and man-handled her inside before she realized what was even happening.

"No!" she said, fighting back. "I won't hide while you meet the enemy!"

"I'm not going to fight anyone," he said. "I will lead them on a merry chase through the woods. Once I have them chasing their own tails, then I will come back for you. I promise."

It was a suicide mission. They both knew that. She fought against him again until she saw his eyes. They were pleading with her to allow him to do this. They had been partners a long time, and she understood what he felt. He wanted to save her, just as she would have wanted to save him if the roles were reversed. She didn't want to lie and wait in the moldering dark doing nothing, but she surrendered and allowed him to tuck her inside and cover her with the leaves. Once she was hidden, she heard him pause a moment before dashing into the night.

Then she was alone in the dark with nothing but her pain.

The air was dense as she breathed through the rotting leaves and fought the rising nausea they magnified. She subdued it in time to hear footsteps approaching. She stiffened. It was dark, and there was no way anyone could see her hiding spot. Yet a cold sweat ran down her spine. The intense silence of the night was the only sound to greet her ears. Then, soft as a cat, the footsteps began again. They were coming toward her and stopped only a few feet from her hiding place. Terrible foreboding wrapped itself around her as the stillness deepened. She closed her eyes, bracing herself for whatever would come.

ANNE WOKE, DRENCHED in a cold sweat. She shivered even though the night was temperate. The dream, the memory, had come back to her with all the vivid details she had forgotten since she had been seventeen. Her hand crept to her left side and felt the raised scar running all the way to her navel. Being in Aiden's house brought back all of those memories, both good and bad. Most had been good, but it was the bad ones that haunted her sleep.

She thought of Criheast, Scaina, Ridge, and the rest of her lost patrol. During her time at Decedeo, she had not neglected these ghosts of her past life, but being in Aiden's home put flesh to them. She had once been so sure of herself, and she had remained sure of herself while she had been the Lady of Decedeo. But she had defined herself as the Lady for so long she was unsure she remembered how to be a warrior anymore. She was rudderless in this new life, as frightened as she had been as she hid from the Gruilitians, wounded and alone, all those years ago.

She settled back into the covers. The empty space beside her was a chasm she couldn't bear to come to grips with yet. She had no tears left inside her. They had melted into the abyss of Henry's absence. Within that abyss she was still able to find a song, though. It had never abandoned her. Not when she had been orphaned or left for dead, and certainly not now as her past came careening back into her life. She knew she could be strong for her children with the help of that song and Aiden's steadiness. She also knew how impossibly hard it would be to straddle the rift between who she had been and who she had become. She wondered if, in light of this fact, her dreams weren't banes, but blessings. Perhaps they were given to her to help her remember who she was. Or perhaps they were a call to stand firm. She had to believe there was more to them than reminders of loss. Only time would tell.

Two

SUMMER 261

ROSE'S LIFE HAD BEEN FAR FROM CHARMED. HER SOUL was marred by a patchwork of scars so raised she could almost feel them through her skin. Yet, though they felt unjustly earned, she had learned to live with them in the thirteen years of her existence. Not only to live with them, but also to find happiness in spite of them. She possessed a litany of golden memories that cast her scars into twilight. That is, until now. Now those memories had to be locked away in the name of self-preservation. She could not think of the Poynters or Decedeo. Not anymore, not since she had betrayed the remnants of their family. Yet she longed for them, for they had been her one solace. Before he had been lost at sea, Leonard had been a comfort to her. She had accepted, if not grown accustomed to, his death, and she supposed she would have to do likewise with the Poynters now. No one was left to her but the cold man destined to be her father. She supposed she should have been bitter at the way things had turned out, but she couldn't gather enough emotion to function, let alone feel bitter.

Staring out the window of the carriage, her glassy eyes comprehended none of the scenery. She could no more recognize landmarks than fathom in how short a time her life had been turned on its head. Eight, short days ago she had been happy. Despite the void she felt at not being a true Poynter, she had found the closest thing she knew to peace in their home. Pain warmed on the edges of her stone heart as her happy memories began to creep out of the stronghold she had built for their banishment. Soon the pain would storm her defenses, overwhelm her, and drag her to despair so deep no song could ever find her. She wrenched herself free. The pain of breaking away devastated her for only a moment. Then the comfortable weight of numbness fell back upon her. She gave herself to it, body and soul.

Verderva was only hours away from Decedeo, but it could have been days as far as she was concerned. The woods she had wandered so freely slipped away without even the ceremony of her recognition. When they arrived at the boarding school she saw strange people everywhere. Some grabbed her trunks. Some talked to the driver. A Lord and Lady greeted her. She had the vague impression they were kind people, but she didn't care to know them.

The Lord and Lady led her many places. A classroom. A large hall. A garden. The edges of each were blurry with surreality. The gentle voices of her guides floated as if from a great distance, lulling her to a sleep she now realized she desperately desired. Though they were still walking, she stopped. Falling over her like a blanket, exhaustion started at the top of her head and slowly moved down. Its warmth filled her ears with cotton, and the blurry edges of her vision laid claim upon the entirety of her sight. What little resistance she had to offer conceded defeat as she fainted, and gave herself to the shadow's warm embrace.

She had been deceived though. The sleep she allowed herself was haunted by dreams, both dark and convoluted. She saw strange faces and heard terrible commotion all around. It all fell on her, shattering her into a thousand pieces, and there she lay. Discarded. Expendable. Guilty. She could perhaps still be salvaged, yet she could think of no one who would intercede on her behalf. This was her lot, to be weak and foolish, and thus unworthy of her true name.

Waking in an unknown room, she stared at the dark, foreign ceiling with the memory of her nightmares lingering near. Tears leaked out of her eyes and dragged with them soft sobs which refused to stay demure. With horror she recognized the guttural wails assailing her ears as her own. But she couldn't stop. It was the first time she had cried since the night her father had locked her in the cellar. She found the tears released pressure, but relieved no pain, like pus from a wound already turned septic.

Then, underneath the weeping, she heard something so familiar it almost instantly filled her with comfort. It was a song someone had sung to her in another life, a life where someone held her and told her they loved her. It quieted her tears enough for her to realize she was being gently rocked back and forth in someone's arms. The song persisted. It slipped past the darkness and burrowed under the guilt until she could almost imagine she had gone back in time and was being held by Aunt Anne. She let the memory wrap her up, and she held onto the song like it was a lifeline, its ending notes slowly disappearing like bright sparks from a campfire.

"I saw you had the poems of Rohirt in your things. A book so dog-eared must be well loved. I am glad you know his songs."

Rose didn't know who this woman was, but her voice was soft and her hands gentle as they stroked her hair. Burrowing deeper into the refuge of those arms, she caught the faint smell of spearmint. Sleep began to steal over her. Natural sleep, lacking nightmares and demons. She felt herself being tucked in.

"There's a good girl. Sleep now. We will see to your other needs in the morning."

For the first time in many days, Rose obeyed something other than the voice of despair which had consistently called to her. She slept. She woke a few times, always to a different time of day and different faces, yet she always slipped into the comfort of sleep. When she finally opened her eyes without the nag of exhaustion hovering near, it seemed to be morning. A woman was seated beside her bed, engrossed in reading. Rose, while still unnoticed, studied her and saw she was older than Aunt Anne, but wasn't an old woman. Her features had been molded by kind wisdom scrupulously gleaned through the years. With everything about her radiating comfort, Rose's first inclination was to fall into this woman's embrace and confess every detail of her miserable story.

Rose shifted in bed, and the Lady's eyes immediately snapped up from her book. Caught unawares, Rose withdrew instinctively. The friendly desire she had so recently acquired absconded like a thief in the night. The woman's eyes were kind and her smile genuine, but she seemed so pure. Rose couldn't bear the thought of desecrating her with something as dirty as her confessions. She suddenly wanted this woman to leave. It would be safer to never know this kind woman than risk being rejected again.

"Good morning, Rosemary. I am thankful to finally have the opportunity to meet you properly. How are you feeling?"

"Fine," Rose said hoarsely as she sat up in the bed. She hadn't realized how ravaged her throat was until she tried to speak. She couldn't remember the last time she had eaten or had a drink. She grew dizzy at the thought and felt herself falling backwards. The woman lowered her to the pillows. Then, as Rose regained her bearings, the woman fetched a glass of water and helped Rose drink. The water was what she needed, but, believing herself unworthy of concern, she again yearned for this woman to leave.

"Thank you," Rose said. "Where am I?"

"Verderva. Your father sent you to us to learn. I hope you will adjust quickly."

"I hope so as well."

"Can I get you anything right now? You must be hungry."

"No thank you, Lady..."

"Forgive me, I never introduced myself. My name is Lady Diane."

"No thank you, Lady Diane. I am fine for the moment."

Lady Diane searched her over, pity mixing with intrigue. Rose flushed. She recognized Lady Diane's voice as the one that had sung Rohirt and calmed the nightmares. She was grateful, even in all she didn't deserve, but gratitude couldn't cover her intrinsic sins. Lady Diane must go. Somehow, the Lady seemed to understand. Patting Rose's hand, she left her alone. Rose had wanted her to go, but, as she watched her walk away, a part of her wished she would have stayed.

The next day, Lady Diane took her to class and introduced her to hordes of girls. Rose had never known there could be so many girls her age! She shrunk away from their curious looks, longing to disappear. She darted to an empty seat, followed by all those eyes. The teacher called the class to attention, giving Rose a reprieve from their glances. Though the teacher was talking, Rose couldn't hear past the ringing in her ears. Suddenly a folded piece of paper was on her table. She stared at it, uncomprehending for a time, before daring to open it. The message was a simple one, drawn with a loopy hand.

"*Hi Rosemary. My name is Elizabeth. Would you like to be my friend?*"

Casting a glance at the writer, Rose found her to be a brown haired girl with lively, green eyes. The girl, Elizabeth, smiled, stretching the freckles across her cheeks even wider. Rose started to smile back, but the action caused her cheek to smart in pain. Memories from another life crashed over her—memories of her father striking her down to the ground before a crowd of impassive men—men he had chosen instead of her. Anticipating tears, Rose turned away in time to hide them. This was all too soon. Her hands were still healing from the barrage of the cellar door. She could still imagine the feel of Hope's feathery hair tickling the underside of her chin and the strength of Mark's hand helping her into their tree house. She put her face down, leaving Elizabeth's question unanswered.

Days passed this way. Rose didn't know how many—she didn't care to count. She fared acceptably in class. It was hard to pay attention when there was so much going on in her head. Every day found her waking to thoughts of the Poynters. Her mind drifted back to the old routine she had always known with them, and, at the correlating times, she would say to herself, "The Poynters would be eating breakfast right now," or "Mark would be finished with his studies soon," or "It is almost time for me to go home." With her mind distracted by a life that could be no more, she didn't forge any friendships. Not even acquaintances. She couldn't befriend any of the girls as they gossiped amongst each other and giggled over boys. None of that mattered to her, so she vaguely listened before disappearing into her mind again. The girls attempted to call her back at first, but soon they stopped trying. Desiring to be alone, Rose saw it was for the best.

She saw Lady Diane everywhere. As headmistress, the Lady

was a busy woman, making it nothing unusual to see her two or three times a day. Each time the Lady seemed to know Rose was near, found her out, and smiled at her with the radiance of sincerity. Rose cowered from her, unsure why she did, even as she did it. With apprehension she acknowledged their second meeting couldn't be avoided indefinitely.

Lady Diane knew some of the healing arts, and, therefore, summoned Rose to her study in order to change the bandages on her hands. Rose dreaded the meeting. She hadn't spoken unless spoken to by the headmistress since her arrival. Silence was safer. It kept her from revealing the truth of who she actually was. But she knew she would have to speak to the Lady. She was one who asked questions near the heart of the matter, and Rose was most afraid of this. When she was bidden to enter the study, Rose took a deep breath before obeying.

"Good afternoon, Rosemary. Please sit so we can begin."

Rose sat as directed, in complete silence.

"Our healer tells me she is encouraged by the progress your hands are making, and would like me to look at them to see if we can leave the bandages off for good this time."

Rose still didn't answer. Seeming to understand, Lady Diane matched the silence. When she began to unwind the bandages, Rose looked away. She was tired of seeing the jagged wounds criss-crossing her hands. They only served as a hateful reminder of the night she couldn't forget. She felt one hand freed, then there was a pause, then the second hand was unwrapped and freed. She winced at the slight sting of the cloth being pulled free and waited for the Lady to release her hands. But it never happened. Irritated, she turned to see something completely unexpected. The Lady merely sat there, staring at her hands. Rose looked at them, too. They would scar, no doubt. They would scar as badly as her face had after her father had pushed her into a table. Her scarred face and hands would serve as a testament that proved how broken living life was.

"Your father never told us what happened to your hands."

Irritation blossomed to anger before Rose even realized what had happened. It was a question, not a statement, and she wasn't ready to give an answer to it. It was nothing to concern of the Lady. Rose jerked her hands from that gentle grasp and turned to walk away. She paused at the door, her face set toward the timbers.

"Am I free to go, ma'am?"

There was no reply at first, which caused Rose to grind her teeth in rage. She didn't know where these emotions had sprung from, and, in the moment, she didn't care. She wanted to be somewhere where she could be broken in peace.

"When I saw Rohirt's songs in your belongings, I was sure a day would not pass without your voice singing one of them. And yet, I have not heard you sing. Not once since you have been here. Why is that, Rosemary? I pray you have not lost your song."

Rose bolted. Heedless to everything but her need to be alone. Ducking into the first venue of solitude she found, Rose immediately began weeping. Her anger dissolved in those tears, only to be replaced by shame. She had forgotten. She had forgotten all Aunt Anne had ever taught her. She had seen hard times before, but she had always managed to sing. Aunt Anne had been there in those moments, encouraging her song to life. But now, with her mother figure gone, she needed to know if the song had ever been her own or merely borrowed.

She delved into the pit of her mind with purpose for the first time in a long time. She pushed past her usual misery wallowing and searched deeply in the archives of her memory. There, buried just below the haze she allowed to hold her captive, she found her song. Grasping the melody with her intellect, she felt its familiar weight. But she was afraid to sing. She was afraid singing would bring more pain or be a well of cursed water. The choice to sing was a difficult one, especially when she remembered how easy anger had been. Her heart's cynical edges reveled in anger. It would be simpler to allow these growing callouses free reign.

It would be simpler, yet she knew it wasn't right. The hope she had professed to could allegedly transcend any circumstance she found herself in. The question now was if she could have faith in it. Did she or did she not believe the stories of the Great King? She found her answer laying inches inferior to the question's skin. Of course she believed. She had claimed personal rite to belief years ago. The truth hadn't changed, which meant it could still be found in the exact same place.

The first few notes were hard. They had to push their way past the cynicism and defenses she had built. Even when the tune finally came free, it escaped with tentative steps. She sang to the end of an entire verse before stopping. Her defenses pushed back against the melody, making progress difficult, but it was a start.

Weeks trickled by after her first song. She attempted to sing everyday as the now familiar numbness threatened to overpower her. Some days she gained ground and others she lost it, but she persevered. She persevered even on the days she could hardly drudge up a tune, though through no strength of her own. The dog eared pages of Rohirt became exceedingly more so as she poured over them. She could almost hear Aunt Anne's voice reading the words as they ran through her brain. With the passing of the weeks so too passed the anger in her heart. She was weary, confused, and hurting, yet the anger had been sung to sleep.

She began to realize something about herself in those weeks. She needed help. There was so much she didn't understand, and if she could speak it to someone then maybe it would help order her thoughts. However, she was terrified to be fully known. If anyone truly knew her, knew her failure and treachery, she would be despised. It was her lot, she understood as much; however, she abhorred the thought of Lady Diane's looks of pity changing to disgust or Elizabeth's freckled smile falling into a scowl. Yet she couldn't carry on much longer with the weight of her entire story crushing her. She knew who she needed to tell. She stood outside the Lady's door screwing up her courage to knock, knowing that as she did she was passing the point of no return.

"Rosemary! What a pleasant surprise. What can I do for you?"

Rose didn't pause; she feared she would leave if she did. With abrupt purpose she sat before Lady Diane. Her heart raced as all her fears scrambled to find a home there. But she knew this couldn't wait any longer if she was going to survive.

"There is something I need to tell you. It's about something terrible I have done."

She started at the beginning and left nothing out. She talked about her early life, how lonely it was with her father noticing only to belittle her, and Leonard ignoring her for the most part. Then their move, her meeting with Mark, and how terribly insecure she had felt with him. Yet he had been her friend when everyone else had cast her off. She talked on and on about the safe place she had found with Uncle Henry and Aunt Anne. Her own home became a solace when Leonard began to change. But then he had died, and she had been discarded, forgotten, and told she'd never been wanted. She even spoke of her conflicting emotions toward Hope. She was ashamed even as she spoke of feeling replaced by the child, but she couldn't stop the avalanche of words now. She steamrolled on to the awful moment when everything had changed, not sparing any detail of her cataclysmic failure.

It was done. Hours had passed, and she hadn't stopped speaking in any of that time. Everything about her, everything she felt and feared had been shared with this woman who was more stranger than anything else. The weight upon Rose's chest had lifted making her breath come easier, but she couldn't look up. She was so afraid of what she would find in the Lady's face. Her courage spent after her confession, she stood without even looking up.

"I'm sorry," she whispered before turning away.

"Stop!"

The voice sounded as if the owner had just wakened from a dream. Rose turned back, not knowing what to expect. She was shocked to find Lady Diane's cheeks wet with tears. They regarded each other tearfully for a time before the Lady opened her arms to Rose.

"Oh child," was all she said and all Rose needed. She entered the embrace, and the two of them cried silently for a time. Rose reveled in being known, fully known, and accepted nonetheless. For such a thing to be true was unimaginable even in the wildest of her daydreams. Her song gathered strength in the Lady's embrace, and it was only then she realized how perilously close it had come to dying altogether.

Little else was said that night. Little else needed to be said. Outside the study, she paused with her hand on the doorknob and pondered the mess of healing wounds there. The cuts had closed up leaving a landscape of pink scars behind. Their haphazard wanderings were as confused as she. They would probably always be there. But as she looked at them now she was convinced they weren't as wide as they once had been. Slowly, from the edges, the scar tissue was morphing back into skin as pure as if nothing had happened. She was too weary to smile, but her heart lifted.

The next day she went to class and sat in her normal seat. Her loneliness had followed her as usual, but today it bothered her. She didn't want to be alone anymore. She wanted help in the dark places she was sure to face. She scribbled a note on a piece of paper, and slid it onto Elizabeth's desk. The girl looked confused at first, before meeting Rose's eye. Rose's heart fell slightly until a verse of Rohirt sprang from her mind. Elizabeth opened the paper to read the simple message.

"Is it too late to be your friend?"

Elizabeth's ready smile soon stretched her freckles across her nose while her green eyes danced in delight. Rose couldn't help it. She smiled back.

Three

*L*EONARD STARED NORTH. WHENEVER FEDIC WASN'T wrenching his arm from its socket, or Intoya wasn't finding work for him to do, Leonard could be found staring toward Deteen. He found no answers in the endless blue. He heard no whispers in the humid breeze. He found no steadiness beneath his feet no matter how much he desired it. But it was comforting to look toward everything he loved. He feared that if he didn't look north, he would forget everything and everyone he loved. He couldn't do that. Not when there was so much, so many people, he wanted to remember. People like Clint, the Poynters, and his father. And Rose. Little Rose he had promised to take care of. He could never forget her.

Fedic appeared beside him. No words were said, yet Leonard winced instinctively. The healer of the *Exem* didn't like him, and he found ways to take his frustration out on Leonard. Namely the *exercises* he said were necessary to regain full function of Leonard's arm. Leonard knew little of the healing arts, but he knew the exercises to retain his range of motion made tears come to his eyes, leaving him miserable for hours. Leonard never uttered a complaining word though. Whenever the healer was particularly vicious, Leonard fought to bite back the angry words that sprang to his lips. Being a stranger in a strange place, Leonard could little afford to gain enemies with people who were eager to hate him. He submitted for a deeper reason, though. In a way, Leonard understood Fedic. The healer was being asked to care for a man who had killed his countrymen. Leonard remembered the boy he had killed during his first battle. He had watched that boy die with his sword, buried to the hilt, in his chest. That boy could have been Fedic's brother, or cousin, or friend. If not Fedic's, then he was someone's son who would never return to Staveen. So Leonard bore Fedic's retribution patiently, hoping to gain redemption if there was any to find.

"Do you have another round of exercises today?" Leonard asked, praying for a negative answer.

"No. Your arm is doing better. We should be able to scale it down to working it every other day."

Leonard allowed himself a small grunt of approval, though inwardly he was dancing for joy.

"Then, to what do I owe the honor?" he asked, when the healer was reticent to be forthcoming with further information. Fedic was silent, his arms crossed in front of his chest. Leonard waited. He knew the man would speak when he was ready, and not a moment sooner.

"We will arrive in Telyon tomorrow. Captain Intoya wants me to answer any questions you may have about our way of life. Apparently, he doesn't want you to feel anymore out of place than necessary," he said with a snort. "I told him you will stand out, no matter what we do to you."

"Your confidence is inspiring," Leonard said dryly.

Fedic rounded on him with surprising vigor. There was barely controlled anger emanating from every pore of his body.

"This isn't a task I relish. I came aboard to heal my countrymen who had been wounded, not babysit the one who had inflicted the wounds. You're right, I have no confidence in you. You have proven yourself to be a barbarous people who kill first and ask questions later. Intoya believes your story about being deceived, but many don't. Many of us would prefer to see you indicted rather than instructed. But my captain has asked, and I will obey. So I ask again, is there anything you want to know about Staveen or can I declare this meeting over?"

Leonard bit back his own anger at the unjust accusation. Fedic wanted to fight. Everything about him screamed his desire for Leonard to throw a punch. Any excuse to loose his venom on him would do. Anger wouldn't solve this problem, though. A verse from Rohirt drifted through his mind, and he closed his eyes to better hear it. He didn't realize he was humming audibly until he opened his eyes. The blaze of Fedic's fire had gone out, though the heat remained. Leonard wondered if progress was being made with this proud man.

"All I know of your country is it is filled with valiant men whose swordplay exceeds our own. Anything else you wish to tell me, I would be grateful to know," Leonard said.

Fedic turned to the north with a set jaw. Leonard repressed a smile when he saw how striking a resemblance his companion made to a sulking child.

"It is best we begin at the beginning then," Fedic said, still staring north. "As you know, Staveen is a country of island nations. There are ten islands all together. Cej is the farthest island to the north, and because of that we have very little contact with them. It is also the second largest island in all Staveen. The largest island is simply called the Mainland, and the remaining eight islands surround it. We are from the island of Telyon, and the others are called Kirat, Rolosa, Detda, Triyer, Cordavi, Samew, and Micoo."

Leonard's head swam as new ideas and names assaulted his mind. He wanted a map to look at so he could sort all the islands into some semblance of sense. He had no such luxury, for Fedic was already continuing with his lesson.

"As you can imagine, each of these islands has limited resources due to their size. We have always been people of the sea. In fact, legend says our ancestors sailed from Peros to escape the power of the Lessernoms. Legend also says the islands used to live in harmony together," he said with a humorless laugh. "It is assertions such as these which make me doubt the legends. If there ever was a time of peace amongst the islands before now, then it has been lost in the storyteller's tales."

"But you call yourselves the Allies. How can this be if you have always been at war?" Leonard asked.

"I will come to this in a moment. There is a little more history to cover before we come to the present. Like I said, with limited resources and a history of sailing, we raided each other in times of war and bickered with each other in times of tension. The Mainland, as the largest island, houses the necessary resources we all covet. Each island staked a claim upon its soil, and that soil was irrigated with generations of bloodshed. We were on the verge of destroying each other completely. Even the simplest of children could feel the stirring of the dark magic."

Leonard's brain stopped working for half a second before whirring into action at a thousand miles an hour. Dark magic? It existed still? He had read of it in Rohirt, but he had assumed it had disappeared with the Magic. He struggled to find the right question to ask first, but it was too late. Fedic was moving on again, and Leonard had to pay attention to stay abreast of him.

"There were men who saw how close to oblivion we were. They saw, and they took action. They called for, begged, advocated, and demanded a cease to the hostilities. If it had been a few men on a few islands, nothing would have come of it. Thankfully, it was men from every island who banded together to this cause. It took years of diplomacy, but a central council was established on the Mainland. After more years passed, the council came to a unanimous decision to come together. The Alliance breathed its first breath a mere twenty-five years ago. It was a shaky breath, but it was alive."

"That was an eventful time for both of our countries it seems," Leonard said. "That is only a few years before the Gruilitians raided our northern border."

"Perhaps it was the powers that be balancing the scales. Peace here necessitated war somewhere else."

"Hmm. Well, if you could send us a message next time something major happens in Staveen so we have time to prepare, we would appreciate it," Leonard said. He looked from the corner of his eye to see how the stern man responded to the joke. He was encouraged to see a half-smile pulling the corner of his mouth.

"Our alliance has been tenuous at best. Some years have been better than others, but recently it has been a strain to remain cordial on the Mainland. The central council can hardly find anything to agree upon anymore. One thing we could all agree upon was our contempt of Cej. They had refused to join our alliance, preferring their own raiding parties. They kept to themselves, but they managed to find time to harass us every so often. Every island in the Alliance is militarized for the most part, but only as a combined force did we stand a chance of launching an offensive against them. And, even with all of our pooled resources, we could not be sure of victory in the end.

"About two years ago, a Telyonian council member suggested to the council that we sail to Agumbra, namely Deteen or Raboneetha, to seek an alliance. With either of these countries on our side, we would have a sufficient force to destroy the Cejan threat. With our shared contempt of the pirates, you would think it would be a relatively easy endeavor to persuade the council toward this course of action. Unfortunately, the council can never make anything easy. Three factions soon appeared. Triyer, Micoo, and Kirat adamantly opposed any course of action, stating the pirates did not meddle in our affairs enough to risk open warfare with them. Rolosa and Samew were not against the plan, but they were wary to say the least. Cordavi, Detda, and my home of Telyon wished to seek immediate implementation of the plan. Back and forth they argued until a majority agreed to send a small envoy of ships to Deteen. Rumor said they would be more accepting than Raboneetha.

"The rest, as they say, is history. We arrived only to find ourselves ambushed by pirates on Deteenian ships. We retreated and yet we were followed by these same ships a few months later. We did not wish to fight, for, though we outmatched them in skill," he said with a pointed glance toward Leonard, "Their numbers were far greater than ours. We sustained heavy losses.

"Needless to say, the council was less than impressed. Since we returned a year ago they have been doing nothing but debating the best course of action. Though now, any civility they once had has been thrown to the wind. Some want to try again — Captain Intoya being one of them. He was actually the last ship situated so far north when he found you. Most disagree. In fact, they disagree about everything. This venture has taken an already shaky alliance and placed it in a hurricane. There have been rumors..."

Fedic's words trailed into oblivion. It was almost as if he had forgotten he was talking to Leonard at all. With wistful eyes, he stared out at the sea he called home. Leonard waited in silence. He wanted to hear more, but he was afraid the spell would be broken if he spoke. He waited in vain. Something clicked into place in Fedic's features. When they became the hard lines Leonard had grown used to seeing, he found it hard to mask his disappointment.

"I have said too much," the healer said. "Is there anything else you would like to know?"

There were ten billion things Leonard wanted to know. However, looking at Fedic's face, Leonard knew he would be allowed only one detail. He sifted through all the information he had just been given to pick the best question.

"You spoke of the dark magic. Does that mean you are privy to the Magic as well?"

Fedic, making no effort to hide his confusion, looked him over as if to assess his earnestness.

"Of course we are. Not many believe in its usefulness anymore, and choose not to contact it. Mainly our wielders, who are most in tune with its power, interact with it. It's only a matter of the depth of your relationship with it."

"Relationship? You don't control it?"

"Of course not. When you have a relationship with it, then you are able to ask of it. We could no more control the Magic than we could control the sea. Do you mean to say you have no experience with it?"

Leonard felt an ache he hadn't realized he had. The more he

nosed into the feeling, the more he realized it had been there his entire life. He felt the sudden need to weep, to mourn this emptiness he'd never known was there. He turned his shining eyes away, ashamed for Fedic to see them. Fedic was surprisingly quiet. Leonard appreciated that.

"I think the Magic has been dead in Deteen for a long time," Leonard said, his throat clutching. Fedic made no response. Rather, the pair stared across the waves again.

"We will arrive in Telyon tomorrow. It would be best if you kept to yourself for a while once there," Fedic said. Concern was a strong word for the emotion twining in his words, but they were softer than any he had ever spoken to Leonard. Once alone, Leonard continued his northward watch, mentally preparing himself for the unknown paths before him.

THE SPECK ON the horizon had grown larger and larger as the day progressed. Leonard, not having been given anything else to do, watched it. The sailors of the *Exem* had grown used to, if not accepted, his presence aboard their home and left him alone. Some had even begun to jibe at him as they did each other. It was awkward and intermittent, but Leonard didn't mind. He was building a good reputation among them. Hopefully, he could continue this work once he was on the island. Tracings of an idea were forming in his mind. If he could establish himself as a peaceful man who had been deceived by a mutual enemy, then maybe he could become an ambassador for his country. Leonard remembered the eyes of his king as they met his in the council hall. There had been a desire to end hostilities there, Leonard was sure of it. If he could convince the allies of Staveen of this, maybe he could go home. That was his ultimate goal. No matter what else, he had to go home.

As they were approaching the dock, Fedic appeared at his side. Leonard knew he didn't have to acknowledge the healer, so he continued to watch the scurry of activity on the pier. Deteen's navy had never been strong, and her fishermen explored the Nameless Ocean in boats half this size. There was always activity on the docks, but nothing compared to this. These men had been raised with a singular heritage. Their fathers had been sailors, as well as their fathers, and their fathers before them. They moved with purpose and speed, and speech didn't seem to be a necessity between them. Everyone knew his purpose and trusted his companions knew theirs. As he watched them work, Leonard truly felt the gravity of his nick-name; Land-Walker.

"Your people know their trade well," Leonard said.

Fedic merely grunted. His eyes were narrowed, as if he were trying to figure out a particularly difficult problem. Leonard didn't push any further. He knew he could never force a confidence from this man. When they were secured into port, Fedic finally spoke.

"Something is wrong," he said. "Stay with me, Leonard Clifton."

Leonard obeyed. He didn't know why Fedic was acting with such caution, and he didn't want to discover the reason in a way he would later regret. The *Exem's* gang plank was lowered onto the dock, and her sailors walked down it gratefully. However, Leonard noticed their joviality had dampened significantly. Feeling even more like a foreigner, Leonard tried to figure out what the others saw that he did not. Fedic walked to the dock where he was a approached by a man about his own age. Each of them touched two fingers to their foreheads then their lips, in greeting. Then, with a smile, they embraced.

"Vicene," Fedic said. "It is good to see you again, cousin. It's been too long."

"It has. I am glad you're home. Many things have happened since you've been gone."

Leonard was studying Vicene. He could tell the men were related. They shared the same black hair, lanky arms, and strong jaw line. He was still comparing the two when Vicene caught sight of Leonard. His face immediately darkened. Noticing at the same time, Fedic and Leonard were equally put on edge.

"Who is this?" Vicene asked.

"A land-walker we pulled from the sea," Fedic said, moving between the two ever so slightly. Leonard didn't know if Fedic's action was conscious or not, but he was grateful for it nonetheless. Vicene appeared stormy.

"You should not have brought him here," Vicene said.

Leonard began to notice his surroundings. The other sailors of the *Exem* had greeted cohorts as Fedic had. As they told tale of who they had pulled from the sea, the other Telyonians became wary, even angry. They were looking at Leonard with suspicion and hostility. Some were beginning to stand in a knot and talk amongst themselves. Some scurried away, obviously intent on fetching something, or someone.

"You could not have chosen a worse time to bring a land-walker here, Fedic," Vicene said.

"Why? What happened?" Fedic asked, urgency slipping into his voice.

A knot of men were approaching now. Those who had disappeared had returned with men in uniform, their swords menacing on their hips. Leonard felt his mouth go dry.

"The Alliance has broken, Fedic!" Vicene said. "The council finally broke it apart while you were gone. Everyone is on edge right now. Those who aren't worried about war are furious at the land-walkers for attacking us. It will be an act of mercy if all they do is throw him in prison!"

The men had arrived. They glared at Leonard, and Leonard did his best to stand his ground beneath their looks. One of the uniformed men approached, walking directly toward Leonard. Intoya was there now. He had obviously been informed of the situation, for he stood squarely in front of Leonard with his arms crossed. The armed man hesitated at this defensive show from the captain.

"Captain Intoya, I must arrest this man," he said, respectful yet unapologetic.

"What crime could he have possibly committed? He has only just stepped off the ship."

"He's a land-walker, an enemy. Telyon has declared a state

of war since the alliance broke. He must be incarcerated on that basis alone."

"I will vouch for this man. He is no enemy. His people have been deceived by the Cejans. They did not know what they were doing."

"So he says," the armed man said with a scowl. "But anyone who allies with pirates cannot be a man whose word I trust."

"This is an outrage! He is one of us! He has done nothing wrong!"

Intoya was shouting now. The man and the crowd behind him were growing increasingly hostile toward the captain. Leonard could tell the armed man respected Intoya, but that would only stay his hand for so long. He had a job he felt justified in doing. This mob was scared and angry, and they wanted blood. They would prefer only Leonard's blood, but if it needed to come to Intoya's as well, Leonard believed they would take it. Leonard could not allow that to happen. He placed a hand on Intoya's shoulder.

"Captain, it's all right," he said, stepping out from behind him. Intoya began to say more, but Leonard begged him with his eyes to stand down. The message relayed itself, and the captain bit his lip instead of speaking. Fury and concern mingled in Intoya's face. Leonard stepped toward the armed man, who wasted no time spinning him around and jerking his arms behind him to bind his hands. Leonard's sore shoulder screamed in pain, causing him to instinctively pull away. The next thing he knew he had been forced to the ground with the guard pressing his head into the dock. His ears were ringing from the blow, but he could still hear Intoya shouting.

"What are you doing?" the captain bellowed.

"He jerked away from me. He could have been reaching for a weapon."

"He was shot in the shoulder, you fool!" Fedic said. "I have been working with his arm, but it is still painful. He jerked away because of you jerking him."

"I am well within my rights as an enforcer!"

"To ruin all I've accomplished as a healer? Remind me to not bother attempting to heal anyone while you are working since you'll only break them again!"

Things were getting hot again. Leonard's head was aching, but his ears were done ringing, and he was able to gather himself enough to speak.

"Fedic, no!" he said as best he could from the ground. "I'll be all right. Let him alone."

From his prone position, Leonard couldn't see the interactions of the others, but the silence which followed his speech encouraged him. He felt his hands being bound behind him before he was dragged to his feet. He saw Intoya was furious still, but remaining silent. Fedic looked at him with a new expression that was impossible to read. Leonard nodded to him instead of trying to discern. Then the enforcer pulled him away. Leonard grit his teeth in pain as his wounded shoulder was twisted while he was led forward. He saw a few of the crew of the *Exem*, but he was moving too quickly to see their expressions. Traversing on, the enforcer led him through town to what seemed to be the center and there he pushed Leonard inside a cramped building. Upon entering the oppressive space, Leonard saw there were a few empty cells around the perimeter of the room. The enforcer cut Leonard's bonds before pushing him in one. Then he left Leonard alone. Sitting on the floor of the musty cell, he massaged his shoulder and tried to figure out what had gone wrong. The alliance of Staveen had broken. He was a prisoner of a war he hadn't known existed. He wasn't going to be an ambassador. He wasn't going home.

Days passed. He couldn't be sure how many. There were no windows in the building, and the meals appeared sporadically. He waited, and tried not to think of home. It was hard because home was all he could remember. He hoped little Rose was faring better than he. What he wouldn't give to be with her again! When he was beginning to think he couldn't stand the solitude any longer, he received a visit from an unlikely person. There, in front of the bars, stood Fedic assessing him. Leonard looked back and waited for the healer to speak first.

"You are a remarkable man, Leonard Clifton."

"You sound reluctant to admit as such," Leonard said.

"I am. Against my better judgment, I trust you. I have never seen a man bear unjust pain as patiently as you have."

The healer pulled a set of keys from his pocket and unlocked the door. Leonard, though confused, stood and walked to Fedic, facing him eye to eye.

"Does this mean I am free?" Leonard asked.

"No. Not in the truest sense. I have bound you to me. I was advised not to, but I have."

"What does that mean?"

"That means you are free due to my good standing as a citizen. I have agreed to share responsibility for your guilt. Whatever crimes you commit, I will also be punished for them, because I have agreed to accept you as mine. In return you are allowed to walk among us under the protection of my citizenship."

Leonard looked at the stern man standing with his arms crossed and his eyes glaring. His entire posture spoke of a man acting against his own reason. Leonard didn't fully understand the magnitude of the gift Fedic had given him, but he understood enough to know it was a true sacrifice. Whatever it was or wasn't, it was a lifeline of hope to Leonard. Now he had a chance to prove himself to these proud people. Now he had a chance to go home. He bowed his head in respect.

"You will not regret it," Leonard said.

Fedic snorted, and turned toward the door.

"I better not," he muttered.

Four

$\mathcal{T}$HE DARK CEILING HUNG UNCOMFORTABLY CLOSE. AT first, Mark had thought he was uncomfortable because he was in a new home. He and Morgan had beds on the main floor, while his mother took residence on the second floor. That meant his ceiling was not as tall as his mother's was, and he blamed the cave-like resemblance of the low ceiling for a time. But, as he gazed at the imposing entity above him, he realized neither of these were the reason. It was something deeper and more recently acquired.

He heard the timbers above creaking. He pressed his eyes shut until they hurt. His mother was dreaming again. A month after their world had imploded still found her tossing and turning through the night as if in hopes of outrunning the frightening thoughts in her mind. Some nights she would wake with a stifled cry. Usually, she bit it back so quickly he wondered if he had actually heard her. He didn't mind those nights, though. It was nights like this one that ground down something inside of him. He knew she couldn't escape her agony, no matter the depth of her desperation, and that meant she was human, with human weaknesses and fears. She was still the strong woman he had always known, but now he was seeing the weakness his father had always shored up.

When the creaking continued, he had to be somewhere else. It was suddenly imperative. He slipped outside without Morgan stirring. Morgan had a small barn for his horse. Mark thought about stealing inside to find comfort with Armon, but claustrophobia clawed up his throat. He couldn't be inside right now. He needed to be somewhere where it was open. He needed to feel the wind on his face. He scrambled up to the top of the barn, wrapped his arms around his legs, and waited for the comforting touch of the wind.

Ever since he had been a little boy, the wind had fascinated him. Its very essence was a mystery. Its force was capable of gently soothing a baby, or powerfully bowling over livelihoods. It was a respecter of no man, yet it allowed itself to be captured in the sails of a boat. However, the wind's dichotomous nature wasn't what interested him the most. Nor was it the invisibility of its hand as it shifted the tangible in its path. It was the stories it told as it whistled past him that captivated him. There was no telling where the wind had been before it had found him. Perhaps it had come from the depths of the Hytines or maybe it had swept across the swells of the Nameless Ocean. The possibilities were as long as the distance it could travel. It could have touched the life of another and brought their song to him.

If that were true, then perhaps the wind was taking pieces of himself and giving them to others. Maybe the same breeze drifting across his face had first touched a member of his lost family.

He clung to such a tether between what had once been and what was now — a tie that grew more tenuous each day. The world was changing, as was he, through avenues he didn't fully understand. Some days he felt young and healthy, and other days he felt dreadfully old. On the good days, he still saw the turret of smoke roiling from the heart of Decedeo whenever he closed his eyes. On the bad days, all he could see was Sir Richard's icy eyes preparing to kill him. Every time he remembered that unspoken death threat he felt the same shaky feeling in his knees. He hated how weak it made him feel, but he couldn't stop the feeling once it started.

And those were just his waking nightmares. The night afflicted him with more acute tortures. It was then that he dreamed of Rose. Some nights he dreamed of the sweet moments they had shared; the ones she had willingly chosen to disregard. Other nights those idylls were ripped apart, and she became a monster or phantom who laughed at his pain. Those were the nights he woke with burning tears in his eyes and a wrenching rage inside him that felt like it was twisting him apart.

The mornings following those nights always brought guilt. He wanted to believe in the existence of another explanation, one that cleared Rose's name. Yet everyday was filled with overwhelming silence. He tried to fill the silence with activity, stifling the screaming accusations that threatened to rip through his mind. He couldn't keep his wrath boxed away when he heard such screaming. He felt himself baptized into it, and it was like a fire that burned bright, even when he managed to box it away. And so he enveloped himself in numbness.

All Agumbra had once been a safe and beautiful place. And it still could be, but it was harder to see. Because of all that had happened to him, he had been able to peer behind the curtain into the inner workings of all he'd taken for granted, and his line of sight was littered with broken vessels which had once held joy. Now he awoke in the mornings, stared at the ceiling, and, almost physically, picked up the burdens he had dropped the night before. There was no joy in greeting the morning now — only low-grade despair, world weariness, and mental calculations of what he should do.

He tried to sing the old songs, but he doubted their message now. It was hard to believe that everything had once been wholly right when it was now wholly wrong. It was too hard to believe in a land called Peros when Agumbra was so jarringly cruel in its reality. It was hard to have courage when his heart had left him. It was hard to forgive when anger felt so much more satisfying. It was hard not to be cynical when disappointment hurt so much. He was realizing it was hard to do a lot of things.

For the past month he had been working hard to escape these thoughts. He had worked hard at whatever task was given him and tried to make it perfect. Morgan was patient in his own way, never belittling, but seldom vocal in his praise. Mark took his silence as disappointment and strove for his godfather's approval with even more fervor. He didn't mind. On the nights he was completely exhausted he could sometimes escape his nightmares, but it wasn't enough. It all felt meaningless.

The wind blew around Mark's ears and he shivered. He didn't know how long he had been sitting on the roof, but it was long enough to leave his joints stiff. Surely his mother was done with her silent struggle by now, and he could spend what few hours were left of the merciless night in the relative peace of his bed. His climb down was more treacherous now that his limbs were stupid with cold. Part of him wanted to fall and trade his mental agonies for mere physical pain. He trudged to bed, fell into it with his shoes still on, and dropped into a restless sleep.

Mark woke to Morgan shaking his shoulder. He blinked owlishly trying to make sense of his surroundings. The soft life of the young morning peeked through the windows as the heaviness of insufficient sleep cloaked his eyes. Momentarily, Morgan's face registered before him. It was difficult to discern the emotion in those stern features, but Mark was positive it was disappointment, yet again.

"Mark, why did you wear your clothes to bed?" Morgan asked.

"I went out last night when I couldn't sleep," he said. The answer caused Morgan to purse his lips.

"That was not a wise idea. We cannot know if you are being watched by the king."

So he was disappointed. Mark should have known. He didn't bother to answer as he sat up in bed. Morgan continued to gaze at him until Mark grew uncomfortable.

"Did you need me for something, Morgan?" Mark asked.

"Yes," Morgan said after a pause. "Yes, I need you to go to town to pick up some supplies. I also need you to find the Hemming boy."

"What do you need Robbie for?" Mark asked, jealousy slipping into his voice.

"I don't need him. You do," Morgan said, turning away.

Mark baulked at the insinuation. He didn't want to need anyone. Rather than enter a pointless argument over the fact, Mark dutifully ate his breakfast before journeying into town. He allowed his mind to wander as he went to the appropriate shops. He still was faced with the same problem he had faced this morning. Nothing he did seemed like it mattered. Agumbra was still broken, and he still could do nothing but watch. He ruminated on these things until he had completed his errands and found himself in front of Robbie's house. Mark almost refused to enter as he remembered Morgan's words. But he missed his friend. They hadn't seen each other since the day Mark had learned of Rose's betrayal. If anyone understood the war inside of his mind, it would be Robbie.

He entered the shop to find a surprise waiting for him. Robbie was there, but he was dressed in the characteristic, blood-stained apron of a butcher. Mark approached the counter, unable to understand. When Robbie saw him, he gave Mark a radiant smile.

"Mark! It's been too long!" he said, stepping around to greet him.

"I guess it has," Mark said, looking his friend over from head to foot. "What is all of this about?"

"I turned thirteen a few weeks ago, so my father began my apprenticeship!"

That was the answer. It struck Mark between the eyes as if in accusation for missing something so obvious. He would be thirteen in a month. He would need an apprenticeship, and Morgan had no pupil. Mark would learn to be a healer. He could think of nothing better to do than to face the brokenness of Agumbra than with healer's hands. He could finally fight back against the darkness that sought to crush him.

He remembered muttering some excuse to Robbie, but not much else. He ran all the way back to the cottage where Morgan was tending the herb garden. He stopped as Mark whirled into view.

"Morgan, will you make me your apprentice?" Mark said before his elder could speak. Morgan was at first surprised, then contemplative. He looked Mark over as if for the first time.

"Walk with me," he said after a while.

He's disappointed in me. He doesn't want me, Mark thought. Dejected, he turned to keep pace. They walked as Morgan, per usual, was quiet with thought. Mark willed himself to be patient, though his hope was fading.

"Why do you wish to be a healer, Mark? You have never

shown an interest before."

Mark didn't want Morgan to know how deeply he was struggling. He wanted to appear strong to his godfather. He chose the safest answer.

"I'll be thirteen next month and in need of a trade. It seems only natural I would study with you."

"Why not ask Andrew to teach you about training horses? You work well with Armon."

"I don't want to be Andrew's apprentice. I don't want to break horses."

"Why not? It is a trade, one you enjoy and have inclinations toward. He is looking for someone, whereas I am not."

"I want to be a healer. Nothing else," Mark said. He was surprised when his eyes began to well with frustrated tears. He had to look down to hide them.

"Then tell me why. Why do you want to be a healer?"

Mark knew he must be honest if he were to stand a chance. He took a steadying breath.

"I'm tired of not being able to fix things. I'm tired of feeling helpless. I want to help."

Morgan received this in silence. Mark allowed himself a shred of hope. The healer hadn't shot it down immediately, which meant he was seriously thinking about it.

"I understand those feelings, Mark. I became a healer for many of the same reasons. But, while this can be very rewarding and useful work, it is also some of the hardest work there is."

"I am not afraid to work. I want it to be hard."

"You aren't understanding me. I can teach you all I know, but you will still be faced with problems that have no answers. You will watch people die, despite your best efforts, and you will not be able to stop it. There will still be times when you feel helpless."

"But not all the time!" Mark said before he could censor it. His confession hanging between them, Mark didn't dare to study it lest he meet Morgan's eye.

"Look at me, Mark."

Mark obeyed. Meeting Morgan's scrutinizing gaze, he did his best to hold his ground. Morgan seemed to strip him bare.

"All right," Morgan said slowly. "I will apprentice you under these conditions. We will not start until you are thirteen. In that time you will learn to appreciate rest. You must enforce this upon yourself. If your birthday comes and you have not learned to respect healthy rest, then we will not begin anything. Understood?"

Mark nodded, confused as to the benefits, yet willing.

"Well Mark? Can you accept these terms?"

He decided. He knew what he wanted.

"Yes sir."

"Good. Then we have a deal."

It was with reluctance that Mark faced his final month before turning thirteen. He couldn't maintain his facade of well being without mind-numbing work to hide behind. The poison in his mind began to stagnate in the hours of rest he imposed upon himself. After suffering this way for a few days, he could stand it no longer. He ran to the solitude of his woods, hoping they were still a familiar friend. For the first time in a long time, he suffered no disappointment. The quiet life-thrum pushing up through the roots kept his angry hollows of silence at bay. The wind swept through the tops of the trees, and he swayed with them until their beckoning branches overwhelmed his resolve, and he scrambled to the tallest apex he could find.

Soon the landscape was in view. He wrapped his legs round a branch in preparation for the wind to blow again. He didn't know what he hoped to find this high off the ground. Rose had once told him he had a gift for deciphering the message of the wind. Maybe that was why he had come. Maybe he was hoping the wind would whisper the secret answer to everything wrong in his life.

He saw the wind brushing the ceiling of the forest as it rushed toward him. He hunkered down in preparation for its blow. It hit him full in the face with an unexpected strength. He dropped his hands for further support as the gale pulled tears from his eyes. It seemed to bear the smell of ash and smoke — perhaps the lingering remnants of his home. Whether he actually smelled these things or not didn't keep the pain of the sad memory from washing over him anew. He gripped the rough bark until his hands ached. Then he realized he had been wrong to ascend and open himself to the agony of remembering. There were no answers to be found here.

The wind ceased at last. However, he didn't have time even to wipe his watering eyes before another, more powerful blast was upon him. This one took his breath and carried it far away. He reflexively closed his eyes and concentrated on listening. He couldn't be sure, but he thought he heard something in the blast. The more he listened the more he was convinced he knew what it was. It was the sound of voices from the village or from a village miles beyond that. It filled him with the unknown longing that had oft haunted him. It made him want to peel back all he could see to find a truer world from whence these voices wove their song. He imagined it was a place where the ache he housed in his chest was an unwelcome intruder under permanent eviction. The thought of a truer world thrumming beneath the broken one filled him with hope he hesitated to embrace. He didn't know what he felt, still such a release of feeling couldn't pass without commentary. He tried to bellow into the wind but found his voice already taken from him, miles away to be heard by another who was astute at listening.

He couldn't explain it, but his encounter on top of the world somehow made his days more tolerable. The wind hadn't answered any of his questions, but it had reminded him there were deeper forces at work. He could either hide in self-pity, or he could take action for the cause of the unbroken world just out of his sight. He wasn't peaceful, but he could find quiet again. In those quiet times he found a semblance of peace, and, for him, it was enough.

It was enough for Morgan as well. Mark's thirteenth birthday came without pomp or circumstance. The lack of ceremony didn't matter. What mattered was that his stoic godfather quietly summoned him to officially begin his apprenticeship. Mark was ready for the work. He was ready to have purpose to his days again. He was ready to learn the skills necessary to save lives. Most importantly though, he was ready to do his part in the fight against the evils which had befallen his family. As far as he was concerned, he would make it so that such evils couldn't fall upon them again. Ever.

Five

*M*ARK SAT BACK TO MASSAGE HIS EYES. HE DIDN'T know what he had been expecting when he had asked to become Morgan's apprentice. He had imagined long days wading through the sick and dying. Morgan would reach into his bag to find the perfect cure which would drag the patient from the jaws of death. He would give Mark a part to play, and Mark would learn in a trial by fire. Those were the most dramatic of his daydreams, but even his tame dreams were more exciting than what he actually was doing.

Morgan had assigned him a daunting pile of books to study. He had told Mark that hands on study would only begin after Mark showed a proficiency with the information the books contained. Looking at the stack now, Mark despaired that he would never know everything he needed to know. If he were fair, he would have to admit the work wasn't consistently discouraging. A large percentage of the time he spent studying was willingly given. He was not only learning how the body worked, but also the ten thousand ways it could cease to work. It was fascinating most days. Today was not most days, though. His eyes felt like they were crossing after hours of reading the cramped writing which filled page after page after page. The headache which had begun in his temples an hour ago was expanding outward now. It felt as if his head would split cleanly in two with the increasing pressure.

He stepped away from his work station. The house felt too cramped still, so he stepped outside into the chilling air. Fall was in her crowning glory. The path to town was weighed down with all the colors of the branches, making the path seem warmer — like a friend leaning in to whisper a secret. Yet, despite the cozy aesthetics, Mark felt his temper grow more foul. This road was a mockery of the trails Decedeo had boasted. There, the fall revealed trees with breathtaking hues around every curve. The fort he had been building with Rose was sheltered in the one tree in a half-mile radius that turned a fiery red. His father had joked it was always easy to find the pair. All he had to do was find the most elaborate flush of color.

Mark flushed. None of those things existed anymore. Decedeo. His father. Rosemary Clifton. It had been four months, but he still couldn't think on those things.

A strange sound deeper in the woods caught his attention, pulling his mind from the shadowy corridors it had begun travelling down and engaging it fully. He forgot his blossoming headache and fouling mood as he followed the sound. It sounded like metal striking metal, but it was too fast to be a blacksmith. If he didn't know better, he would have said it sounded like two people sparring. But he didn't know anyone who could handle a blade with the ferocity the sounds portrayed.

He was only partly wrong. It was two people sparring, but he realized he knew them both. Or at least he thought he did. Morgan and his mother were trading blows at such a rapid pace, it was hard to follow their movements. After a time, he gave up trying and focused solely on his mother. He had never seen her like this. Having grown used to her reserve these past four months, he had begun to think of her as someone who needed extra care lest she break. That wasn't the woman he was witnessing now. This woman was intense to a level that almost frightened him. He was still trying to reconcile these two sides of his mother, when Morgan surprised them both by disarming her. She snorted in frustration as she went to pick up her sword. Morgan sheathed his with an easy grace.

"You cannot be hard on yourself, Anne. It has been years since you sparred with anyone. Not to mention your shoulder, which still needs some work. I am pleased with how much you are still able to execute."

"But it still will not be good enough if Richard decides to send his men for us," she said. "I may as well not have a sword if I cannot stop a single man."

"I think you are underestimating yourself. I know several guardsmen who would have fallen under the onslaught you just put me through."

"Don't patronize me, Aiden!" she cried, pointing her sword

at him. "I want my mentor, not a yea-sayer. I need to be able to protect my son if they come to take him."

"I have never patronized you, and I don't plan on beginning now," Morgan said unperturbed by her display. "You have always tried to accomplish two days' work in one, and I have always told you what you needed to hear. Yes, you need more work, but you have retained more than you give yourself credit for."

"I forgot how infuriating your consistently calm answers were," she said with a wry smile.

They were going to banter. Mark could tell by the small grin on Morgan's face. The thought of the stern healer joking was a foreign concept in and of itself, in addition to everything else Mark had just seen. There was so much he didn't understand about his mother's past, his godfather included. As he tried to muddle through the mystery, he leaned too hard on a branch and broke it. Both swordsmen snapped to attention, their swords drawn and pointed at Mark. Recognizing Mark they lowered their weapons.

"Mark! What are you doing here?" his mother asked.

Mark stepped into the open. He could answer her question, but then it was unlikely he would receive an answer to any of his.

"What were you doing?" he asked, choosing the proactive approach. Her face fell into troubled lines at the question. She looked to Morgan for support. Morgan merely looked back at her, a question of his own written in his eyes. His mother sighed, resigning herself to do this task alone.

"We were practicing. That's all you need to know."

"But where did you learn to fight like that?" he persisted.

"All you need to know is I learned it a long time ago."

"Did Morgan teach you, in the place where you are from?"

"I have told you everything you need to know for now, son," she said, a rare line of anger bridging her eyes. "I will tell you the rest when you are older."

Mark felt hot words rising in his throat. For the first time in his life, he wanted to fight with his mother. He almost allowed his angry words to overflow — to poison the air between them, but he was confused and also wanted to obey. Then he saw her. The stubborn line still furrowed her brow, but underneath it he could see how tired she was. She didn't want to fight, but she also couldn't back down from the position she had taken.

With an effort, he walked away, his head pounding. He had thought that if he turned away he would feel better, but he found now it wasn't true. The frustration he had allowed to build in his chest was only growing. With each breath it swelled until he was breathing in short gasps. He needed a vent of some sort or he was likely to explode.

His feet carried him down the path to town. He hardly recognized where he was going, but the movement kept his anger at bay. By the time he reached town his head was enveloped in wrathful pain. The noise of the square only exacerbated it, and he suddenly wanted a quiet place to put his head down. Thinking there would be no peace at home right now, he decided to visit Robbie. He knew his friend would let him stay without asking many questions.

He had every intention of following through with this plan of going straight to Robbie's house, calming down, and preparing an apology to his mother. No other thought tempted him. Until he saw Caleb. The boy was just standing at the side of the road, but he was sneering at Mark. The sight of that sneer snapped the thin thread of self-control Mark had salvaged. Seething rage overwhelmed him as he walked toward his foe. He realized he had left one fight to pick another, but, casting all reason aside, he walked to within a foot of Caleb.

"Can I help you?" Caleb asked.

"I don't like the way you are looking at me," Mark said.

"I will look at you any way I like."

"You will if you want me to knock your expression off your face."

"I would love to see you try," Caleb said, provoking Mark even more.

Mark didn't remember throwing the first punch. It was a wild attempt, easily blocked, and even easier to counter. Mark saw stars before he felt himself collapse to the ground. He shook his head to push past the pain trapped inside, and got up to tackle his nemesis. Mark had fought Caleb twice before, and he had won two times before. He fully expected to win a third time without an issue. But his rage wasn't enough this time. No matter what he tried, Caleb always had the upper hand, and it wasn't long before Mark was pushed into the ground with his arm pinned behind his back. Snarling with rage, he fought to regain his advantage but could not triumph over his enemy.

"Yield," Caleb panted.

Mark continued to struggle but without success. Caleb twisted his arm farther behind him until Mark could feel a terrible strain in his wrist.

"Yield!" Caleb demanded.

Still Mark refused. Instead he buried his face into the dirt in resignation to all his defeats and impossible desires. He couldn't forget the terrible things he had seen, he couldn't know the secrets his mother harbored, and he couldn't break free of Caleb's hold. A morbid insight crossed his mind as he remembered reading about broken wrists in Morgan's book. He growled in expectation of learning about them first hand. Caleb, sensing this, obliged by pulling harder on Mark's twisted arm. Just as Mark was sure his bones would give, the pressure was released, and Caleb got off him. Mark, allowing himself only a few moments to manage the pain emanating from his wrist, scrambled to his feet, anticipating another attack from his enemy. Surprisingly, he found Caleb struggling with none other than Robbie. They weren't trading blows, but Caleb, intent on beating Mark, was grappling to free himself. Mark watched, massaging his wrist and opting to stay out of the fight.

"Let me go, Robbie! This isn't your fight!" Caleb snarled.

Robbie didn't answer. Instead, he gathered a handful of Caleb's shirt and shook him hard. When his squirming ceased, Robbie pushed him away. Caleb grasped his head and continued scowling at Mark. Robbie refused to move from his place between them.

"I don't know who started this, but enough is enough! You were going to break his arm if I hadn't dragged you off of him!"

"He wouldn't yield!" Caleb said defiantly.

"Go cool down, Caleb! You two have done enough for now."

Robbie, no bigger than Caleb physically, had gained the influence in their group and was able to sway the irate boy. Spitting in Mark's direction, Caleb stalked away. Mark scowled in turn, still massaging his sore arm. Robbie continued standing as a buffer until Caleb disappeared from sight. Then he rounded on Mark, righteous indignation in his eyes.

"Why do I have the feeling you began that mess?"

Mark's headache began overtaking his senses again. Losing to Caleb served to worsen his temperament even more. He didn't want a moral compass right now. He wanted solitude. He began to stalk away, but Robbie had other plans. He ran in front of Mark, blocked his path, and placed a hand on his chest.

"Get out of my way, Robbie," he snarled.

"Or what? Will you hit me, too?"

Mark shoved his friend's hand away, but made no further attempt to pass him. Something in his manner stopped Mark cold, fury and all. The friends studied each other in silence.

"You've changed, Mark," Robbie finally said.

"Many things have changed. I simply followed suit."

"I understand your life has been completely upended. I was there, Mark. I saw what they did to you and your family. I watched Decedeo burn, too. I did everything I possibly could to help you. I still am, for that matter. I have been, and will continue to be, on your side. But Mark, you are becoming someone I don't recognize. You hide away and refuse to do anything with the boys and me. Whenever you do venture out of your self-imposed solitude you're vexed or distant. As far as I can tell, you are so consumed with everything you have lost that you don't see everything you still have."

"Don't condescend to me! What do you know about everything I have lost? How can you stand there and dare to empathize with me?"

"All I know is I miss my friend Mark! I know he had to disappear for a while to survive, and I know he will not be the exact same person as he used to be if he comes back. But I also know I don't like the brooding fool I'm looking at right now. I want to wait for Mark, I really do, but I need to know he's coming back eventually. If he isn't, then I need to know, because I don't want to be around whoever took up residence in his place much longer."

Mark wanted to scream. He wanted to push Robbie aside and storm away to whatever lonely haunt he could find. But he didn't do either of those things. Instead, he silently refused to meet his friend's eye. It wasn't as much from obstinance as it was from shame. The words hurt to hear, but they were the most honest ones he had heard in a long time.

"I want to be your friend, Mark," Robbie said, putting a hand on his shoulder. "You just have to let me."

He paused, allowing his words to grow and gather meaning between them. Mark still wouldn't meet his eye. Robbie sighed before saying, "The boys and I are going to test our boat on the river tomorrow. Will you come?"

"I'll try," was all Mark could muster. It was enough to satisfy Robbie, who finally let him pass. Mark trudged home, his anger brewing, and his pride smarting as much as his arm and head.

MARK WATCHED FROM the trees as his friends prepared their unsteady vessel. They had been working on it, off and on, for almost a month, combining all the efforts of their twelve-year old ingenuity. All of them were inordinately proud of the rickety ship they were now preparing to take down the river. Mark could hear snippets of their conversation as they traded friendly jibes across the bow. Their carefree demeanors intensified the knot in his chest. When he raised his hand to rub it, his shoulder convulsed in pain.

Robbie's words had ricocheted in Mark's mind all night, darting into his anger and leaving pinpoint breaches in his defenses. The truth of those words grappled with his tenacious desire to cling to his angst. The boys began climbing into the boat. As he watched them, Mark continued vacillating. Just as he began to step out of the woods to join the motley crew he caught clear sight of Caleb. The breaches which had grown during the night cinched shut at the sight. The boat drifted into the current without him, and Mark resigned himself to the aching knot in his chest. He stood gazing at his friends and found he couldn't leave.

As he watched, Mark could tell something was wrong. The boat wasn't remaining steady now that it was free in the water. Though the river wasn't wild, its gentle rapids were proving too strong for the handmade craft. Overcompensating, the boys began scrambling to correct the problem, and though well intentioned, their actions proved detrimental. The ship listed hard, dropped into a wave sideways, and flipped. The boys all fell into the water in hapless array.

One by one the heads of the unfortunate sailors bobbed in the water. All except one. Mark didn't see Caleb. Completely engrossed in their attempts to right their boat, the boys didn't notice their missing comrade. Mark's eyes swept the water and spotted his nemesis. He was floating downstream, face down, toward rougher waters, and though buffeted, he remained as listless as a rag doll.

All Mark's hard feelings toward Caleb dissipated in that instant. Mark was moving without knowing it. He ran along the bank, attempting to get ahead of Caleb. Mark knew he had to get to him before he was pulled into rapids that would make navigating a rescue difficult. Finally managing to pull ahead, Mark turned sharply and dove into the water. He cut through the water with powerful strokes and caught Caleb's limp body. Mark could feel the water's undertow beginning to pull at his legs. Flipping Caleb onto his back, Mark also laid on his back and pulled his feet up. Scanning the river, he noticed an eddy to his right, but he had to move quickly if he was going to make it.

Gathering his strength, Mark positioned his arm around Caleb's chest. He breathed once. Twice. Three times. Then he burst forward with a vicious kick. He pulled at the water with his free arm, but it seemed that his efforts didn't accomplish anything. Still, he kept going, desperation aiding his quickly flagging strength. Only when he noticed how close he was to the eddy, did he realize how far he'd come. Just a little farther now.

A surge of victory thrummed through his body as he broke the eddy line. But it was quickly swallowed as he felt the water pull hard on his legs. Clinging desperately to Caleb's listless form, Mark struggled to keep them both afloat in the relentless deeps that pulled harder and harder, first at his legs, then at his hips. He gasped for air but found only a mouthful of water. Something primal roared to life in Mark's brain. His grasp was slipping on Caleb's chest, as was his view of the afternoon sun.

From somewhere deep in his mind, Mark remembered something his father had taught him. Instinct, more than cognizant thought, caused his arms to wrap tighter around Caleb's chest. Without thinking, he willed his body to roll. It was hard to overcome the pull of the eddy at first, but he managed to produce enough momentum to put them both into a sloppy roll. The water's hold on his body broke enough for him to perform a second, more concise, roll. The water released the two boys, and Mark found himself floating in the gentle water of the eddy. Relief washed over his adrenaline shredded nerves.

"They're here! Help me!"

Mark heard splashing as several boys crashed into the water. Relinquishing his hold on Caleb, Mark allowed himself to be dragged to shore. As he lay on the beach, he saw Robbie smiling beside him.

"You're crazy, Mark! Truly! But you saved Caleb's life."

"How is he?" Mark asked, sitting up with a groan.

"He hit his head, but he seems to be coming around now."

Mark looked around and found Caleb. There was a bump on his forehead, but he seemed okay otherwise. The two locked gazes. Mark could see understanding burgeoning in his nemesis' eyes. As he watched it grow, Mark realized he wasn't sure they were enemies anymore. He didn't think they were friends either, but he knew something was different because of the choice he had made without thinking. The only thing he knew for sure was that the knot in his chest had finally begun to dissolve. Their line of sight unbroken, Caleb gave Mark a nod. For the second time that day, Mark acted without thinking. He silenced his anger by calling a truce with Caleb.

Six

*R*OSE BREATHED INTO HER CUPPED HANDS IN AN attempt to warm them. The effort only worked for a short second. The winter wind mocked her attempts to hoard her body heat. Verderva was lower in elevation than Decedeo, which meant winter's fury was far more fearsome at home. Such thoughts stifled any complaints that tempted her lips. That is, until the wind roared past again and left her ears numb with cold.

Yet, despite the chill, she loved this time of year. She loved every season while she was in the midst of it for different reasons, yet this time of year was particularly precious to her, if not for the weather, then for the milestones it held. A new year would be beginning soon, and Rose had always loved the changing of the years. She believed there was something poetic about standing on the threshold of a new year and imagining the possibilities therein. And then, as if to celebrate new beginnings, Uncle Henry's birthday was only a few days after the new year began. He never wanted to honor his birthday with a celebration, but Rose had loved making him a gift. He always accepted them enthusiastically, no matter how small the trinket.

The calloused wind breathed a particularly vicious gust into her face. It stung her eyes and caused tears to well in them. She was thankful for the excuse. Thinking of Uncle Henry was dredging up a different sort of crying. Though she had been at Verderva for almost six months now, time was no closer to healing the anguish of her mind than to healing the scars on her hands and face. To be sure, just as it had softened the raised, unfeeling flesh, it had also taken the initial sting from her sorrows. She found, though, when she looked at her hands in this moment, the cold had mottled them, accenting the harsh scars that covered them. She knew the same mottling would show on her cheek. Hoping to hide the contrast, she breathed into her hands again, despite its vanity, before concealing her face in her scarf.

"Rosemary! Wait for me, Rosemary!"

The sound of Elizabeth's voice stopped her in her steps. Red from both the wind and running, Elizabeth was soon by her side. Far more demonstrative than Rose would ever be, Elizabeth immediately slipped her arm through Rose's, and the pair began walking toward their room.

"Let's hurry and get out of this wind! I must say, it is far colder today than it has been yet this year. I heard Kerri Turley say, yesterday, that she heard from her father that it was going to get much colder before we could expect it to get warmer. She said, that he said, it was this way because the caterpillars were especially fuzzy in the fall. That's supposed to mean it's going to be a wickedly cold winter. What do you think? Do you think how fuzzy caterpillars are in the fall is a sign of how cold it will be in the winter? Or do you think it's just an old wives' tale? I don't know what I think about it. I've seen plenty of caterpillars in the past, who were as fuzzy as could be, but then we had a mild winter or a lingering summer. But then there are winters like this one where the wind seems to freeze the very tears it brings to your eyes."

Rose smiled into her scarf. Many found Elizabeth's constant chattering a nuisance, but, to Rose, it warmed her more than any winter coat. Rose was still reticent to share her story with anyone besides Lady Diane, so having a friend who carried the majority of the conversation was a relief. Rose regarded her friend as she chattered away. She was tall and willowy, like someone had taken a hold of her brown pigtails and pulled her before she was quite ready. Much to Elizabeth's chagrin, her hands and feet had grown disproportionally large compared to her slender arms and legs, giving her an awkward, coltish appearance that was accented by her innate clumsiness. But, whatever physical grace she lacked, Elizabeth made up for in friendliness. Whenever her mouth wasn't forming words, it was curved in a perpetual smile that stretched her freckles wide across her cheeks. Her optimism never failed to buoy Rose's efforts to fight against the darkness, and, even if Rose had shared her friend's inclination for words, she could never have found the best ones for saying thank you.

Elizabeth's words were lost in the swirl of wind as the pair entered the dormitory. It took a few moments before Rose realized Elizabeth was speaking to her.

"Rosemary? Did you hear me?"

"I'm sorry, Elizabeth. What did you say?"

"I asked you what you plan to do over your break. Will you go home?"

Rose blamed her subsequent shiver on the outside chill which had crept in with them. For days she had been alternating between fear her father would summon her home and the pain he wouldn't. She didn't know why she had thought he would send for her. If she were honest with herself, she knew he wouldn't, but that didn't make his absent invitation less noticeable. What she really wanted was some sort of correspondence with Mark. She hadn't spoken to him since that afternoon at their tree house. She could still imagine his resolute face, suddenly pale from the news Robbie had brought, looking at her as he promised to find her. She wondered what had become of her friend. If she knew how to contact him she would write immediately. As this was not the case, she resigned herself to waiting for word which may never come.

"Rosemary? Are you all right?"

Elizabeth's question was soft, but it still jarred Rose back to reality. Glancing toward her friend, she saw that her lively green eyes were narrowed with worry. Rose smiled sheepishly — an attempt at banishing that worry. The effort was as in vain as her earlier attempt to warm her hands.

"Yes, I'm all right. Forgive me, but what did you ask again?"

"I asked if you were going to go home over break?" Elizabeth asked, still looking concerned she had missed something important.

"No," Rose answered, forcing lightness. "I was planning to stay here."

"You cannot stay here!" Elizabeth said, completely aghast. "How terribly lonely it will be to be the only girl who doesn't go home. Why, even Nancy Huss is going home! She lives south of Port Havenda, and never gets to go home over break because of the distance. Oh, I couldn't bear to think of my best friend stuck here for three whole weeks. You must come with me! I know father and mother would approve. They love having a full house. Mother always says it feels more like home when there are plenty of people filling it with their voices. Oh, do come! It would be such a delight to introduce you to my brothers. They're all coming home, too, and it will be the first time we will all be there in ever so long. They will love you, I'm sure of it. And perhaps even my friend, Peter, will be there," she said with a blush.

Rose initially balked at the suggestion. To face a house full of rowdy boys, for Elizabeth had told her stories about her brothers, seemed overwhelming to Rose who was still struggling to build relationships with the girls at school. She couldn't deny it would be lonely at the school when everyone left, but it was easier to face the silence than make an effort to invest in people who would, in turn, ask questions she wasn't ready to answer.

Then Elizabeth squeezed her hand. Looking into her friend's

face, Rose saw the perpetual smile coupled with clear, green eyes and was encouraged to face her fears. Before she realized what she had done, Rose nodded her assent. Squealing with delight, Elizabeth gathered her into a hug. Rose returned it willingly even as she pondered the bewildering predicament she had agreed to.

MONTRIST ESTATE WAS northeast of Verderva. Positioned on the Marest River, the estate town harnessed the power of the water for running the mills which contrived its livelihood. The estate itself was nestled in a valley in the wildest section of the Lachian hills. This far north, the famous, rolling slopes more resembled the jagged edges of the Hytines. To Rose, it seemed like a fairy land. The trees, their boughs heavy with ice, bowed in welcome to her. The winter sun darted between these icy branches as shoots of rainbow seeking a home to lay its merry head. Even the trickle of the water beneath the frozen creek laughed like a mirthful sprite in defiance of the bitter cold.

Elizabeth, who hadn't ceased talking since they had entered the valley, was relaying a story about something she had once done in the creek with her brothers. Rose, preoccupied with the wintery scene around her, only caught every other sentence. She sighed, wishing desperately Mark was there to see these things with her. What adventures they could have here! Every tree seemed to house a druid who beckoned her to search each bend in the path to discover their secrets. Amused laughter brought her back to herself.

"You haven't heard a word I've been saying. Have you?"

"I'm sorry," Rose said with a blush. "Truly I am. I've just never seen anything so beautiful in my life. I keep expecting to see one the of Magic Folk appear at any time."

The beginnings of a frown creased the line between Elizabeth's eyes. It disappeared so quickly that Rose wondered if she had imagined it.

"I'm so glad you like it! It's lovely to have someone love what you love."

The rest of the ride was spent in silence, each of the girls looking out the carriage windows. Montrist was a tidy building which seemed to be made completely of turrets built on turrets and fashioned with sundry steeples rising toward the sky in fairy tale style.

"Rosemary," Elizabeth said as the carriage pulled in front of the main steps. Smile on her lips, Rose faced her friend only to find the persistent smile momentarily gone. The green eyes, usually so vivacious, were troubled. Rose took her friend's hands.

"Whatever is the matter, Elizabeth?"

"Oh dear, there is no need to look so grave," Elizabeth said, laughing self-consciously. "I only wanted to warn you about something before we went inside. I know how important Rohirt's stories are to you, and I respect that. My family doesn't believe in them though. My father, in particular, can be rather scathing when he speaks on the topic. It doesn't come up in conversation very often, but I wanted to prepare you in case it does. Oh, I hope it doesn't put a shadow on your visit. I so want this to be a pleasant visit for you."

"Thank you for warning me," she said with a smile. "I know to prepare for the possibility now. I still plan on having a pleasant visit. How can I not when I have as good a friend as you to share it with?"

Elizabeth's smile was back, all traces of worry gone from her eyes. A noise sounded from the great stairs, causing those eyes to flick past Rose. If it were possible, that wide smile grew even wider. Rose looked behind her and saw a boy running down the stairs. He was hatless and coatless in the bitter cold, but it didn't seem to hamper his progress at all. Elizabeth, scrambling to reach around Rose, flung the door open and, leaping from the carriage, met the boy in a fierce embrace.

"Xan! It's so good to see you! But what are you doing without a coat? You'll freeze to death, you silly clout."

"You were taking too long to get out of the carriage, Bethy. I tried to be patient. Honest I did! But I couldn't take it any longer, and I had to see you."

The boy's brown curls, which fell over his ears and down the back of his neck, and jade eyes made him a picturesque image of childhood innocence. His features were still round, and a growth spurt hadn't yet found favor in him. Regardless, it was obvious the merry boy could be none other than Elizabeth's brother.

"But where are my manners?" Elizabeth said, turning her brother to face Rose. "Xan, this is my friend Rosemary. Rosemary, this is my brother Alexander, or Xan for short."

Xan attempted a dignified face as he bowed low to Rose. Amused, Rose returned it with a curtsey. Appearing pleased, Xan pulled his sister's ear to his mouth.

"Did I do that right, Bethy?" he asked in an audible whisper.

"You did perfect," Elizabeth said in a conversational tone. "Now let's go inside before you freeze to the stairs."

"I won't freeze to the stairs. I move too quickly for that!"

To prove his point, Xan sprinted up the stairs into the house. Laughing, the girls followed him out of the cold. Xan and three other people waited for them. Just as it was apparent Xan was Elizabeth's brother, so, too, it was obvious these three were her relations. Her father, who managed to be tall and portly at the same time, stood beside her mother, whose brown hair, green eyes, and willowy form matched Elizabeth's perfectly. Beside them was a teenage boy who looked like he was still growing accustomed to the tall frame and long limbs he had acquired. The entire family beamed at the girls as they entered.

"There's my Beth!" her father said in a voice that shook the room. Elizabeth shrieked with delight and flung herself into his arms. He spun her around, their laughter mixing in the hall. "It's about time we had more girls around here! Your poor mother has been sorely outnumbered since Alfred and Nico came home yesterday."

"Heel and Nico are home already? How marvelous! I didn't think they would arrive until tomorrow."

"That wonderful king of ours said they could come home early. Said there was no point in them guarding a shoreline that

89

wasn't going to be attacked by pirates anytime soon."

"Elizabeth, would you be so kind as to introduce us to your friend," Elizabeth's mother said. "We have all been anxious to meet her since you wrote she would be joining us."

"Forgive me," Elizabeth said, catching her breath now that her father had put her down. "Rosemary, this is my father, Lord Alfred Winston, and my mother, Lady Bethanna Winston. The rogue there on the end is my older brother, Fred. Family, this is my dear, dear friend Rosemary Clifton! I do hope you will make her feel welcome while she stays with us."

"Why of course we will," Lord Alfred Winston boomed. "Any friend of our Beth is more than welcome here at Montrist. We will especially covet your company, Miss Rosemary, as you bring yet another female presence to this wasteland of ugly male visages."

"You realize you do yourself a disservice with such a statement, father, seeing as we all resemble you," Fred said, his eyes glinting with mischief. Their father broke into a hearty laugh and clapped his son on the shoulder.

"I believe you are right, son. Well played, sir. Well played!"

"Where are Heel and Nico? I thought you said they were home," Elizabeth asked.

"They went out for a ride. They should be home soon, though," Lady Bethanna Winston answered. "While we wait, let us retire to the study for tea so we can hear all about your journey."

Taking her mother's arm, Elizabeth began bemoaning their

lack of adventures on their journey. Rose began to follow, when an arm was suddenly offered to her. She looked up to see Fred's mischievous eyes smiling at her.

"May I escort you, Miss Rosemary?"

"There's no need to call me 'miss.' Rosemary is fine," she said with a blush.

"Very well, Rosemary. May I have the honor?"

She took his arm, and he began to lead her after his family.

"It is excellent to have you with us, Rosemary. Elizabeth has never brought a friend home before. She manifests our family's, shall we say, boisterous personality through the medium of consistent chattering. While we find it endearing, there are many who find it irksome. The unfortunate outcome is she lacks many close friends. She is also disadvantaged going to a girl's school when she grew up with a pack of brothers. I speak for the family when I express our gratitude to you for your faithfulness to her."

"It's far from a chore. She is very dear to me."

"Again, I am pleased to hear you say so. I pray our family doesn't overwhelm you during your visit and so change your mind. It can become a touch rowdy when all of us are home."

"Elizabeth has told me stories, but she has never given me all the details."

"That is probably for the best, though you may still have some questions. Are there any I would be able to answer for you?"

"Well, to begin with, how many of you are there?"

"I am pleased to inform you there are only five of us

children, though I am sure it feels like many more at times," Fred said with a laugh. "Alfred, my oldest brother, is twenty-one. He is a guardsman for the king at the palace. Nicolas, or Nico, is next, at eighteen. He recently joined the navy and was assigned to a ship not long ago. I hold the honor of the middle child, and Elizabeth comes next. Finally, little Xan brings our entourage to a close. He was my parent's surprise, but we have yet to regret it."

"He does look young. How old is he?"

"He'll be eight in a few months."

"It must be exciting to have so many siblings. Tell me though, why did Elizabeth call your oldest brother Heel?"

"An excellent question which has a fascinating, if somewhat long, answer. Alfred has never liked his name, though it is an honor bestowed upon all the firstborn sons of our family. Father would not hear of him shortening it, though. Then, when Xan was born, Nico made an interesting discovery. Alexander can be shortened to Al, and I have always gone by Fred instead of Frederick. As I'm sure you already noticed, Al and Fred are two different ways Alfred can be shortened. So between the two of us, we make a Nico sandwich with 'Fred bread', and between him and Xan they make a sibling sandwich with 'Al bread.' Nico concluded since Alfred was a piece of bread at the end of two different sandwiches, he obviously had to be the heel of the loaf. This amused my father, who has a weakness for puns, and he allowed the nickname to persist. Heel prefers the moniker to his given name, so he is forever to be our own Heel."

Rose laughed out loud and Fred's eyes danced in pleasure as she did. Nearing the study, Rose could hear the sound of the Winston's banter. Elizabeth was telling an animated rendition of a mishap she had at school. Lord Winston and Xan laughed uproariously, while Lady Winston sat with a smile on her lips that was reflected in her eyes. Fred led Rose to a seat near Elizabeth then sat next to her. Rose had never seen her friend so relaxed and hadn't realized how much she restrained herself around their teasing classmates. When she was approaching the climax of the story — the part where she managed to drop every book she was holding down the center of a spiral staircase — the sound of feet in the hallway caught Rose's attention. Elizabeth, noticing the sound as well, turned expectant eyes to the door.

A trio of young men caroused their way into the room. The older two were tall, but that was where their similarities ceased. One wore the same brown hair and green eyes as his mother and siblings. A full beard rounded his otherwise angular features, but even the angles of his face couldn't repress the joviality in his eyes. Rose imagined Xan would grow to resemble this man. The other man was clean shaven, with his father's red-blonde hair and blue eyes. The last, a boy about Fred's age, had dark features which were, if not handsome, pleasant and currently creased with delight. As soon as they entered, Elizabeth went dashing to meet them. They teased her in characteristic Winston volume. While Rose was watching with a smile, Fred leaned in to whisper in her ear.

"The last of the Winston crew. Heel is sporting the beard, and Nico is my mother's blessing. She always said she wanted a pack of red-headed children to match her red-headed husband. The Fates allowed her only one, but she's been an awfully good sport about it. The little black sheep with them is Peter. His family is close to our family, and he's always been sweet on Beth. If Beth would slow down long enough to notice, I think she'd find she's sweet on him as well."

Rose met Fred's eyes and noticed the impish smile there. Her attention was soon pulled away as Elizabeth properly introduced her to Heel, Nico, and Peter. The party complete, they spent the rest of the afternoon in the study, laughing with abandon. Though everyone was trying to keep Elizabeth's attention, she did not forget her friend. She made conscious effort to include Rose in the conversation, which Rose appreciated even if she still chose not to talk much. This, and Fred whispering droll commentaries into her ear, helped Rose feel included in the family reunion.

There were so many things to say and so many stories to tell, the conversation never waned once as the afternoon slipped away. Rose hadn't smiled so much in months. She loved how these people loved and was drawn to their light like a moth to a flame. Once near, the flame didn't burn her. Rather, it warmed the cold, achy part of her heart which missed the Poynters. Her cares slipped into oblivion for the first time in a desperately long time. And they stayed away from the time everyone changed for dinner, throughout the magnificent feast, and clear through gathering in the study again.

Her cares found her again, soon enough. When they crashed upon her, she had to bow her head beneath their weight. At the time, she was in the study, when the men were smoking their pipes in one of the few contented silences the party had shared. Peter, after time and again insisting he needed to leave, had finally managed to make it out the door with Elizabeth, who had offered to see him out. Rose and the family watched them go, only breaking the silence when the door shut behind the pair.

"Poor Peter, I don't think even he knows yet how much he likes our Beth. If he doesn't at least begin flirting with her soon, I'm afraid I might have to just to inspire some jealousy," Nico said.

"Leave the poor boy alone. He has plenty of time to pursue Beth," Lady Winston said.

"Not if what his brother Antoine says is true," Heel began. "He told me our Peter is considering becoming a guardsman."

"Aah, but brother, I heard from Peter not two days ago he didn't think he was going to consider those aspirations anymore. He said there were other things he wanted to look into first," Fred said.

"I see no reason why he should reconsider," Lord Winston huffed. "Perhaps if that dunce of a king we used to have were still on the throne, but not now when we have a real king to lead us. He should be proud to serve under someone as noble as King Richard."

"I don't believe it is the king's character Peter doubts, just

himself and if being a guardsman is what he really wants," Lady
Winston said in a conciliatory tone. Lord Winston snorted again
before talking.

"I never meant to allude that Peter doubts the king's
character. How could any of us? He's proven himself to be a
worthy man who will care for his people as if they were his own
children."

Lord Winston continued, but Rose couldn't hear him
anymore. The rushing return of her sorrows had muffled her
hearing. She was thinking of that terrible, summer day when she
had last seen the king. She was laying on the ground, her cheek
ablaze from the blow her father had just given her. She had
looked to her father and seen the war he was destined to
concede in his eyes. For one, brief moment, she had thought her
father would keep his word to protect Hope. But then the king
spoke. He had spoken into her father's no man's land and drawn
him from her. As her father drug her to the cellar, she had
caught a glimpse of the king's face. It wasn't aghast at the
violence he witnessed. It wasn't indifferent to see a man betray
the one he should have protected. It had been pleased. Triumph
had curled his lips into a small smile, and his eyes glimmered
with approval. It wasn't the face of a *worthy man*, and it certainly
wasn't the face of one she would like to call father. Not that her
own father was any better.

"Rosemary? Are you all right?"

Fred's whisper brought her back to the room. She looked
past his concerned eyes as she scrambled to find her bearings

again. Nico was talking now, and something he was saying demanded her attention.

"Pardon me, but did you mention something about first mate Moore?" she asked before she had found all of her words.

"Why yes," Nico said, taken aback by her interjection. "I was just telling a story about him."

"His first name isn't Clint, by chance, is it?" she asked.

"His name is Clinton, though I've never personally heard it shortened to Clint before."

"Why? I've heard there's a story behind that," Heel asked before Nico could interrogate Rose.

"All I've heard is hearsay. Apparently, he used to go by Clint, and was a regular jokester. I don't know if that part is true, though. I can't imagine our first mate being anything but serious. Anyway, he had a dear friend who they called Cliff, so together they were Clint and Cliff. Sadly, Cliff was killed in action during the pirate offense, and first mate Moore never recovered. He wouldn't allow anyone to call him Clint anymore since it wasn't the same. Again I'm not sure how much is true. My guess is they made up a story to explain why he's such a hard-nose now. Why do you ask, Rosemary?"

But Rose couldn't answer. She couldn't even control what she was doing. Hearing someone speak of her brother's death had somehow made it more real. It couldn't be relegated to the walls of Decedeo when strangers spoke of it. Though she had mentally assented Leonard was dead time and time again, one gullible part of her heart silently clung to the hope he was still alive. But he wasn't. The Nameless Ocean had swallowed him, and he was never coming home.

Somehow she was standing, making excuses, and walking out of the room. Unsure how she got there, she found herself in her room. Still, she couldn't control herself. She sunk to the floor as sobs rose out of her chest. Trying to silence them, she bit her knuckle but felt nothing but tears dripping onto her hands, and heard nothing but her repressed wailing.

"Oh Rosemary! Whatever is wrong? Your hand! Oh, your poor hand!"

Elizabeth was there, holding her tight. With apathy, Rose saw the bite was bleeding. She knew the jagged cut would scar and add more turmoil to her ruined hands.

"They told me you left the study terribly upset. Nico feels wretched he said something wrong to offend you. What happened? Will you please tell me?"

Fat tears still leaking out of her eyes, Rose debated on what she wanted to tell her friend. There were so many things she could say. She could say how she had killed her mother, how her father hated her, or how her brother had been lost when she had finally found him. She could say how desperately she missed the Poynters even though they could only despise her for her treachery. She could tell Elizabeth how jealous she was of her family who loved her and wanted her. Her lifetime of hurts clambered up her throat, drying her tears and begging her to free her stories through the medium of ungracious words.

But then she felt something new. Though her tears had

ceased, there were tears still falling on her hand, mixing with the blood flowing from her knuckle. Rose knew they belonged to her gentle friend; the one who had offered to share her family's love with her when only loneliness had awaited her. Everything Rose had ever loved had been taken from her. Absolutely everything. But now, literally clinging to her hands, was someone who wanted to love and be loved by her. Rose had been wrong when she had thought her battered heart too sore to love as she once had. It remained battered and wary, but it had already latched onto the girl holding her hands. Rose realized that if she had already allowed herself to become a friend, then she must also trust her friend with a little of her story. Not all, but a little. Rose brought Elizabeth's hands to her mouth for a kiss then dared to speak.

"Elizabeth, I would very much like to tell you about my brother," she said. Her voice, beginning as a mere whisper, grew stronger with every word it spoke.

Seven

*G*UIDED BY THE PALE LIGHT OF A CANDLE, ANNE MADE her way to her upstairs room. She had finally convinced Mark to put away his books and do the same. Her boy took Aiden's dictums for his apprenticeship very seriously. If Aiden had said he needed to know everything in every book in the house, Mark would have manfully begun at once to learn it all. He had come by this stubborn persistence honestly through her. She sighed. She didn't know if Mark took more after her or Henry as he grew into his own.

Henry.

The name was soft as a kiss on her lips. She missed saying it almost as much as she missed seeing the bearer. She tried not to think of him. It was too painful to indulge in too often. Yet, though she managed fair on most days, tonight she couldn't keep her husband's memory away. Tomorrow would be his forty-first birthday. She remembered celebrating his fortieth in grand style. Mark and Rose had decorated the banquet hall with the happy

Hope in tow. Nancy had out done herself cooking a sumptuous feast of all Henry's favorite foods. They celebrated at lunch time so Rose could join them before going home for the evening. They sang and laughed and gave him their gifts. That night, he had pulled her close and whispered, "We'll have to do something equally special when you turn forty in few years."

She sighed again. So much had changed. Her birthday wasn't until the summer, but she knew the only special thing she wanted was to feel her husband's arms around her again. She set the candle down in the window Aiden had put in just for her. Curling her knees to her chest, she sat below the window and looked at the moon. Her thoughts carried her back in time to the horde of memories she shared with her husband. She whispered each one, as it crossed her mind, to the moon. She talked until she noticed her mouth was dry. Taken aback, she saw that her poor candle had burnt to a stump, and the winter constellations shone out clear. The cold of the night had seeped through the window into her bones. Cold and cramped, she shifted and sat on her knees. After watching the flickering candle for a time, she finally blew on it, snuffing its flame.

"Happy birthday, Henry," she whispered. Then she lay in bed and was almost instantly asleep.

SHE DREAMED AGAIN that night. It was so real she forgot it was a dream while she was in it. She was seventeen again, hiding in the cave where Criheast had left her, and the Gruilitians were standing just outside. The leaves, moldy from the rain, made the air putrid and suffocating. Her side throbbed from the wound she had incurred while killing the Gruilitian chieftain. Regardless, she didn't dare move. Blinded by the leaves Criheast had buried her in, she had only her ears to rely on. The Gruilitians were whispering to each other in their native language. Cursing herself, she wished she had worked harder at learning their barbarous language. As it was, she had no idea what they were planning.

Then they were silent. She strained her ears into the void in vain. Because the Gruilitians were infamous for their light tread, she continued breathing in shallow breaths, though it felt like her lungs would soon explode. Unknowable amounts of time passed before she finally heard footsteps leading away from her hiding place. Still, she dared not move. Patience had never been her strong suit, but, in moments like these, she could be one of the most longsuffering individuals in all of Deteen. More time passed. The air was becoming unbearably stuffy, and her side demanded attention. She hadn't heard a thing since the retreating footsteps. Surely, she must be alone. She repositioned and drew a gloriously deep breath.

No sooner had she taken it, though, when it was stolen from her. Something struck her in the gut so hard she couldn't even gasp, let alone breathe. Curled in the fetal position, she tried to pull all the air she could into her lungs. Her ears pounding, she could barely hear the sound of yelling voices and rustling leaves. Instinct told her she needed to prepare herself to fight, but she was just now dragging oxygen into her body. All she could do was think of how she was at their mercy. If she could have, she would have laughed wryly at this thought. The men to which she had fallen captive did not know the meaning of mercy.

Her cover of leaves stripped away, she saw painted faces and large hands reaching for her. Those strong hands wrapped themselves in her hair and on her arms and pulled her into the night. She caught a glimpse of a group of men standing in a half-circle around the cave. A few of them held torches that cast eerie shadows over their scarred bodies. Their white teeth gleamed in the darkness as they smiled at her in mockery, and she knew she had fallen into the worst of nightmares.

Something struck her behind the knees. A small cry escaped from her, along with precious air, as she fell to her hands and knees on the ground. She felt blood flowing from her injured side again. Even hot pokers buried under her skin could not have hurt more. In pain and defiance, she rasped into the dirt. The leaves were still wet from the rain. She felt the damp seeping through her clothes, and she thought of the last time she had hunkered down like this. It had been before they found the village of massacred bodies; before their quest for justice. She had been joking with Aiden and Ridge. Hadn't that been a lifetime ago? Two?

She returned to the present nightmare when someone's knee in her back forced her flat to the ground. The pitiless appendage dug into her spine as the bearer pushed against her back with his full weight. More hands seized both of her wrists. Completely overpowered, the resistance she offered only amounted to a laughable show of force. She may as well have tried swallowing the ocean for all the good it did. Binding her hands so tightly she could already feel them going numb, her captors hauled her upright by her hood only to knock her down again with a back hand across the face. Stars danced before her eyes as she lay gasping in the wet leaves. Before she could regain her bearings, she was grabbed by the scruff again and jerked to her knees.

Her world was spinning. She tasted blood in her mouth. Her breath was still coming in painful gasps. The wound on her side throbbed relentlessly. Having no power to stand on her own she leaned into the hands holding her upright. It was her injuries, not any concession of her will, that caused her to hang her head. She was aware of someone squatting in front of her, but didn't give him the satisfaction of meeting his eye of her own accord. When fingers twined in her hair and raised her face, she locked gazes with a set of painfully blue eyes shining out of a mask of black paint. Thankfully, she felt no fear, only defiance.

"Tell us where your patrol is," he said, weighting each word with menace. She spat blood on the ground between them. Then, as best she could, she took slow breaths.

"No."

She watched several emotions flicker in the barbarian's eyes. Confusion, then disbelief, and finally anger. Understanding she was completely in his power, Anne knew she should fear the anger she saw in his eyes. But she didn't. Blaming it on the adrenaline pounding in her ears, she allowed herself a small smile. Her captor noticed, and the fury in his face deepened to an unsettling level, as his eyes glanced down at her side. Her wound was bleeding, she could feel its warmth caress her side. The blood had soaked through her jerkin to be noticed by all. Blue-eyes moved her garment aside to see the clumsy bandage Criheast had applied. With a meaningful glance, her captor raised his hand with his thumb up. He made sure she saw it before slowly, deliberately, mercilessly, pressing his thumb into her side. Her heart leapt into her throat and blocked even her cry of agony. He pressed until she saw white-hot flashes of light. The light grew until it consumed her sight and she knew no more.

Such rest was not destined to be hers long though. She coughed as cold water was thrown in her face dragging her back to consciousness. The smell of the musty leaves pressing into her cheek was her only touchstone to the world. The rest was pain and chaos swirling into a maelstrom that threatened to consume her. Again she was scruffed, and again she was on her knees before the furious, blue-eyed man.

"When I ask a question, I expect to be answered. Tell me, where is your accursed patrol?"

She was still struggling to orient herself. Everything about his face was contorting before her. Everything except his eyes. They remained bedrocks of hate that she used to tether herself to the tangible world in order to answer him.

"No."

Her second "no" was softer than the first, but no less determined. If she was going to die at this man's hand, she refused to help them find her fellows. All she wanted now was for him to kill her quickly. Her monosyllabic response seemed to put him in the mood to comply with her wish. His hand crept to his belt, which housed a wicked-looking blade. The other Gruilitians saw the movement and were motivated to speak in their native tongue. Blue-eyes became, if possible, even more wrathful. In the end, though he argued demonstrably, he lost. Scowling at her, he sheathed his knife.

As if that motion were a signal, the group began to move as a collective. Anne was pulled to her feet and pushed forward. She tripped, falling in an ungracious heap to the earth. As she cried out in pain a hand was firmly held across her mouth, stifling her moans. Blue-eyes filled her line of sight, animus freezing his already cold eyes. Using his free hand to help her stand, he first ran his fist along the length of her wound. His hand across her mouth suffocated the groan that escaped her. Anticipating another shove, her stumbling steps landed underneath her this time — a small victory that went unnoticed by blue-eyes as he prodded her forward.

Running had been hard enough while holding onto Criheast. Now it was a blur of agony. She fell several more times and was always brought to her feet by unseen hands pulling her arm, or hood, or hair. Whenever this assistance was accompanied with some added cruelty she always knew it came from blue-eyes. One time, he dragged her by her hair for a body length before she stood on her feet again. Eventually, after what seemed a lifetime, the torturous march came to an end. She crumpled, exhausted, before a bear of a man, and was finally shown some mercy when they let her lie there. They had returned to the Gruilitian camp she and Criheast had attacked earlier, but she had no lingering gazes for it now. She was too busy vomiting, each retch burning a path up her throat and down her side. Too miserable to care, she collapsed in the grotesque mess. She wanted to die, but death was avoiding her. Fickle Death, leaving those who would welcome it in favor of those who wanted to live.

The Gruilitians were talking in their harsh language again. She didn't care so long as they left her alone for a few more moments. And they did for a time, but all things must end. Too soon, and she was rolled onto her back by a heavy foot. Her bound hands, which she had thought were numb, prickled in pain as she lay on them. The Gruilitians continued talking amongst themselves, and their words grated on her ears. She tried to listen past their voices to the sound of the night beyond, but their ugly words muffled the soft whispers of the woods. She turned her head to study the dark trees.

That's when she saw him. Barely visible in the flickering torchlight, Criheast stood on the outskirts of the camp. Everything seemed to grind to a halt around her. There was only her and her partner, staring at each other across an infinite void. She begged him with her eyes to stay where he was. He couldn't save her. No one could save her. Criheast knew that as well as she, but it didn't seem to matter to him. His hand was on his sword, his eyes measuring the obstacles he needed to overcome.

Her battered body wanted to move, to somehow tell him to avoid this madness. As it was, the plans of both of them were foiled.

More hands materialized and drug her toward the center of camp. In the middle of everything, yet still away from the fire, blue-eyes, carrying two lengths of rope, deposited her. He propped her in a sitting position, and kneeling in front of her, bound her knees and then her ankles together.

"I don't understand. Why don't you just kill me?" she asked, her voice husky with pain.

"We have other plans for you," he said. "You killed our chieftain, and our traditions demand certain recompense. In order for him to be laid to rest properly there must be a blood sacrifice. It can be done with any enemies' blood, but he enters the afterlife triumphantly if it is the blood of the one who killed him that is spilled. He must rest for three days as we prepare the ceremony. Then, and only then, will you die."

"Well, if you are going to keep me alive, then you should have a healer look at my side. You don't want your precious sacrifice to die before the appointed time, right?"

Finished with the knots on her legs, he pulled some cloth from his pocket. He shoved it in her mouth and secured it with another cord. He looked her over with obvious satisfaction as she choked on the gag.

"You only need to be alive in three days. It doesn't matter how close you are to death, it only matters that you can still draw breath. Your last three days will not be pleasant ones, but you won't die until we want you to. That's a promise."

He left her with his threats ringing in her ears. In an odd way, it was comforting. It gave her something to think about besides her physical pain. Exhausted, she curled into the fetal position on her uninjured side. Stranded in the middle of camp as she was, there was no need for anyone to guard her. She was in the middle of camp, making it impossible for her to slip away, even if she were free and uninjured. Gruilitians were bunking down for the night, but she found she couldn't follow suit. The night was as merciless as her captors. The areas of her clothes that had remained dry after water was thrown in her face were now soaked through by the wet ground, and the spring wind still carried winter's bite. She shivered, her misery complete.

The Gruilitians slept as the night deepened. She curled tighter, and was hoping for the relief of sleep when she heard a familiar bird call. It had to be Criheast; she knew it had to be him. Unswervingly determined, he was still trying to rescue her. She wholly believed there was no way he could save her, but perhaps there was a way she could save him from this futile errand. She didn't bother finding him with her eyes. Seeing him wasn't necessary to her plan, and, if she saw him, she might lose her resolve for executing it. Stretching her arms down from their bound position behind her back and pulling her legs tightly to her chest, she muffled her groans of pain against the gag as her wounded side throbbed in relentless agony that threatened her with blacking out. Slipping her hands past her rear, she pulled her feet through her arms. Her hands now in front of her, she panted to steady herself, then sat up. Now she looked for Criheast. There he was, on the edge of camp, no more than a hundred paces from her. It might as well have been miles. He caught her eye, and she saw both worry and guilt there. She had to stop him. She had to stop him before his guilty conscience got him killed.

She fumbled with the gag, but it was no use. It had been tied too tight. She gave up and began gesturing to him. He stopped in an effort to understand. First, she held up three fingers. When he nodded, she drew an arc in the air in front of her. Then she pointed at herself. He nodded again, and she finished by drawing a finger across her throat. Alarm registered in his face. He began to move forward again with new purpose, but she gestured him to stop. Making sure he was paying attention, she pointed at him and then to the woods. Her last gesture was to make a cross as best she could with her bound arms. Criheast frowned and shook his head. The message had been *Three days, I die. You go get help.* He understood, but didn't agree. He kept moving forward.

She had to do something drastic to stop him. She looked around her, and saw a rock that appeared to have a somewhat jagged edge. Making sure to make as much noise as possible, she began to roll toward it. Clumsily, she made it to the rock and began loudly sawing at the ropes on her hands. She saw Criheast freeze, panic plain on his face. He gestured wildly for her to stop, but she ignored him. Her nearest captors were beginning to stir. She redoubled her efforts.

She surprised herself by snapping the cords free. Tears

sprang into her eyes as blood rushed back into her hands, but she only allowed herself a moment to feel the pain. She pawed at the gag with her useless fingers, never expecting to actually get it off. Someone dealt her a vicious slap across the face before her hands had even regained full feeling and she felt a warm trickle of blood leak from her nose as she fell to the ground. Quicker than she thought possible, she was dragged to another part of the camp where a thin, but sturdy, tree stood. Someone tied her to it with a cord around her chest, her hands, and even her neck. And, though she was sick from the pain, she felt happy. Criheast was out of sight. She had at least been able to save him.

The next three days were nothing but a hellish montage set on repeat. The Gruilitians gave her food and water when it suited them. Otherwise, they left her alone. Sitting against the tree, her extremities growing numb, she tried to think of anything but the pain and cold. She could feel that the avulsed skin on her side was infected. One moment she was dripping sweat and the next she was shivering with cold. Her thoughts ran together in a torrent of madness until she could no longer parse them. She began to fear sleep when the shadows started calling her. At some point, she was sure, they wouldn't let her return to life. Despite her efforts to retain her sanity, when the sun set on the third day, she was so far in the grip of the fever she couldn't tell what was real anymore. All she knew for certain was Criheast hadn't come back with help. She was going to die, and she was going to die alone.

Night was king when she was finally cut free. Though she

was completely flaccid from being tied to the tree, her enemies dragged her listless form to a crude altar in the middle of the camp. They kept her limbs bound, though she could hardly stand, let alone run. The man she had killed three days earlier laid on the altar, decorated in barbarous glory. They laid her beside him, the smell of his rotting flesh drawing tears to her eyes. Demons, masquerading as men, danced in dizzying circles around her. Flames from torches swirled around them, licking their bodies but never consuming them. Their drums resounded in her chest and shook her until she felt like she would fall apart. She wanted to fall apart. Anything to stop the madness raging in her head and body.

The noise of the drums ceased, but their beat continued shaking her body. The demons had vanished into a night now full of clashing metal and yelling men. The fire retreated to a distance it couldn't consume her from. She begged it to return. She wanted to die. Why hadn't she died yet? Why weren't the flames consuming her and freeing her from this agonizing existence? She could tell there was madness engulfing her peripherals. It must be more of the fever dream. She paid it no heed, choosing instead to wait. She waited on the altar for Death to finish the work it had painstakingly wrought in her.

A man's face appeared before her. Everything had blurred edges, but she could tell he wasn't a Gruilitian. He was dressed as some sort of Deteenian soldier. There was rank worry in his face as he fumbled with her gag. She breathed deep, clean breaths as he worked on freeing her from her other bonds. She knew her arms and legs should hurt after being tied so long, but she couldn't feel anything anymore—the raging heat was now ravishing her body. Hopefully the fire had found her at last. Now it could consume everything about her. The Deteenian's face still swam before her. Though he was saying something, she couldn't hear him. Normally, the fear, bright as fire, in his features would have concerned her. But the Siren's voices she had avoided for so long were calling to her from the darkness, and it was easier to go to them than care for this soldier. She heard nothing. She saw nothing. She was nothing.

No dreams adulterated the darkness she found herself in. Pale memories resembling cognizance was as close as she came. After what could have been an eternity, she awoke in what she assumed was the afterlife and found herself laying in a comfortable bed, in a cozy room. The sun was filtering in through the windows and she could hear the sound of cheerful birds. She found it wasn't the afterlife when she tried to move and stiff pain greeted her. Drawing a deep breath, she noticed how dry her mouth was.

"You're awake!"

She looked to see the man who spoke. Sorting through her shoddy memories, she recognized him as the last man she had seen before succumbing to the darkness. He had a kind face, sandy hair, and gray eyes. He could have been an angel after the demons she had faced. Demons with blue eyes and harsh hands. Like a breaker, memories of her captivity crashed upon her, and she felt a sob rising in her chest. Whether it be from relief or from being overwhelmed, she was soon weeping. She hadn't cried this uncontrollably since she had been a little girl, and the untamed tumult of her emotions frightened her.

She felt arms go around her. Gentle arms. Comforting arms. She leaned into the man's chest and cried like a child. He rocked her back and forth, whispering all the while.

"It's okay. You're safe now. No one is going to hurt you anymore. You're safe."

Intrinsically, she knew it to be true. There, in the refuge of this stranger's arms, she felt protected like she hadn't felt in years, not even with Aiden. She felt destined to know this man. How else could she explain the feeling of belonging she felt with him? So she allowed herself to be comforted by the man who held her. The same man who would later introduce himself simply as Henry.

ANNE WATCHED MARK disappear down the road. The boys in town were going on some sort of caper, and they wanted Mark to join them. She was glad to see him go. Though Robbie extended many invitations, Mark only accepted a few. Not wanting her boy to be lonely, she wished he would accept more.

The sun was making its way down in the sky for its early retirement. Watching its path, she shivered in the frosty air. Though it nipped at her nose, she continued her vigil. Aiden would be home soon. He had left the day before to travel to the next town to buy supplies. The house yawned empty, like an open grave, and she didn't want to go back inside it yet.

Last night's dream was still sticking to her skin. She had forgotten so much about those days that it had almost been like living them over for the first time. She ran her hand down the scar on her left side. Even though time had taken away the other hurts, it had left this scar as a memento to the past life she had shared with Aiden. But it wasn't her old life or memories of being a captive that had held her thoughts ransom all day. Instead, she thought about Henry. She had spent his birthday wishing he was here with her so she could thank him for saving her life.

Aiden was coming up the path now. He waved when he saw her. Returning the wave, she met him halfway and embraced him. The wind-blown smell of the open road clung to him like a skin.

"Welcome home, Aiden. Did you get everything you needed?"

"Yes, and more," he said with a smile. "But first, why were you standing outside? It's freezing."

"I was thinking about Henry. Today is his birthday," she said, looking away. "My thoughts seemed easier to bear when they weren't confined to four walls."

Sobering with her, Aiden didn't say a word. He just drew her close again.

"I dreamed of him last night, Aiden. I dreamed about how he saved me from the Gruilitians. Though, the more I've thought about it, the more I have realized I need to thank you for that rescue as well. How else could Henry's men have known where to look for me?"

"It was Criheast's idea. He knew we needed more swords than our seven to free you. I was only the one who relayed the message."

"Regardless, thank you," she said, stepping back enough to kiss his cheek. "Now, let's go inside, and get you warm."

"Aren't you going to ask me what else I brought home besides supplies?"

He looked eager as a school boy. Amused, she faced him with a smile.

"All right, I'll play along. What else did you bring home, Aiden?"

His craggy face broke into the widest smile she'd seen on it in years.

"I brought us a lifeline to Hope."

Her world slowed, and her breath caught in her throat. It was a while before she could respond.

"Hope? But how? She's in the palace a day's ride from here."

"Nancy," he said, pressing a note into her hand. "I've been trying to establish communication with her since you arrived here. It took months, but we finally have a secure system by which we can communicate. It can't be often, or else it will arouse suspicion, but it will be enough to coordinate efforts to rescue your daughter."

Anne was already reading Nancy's report on Hope.

"Oh Aiden, she's finally learned to say 'dada!' She hadn't

learned that yet, and always called Henry 'mama.' She's already trying to walk, and she's…oh Aiden!"

She threw her arms around his neck, laughing like a child. Aiden bent to whisper in her ear.

"We are going to get your daughter back, Anne. You will see her again."

Clutching Nancy's note in her hand, Anne allowed herself to truly believe that idea for the first time in a long time.

Eight

*W*ATCH YOUR STEP, LAND-WALKER!" A VOICE CALLED from above.

Leonard barely avoided tripping over the coil of rope which magically appeared in front of him. With a suspect already in mind, he raised his eyes aloft. Sure enough, Montrey grinned down at him as he hung from the rigging with only one hand and a few bare toes despite the cold. "Monkey Montrey" was always looking for an opportunity to give Leonard a hard time, and Leonard smiled at the man who was as small and agile as his namesake.

"Thanks, Mont! Though you spoiled a dream of mine. I've been longing to trip over some rope for months now. Just like I did all the time when I first came aboard."

"If such is the case, then I am positive something can be arranged to see that dream's fruition."

Then he disappeared into the rigging to whatever nest he had created for himself aloft. Smiling to himself, Leonard wondered what mischief he had brought upon his own head. He was not the only one with such musings.

"You've asked for it now, Clifton. Mont won't rest until you've been sprawled over the deck at least half a dozen times."

"That's why I have friends like you, right Rontei? You'll keep an eye out for me to make sure it doesn't happen."

"We can only do so much," another man, Priscink, said. "You know how fast that little monkey is, and sometimes he slips something past us."

"Besides, land-walker," Rontei said with a smile, "We don't want to make it seem like you're one of us. That would suggest that we actually like you."

"Come now, gentlemen, I've been with you for eight months now. Surely there is a place for me within your stout hearts," Leonard said, dramatically placing a hand upon his breast. Rontei and Priscink both laughed at this added flair.

"Well, that could be part of it, don't you think Priscink?"

"Perhaps a small part. I think the main thing that keeps us from tossing him overboard is we've grown accustomed to his face, even if it is a particularly ugly one."

"I think the reason you don't throw me over is because you know I would come back to haunt you. Then you would have to endure an existence constantly riddled with facts about farming."

"That would be dreadful. Can you imagine? It would be the first recorded death where a ghost bored his victims to death!"

The trio laughed with each other. Of all the comrades he had made, Leonard was closest with these two. Their interactions reminded him of his time with Clint. Leonard thought of him now. Was he still sailing for the king, or had he lost his taste for the sea? Loneliness, rising from the deepest part of him, nudged at his heart when he thought of Clint wintering at Port Havenda. Though Leonard knew the waters were full of Cejan, Staveenian, and Telyonian ships, the vast sea felt empty to the lone land-walker caught in its arms. Having grown up referring to these waters as "The Nameless Ocean," Leonard still retained some of the feeling of quiet menace his people had always felt toward the water, despite his months traversing its plane. Maybe things would be different in the spring. Then he would know that his friend was sailing the same waves he was, and the lonely feeling would retreat. Maybe, one day, they would see each other again. He tried not to think about how many years stood between him and that dream. It might have been faster if the Allies were still united, or he had earned his citizenship. As it stood, neither of those things were close to happening.

"Apparently our company isn't enough to hold Clifton's attention," Priscink said. "Maybe we should throw him overboard after all."

Leonard came back from his musings as Rontei slapped his shoulder.

"I'm sure there's a good reason Mr. Clifton decided he couldn't be bothered to listen to us anymore," Rontei said, digging into Leonard's ribs with an elbow. "What do you think could occupy his thoughts in favor of our lovely conversation,

Priscink?"

"I don't know, Rontei. Could it be a certain maiden he keeps insisting he has no eyes for?"

"Enough, you two," Leonard said, exasperated that they were returning to a topic he was tired of being teased about.

"It appears we have struck gold! Are you going to say, Mr. Clifton, you still deny any interest in the lovely lady who happens to reside with you?"

"You best keep your voices down. If Fedic hears you two, he won't be happy," Leonard said, pushing them away as he felt vaguely uncomfortable.

"Does he still not know that you favor his sister?" Rontei asked.

"He would know if there was any interest on my part, which, I would like to add, there isn't," Leonard said. "Besides, you act as if he is the only one who would have to approve any feelings on my part. Asuwith has taken pains to tell me her opinion toward me. If you remember, it is less than flattering."

"Ahh, the woes of unrequited love," Priscink said, draping an arm over Leonard's shoulder. Leonard tried to shake him off, but his teasing friend would not be displaced easily. "Perhaps she will find you less repulsive once you have earned your citizenship."

"Because we all know how close I am to earning that," Leonard scoffed.

"I think you're closer than you think, my friend," Rontei said, switching to a serious tone. "You've given Fedic no reason to be ashamed of extending his citizenship to you. I'd say you've been quite a credit to him."

"The sea will boil the day Fedic admits as such, though anyone with any sense can see it's true," Priscink said, matching Rontei's tone. "Sometimes I wonder why he offered since there are times when he doesn't even seem to like you."

"You two aren't being fair," Leonard said. "You're right. Fedic has never pretended to be overly fond of me, but he saw more of the attacks my country staged against yours than you, and part of him is still bitter about it. Regardless, neither of you can say he has been unjust or unfair. I think it would be easier for him to cut off his own arm than for him to be either of those things. If the opposite were true, he never would have offered his citizenship, and I would still be in custody. I trust he has not brought my case before the council for very good reasons. You forget, comrades, but I have only been with you for eight months, and the crew of the *Exem* are in the minority when it comes to good graces toward me."

"Because they're a lot of blockheads. We're a proud people, Clifton, but sometimes we aren't able to see the truth, even if it's as plain as day," Rontei said.

"Careful, sir. You may be paying me a compliment."

"We best recant then. We cannot stand for that!"

The voice of the first mate barked across the deck, surprising the trio.

"Is there a need to issue invitations or are you three almost done with your get together? I hate to be the bearer of bad news, gentlemen, but we are on a ship and there is work to do. You may enjoy taking in the brisk, winter air, but your shipmates would rather be home in the warmth of their own beds. So why don't you look lively and help them in that pursuit!"

"Yes sir!" the three said in unison, smiling like school boys caught playing truant. When Leonard turned to his post, he saw Fedic. The healer was considering him with his dark eyes. On the sight of Fedic's serious face, Leonard's smile vanished, and the two locked gazes for a moment. Then, as if annoyed, Fedic shook his head and walked away. A sinking feeling fell upon Leonard's heart. He had tried as hard as he knew how, but he still disappointed his protector daily. Rontei and Priscink's words tumbled in his mind, but he pushed them away. He trusted Fedic's sense of justice and believed it would steer him to present his ward's case for citizenship. Leonard just had to be patient for that day. All his desires rested in that hope. What else could he do?

LEONARD WAVED TO Rontei and Priscink from the pier. He would see them soon enough—there was bound to be another scout soon—but Leonard would miss seeing them in the close quarters of the ship. Though known as a land-walker, Leonard was becoming more at home on the deck of a ship than in port. At least on the confines of *Exem* he was looked at with, if not congeniality, respect. On shore, he was seen as a leper, or a sad, stray dog. Passersby gave Fedic sympathetic glances, pitying him for having been saddled with such a burden. Leonard did his best to ignore their condemning gazes. He knew the road to acceptance was going to be long and uphill, and he was ready to weather it. With thoughts of his homeland ever present in his mind, Leonard performed all the duties of a responsible citizen without the recognition of being one.

Silent as usual, Fedic led the way to his house. Leonard followed, smoothing his hair as he did. It refused to lie flat, especially after being blown by the ocean winds. He could feel the roughened skin on his cheeks where those same winds had chapped his face. Fedic noticed, but only raised an eyebrow. Though it made him blush, Leonard still fought his unruly hair as Fedic entered the house. He entered too, his hair still unkempt.

Fedic was embracing a tall, dark-haired woman. She shared his strong features, including the jaw line, which was almost too masculine for a woman. The family resemblance extended even to most of their expressions—generally stoic. But now both countenances split into wide smiles that softened their features. It was a particularly pleasing effect on Asuwith. With her tall, broad frame, Asuwith didn't fit the typical stereotype of beauty. Fedic blamed this and her fiery personality for her lack of suitors. Generally, he spoke of her singleness with annoyance, but everyone could tell Fedic loved living with his sister. Leonard stood in the shadows and watched them in silence, hoping to stay unnoticed for a long while.

"It's so good to have you home again, brother! It seems your scouting ventures grow longer and longer the more you go on them."

"Someone has to patrol the northern waters to make sure those pirate rouges stay away. Intoya is the only one who volunteers for the task anymore. Never fear, he said we would be home for a good long while this time."

"It's about time. I was preparing to introduce myself as a maritime widow to any who would ask."

"I'll say it again, you can resolve much of your loneliness by finding a man to settle down with," Fedic teased.

"And I'll say it again, I haven't found any with which I would like to settle. Besides, why would I want a husband when I have such an excellent brother?"

Before Fedic could respond, there was a knock at the door. Brother and sister turned and finally noticed Leonard. Asuwith, with a line creeping between her eyes, caught sight of him as he turned to answer the door. Still self-conscious because of his ruffled hair, he was now grateful of his windblown face, since its redness hid the blush that had crept into his cheeks. He tried to will the blush away, but the thought of that line between her eyes kept his face hot. He comforted himself with the knowledge that her initial, and rabid, dislike of him had mellowed to something between indifference and annoyance. As he put his hand on the doorknob, he wondered why he cared so much what Asuwith thought of him. Why was she special? She was just one of many he was trying to prove his character to...wasn't she?

When Leonard opened the door, he was greeted by a

messenger boy. He recognized the lad as the one who ran errands for Captain Intoya. Just a few years younger than Rose, maybe ten or eleven, he eyed Leonard with the same fascination as most of the Telyonians—as if he were some oddity who would suddenly break into marketplace tricks like the roaming jesters. Leonard preferred their looks of curiosity to the distrustful ones he usually received. Having recovered from his gaping, the boy handed a letter to Leonard, who pulled a silver coin from his pocket in exchange. The boy's eyes widened at the generous gift. When he looked up at Leonard, he saw the odd, ruffled-haired man give him a wink as he pressed the reward into the little messenger's hand. Leonard watched him go, a smile stealing over his face at the boy's obvious joy.

"What is it, Leonard Clifton?" Fedic said.

Leonard sighed at hearing Fedic use his full name. His protector never called him by any other. It was as if the healer was trying to maintain as formal a relationship between himself and his ward as possible. He supposed he should be thankful. Most outside the *Exem* either called him land-walker or something derogatory. Usually unphased by the nickname and jeers, he appreciated the moments when he felt known and accepted for who he was instead of mistrusted because of what he represented.

"It looks to be a letter from the captain for you," Leonard said, shutting the door. "It seems odd he would already be corresponding with you."

Choosing not to respond, Fedic took the note and read it in

the kitchen. Fedic was reserved in his emotions, but Leonard had learned to read him in these last eight months. Now, as he watched his protector and saw black slowly gather in his eyes, Leonard could tell it wasn't good news. Asuwith noticed as well, but she knew to remain silent. With a scowl, Fedic jammed the letter into his pocket before reaching for his coat. As he threw it around his shoulders, Asuwith broke the silence.

"What is it, Fedic? Why are you acting like this?"

"Something has come up, and I need to speak to the captain about it."

It was obvious he was done discussing the subject, but it was also obvious Asuwith did not want to tolerate remaining uninformed. Bristling until she had almost grown larger, she was beginning her counter-attack when Fedic held up a hand.

"Please don't, As. I'm hoping this is a misunderstanding, but I won't find out if I stand here and quibble with you. I shouldn't be gone long, and once I return I will tell you everything."

Before she could retort, he swept out the door, leaving Leonard with the indignant Asuwith. With a huff, she returned to her dinner preparation. Leonard knew better than to try to speak to her when she was in such a black mood. Instead, he went to the well to draw water for her. Then he brought in more firewood and stoked the fire. When he asked if he could help, she pointed brusquely to a pile of vegetables that needed chopped. He complied to her unspoken command with equal silence.

They worked that way for a long time. Leonard could feel

tension growing between the two of them, and it caused heat to rise up the back of his neck. Her terse movements made him jumpy, causing him to knick his finger. Gasping, he pressed the wound into his shirt. Asuwith didn't even acknowledge he had breached the silence.

He wouldn't mind these moods of hers as much if she would deign to speak to him. If she would only let him, he knew he could cheer her. But she remained walled-off and distant. He hated the tension between them—the tension he was sure only he could feel. His finger had stopped bleeding now, and he rinsed it off before returning to the vegetables. He found he couldn't return to the silence, though. It was too deadening after the activity he had been surrounded with on the ship. Softly, he began to hum a song of Rohirt. He had sung many of the bard's songs these past eight months. The tune reminded him of Deteen and Rose, everything he wanted to return to, and everything he wanted to preserve. It was a small piece of home he could carry with him wherever he went.

"It always surprises me how much of Rohirt you know," Asuwith said, breaking the silence.

Leonard almost cut his finger again in surprise. Turning to look, he saw she was looking over her shoulder at him. Her set jaw revealed she was still peeved at Fedic, but her conversational tone indicated she was trying to overcome it. All Leonard could think of was how his stomach knotted in a pleasant way when she spoke to him.

"Yes. My sister taught me much of his work before I left."

"A sister? I didn't realize you had a sister."

"Yes, I have a sister," Leonard said. "Her name is Rose. She'll be fourteen this spring."

His stomach was knotting again, but it wasn't pleasant this time. Though he had thought of Rose often during his time in Telyon, he had never spoken of her. He hadn't told anyone about the details of his life in Deteen. He felt that if he spoke of Rose, his father, Decedeo, or even Clint his separation would solidify into a cold, hard fact. He could feel it happening now. He was going to miss Rose's birthday again. Was she really going to be fourteen? A vicious pang throbbed his chest as he wondered how many of her birthdays he would miss. Would she be a woman before he saw her again? Would he ever see her again?

"A younger sister? I'm sure you never refused to take a minute to explain a situation to her. You probably never left her alone while you did important *man stuff*. You were a good enough older brother not to…"

She had ceased to speak to him in favor of listing her grievances against her own brother. Leonard couldn't hear her anymore, though. With his hands braced against the table, he tried to maintain steady breathing as he hung his head, his promise to little Rose running non-stop through his thoughts— his promise to take care of her and to come back and make a true home for her. But he couldn't do that now. He had abandoned her to the care of their casually cruel father. Asuwith had not been talking about him, but her words were still true. He had left his sister alone. So very alone.

"Land-walker? Are you all right?"

Asuwith's voice was soft, softer than Leonard had ever heard it be. It brought his mind back around, and that's when he noticed how far he had hunched over the table. The muscles of his back were sore from mindlessly clenching them but, thankfully, his eyes were dry. Even though his back was to her, she would have been able to tell if he had been crying. He refused to give her another reason to show her contempt of him.

Fingering the dirt he had brushed off the vegetables earlier, Leonard remembered that his father's hands were always stained with dirt. And not just any dirt, but the rich, black soil of Deteen. That soil would be sleeping beneath a layer of winter frost now. Though sometimes the winter seemed to hold on forever, the soil would always awaken with Spring's sweet kiss. It remained immutable whether times were good or times were bad, or whether it held forests of trees or seas of crops. The land would always be there, following its seasonal patterns even if he was not.

Without a word, Leonard dashed to the door, retaining his presence of mind long enough to grab his coat before bolting outside. The winter sun had already set behind the watery horizon, but Leonard knew the streets well enough to avoid getting lost. While not warm, the night was not as cold on land as it would have been on the water, and Leonard found he didn't need to bury his face in his collar. But hoping to go unrecognized and unaccosted, he hid his face anyway. He wanted peace so that he could lose himself in his misery for a while.

Aimlessly wandering the empty streets, Leonard wallowed in the despair he had put to the side for so long. Never had the words "bitter-sweet" meant more to him than they did now. He wanted to remember everything, even if those memories hurt like the debriding of a wound. Immeasurable amounts of time passed as he traversed the streets. He walked until his feet were sore and the tip of his nose was numb. Part of him didn't want to return to his foreign abode because of the quiet he had found on this lonely haunt. The other part of him was embarrassed to face Fedic and Asuwith. They must think him such a fool! Knowing he couldn't avoid them forever, he finally turned his feet toward his new residence.

Leonard slipped inside as quietly as possible. Sitting by the low light of fire, Fedic was smoking his pipe. The two men acknowledged each other from across the room.

"You were out late."

Not wanting to defend his actions, Leonard remained silent, and a few long moments passed between them.

"Well, whatever is the matter with you, be sure to get good rest tonight. We are sailing again in the morning."

"What? Where?" Leonard said, breaking his silence out of sheer surprise.

"A group of the council members are sailing to the Mainland in order to meet with delegates from the other islands, and they want Captain Intoya to go with them. They seem to think if they talk some more they will find some way to make peace," he said, laughing bitterly. "We all know how useless such talking is. One reckless choice and Staveen will be engulfed in war again…just when she should be healing from our northern failures."

Pausing to gather himself, Fedic took a few easy breaths. Leonard, who was still in the throes of longing for his homeland, felt himself grow defensive at the mention of the north. Fedic, who had finished composing himself, seemed to notice this and eyed Leonard with curiosity, as if trying to gauge how he would respond. Leonard matched his breathing to Fedic's to steady himself.

"How does this affect us?" Leonard asked in a level tone.

"Intoya has asked me to come along to be an advisor to him. Since I am going, then you must go with me."

"I can't be trusted since I'm not a citizen, can I?" Leonard asked brusquely.

Fedic's silence was the answer. Leonard looked to the ceiling as he worked his jaw. He thought of the defense of his protector he had presented to Rontei and Priscink earlier that day. It assuaged him some, but not totally. Leonard knew Fedic would do right by him. His sense of justice would allow nothing less. Leonard was tired, though—tired of seeing Fedic measuring him up and always finding him wanting, tired of Asuwith's disdain, and tired Telyonian aversion. He was tired of being a stranger in a strange land. He was tired of being no closer to going home. He was tired, and he felt it in every bone in his body.

"The time is not right, Leonard Clifton. I will present your plea for citizenship one day, but not until the time is right."

Fedic said no more, and Leonard, knowing the subject was closed, left the room without a word. His disappointment and frustration balled up in his chest and kept him awake long after he lay down in bed.

Nine

$\mathcal{W}$HEN LEONARD WOKE IN THE MORNING, HE FOUND the night had taken the sting from his woes of the night before. They were still there, he was sure they always would be as long as he was away from home, but they seemed manageable as he began the new day. The discovery was met with gratitude since he was sailing again today—his time for the Mainland. He would have preferred to be traversing the northern waters in search of pirates instead of sailing half a day to the south to the nucleus of Staveen's woes. Tension had been rising on the Mainland ever since the Alliance had broken, filling the air with palpable unrest. The few times Leonard had gone ashore on the Mainland left him frustrated and displeased, with no desire to return. His feelings were secondary, at best, though. Fedic had said he was going. That was the end of the matter.

Since they were planning to return in the evening, he didn't pack much—just a light, shoulder pack. Then he reported to the kitchen. Asuwith was there, but Fedic was nowhere to be found.

Asuwith's gaze lingered for a moment longer than usual when she turned to see who had entered. There was something stirring in her dark eyes, but she turned away before he could identify it. When her glance created butterflies in his stomach, Leonard cursed himself. He still couldn't find the resolve to steel himself against her opinion. He desperately wanted her to think well of him.

"Good morning, Asuwith," he said, trying to breach the distance between them.

"Good morning."

She didn't turn around when she answered. Leonard felt himself color in embarrassment. He had made a fool of himself last night by rushing out into the street. He was resigning himself to what he hoped was a dignified silence, when he noticed her fidgeting fingers. They were dancing around the charm Fedic had given her when they were both younger. It was a sea dragon pendant, and it was never seen far from her. Right now it was threaded on a plain string bracelet she had woven for it. The charm required a simple bracelet because, whenever she was uncomfortable, her fiddling fingers found it and toyed with it until the bracelet broke. Did that mean he had made her uncomfortable with his outburst last night? The thought grieved him more than he knew it should.

"I'm sorry if my irregular behavior last night made you uncomfortable."

Her fingers continued to twist the charm back and forth as silence rested between them. He was bending to lace his boots when she finally spoke to him.

"You miss home very much, don't you?"

Lowering his head to hide his face, Leonard kept lacing his boots.

"I'm thankful for everything you and your brother have done for me. If not for you, I would still be a prisoner of war."

"That's not what I asked though," she said, turning to face him. "I asked if you missed home. Your home across the waters."

Leonard paused as he reached for his other boot. As was typical of Asuwith, she had skimmed past the diplomatic answer in favor of the heart of the matter.

"Yes. Yes, I miss Deteen very much," he whispered.

"And your sister?"

"Especially my sister."

He heard a quiet curse. Looking up, he saw she had broken the charm free of her bracelet again. They stared at it, both of them frozen in time, as if to figure out what it meant.

"Did you break it again, As?" Fedic asked as he entered the room. His entrance broke whatever spell had fallen over the room, and the pair looked away from each other like guilty children.

"One day I will buy you a taramute chain. Telyon may not agree with the miners of Samew about much, but their craftsmen have learned to forge incredible things out of a material that is supposedly unbreakable."

"You say that every time I break whatever my charm is on,

and I always tell you the same thing. Don't bother. It's a waste of good silver when I can make do with the materials I already have," she said, her voice regaining its plain, mater-of-fact tone. Fedic chuckled at her change in demeanor.

"Will my little sister ever let me spoil her? Even once?"

Scoffing as if nothing could be more ridiculous, Asuwith turned to her brother to hand him a sack with some provisions in it.

"I'm not little anymore, brother, and I don't need pampered like a child. Now go. It's best not to keep them waiting."

Despite her curt words, she smiled when Fedic gave her cheek a kiss. Then, with a signal for Leonard to follow, Fedic stepped into the chilly morning. Asuwith approached Leonard with another sack for him. Their hands brushing lightly during the hand off, she drew back as if shocked, and the traces of a blush appeared on her face. Leonard could have tried to ascertain the root of her blush, but he was too busy trying to figure out why the warmth from her momentary touch was creeping up his arm. As he tried to cover his confusion with a grateful smile, her eyes adapted their customary aura of annoyance.

"See you tonight, land-walker."

He turned to follow Fedic. It seemed nothing had changed between he and Asuwith since the events of last night. Gratefully, he acknowledged to himself that at least her esteem of him didn't seem lessened. The warmth from her touch was lingering in his arm, and he wished he knew why. He also wished he knew why he felt the urge to look back at her before he left again. He told himself not to be foolish and walked to the door. Yet, when his hand touched the latch, he could no longer repress the urge. Casting a glance over his shoulder at her, he saw she was no longer looking at him. Rather, she was inspecting the bracelet she had broken, disappointment in her eyes. He left then, her expression searing itself into his mind's eye.

Fedic and Leonard made their way to the ship in silence. Though it was early, the docks were already stirring to life. Today was a market day, which meant a majority of the island would gather here to barter, buy, and sell. Leonard liked market days. On those days he was only a face in the crowd, able to slip to and fro as he pleased without being hounded by wary glances. As it was, the few who acknowledged him now did so mostly with distrust in their eyes.

Leonard found no relief once aboard. The ship was named the *Obaac*, and it was run by a skeleton crew. Leonard knew all the crew members by sight, a few of them by name, and none of them as ally. He ignored them as he set about doing his job. He was more than capable in the work of a seaman. He had been on ships for a long time now, but he missed the friendly jibes he usually traded with Rontei, Priscink, and Montrey. No matter, they were soon underway.

Telyon disappeared as the ocean engulfed the *Obaac*. In Deteen, they had always called the water the Nameless Ocean. It fit their understanding of the mysteries that lay beyond the watery horizon. Staveenians, who loved and respected the ocean, had named it Brophileo. Leonard liked giving it a name. Though he had always loved farming with his father, the waves called to him with a sweeter song. Giving the ocean a name made it more of a friend than a foreboding enemy.

Yet, no matter how much he had wanted to leave a sense of foreboding behind him, it had found its way aboard the *Obaac*. Leonard knew it had nestled deep in the hearts of even the saltiest of the sailors sailing with him to the Mainland. The island of Kirat had been taking an aggressive stance against those who still desired to patrol near Cej. Telyon, being the champion of that cause, had not endeared itself to the Kiratians. This tension was magnified by the strong but competing influence both Kirat and Telyon held among the islands in Staveen, and, if either declared war on the other, the remaining islands would quickly choose a side and plunge Staveen into a civil war.

As the ship neared the Mainland, the captain called the crew together. He eyed them all as sternly as a school master before unruly pupils.

"Listen up, lads. I'll not have any of you going ashore unless you are going to the council. The last thing we need is for any of you hot heads to pick a fight with a Kiratian. You will be ready to set sail for home as soon as we are back aboard. I'd honestly prefer you hoist the gang plank and hunker down in your bunks until we return. The fewer chances we have to interact with anyone ashore, the better. Am I understood?"

"Yes sir!" the crew replied in unison.

The crew dispersed to their posts. Leonard was doing the

same, when he noticed Fedic pulling the captain aside. Angling himself to hear their conversation, Leonard strained his ears to listen. He couldn't hear what Fedic had to say, and, at first, he couldn't hear the captain's response. Near the end, though, he heard what he had been expecting to hear.

"I don't trust the fellow. He'll come ashore so I can keep an eye on him."

Fedic said nothing to the contrary, and it was decided. Leonard didn't relish the idea of going ashore, but he would do it without complaint. No doubt he would be locked in a secure outer room, like a prisoner or a bad dog. It riled him to think of it, but there was nothing to do but bear the indignity of it all. At least he wouldn't spend all day waiting below decks. The weather was still cold, but not nearly as bitter as it had been. Even on the water, Leonard decided to forego gloves and a hat. He kept his coat, though. It wasn't nearly warm enough to abandon that yet.

Leonard remained stoic when Fedic told him the news he already knew, when the Mainland grew larger and larger on the horizon, and when they finally docked. Under the scrutiny of everyone who was going to the council, Leonard stepped ashore with his head held high. He didn't want to draw attention to himself here, and one of the best ways to blend in was to swagger some. Staveenians were proud people, making his farmer's modesty stand out all the more. They walked through the main square as a tight group in order not to lose each other. There were so many people here! A representative from every island was crammed into the small space. Apparently it was market day here as well, and Leonard was fascinated by the bustle of life which surrounded them. He had never seen so many different kinds of people, nor so many different wares. One booth in particular caught his eye. It was a merchant from Samew, who was selling various items crafted of the unbreakable taramute. There were mail shirts, horseshoes, and everything else of the like, but what really held his attention were the slender chains designed for holding pendants. As Asuwith's disappointed face flashed before his mind's eye, he stared blankly into space. Intoya paid him a small wage for sailing aboard the *Exem,* and Leonard had saved enough of it to possibly buy one of the treasures for her. When he finally returned to himself, he realized he had met gazes with a Kiratian sailor across the crowd. Recognition of Leonard's foreign heritage swept across the man's face the longer he looked at him. Smiling wickedly, the man turned to his crew mates, and they in turn looked at Leonard with hungry eyes. Leonard turned away. He didn't know what they were thinking about, but he knew he didn't want to be a part of it. Looking away, he attempted to hide himself within his own group. Still, even as they moved away from the leering Kiratians, Leonard felt their eyes boring into his back.

The council hall they were heading toward was not far from the main square. Most of the structures on the Mainland were narrow and crammed together, maximizing the limited space. The council hall was the one exception. It flourished like a flower that had been given free rein to grow as it liked. It was still smaller than most of the estates Leonard had seen in

Deteen, but after months of seeing only ship's cabins and pinched houses, the structure loomed large before him. Awed, Leonard felt his first rush of excitement since learning about this trip. Though he had been to the Mainland before, he had never been inside the council hall. He knew he was going to be relegated to some far, back room, but at least he would get to see some of the inside first.

Guards stood beside the doors—their set faces hardened into stern grimaces by years of duty. Leonard understood them. There hadn't been much to smile about in recent years. They eyed the captain as he approached them.

"We are the representatives from Telyon for the council being held today," the captain said.

"Telyon?" the soldier asked as he looked into the group. "We were warned you might have a land-walker with you. Is he here?"

No one spoke, but nearly everyone surreptitiously glanced at Leonard. Trying to appear as if the implications of the guard's question didn't bother him, Leonard stood a little taller. The guards narrowed their eyes and looked back to the captain.

"Only citizens of Staveen are allowed into the council hall. We cannot allow him to pass."

"He is under my citizenship," Fedic said, stepping forward. "Surely that is enough."

"It may have been in the past, but times have changed. The land-walker does not enter."

Fedic was going to speak again when Intoya placed a hand

on his shoulder. The captain of the *Obaac* seemed confounded. Head bowed deferentially, Leonard approached him.

"Captain, I can return to the ship. I believe that would make you feel more comfortable than if I waited outside. I give you my word I won't stray from the path."

The captain was torn. He didn't want to trust Leonard, but he also knew Leonard was right. The captain deliberated in savage frustration, then Fedic intervened.

"He is trustworthy, captain. If he says he will return straight to the ship, then he will."

The captain battled half a second more but finally nodded to Fedic. Then he pushed past the guards into the council hall, his crew following him in dignified silence. Fedic was the last to enter, and before he disappeared into the hall, he looked at Leonard a final time. Everything about that look said *Don't prove me wrong, Leonard Clifton.* Then the doors shut and Leonard was left alone in the cold street with two soldiers who obviously hated him.

Disappointment and relief collided in his chest and somehow gave birth to anxiety. Word was out that the Telyonians had a land-walker with them, which meant he was a marked man—especially now that he had been sent away from the council hall. The chance of being recognized and accosted rose with every passing second. The guards were glaring at him in a way that made him feel exposed. Hoping to outdistance those glares, he began walking toward the ship. Soon the guards disappeared into the background, but now Leonard was presented with another choice. Did he walk through the crowded square or choose a quieter side road to take him to the safety of the ship? Realizing the danger of being discovered alone on a side street, he chose walking through the square and hoped the multitude of milling people would provide protection and adequate cover.

Upon entering the square, his dark feelings lifted some. The people had compensated for the bleak, winter day by dressing the buildings in brilliant colors. Even the people themselves were dressed in colorful array that added to the exotic air of the town. Every island was represented by a different color palate displayed in a wide variety of clothing styles. And it was loud— loud with the noise of a throng of people in a limited space. Leonard wondered if the market day coincided with the council meeting on purpose. It was as if everyone had made a silent truce for the day as their leaders gathered to attempt peace. That didn't mean it wasn't tense. Leonard believed he could put his fingers on the collective body of these people and feel the pulse of their tension validating their existence. It was an unhealthy heartbeat, even if the body showed no signs or symptoms of its ailment.

Putting his head down to make his way through the crowd, Leonard had every intention of walking straight through, looking up only to get his bearings every so often. Those intentions faltered as he passed the taramute stand of the Samewites. Up close, he could see how extraordinarily delicate the necklace chains were. Not only that, but somehow their melders had found a way to change the colors of the taramute as they formed it. Every color of the rainbow seemed to gleam from the precious metal, indicating the level of mastery and high quality of the chains.

He had mustered his will to walk by the stand when he saw a chain unlike any of the others. This one was actually three impossibly slender chains braided into one. One strand was standard gray taramute, but the other two had been dyed, one blue and the other green. The colors were the same as those in Asuwith's sea dragon pendant. Her disappointed face from this morning filled his mind's eye again. He knew then he had to buy it for her, even though he didn't think the gesture would put him in her good graces. In fact, if he knew Asuwith, there was a good chance she would scoff at the gift and distance herself even further from him. But Leonard had an overwhelming desire to give her good things. He flushed at the thought, but the desire still remained. Against his better judgment, Leonard approached the stand.

He traded quickly with the man. The chain was elaborately priced, but Leonard was able to bring the price down by bartering a ring he had brought from Deteen. Thankfully, though it wasn't a particularly valuable ring, its foreign origin increased its value. Still, the Samewite asked a high price, requiring nearly all the money Leonard had saved while in Staveen. Leonard knew he could have bartered the merchant down more, but he was in a hurry to return to the ship. He had already stayed too long in the square. Folding the chain in his hand, he discovered it was flexible enough to be entirely enfolded in his palm. Having never bought anything so fine before, he wondered what in the world he was doing.

Thanking the vendor, Leonard turned to go, but was abruptly stopped by three men who unbeknownst to him, had silently sauntered up behind him and were now standing nearly shoulder-to-shoulder with him. Beginning to apologize, the words froze on his lips when he raised his eyes to see who he had run into. It was the Kiratian sailor he had locked gazes with earlier that afternoon. The malicious, self-satisfied grin was still spread across his face, making Leonard feel sick.

"How do you do, land-walker?" the sailor asked.

Leonard didn't reply. Knowing the swaggering air he had adopted would only make matters worse, Leonard ducked his head as he tried to step around the three men. He should have known it couldn't end that simply. The biggest of the three blocked his path and placed a heavy hand on Leonard's shoulder.

"Did you see that gents? The land-walker was very rude to us just now. Completely thankless, even after his miserable life had been spared. Not only spared, but improved! If it had been up to me, I would have run his worthless hide through when I first found him, not offered him the protection of my citizenship."

As if on cue, the third man had circled behind Leonard, forming a complete entrapment. His blood beat hard in his head, making it hard to think clearly. The only thing he knew for sure was that, no matter what happened, he could not retaliate in any way. Because he was not a true citizen of Staveen, this man could abuse him anyway he pleased, excepting murder, without fear of retribution by the law. But if Leonard attacked a citizen, it would be an outrage that held the potential to incite the civil war the nations were teetering on. Leonard wasn't the only one who knew these things. The Kiratians knew them as well, Leonard could see in their eyes they did. But it wasn't any of those facts that froze his blood. No, it was the pleasure he saw in the Kiratian's eyes that did.

"Why don't we tell everyone how rude this land-walker has been to us. They deserve to know what kind of man has been hiding among them."

Before Leonard could move, the man behind him pinned his arms behind his back. Leonard struggled instinctively, but his efforts were soon cut short by the big man driving his fist into his victim's stomach. As he tried to catch his breath, the three men drug him to the middle of the square. Quickly they mounted the raised platform which stood there. Doubled up as he was, Leonard could still tell most of the eyes of the Staveenians were locked on him and an eerie quiet had begun to fall. The Kiratian sailor noticed this as well and raised his hands for silence. The crowd soon quieted for him, and the people gave him their attention.

"My fellow Staveenians, I don't know if you have had the pleasure of meeting this man. This is a land-walker—one of those barbarous men of the north who allied themselves with pirates in order to kill our brothers and sons."

Leonard began to panic. The sailor was inciting the only form of union the Staveenians could hold in agreement. Almost all of them had lost someone in the battles Leonard had participated in against them. It was possible his sword had created some of the widows who stood looking at him now. Such a crowd could rend him, limb from limb, with ease. As fear crept up his neck, the only thing that calmed him was the feel of Asuwith's chain in his hand. He refused to act in any way that would shame either her or her brother.

"Perhaps you can't recognize him with those Telyonian clothes on. Maybe this will help."

Roughly, the other two sailors stripped Leonard down to his underclothes. The chill of the air, bearable in a coat and warm pants, pricked his bare skin even as hot humiliation washed over him.

"How about now? Do you recognize him as the butcher he is?"

There were murmurings in the crowd. People were gathering so close that Leonard could see their angry eyes from the platform. He shivered with cold and dread.

"I think a little stay in the stocks would give him time to sit and think about what he's done. Don't you?"

A roar of approval erupted from the mob. Quicker than Leonard thought possible, a pillory appeared before him. Amidst great yelling, Leonard was forced to his knees. He didn't resist when they put his head and hands into the wooden prison and locked it shut. The Kiratian sailor, smiling smugly, knelt in front of Leonard to look him in the eye.

"This is for my brother, you son of a whore," he said, menace dripping from every word. Then he hit Leonard so hard across the face that Leonard feared he would black out. The sailor stood, smiling smugly, and left Leonard, bleeding and bound, before the mob. It wasn't long before objects were being thrown at him—muck from the gutter, rotten vegetables, dog droppings—it didn't matter what it was as long as it hit him. Leonard closed his eyes, turned his head away as best he could, and bore the onslaught in silence. Humming a song of Rohirt to himself, he tuned out the noisy crowd at least a bit. The song made him think of Rose and her steely will. Borrowing courage and endurance from her memory, he was almost able to forget the shivering cold and the cursing mob.

Whatever misery his torturers thought he lacked was soon supplied by a bucket of cold water that was thrown in his face, immediately dousing his memories of Rose. Leonard gasped for air, his breath appearing in white clouds before him.

"Wake up, land-walker. We can't have you going to sleep on us."

The people, pleased, began cheering again. Leonard was shaking uncontrollably with cold now, and doubted he would ever be warm again. Unable to move his numb hands, he prayed Asuwith's chain was still clutched in his fist since he could no longer feel it. Still, he remained silent.

As several lifetimes seemed to pass, the shivering began to

ebb, but the cold deepened. Glancing at his hands, he saw they had been blanched white by the winter air. His thoughts had begun congealing in his mind, like blood clotting in a wound, when he noticed someone working beside him. Soon, the pillory was lifted and he was being assisted out of it. As a coat was placed over his shoulders, Fedic's face filled Leonard's vision. His healer eyes were raking over him, assessing the damage. Leonard tried smiling to assure him that he was fine, but his face was still numb and uncooperative. His only movement was involuntary shaking that racked his body. His assessment finished, Fedic's eyes shifted from those of the inquiring healer to disappointed and angry mentor. Ashamed and unsure why, Leonard looked away. Fedic, his face grim, stood and faced the crowd.

"Who did this?" he said, his voice as firm as steel. The Kiratian sailor had already joined them on the platform, everything about him smug.

"I did."

"What was his crime?" Fedic asked. Leonard could tell from Fedic's tone and demeanor that he disagreed with the severity of the punishment, but not the punishment itself if it was deserved. Leonard could see the small crew from the *Obaac* standing near the platform—their posture ready, their eyes alert, and their agreement with Fedic etched in their jaws. The Kiratian sailor smiled back at Fedic, his eyes gloating.

"There was no crime besides that of being a land-walker. Surely that is enough, though."

It took a moment for Fedic to understand what had been said, but, when he did, Leonard saw him turn white with rage. Then Leonard's chest tightened. A pale visage was the only warning Fedic ever gave when his anger had become murderous. The healer didn't change his stance on the platform, but deliberately drew his sword. The square was quiet now, and the sound of the scraping metal echoed in the square as eerily as the cry of a lone child.

"You mean to tell me, this man was treated as such on a whim?" Fedic said, his voice deceptively even.

"And if he was?" the Kiratian asked quietly.

"That is outrageous! He is protected under my citizenship and cannot be treated this way without cause."

"Perhaps not on Telyon, but here on the Mainland, that means nothing. He is not a citizen. That means I can do to him whatever I want, whenever I want. He's a common butcher, and you are a fool to defend him. To defend him is to defend our countrymen's murderers!"

Leonard saw many hands creeping toward swords. Some of the *Obaac's* crew had already drawn their weapons, their countenances angry. Fedic was shaking with rage now, and Leonard could tell he was preparing to engage their nemesis. Something in the back of Leonard's sluggish brain realized how cataclysmic such a rash action would be. It would lead to war, more bloody war where more women would be reduced to widows and more children left fatherless. Intoya had helped Leonard stand, but by now his hand was on his sword as well.

Leonard, breaking away from Intoya, stood between Fedic and their tormentor. The silence was palpable.

"Stop, Fedic! It isn't worth it," he said with his heavy tongue.

"Stand aside, Leonard Clifton," Fedic ordered. As he attempted to step around his ward, Leonard pushed him back into his stance.

"No! No matter what you feel right now, he is your brother. I refuse to be the impetus of a civil war. I refuse to have any more Staveenian blood on my hands!"

There was a hush in the crowd, as if every onlooker was holding his breath, but Leonard focused his eyes on only one man. He prayed his protector would relent because he didn't have the strength to fight him if he didn't. At last, something strange passed through Fedic's features, and he sheathed his sword. The crowd sighed with relief. No matter how angry they had been, they hoped for something better than civil war. Fedic took Leonard's arm, leading him off the platform and away from the disappointed sailor. Once they joined their crew, they began muscling their way to their ship. Leonard followed, feeling warmer in the coat, but still shivering badly. Fedic noticed, as he noticed everything, and, drawing near, spoke so softly that only Leonard could hear.

"You aren't a butcher, Leonard Clifton. You are a good man. Perhaps one of the best I know."

Leonard allowed himself a smile then, but he wasn't sure if it was because of Fedic's praise or because he could once again feel Asuwith's chain in his clenched palm again.

THREE DAYS HAD passed since the incident on the Mainland. Three days, yet it seemed too short a time for all that had happened. Leonard thought back on them, trying to decide which event had impacted him the most.

It wasn't the amputation, though that would continue to impact him for the rest of his life. When they had returned to the ship, Leonard's left hand was slow to regain color or feeling. Fedic worked tirelessly in Leonard's recovery, but in the end it was decided that Leonard would lose the little finger of the afflicted hand. The bulky bandage still swaddled his hand, but Leonard counted himself lucky. His circumstances could have ended much worse if he had been left exposed for much longer. Rontei and Priscink had already bestowed the nickname of "Niner" on him, which made him feel less like an outsider.

He now saw begrudged respect in the faces of the Telyonian's. Word had spread quickly of Leonard's actions to stifle the fight which could have induced war. They no longer doubted his loyalty, and, if ever they did doubt, their eyes only had to travel to the white bandage wrapped round his left hand to know what price he was willing to pay for their country. Even citizens on the other islands had shown him their respect. The most memorable occurrence had been from the Samewite merchant he'd bartered with. He had sent Leonard back his ring and all his money, along with a simple note that said, "A taramute chain is well worth my son not going to war."

In fact, Fedic had informed him there had even been a shift in the political arena. Though the islands of Staveen were far from calling a truce, tensions had lessened. Having hovered so close to the brink of war scared the populace, and that fear made room for more communication, even if disagreement was still strong.

However, Leonard's favorite moment of the three days was the look on Asuwith's face when he had given her the chain. Fedic had been away, giving Leonard the courage to tell her how grasping the chain had given him strength while in the stockade because it reminded him of her. Her face had flushed and her eyes filled with wonder as she studied the precious chain. The blush in her cheeks and amazement in her eyes softened her face and made Leonard's heart beat faster. In that moment, she remained quiet, but she had thanked him in two far better ways—she hadn't taken the necklace off since putting it on, and she had begun calling him by his name.

But even that paled in comparison to this present moment. He was standing outside the delegate hall still wondering if it was all real. But it was real. The council had called him before them with news that the case for his citizenship was being formally processed. How had they phrased it? He had "exemplified Telyonian standards" and had "proven himself a credit to their community." He hadn't imagined such words even in his dreams.

"It appears you've received the good news," Fedic said as he walked toward him, stoic as ever. Leonard met him with the standard Telyonian greeting, but it didn't seem enough. He wanted to embrace him, but he knew the healer would be opposed.

"Thank you, Fedic. I don't think you know how much this means to me."

"I think I do. You have a heart set on peace, Leonard Clifton, and I believe you will use your citizenship for pursuing that ideal. First between the islands of Staveen, but then with your homeland. Don't doubt, Leonard Clifton. I believe you will see your homeland again. No one can love something so much, and not have it so. Until that day, I hope you are able to find a home here in Telyon."

As he extended his hand to Leonard, the smile in Fedic's eyes almost crept to his lips. Leonard grasped Fedic's forearm just the way he used to do with Clint. Fedic nodded and began to walk away. Pausing after a few steps, he looked over his shoulder, a mischievous smile finally claiming one corner of his mouth.

"And Niner? Now that you are going to be a citizen, you should probably begin courting my sister properly. I think the season where you attempt to hide your feelings for her should probably come to a close."

He walked away then. Leonard watched him go, smiling like a fool, finally feeling as if he belonged to something again.

Ten

SPRING 262

CURSE IT ALL. CURSE THE CHILL THAT CLUNG TO THE DAYS despite spring's arrival several weeks ago. Curse the boy he had been assigned to watch. Curse his own low rank, which had made him the first choice for this post. And the rain! May the rain be three times accursed!

Barinne shook some of the water from his cloak. The rain, which hadn't ceased for three days, had turned the roads into quagmires of mud that infiltrated his sodden boots as easily as if they were made of rags. Grumbling to himself, Barinne thought of the town's inn with its warming ale and welcoming fire. His assignment had allowed him to visit it only a few times in the two weeks he had been here. A shiver passed through him, knocking loose the comforting thoughts of the inn. One more week and he would be done with his rotation. One more week and he would be free to visit as many ale houses as his stipend from this assignment would allow.

Barinne cursed again as water ran off the brim of his hat and down the back of his shirt. Maybe this post would be worth its trouble, if the boy did anything interesting. He did what the average apprentice did. He read what his mentor told him to read and spent precious few hours practicing the hands on skills he wanted to learn. Barinne had been watching the Poynter boy for so long now that he felt as if he knew him better than the boy knew himself. Unfortunately, everything he knew was incredibly boring.

Barinne was unaware of the king's reasons for having the boy and his mother watched. All he knew for sure was that the boy's father, who had supported the old king, had been imprisoned for treason, and the family had been separated during the power struggle. The daughter had been taken to the palace to be watched over by the king personally. Somehow, the wife and son had managed to escape and were living in reduced circumstances. But now the king wanted to know what the boy was doing at all times. None of it made any sense to Barinne, who cursed again in order to distract himself from his misery.

The day was coming to a close, though the long stream of gray, overcast days made it hard to tell daytime from dusk. But the gray was dimming now. Settling in for what promised to be a cold night, Barinne pulled his cloak tight around himself. Having just gotten snug, he spotted the boy outside hunching against the rain and moving quickly toward town. The rain forgotten, Barinne began stalking his prey.

Remaining undetected was easy. The boy, having tucked his head in his cloak to ward off the wind swirling around his ears, was rendered nearly deaf. Undeterred, he moved with relentless purpose at nearly a jogging pace. Barinne wondered what errand could have drawn the boy out of his dry house this close to eventide and in the rain. His task was not to figure out the inner workings of his subject's mind, though. It was merely to follow and report, and, for the first time in days, his subject was doing something unexpected. So Barinne followed, grateful to do something other than sit in the rain.

Upon entering the village, the Poynter boy walked straight to the postmaster's house. Barinne smiled to himself. He had acquired the postmaster's allegiance soon after arriving for this assignment, thus whatever the boy was trying to send would first undergo his inspection. Barinne hoped that it was something more than the old healer writing a neighboring colleague to send supplies. Barinne thought he may have found some excitement at last because the boy handed a couple of letters to the postmaster, who haggled with him over the price for a time, but not long. It was too wet outside to warrant anything but perfunctory bartering. Paying the agreed price, the boy tucked himself back into his cloak for the trip back to his house. Barinne didn't follow him this time. His subject had left something behind that was far more interesting than anything that waited at his return destination.

Waiting until the boy had disappeared, Barinne approached the postmaster's house. He knocked once and entered without waiting to be admitted. Having expected the spy's appearance, the postmaster barely acknowledged Barinne's arrival. The letters were laying on the table, slightly damp, but otherwise in good condition. The postmaster, a man of few words, merely looked at Barinne, an eyebrow raised in question. Barinne placed a couple of gold coins on the table in answer, and the postmaster looked away. Barinne, now completely unfettered, inspected the letters the boy had so carefully delivered.

On the first he recognized the bold handwriting of the healer. Barinne recognized the name of the recipient as another healer the old man consulted with at times. There must be an especially sick patient he was concerned about, or he wouldn't have sent the boy to deliver the letter now.

The second letter was far more interesting. The four words that darkened the front were in the boy's nigh unto illegible hand. *Rosemary Clifton. Verderva School.* That was all it said. Clifton was the name of the man who had taken the lordship of Baymontiac. He had been the overseer of Decedeo Estate before then. This had to be his daughter, then. What did the son of a displaced lord have to say to the daughter of an upstart noble?

Barinne picked up the letter. The postmaster's roving eye was turned away again by the appearance of a few more coins. Breaking the seal, Barinne scanned the letter's contents. As he did, a smile spread over his face. This was something the king would want to see. This was something that would distinguish him and perhaps get him reassigned to a more illustrious position. The past two miserable weeks fell away like a bad dream as he pocketed the letter. Things were going to get better for him soon. Very soon.

ROSE,

It's been a long time. Maybe it's been too long. Part of me wants to believe it hasn't. The other part of me doesn't know what to believe. It knows what it wants to believe. It wants to believe the best in this situation; in the way everything turned out. It wants to believe the best in you.

Rose, I don't know what to say to you. Civil words don't come naturally to me when I've been angry for so long. But that's why I'm writing this to you. I want to hear your side of the story. I need to hear your side of the story. Bear this in mind as you read this letter.

I don't understand, Rose. I have tried to understand, but I just can't. The king's notice thanked you for your "invaluable service" in the kidnapping of my sister. How can that be true? Did you want your father's love so desperately that you were willing to sacrifice my family for it? Not just my family, but yours as well, for I have always considered you my sister. I thought you felt the same toward us. Did I misjudge you? Did you see Hope as something less than your sister? And how could you choose your father, the man who left that scar on your cheek, over Hope? Over me?

I don't want to fight you. Neither do I want to hate you, but I'm drowning in all the things I don't understand. I'm begging you to send a life boat to me. Write me. Tell me what happened through your eyes. If the king was right, if you have outgrown our friendship, don't bother writing back. Your silence will be enough, and I will prepare a speech which will be far from civil next time we meet. But if I'm wrong, tell me. I beg you to tell me! I miss my friend, almost as much as I miss my father and sister. If my friend, Rose, is still there, will she send her answer by the soonest post? I can *only keep the anger at bay for so long, so, please, write with haste.*

Mark

Richard read the letter again. He had been waiting for the Poynter boy to make a move like this. The only surprising thing was how long it had taken him. And, while Richard was pleased, it was disappointing how innocuous the boy had chosen to be. Having expected a far more rash course of action, Richard began to think he had misjudged the boy. He remembered the spark of defiance in the boy's eyes at their last meeting. Fear had mingled with that defiance, but it hadn't been strong enough to cover the anger smoldering beneath.

Richard was sick at how much the boy resembled his father. Not a day passed when he didn't regret his decision to spare him at Decedeo. Things were complicated now. Dragging the boy into the streets to kill him would jeopardize his goodwill with the people. Richard couldn't lose that, not when he had such masterful plans for this country. But there was the boy, a symbol of the man he hated, walking free to mock him. It was almost more than he could bear. Almost.

But he hadn't risen to his position as king with haste. On the contrary, patience was a virtue in which he was well-schooled. Waiting for the boy to make a mistake, while tedious, was the safest option. When the mistake occurred, Richard could present himself as the enforcer of the law rather than the aggressor. And there was no question whether the boy would make a mistake or not, Richard had seen the reckless anger in his eyes. It was only a matter of time, and, when it happened, Richard would know, and he would bury the boy with it.

Richard traced the adolescent handwriting with his eyes. Unintentionally, the boy had actually solved a problem the king had been wrestling with for some time. It had been a triumph when he had brought Henry's daughter to the palace. She was a piece of this game he could manipulate anyway he pleased. Looking to the future, he knew she would be the perfect bait for bringing about the downfall of the Poynters. He wasn't sure how he would use her quite yet, but he knew he could use her. His problem was what to do with her in the interim. Having managed to endear herself to the servants, the girl unknowingly created a support base for her family. The loud woman who had volunteered to be her nanny used this to her advantage. She did not speak openly about the Poynters, but she used the girl as a means to surreptitiously champion their cause. It was imperative the girl be relocated before a movement within his own staff could amass against him. However, until a position that allowed her to be used as leverage presented itself, he had been loath to move her.

The boy had inadvertently revealed a position of leverage. His letter showed a tenderness toward his sister Richard could exploit. If the boy thought there was a way he could rescue his sister, he would jump at it without hesitation. All Richard had to do was provide the opportunity, then he would have the Poynter boy.

The girl would go to Baymontiac, his old estate. There

would be no show, no announcement, just a discreet transfer of care. Then, not only would sympathies for her in the castle wane, but news of her arrival eventually would reach Decedeo; proximity would necessitate it. That fool he had left to run Baymontiac, Clifton, was malleable and could be trusted to give an accurate account of the girl. While it could take years, Richard knew the temptation to act would prove to be too strong for the boy.

Richard looked at the letter one last time. He could still post it. He could still send it to Verderva, to the boy's friend whom Richard had used to his advantage. He could allow reconciliation a chance to thrive between the two. There were so many things he could do with this letter.

He held the pages of sloppy, yet sincere, print over the candle, allowing them to ignite. The fire ate away at the body of the letter until there was nothing left to consume. Richard watched it burn in silence. Let the boy remain without an answer to his plea. As the days slipped into weeks, the pain of his friend's silence would sharpen the edges of the anger the boy had revealed in his eyes and his words. And Richard wanted him angry, for wrath to be the Poynter legacy. The players were set for this plan to become a reality, and all Richard needed to do was wait. And he would wait. He would wait for as long as was necessary.

Eleven

*I*T HAD BEEN A MISERABLE DAY. ROSE SUPPOSED SHE should be thankful for the spring rains since she could remember the years of drought. Still able to feel the uncomfortable pinch consistent hunger had left in her stomach, she felt some thankfulness for the puddles she stepped around, but she dredged up the sentiment with effort. However, it took no effort at all to dislike the trickle that ran down her back and the cloud layer that hid the sun. She had so needed to see the sun today.

It was her birthday. She was fourteen. She was still getting used to the changes her body had undergone — changes that marked her as a woman. This should have been an exciting birthday, one that she celebrated with her family in honor of her coming of age. For her, it could be nothing but the opposite. She had no family left to her. Leonard was dead. Uncle Henry was probably dead. Her mother was dead and had been for exactly fourteen years. Hope was gone. She had not heard from Aunt

Anne or Mark in the ten months she had been at Verderva. For all she knew they could have returned to that place Morgan described. Then there was her father.

She swatted at the moisture on her face and blamed the rain for its presence. Her father might as well be dead. Or, better said, she might as well be dead to her father. She didn't know why she had expected him to send anything. As it was, she had been disappointed, once again, by his negligence to send her a word. Perhaps things would have been different if her mother were still alive. She would be home now between her parents and brother. They would sing the coming of age song while she presided over a cake her mother had made. Her father and brother would bellow the tune in their toneless voices and her mother would salvage the song with her sweet voice. Then they would laugh and tell funny stories about their Rose. They would say her name, her true name, even while they told her they loved her.

"Stop it!" she told herself with a vicious shake of her head. Oh, why was her foolish heart so bent on being broken? But knowing the dream of her father's love was a fantasy couldn't stop her from hoping for it. Sometimes she tried to callous that part of herself against him, but was unable. Having forgiven him the night Lady Diane had listened to her confession, she couldn't feel angry toward him. Confused and hurt, but not angry. There were fleeting moments when she wanted to be angry at him, just like he was angry at her. Then, maybe, her heart could finally stop expecting things he would never give. Instead, it seemed she must resign herself to heartache.

She hadn't told anyone it was her birthday. Her heart as overcast as the sky, she didn't feel like celebrating. She had been preemptively glum all week in preparation for today, and poor Elizabeth was at her wit's end to guess why. Rose would apologize to her sweet friend tomorrow, when it wasn't the anniversary of the murder she had committed fourteen years ago. For today though, she felt entitled to be miserable.

It was dark in her room when she arrived. Heavy curtains hung at the windows and blocked what dim light the day had to offer. Elizabeth had forgotten to open them. Rose debated leaving them drawn, of crawling into bed and sleeping until her wretched birthday was complete. But, even in her grim state of mind, such an idea seemed too melodramatic. She would spar with today as long as it was today knowing it would be over soon. So with determination, she crossed the room and opened the curtains.

"Happy birthday!"

Several voices greeted her with these words. Rose, astonished, spun around in time to see Elizabeth and a handful of girls she had befriended stepping out of their hiding places. One of them held a cake with a candle stuck in it, which another girl was attempting to light. Elizabeth, her perpetually wide smile firmly in place, enveloped Rose in a hug. Hugging her back, Rose felt her miserable feelings begin to fall away.

"How did you know?" Rose asked when she regained her powers of speech.

"I have my ways," Elizabeth said, her face bright with a secret.

Lady Diane. No one else could have told her because no one else knew. Rose felt warmth beginning to radiate to her extremities.

"You did this for me?" she asked in an undertone only Elizabeth could hear.

"Of course I did. You're my friend, and I couldn't let such an important birthday go past unnoticed!"

Of course. That's what Elizabeth, her dear friend, had said. Of course. As if this display was the rule, not the exception. As if it were only natural people would want to celebrate you on your birthday. Of course.

But what had her foolish heart been thinking? When Rose thrust her books and music away from her because they reminded her too much of the Poynters passion for such things, Elizabeth always put an arm around her and hummed Rohirt. Elizabeth was the friend with a million questions about Rose's past in her face, yet deferentially never asked one. Of course. Elizabeth had said, "Of course."

Rose went to her cake, her miseries momentarily forgotten. But her foolish heart would have one last say in the matter. Surrounded by friends, Rose couldn't help but wonder if her father had thought of her at all today. Had he taken the time to remember he had a daughter—a daughter who looked like her mother—and that today was her birthday? Or had he put it from his mind—wishing instead for the son and wife who were dead?

She couldn't think of these questions for long. Not when the girls were urging her to blow out the candle. Deliberately choosing to drop her melancholy for a time, Rose complied.

JOHN SHOOK OFF his wet cloak as he entered the palace. He should have taken the carriage, but it hadn't started raining until he was an hour out. He would ask the king for a room if it didn't let up after their meeting. A servant took his cloak, calling him "sir" as he did so. John liked to hear himself called sir. He enjoyed the position of power he had grown accustomed to these last ten months. Being a strict, but fair lord to those in his charge gave him pride. While he wasn't loved, per se, he was respected and far from hated. He allowed his workers certain freedoms he had always desired from the lords he had served under in the past, and some people were actually attempting to move to farms in his jurisdiction. In short, he worked to be the opposite of everything he hated in the nobility.

A young guard met John by the door with brown curls spilling out from underneath his helmet. Those curls and his full beard managed to soften what could have been a harsh, angular face. John amended this thought the longer he looked at the young man. His face didn't seem harsh at all once his merry green eyes were noticed. The soldier led him on in silence while John continued considering him. He looked to be about Leonard's age. That is, if Leonard weren't dead. John stopped himself as he began to imagine his son being friends with this boy. John didn't have a son anymore. He didn't have any children anymore.

That isn't true.

The little voice he couldn't silence spoke in its distinct voice. It was the voice of the man his wife had tried to cultivate; the man the bitter stranger had overwhelmed. Refusing to disappear into the shadows, the better man would whisper to John when he least expected it. Today especially, since it was the girl's birthday. It was difficult to forget the day he'd been forced to make the worst trade of his life, though he tried hard. He even remembered how old she was. She was fourteen today. This probably would have been her coming of age birthday. John silenced the better man before he continued. No more thoughts like this. It was better if he forgot he had a daughter, even if there were sparse moments when he missed her presence.

John forced himself to think on the king's summons instead. Having summoned him the day before, the king refused to give John any information. All he said was to come the next day to receive an important mission. His ego stroked, John had tried to imagine what the king would have called him for on such short notice. Perhaps he had noticed how well he had been doing with Baymontiac, and he was going to entrust more land to John's care. Perhaps he was calling John in order to seek advice for a problem he couldn't solve. Giving his imagination free rein, he allowed it to run wild with possibilities before contenting himself with not knowing. He was here now, and all his questions would soon be answered.

"Lord Clifton?"

It was the young soldier. He had been sneaking glances back toward John for several minutes.

"What is it, son?"

"It's a pleasure to meet you, sir. I believe your daughter came to my house this past winter. She is friends with my sister at Verderva school. Rosemary spoke well of you."

The bitter stranger didn't understand. How could she speak well of him? He would have preferred to hear she had renounced him as her father, decrying his actions from the rooftops. It would be easy then to say he had no daughter. But to hear she spoke well of him flew in the face of everything he had come to expect from the world. The thought of her forgiveness filled him with anger, the same anger she refused to feel.

"She's a sweet girl. You must be proud of her," the soldier said. John focused his eyes on the young man, his words becoming sharp.

"What is your name?"

"Alfred Winston, sir."

"Well, Alfred Winston, I would advise you not to make comments about things you know nothing about."

Winston looked stunned at how fast things had changed. He led John the rest of the way in silence. He was equally as silent as he let John pass into the room with the king. John could see more of the angles of the young man's face and noticed that his eyes weren't laughing anymore. With a flash of regret crossing the wasteland of his conscience, John entered the room with the king. It was John's turn to be disappointed when he entered to find the king was not alone. A handful of other nobles filled the room, and they were pouring over a set of maps. The king briefly acknowledged John and then returned his attention to the maps. He continued this way, ignoring John for several more minutes. Feeling his ire rise at this treatment, John calmed himself with several steadying breaths. After a long time, the king finally dismissed the other lords. Alone at last, the king addressed him.

"Clifton, there is something you must do for me."

John felt himself bristle at this brusque introduction. It was like the king couldn't be bothered to waste two words on someone like John, even though he had summoned him here in the first place. Thankfully John's mask was in place, so the king didn't see any of these emotions flit across his face.

"What can I do for you, sire?"

"I'm sure you remember our friend, Henry Poynter?"

Feeling himself tense, John tried his best to remain impassive.

"Of course, I remember Henry Poynter."

"Then you must remember his daughter. She has been a recipient of my benevolence since the day her traitorous father was removed from power. My situation has changed since that day. It has become apparent to me that it would be advantageous if the girl was kept somewhere other than the palace. Since you have a history with her, it makes sense for her to be removed to

Baymontiac. More importantly, I know I can count on you to give me accurate reports on her, unlike some of my other nobles. What do you say, Lord Clifton? Are you the right man for this task?"

No. That's what John wanted to say. How, in all of Agumbra, could he be the right man to take responsibility for the child of his nemesis? He had proven himself less than worthy to raise his own children, let alone this girl. Part of him still smoldered hot against Henry Poynter and the silver spoon born holding in his mouth. But this was a chance for him to distinguish himself in the eyes of the king. If he did this, if he did it well, then the king would notice and grant him further honors. Besides, the king had only asked him to take the girl. Nothing had been said about raising her or being kind to her.

"Yes, sir. I am your man."

"Excellent. My man will show you where the girl is. She is ready to be transported tonight, but if you would prefer to wait until morning, then I will have a room prepared."

A short nod from the king signaled the end of the meeting. As if by magic, the door behind him opened, revealing the man John was to follow. Bowing to his king, John fell in step behind the servant. A tumult had begun in his chest when he agreed to the task the king relegated to him. He wasn't sure to what he had agreed. The implications, being both deep and convoluted, wouldn't manifest themselves for years. But John pressed all these things into a tightly packed box at the back of his mind. He told himself he wouldn't need to do anything other than provide a roof over the girl's head until she was grown. Nothing said he even needed to see the girl after today. These thoughts comforting him, John, impassive mask in place, did not falter as he walked down the long corridors.

It wasn't long before the servant was opening a door for John to pass through. Refusing to add any significance to the action, John stepped into the room. He shouldn't have been surprised to see Nancy. She had been there the night Hope had been taken—adamantly refusing to be separated from the infant. Even so, John hesitated at the sight of Decedeo's former cook. In her arms was the sleeping child. She was so much bigger than John remembered. It seemed impossible she could have changed so much in so little time. It made him wonder if all of them had changed equally as much since that fateful night at the Hunter's Cottage. Nancy's eyes narrowed when she saw John. Those baleful eyes would kill him if they could. John knew that instinctively.

"It's not the devil, Hope, but it's one of his demons."

"I've come for the child," John said, undeterred. "King Richard has charged me to take her to Baymontiac. He said nothing about you, though."

"You aren't worthy to take this child, John Clifton. I guess that has never stopped you in the past. You weren't worthy to wipe my master's boots or look my lady in the eye. But here you are, a small, hateful man masquerading in noble's attire."

When the servant began moving toward Nancy, John stopped him. He didn't know why since the cook's words had sparked his anger. It was the better man who spared the cook. Annoyed, but unwilling to figure out the inner workings of the decision, John considered Nancy in silence.

"I must say there is one thing you deserve," Nancy continued, "You deserve that traitor daughter of yours. I had never thought Rose capable of such terrible things, but I see now she inherited more than her fair share of your traits."

Something inexplicable panged John's soul. The better man took these words and used them to strike a guilty chord inside him. He had never considered it was more than his own name he had besmirched. His daughter had loved and been loved by these people. Now they thought she had turned against them. He wondered why this thought bothered him so much. What did it matter to him if those who hated him also hated his progeny? But it did matter. He hated that it mattered, but he couldn't change that it mattered. Blast the wretch, especially today on her birthday, for haunting him wherever he went!

Hope began to cry as she woke in Nancy's arms. Love and concern replaced Nancy's fierce demeanor as she comforted the child. John remained silent. They both knew it was time for an event neither of them were ready to perform. As the servant began to approach again, Nancy glared him into submission. Instinctively rocking Hope in an effort to quiet her crying, Nancy stepped toward John of her own accord. Her face free of soft emotions, she considered John. Still, John was silent. With pain-filled eyes, Nancy kissed the child's head one last time. Then, looking for all the world as if she'd rather be falling on her own sword, she passed Hope into John's awkward embrace.

He held her as best he could, as he had seen the mothers in the village hold their children—as he remembered his wife holding Leonard. When the toddler continued to cry, John began humming a tune his wife had always sung to Leonard. Though he didn't know where the memory of the song had come from, the origin of the lullaby didn't matter. As if that was all she had wanted, Hope quieted, her eyes blinking heavily with sleep. A warmth he had forgotten he could feel flickered in John's heart. Confused, he leaned tentatively into it, and it burned steadily while he watched the child sleep in his arms.

When he looked up, Nancy was looking at him as if he were a stranger. She was still wary and angry, but behind her concerned countenance there was something that looked like hope. When the bitter stranger saw that look, he stomped on the warmth in John's heart, extinguishing it completely. John felt his gaze turn cold, and Nancy, gladly reciprocating, gave him an icy glare. She stepped close to John, her entire person demanding attention.

"This is bigger than you, John Clifton. This child is more precious than you can ever imagine. She plays a part in a bigger game. We all do, but her especially. I haven't figured out how, but that doesn't make it any less true. I don't think you are good enough to protect such an important player. Prove me wrong, John Clifton. I dare you to prove me wrong."

Her words clinging to his skin, Nancy and the servant exited, leaving John alone with the little girl. John felt hot at those words until the girl stirred in his arms. Completely unbidden, the warmth in his heart rekindled. He studied her face, trying to reconcile what he saw with what he remembered. Her features, still soft in her baby face, were beginning to solidify, making it easier to see her grown up appearance. She favored her mother, Lady Anne—a discovery that softened John. He had always respected the Lady of Decedeo, as had everyone he had ever known.

John remembered the last time he had seen Lady Anne. She had been unconscious and bleeding in the saddle of a young guard as he rode away from her burning home. He had been disturbed at seeing her flaccid and helpless as a rag doll, especially when she had always moved with such purpose. His pity hadn't been strong enough to stop him from stealing her child, though. The child he now held in his arms.

Violently, he threw such thoughts away from his mind. He didn't regret the decisions he had made to get where he was now. He was the man he had always wanted to be. Others who had fallen in the process didn't matter, no matter who they were. Values the better man wanted to feel—values of truth and honor—didn't matter, nor did the number of times his conscience, albeit weak, nagged him. None of that mattered. This was what he wanted, and if he had to babysit Henry Poynter's brat to further those goals, then so be it.

Walking to the cradle in the room, he laid the sleeping child in it. She flexed, smiled, and continued sleeping, as if nothing in all Agumbra were the matter. John hated how peaceful she was when there was no peace to be found for him. Turning on his heel, he stormed from the room. He wanted to get away from the small girl who made crooked what had always been straight, graying all of his blacks and whites. But, no matter how swiftly he walked, he couldn't cool the warm spot where the child had laid her head, nor the spot in his heart that refused to be snuffed.

Twelve

*M*ARK STILL WASN'T ABLE TO BELIEVE IT. TWO DAYS had passed since the incident, but the time lapse hadn't given him clarity. Unfortunately, he didn't think he could stomach the one fact that had become clear—his mother and Morgan had lied to him. Not once, not twice, but for months. For months they had withheld information that was equally as important to him as it was to them. Thinking of it set his teeth on edge. He had tried his best to do nothing, to bear it calmly, but the effort had proven too much. He had asked Robbie to convene the boys. If no one else was going to take action, Mark and his friends would.

Restraining the urge to constantly check over his shoulder, Mark made his way to their gathering spot in the woods. Having called the meeting in haste, he wasn't sure who would make it. He hoped for enough comrades to carry out the plan he had in mind. Casting a glance over his shoulder again, he couldn't shake the feeling he wasn't alone. But, every time he looked around, he saw only the familiar trees of the wood.

Familiar. The word felt sticky on his tongue—like something too sweet that made bile rise in the back of his throat. He had grown familiar with many things. But how? How had Morgan's house grown familiar? How had Morgan himself become something common when, not too long ago, everything about him seemed mysterious? How had Mark gotten used to waking up in a world where he had neither father nor sister? It had been exactly a year since that fateful day, the day when all he had once counted familiar had been sundered in two. One year and his mind had adapted to make normative what had once baffled him.

But now he wasn't sure what this paradigm he had learned to call normal was—not since he had eavesdropped on his mother and mentor. He knew at the time it was wrong, that he should move along and listen no more, but he couldn't. They were talking of the other place, the place they had planned to go to before Hope's abduction. They must have been speaking in some sort of code. Mark thought that because he couldn't comprehend everything they were saying. But he knew, instinctively, the nature of their subject matter. He had been so engrossed in making sense of their coded talk that he almost had missed the topic they had started speaking of next. It was this last subject, not the first, that drove him into the woods now.

When he arrived to the gathering place, Robbie, Caleb, and all the other boys were already there. Concern in his eyes, Robbie stood when he saw Mark.

"Mark! There you are. Is everything all right? Why did you tell me to get everyone?"

Mark held up a hand for silence. He needed a moment to find the words for communicating his request to his friends. He had been so preoccupied that he hadn't taken time to formulate his question until now. Words came. He didn't know if they were the right words, but they were the ones that came to his lips and would have to do.

"It's okay, Robbie. There isn't anything wrong right now. I'm sorry that I worried you. I've just had some news that has upended me."

"What is it, Mark? What news?" Caleb asked.

"Hope has been moved to Baymontiac Estate," Mark said in a level tone. "She was moved there two months ago."

Mark was grateful the boys understood the magnitude of the news he had given them. He could see the recognition blossoming in their eyes, but none of them responded. They just considered him in silence. His frustration rising, Mark looked around at all of them. Robbie, sensing the mounting tension, stepped forward and spoke.

"We understand how important this is to you, Mark. I guess we don't know what you want us to do."

"Isn't it obvious?" Mark asked. "I want to go get her. I want to rescue my sister and bring her home."

His friends looked at him like he was insane. Maybe he was insane, he didn't know for sure. What he did know for sure was Hope was in closer proximity to him than she had been for a year. He knew if he could manage to bring Hope home, then they would leave for the other place. The hole in his spirit, the one caused by longing for something he hadn't known he'd been missing, would finally be filled in the other place. Mark knew it would because Morgan carried the aura of that place in the folds of his cloak. Breathing it in as he did his chores, Mark knew he would find answers to so many of his questions in that other place.

And what was to keep him here now? He would miss these boys who had become his friends, but they would understand. His friendships had become more fluid after Rose. Like a fool, he had once thought he couldn't move on without her by his side. Apparently, she hadn't felt the same. He had tried to keep the tender part of himself, the part that wanted to understand, open for her response, the one that never came. That tender spot grew harder to open every day, until he was mentally prying it open despite the pain it caused. One morning, he realized he didn't want to feel the pain anymore. Tired of trying, he stopped waiting for her letter. If she could walk away from their friendship, then so could he. That's exactly what he would do when Hope was home. He, with his family, would leave this hateful corner of Agumbra for a place that whispered hope. He just had to get his sister here first.

"Mark, how are we going to do that? We're just a group of apprentices. Surely she's guarded by soldiers. And how would we infiltrate Baymontiac in the first place?"

"Security on her is low," Mark said. "She is watched, but not as stringently as you would imagine."

"How can you know that? How can you know any of this?"

"I heard it from a reliable source," Mark said in a low voice. His mother and godfather may have hidden the information from him, but Mark trusted their words to be true.

"This is madness, Mark! Do you even have a plan?"

"Jack will help us."

The group pondered this idea. After Jonathan had been killed, Jack's family had moved to Baymontiac where he had begun an apprenticeship as a groom. Jack was allowed to periodically travel back to Decedeo town so the boys still saw their companion from time to time. He would be an invaluable resource.

Mark could feel the mood shifting in his favor, but then it froze over again. His friend's eyes blanked out, and several of them took an involuntary step back. Mark felt a presence behind him. The same one which had haunted his steps on his way to the gathering. Tensing himself, Mark turned around. He wasn't surprised to see Morgan standing there, his arms folded across his chest and his piercing eyes flashing dangerously. Sensing the magnitude of the trouble he was in, Mark felt himself shrink back.

"Go home, boys," Morgan said.

There was no question involved, no other option for them to consider. They bolted like guilty men before a lawman. Morgan waited until they were gone, then turned to Mark.

"What do you think you are doing, boy?"

Any shame Mark had felt melted away in the heat of his defiance.

"What you should be doing. I'm doing something to bring my sister home."

"You're a fool who's going to get himself killed."

"But at least I'm doing something!"

"You think because you overhear one conversation you're now an expert on this matter? You know nothing, and ignorance has killed more boys than I care to recount."

"And whose fault is it that I'm ignorant?" Mark said, hardly holding onto his control.

"That was not my decision to make, boy. If it were up to me you would know everything."

"But she's my sister!"

"And she's my goddaughter!"

In the momentary silence that followed, Mark and Morgan commiserated. But the moment passed like chaff in the wind. In that moment, Mark wished again he had hit his growth spurt. He hated craning his neck to meet eyes with his godfather. He wanted to meet those piercing eyes at least on a level plane. Instead, feeling small, he was reduced to projecting himself as someone bigger; someone to be taken seriously.

"Why must you keep secrets from me? How can I trust you if you won't tell me the truth?" Mark asked.

Infinitesimally, Morgan softened.

"I will never lie to you, Mark. Never. There are just some things that are not yours to know in this stage of your life, though they will someday be yours to know. Sooner than you think, you will know everything we know. Now is not that time. Be patient, Mark."

Mark still felt the hot blood pounding in his ears. Whatever softness Morgan had taken on disappeared when he noticed Mark's demeanor. The healer folded his arms across his chest definitively.

"You can't know everything right now, but know this. I will find out if you ever plan another venture to rescue your sister. Trust me when I say I will find out. That day is also the day you cease to be my apprentice. No questions asked. Am I understood?"

Mark glowered at the ground. Disappointment and anger twisting inside of him.

"Am I understood, Marcus Henry Poynter?"

"Yes sir," Mark said, feeling anything but repentant. Nodding curtly, Morgan motioned for Mark to follow him. No more words were said. No more words were needed. Mind whirling, Mark walked behind his mentor. He wasn't going to abandon his plans to rescue Hope…no matter how long it took. He would be patient. He would be wily. He would wait for the perfect opportunity. When it appeared, he would take it. He would do what Morgan refused to do. He would bring Hope home.

WATCHING THE BOY leave with his mentor, Barinne cursed

under his breath. If the healer hadn't appeared, the boy would have made a fool-hearty plan to storm Baymontiac Estate. There, Barinne would have been waiting for him, and capturing him, would present him before the king. That feat would have earned Barinne unending favor with the crown. However, not all hope was lost. Barinne had seen the boy's face as he spoke to the healer. He wasn't going to give up. The healer's apprentice would have to wait, possibly for years, before his chance presented itself. But, when it did, the boy was going to take it. And, when he took it, Barinne would be waiting. Imagining the rewards that awaited him for such a prize, Barinne knew he could wait patiently for the boy's folly. He knew he wouldn't be disappointed either. Folly always revealed itself in the end.

Four Years Later

Time is said to heal
All the past, upon us, has thrust.
Yet we wait, with languishing zeal,
For validation to this trust.

Thirteen

SUMMER 266

HE WAITED IN THE DARK TOWER PEERING INTO THE moonlit night. Though everything was peaceful and calm, he could feel his pulse quickening with anticipation. Tonight would see the culmination of a myriad of his projects, and the prospect filled him with restless energy. Desperately wanting to pace the small room, he willed himself to remain still instead. It was important that the man he was meeting remained ignorant of the personal gratification this would bring. He managed a calm demeanor despite the difficulty. After all, he had achieved his current position by proficiently denying his baser instincts.

Rustling sounds on the stairs outside the door alerted him that his patience would soon be rewarded. Taking a deep breath, he continued to stare out the window, as if bored. He heard a man enter and then the click as the door was shut, still he didn't turn. Instead he kept looking at the moon-dappled landscape.

"Your Highness," an accented voice said.

Richard turned to face a bearded man whose drab cloak couldn't quite conceal the inordinate amount of jewelry around his neck and hanging from his ears.

"Captain Shargon. Thank you for coming to meet with me."

"His majesty seemed to indicate there would be profit involved if I did. So here I am, curious as to the occasion and wondering why it merited such strict secrecy."

"Forgive me for the necessary secrecy. I hope it did not render you any discomfort."

"It will not be a burden to return to my ship, if that is what you are asking."

This cold, diplomatic talk had been practiced over the years of their relationship. Though they remained distrustful of each other they were shrewd enough to know their partnership was mutually beneficial. These opening words were the beginning tests as they prepared to enter into the dance they both knew so well.

"I have a proposition for you, Captain. One not unlike the one I made you several years ago."

"Go on."

"I am in need of another attack from the Allies."

"I'm sorry, your Highness, but I don't know if your tiny navy can withstand another war, imagined or otherwise."

Richard's ears burned at the insult, but he remained in control of his features.

"You are mistaken. I do not need an attack on my shores, but on those of my northern neighbors, the Gruilitians."

Shargon's eyebrows shot up at this news.

"That is an interesting proposition, your Highness. May I ask why the king wishes to quarrel with Gruilit?"

"I do not wish to quarrel. On the contrary, I wish to find myself in their good graces."

"That seems like quite a task when those men are known for the atrocities they commit in the name of their deities. It begs the question if they have any graces, let alone good ones, to acquire. Besides, I am confused about how an attack on them places you in their favor."

"But you see, sir, it will not be me or even my ally, the island of Cej, who will be attacking them. Rather it will be our useful friends, the Allies of Staveen, who will be threatening."

Scoffing, the captain began to look around like his time was being wasted.

"I believe I see where this is going, and I fail to see how this deal is beneficial to me. Honestly, I don't see how it's beneficial to you, either. The last time my men paraded as the Allies it was not my men who bled, and it was not I who lost ships. That honor belonged to you, or do you not remember the massacre of your flagship and the burned corpses of your men? It was several weeks before you were done fishing their bodies from the ocean, wasn't it?"

Richard remembered. It hadn't been his order that had sent Deteen's flagship to that hellish bonfire, but it had been his plan for Cej to masquerade as the threatening Ally force. Though then, as now, his pragmatic mind was able to justify the sacrifice, there were nights when the bloated faces of the charred sailors came back to haunt him.

"Your Highness will forgive me; however, I lack your callousness to knowingly send my ships to be destroyed. Especially when there is no benefit to counterbalance it."

Richard smiled in spite of the resentment he felt at the slight.

"I apologize, Captain. I must have misled you. In my plan there is no loss of life or property. Rather, we both gain."

The pirate's eyes narrowed in suspicion, his cunning mind working through the possibilities behind them. Richard wasn't worried, though. The pirate's curiosity always won in the end.

"Explain."

Richard laughed inwardly. These pirates were so easy to manipulate. They would do whatever you pleased if you hinted at any form of monetary gain. Richard could already see the greedy glint in Shargon's eye, even as the pirate tried to hide it.

"You and I will approach the king of Gruilit and inform him that, in your travels, you have heard rumors of an attack on Gruilitian shores to be carried out by the Allies. Deteen will remain untouched due to our effective defense, however Gruilit remains untested. You informed me, and I, knowing Gruilit's lack of navy, came straight away to offer aid. We'll tell them we have magic to use against the enemy. Gruilit is filled with superstitious people, and the word *magic* will endear them to us.

"We will set up a perimeter and wait for your ships to sail in as the supposed Allies of Staveen. You will then have your wielders perform their magic for the Gruilitians to witness. Then we will give chase in an attempt to run the *Allies* back into the sea. We return as heroes without having spilled any blood."

The Captain was silent in consideration. Richard waited patiently, knowing if he pushed too hard he may lose him.

"I spoke to you of what a delicate art our wielders practice when it was utilized last," Shargon said. "The dark magic is powerful and does not like to be controlled. So, though my wielders are masters at their work, the outcome is at times unstable and unpredictable. I cannot guarantee the safety of my own ships if we turn this power on them."

"I remember. But I also remember you told me that since it is powerful and unwieldy, your men can only project it so far. That's why we had to wait for *The Nightsong* to come close before they could attack it. Gruilit doesn't need to know this. We will tell them that since the dark magic is unpredictable we can't guarantee it will sink the enemy ships. We can guarantee it will strike terror in their hearts. All you must do is stop your ships out of range then have them flee when the fire falls."

"You make a compelling argument," Shargon conceded after a moment. "There is the other matter to consider, though. Do you recall our first conversation?"

"The one that happened right after your first appearance before the nobles? You admitted to me that you were manipulating my predecessor into believing the Allies were coming to fight rather than to form an alliance."

"Yes, and since you recall those details, you no doubt

remember the reasons as to why such an alliance would be detrimental to the prospering of Cej."

"A thousand apologies, it has been many years since we talked on this. May I impose upon you for a retelling?" Richard was delighted to see his question peeved the pirate.

"Such an alliance would give Staveen a staging point for beginning a witch hunt to eliminate us, or at least put an end to our livelihood. If Staveen finds out about our trickery, they will know they have been deceived, and will come back to finish what they started. All those concerns remain current. Now, I agreed to pose as the Allies to repay the debt we owed you for convincing the people to trust us; however, I fear if we do this again we open ourselves to the possibility of discovery."

"My friend, I have thought of this as well. That is why only I, and no one from Deteen, will accompany you. Then it is only Cejans who know of the ruse. You are an accomplished leader. I am sure you are able to maintain your own people."

Becoming ponderous, Shargon paid little attention to the bite behind Richard's words.

"Since you have all the answers, I will impose one more question. If you recall, we barely escaped notice last time. My wielders performed some powerful magic when they created the drought that facilitated your rise to power. Even Staveen's wielders, weak as they are in their relationship with the Magic, felt the energy pull from this use of dark magic. This plot offers the same potential of discovery by Staveen. So I must ask; what does Cej gain? What can you offer that makes the risk worth taking?"

Richard smiled inwardly. He'd won.

"I'm surprised you're still concerned with the Staveenians. It is my understanding that they ceased to be allied years ago. They're too busy bickering amongst themselves to bother sailing north again. Besides, who's to say they would even feel an energy pull from the dark magic this time? My sources tell me that their relationship with the Magic has only grown weaker the longer they fight amongst themselves. They're beginning to abandon it just like Agumbra did generations ago.

"As to why this campaign is worth it, Deteen will pay you your usual fee, which, in and of itself, is a handsome offering. Also, if Gruilit pays us anything, which they most likely will, you will receive sixty percent of it."

The pirate's eyes grew wide. That sum was more than he had ever expected to receive.

"Do we have a deal, Captain?"

Shargon gathered himself behind his mask again.

"I will have to speak to my chieftains, but I am positive we have a deal."

Richard noticed Shargon didn't even pretend to deliberate until morning, and mused that Cej must be desperate for funds. The pirate seemed to realize his mistake too late and attempted to save face by acting indifferent.

"Was there anything else you wished to discuss?"

"Yes. You received the notice of some cargo I need you to take home with you, correct?"

"Yes. It was an unusual request, but easily carried out. To be sure, we are allowed to do with him whatever we like?"

"I leave him completely in your care. All I ask is that he never returns."

"Excellent. Then there shouldn't be any issues."

"Thank you, Captain. That is all that I have tonight. You will be returned to your ship at a time when secrecy can be maintained. We will stay in contact as you prepare your people for the ruse. Then we will be looking for you on the horizon as a warning of the callous attack of those dastardly Allies."

"Yes, those villains," Shargon concurred with a grin.

The pirate turned toward the door he had entered through. His hand had started to open it again when, against his better judgment, Richard found himself asking the corsair a question. Or rather, *the* question.

"Pardon me, Captain. Before you go, I wondered if you had considered the question we discussed in our last meeting. You have had ample time to make a decision."

Shargon paused with his hand on the doorknob, then let it go with a sigh. Turning, he gave Richard a completely unmasked look with all the political wiliness drained away and replaced with honest curiosity...perhaps a touch of fear.

"It was an unusual request, but I relayed it. My Master Wielder, who being as intrigued as I, has some questions for you. We ask these questions to all who seek to learn dark magic, but it seemed particularly relevant to ask you. Why is it you, a king of a country with a long history of denying the veracity of magic, wants to learn what you obviously distrust? And since you obviously believe the Magic is real, why do you seek dark magic? It truly is a sinister force that does not like to be controlled. We don't mind embracing it, humble pirates that we are, but why don't you seek your own magic—the Magic of your precious King?"

Though Richard felt his eyes flashing, he couldn't stop himself. It was only fair to answer these personal questions because he had made a very personal request. But he still didn't like being queried.

"I don't deny the old stories are true. I believe every word of them. It is because I believe them that I come to you. I will not be usurped by those who believe in a greater king, nor even by that King…should he ever show his miserable face again. I will fight fire with fire in that day, and until that day comes, I will cut down the few who believe. This is my kingdom. Zealots who say otherwise will be destroyed.

"I can't do any of those things with a force I have to ask for permission to use. The Magic is dying. It died in Agumbra long ago, and it's in its final throes in Staveen. I have no use for something that weak. I want to control something powerful; something wild and unpredictable. It's the only way I can protect all that is mine!"

Richard spoke with a calmness he didn't feel. He could feel passion welling inside him, even as the words came out smooth. The Captain looked at him in silence for a time, then answered.

"Jubion help the one who crosses you. I will give your

answer to my Master Wielder and will have an answer for you when we meet again."

With that he bowed slightly and left. Turning back to the window, Richard indulged in the pleasure of a wide smile. Everything was going just as it ought. Even his contact in the north had messaged him with news of promising activity. Circumstances at the palace were stable enough that he even felt comfortable leaving to conduct a personal mission. Feeling the night air on his skin, he knew it was time to travel north to his old estate to see the end of a mess he should have ended years ago. No matter. The situation would bow to his will, and he would win. He always won. He made dead sure of that.

Fourteen

STRETCHING HIS TALL, LANKY FRAME, MARK TOOK A moment to feel the spring sun on his face. It had been several days since the sun had deigned to shine, choosing instead to leave the people of Deteen in the clutches of a long string of gray days filled with drizzling rain. Mark was happy to see the cheeky blighter again, even if it had been as fickle as a child the entire length of spring. He allowed himself a rare smile. Nothing elaborate. Just a small, mildly sardonic twist at the corner of his mouth.

"I see we have been reduced to day dreaming instead of working."

Morgan straightened from his stooped position. Neither of them smiled, but there was no tension between the healer and his apprentice as there once had been. Recalling the days after their confrontation about Hope's rescue, Mark remembered a palpable tension. In those days, he had thought he would never forgive Morgan...and he hadn't for a long time. But Morgan had provided a constancy Mark couldn't hold out against. Mark avoided using the word love. It meant attaching himself in a way he was only willing to do in a few cases. Morgan had become one of those cases, though. He loved him for his patience as a teacher, for his willingness to be a father to him, and for his understanding during the times Mark didn't want him to be a father. Mark would be declared a man soon, and it was this man, the one Mark could now look eye to eye with, who would declare him tradesman healer, and Mark loved him for it. Having adapted his godfather's stoicism, Mark never said these things aloud, but he knew it was understood between them.

Yet, despite the quiet love he felt toward Morgan, despite all that was understood, there were still differences that remained unspoken and misunderstood. There were still unyielding spots in Mark's soul that he kept completely secret. Having become calloused, there were times when Mark forgot the soreness was there. These secret wounds smoldered deep into a dull anger he always carried with him. Anger toward the king, anger toward all who ruined his life that day five years ago, anger toward those who had betrayed him, and anger toward those who held his sister captive. He had been working on a plan to rectify this last injustice. While under Morgan's watchful eye, Mark hadn't been able to plan as he would have liked. As a tradesman though, he would be free to pursue this end without fear of consequences.

"Mark?"

Shaking himself back into the present, Mark answered his godfather.

"Sorry, Morgan. My thoughts were elsewhere."

"I find it hard to believe picking herbs hasn't captivated your full attention."

"You know full well how much I enjoy this task. Who wouldn't? Stooping for hours on end while rooting through pungent plant life is a veritable dream."

The pair half smiled at the long standing joke. Feeling the sunlight on his face again, Mark gave himself over to enjoying it.

"Go ahead home, Mark. I'll finish up what's left to do."

"Pray tell, from where does this rash of charity spring?" Mark asked, taken aback.

"It's too nice of a day to be spent picking herbs. You've been working hard and deserve an afternoon off. Why don't you find your mother? She looked like she could use some cheering this morning."

Knowing it was pointless to argue with Morgan, Mark wordlessly accepted the gift of time he had been given. Leaving his herb basket, he made his way back toward home. Spring got the better of him, and he caught himself whistling a tune as he walked, his prone-to-be-too-serious personality relenting enough for him to enjoy the activity. It was too marvelous a day to be overly serious.

As he neared the house, he saw his mother hanging laundry. Capitalizing on her ignorance of his arrival, he studied her for a moment. She was far from an old woman, but the years and her sorrows had taken their toll. She, like him, had grown pensive with the passing of time, and she wore it upon her face. She appeared happy overall, yet it was tempered in a way he didn't recall as a child. Admittedly, she looked less haggard than she had during her phase of stirring restlessly in her sleep, but the edges of her face were sharper now. The graying hair at her temples and the facial scar from Sir Richard's blow magnified that careworn appearance.

Mark had also noticed the appearance of a worry line that served as a bridge between her eyes. Always slightly distracted, those eyes looked past him to something richer; something deeper. It was almost like a deep, visceral part of her had come awake in this place and was waiting for something she believed to be close. It was a bittersweet, desirous look that intrigued Mark as much as it concerned him. He could tell it was the same longing he felt for the other place he still hadn't seen. It was tied to her past somehow—that past he knew so little about. Though she always managed to gently, yet firmly, change the subject when it came up, her eyes couldn't hide the truth within. She wore that look now as she performed the monotonous tasks of everyday life. It made her look unbearably sad. With nothing but trite comforts in tow, Mark felt useless to help her.

Mark wished his father was there. He would know exactly what to do…what to say. She wasn't complete without him, and Mark realized for the first time he was only seeing a part of his mother. Melancholy began falling on him as he realized he would probably never see her completely whole again.

Suddenly, he knew what his father would do. Mark had seen him do it time and time again, especially on such a glorious day as this. It was a foolproof way to make her smile.

Treading as light as a cat, Mark approached her from behind. As he neared, she paused from hanging laundry and stared off into the distance. Mark froze, hoping his presence was still unknown. She stared for a time before resuming her work with a sigh. Mark resumed his approach. Only when he was close enough to make out the pattern of her dress did he spring into action. He leapt forward, wrapped his arms around her waist, picked her up, and swung her around. As he did so, he drowned out her surprised protests with a gusty song.

"Hey, dilly, filly di. I like you.
Hey, dilly, filly. Do you like me too?
Here in my arms
Taken by your charms.
Hey, dilly, filly, di!
Hey, dilly, do!"

As he kept spinning, her hair came loose, getting into his face as well. She was laughing like he hadn't heard her laugh in years.

"Henry! Put me down this instant!" she managed between laughs.

Setting her down, Mark waited for the world to stop spinning. He wasn't laughing anymore. His mirth had been squeezed out by the cascade of emotions that fell on him when he was called by his father's name. In a way the reminder made him grateful he was like his father, yet he'd never know how or to what extent. Since they would never know each other as men, they would never discuss the makings of a good man, or husband, or father. Mark had only wanted to make his mother smile, yet now they were grieving together again. When she turned to face him, Mark saw tears standing in her eyes.

"I'm sorry, Mark. I didn't intend to hurt you. I was thinking of him when you came. And then you sang that song…," she sighed. "He sang that song to me all the time. He surprised me more times than I care to count. After a time though, I knew when he was coming. I could sense it. But then, stealth was not his strong suit," she laughed. "That trait must have skipped a generation because you surprised me completely."

"I'm sorry, too. I only wanted to make you laugh."

"But you did! I miss him, but he isn't completely gone, if we can remember him. I wish you would share my joy because you are so like him. Every time I see you, I see him, and I'm so thankful. You are my living testament that there is still a place for love, beauty, and wonder. How can you not share my joy over these qualities when they are the values your father looked for everyday?"

Mark felt the callouses on his heart growing thicker as his mother's words grated against them. He wasn't sure anything beautiful could come from the pain and anger he felt.

"Please smile, my son. There is so much we have to be thankful for. If your father were here, he'd tell us as much. He wouldn't want us to grieve when we thought of him."

They were quiet with their own thoughts for a while, then

she laughed softly once again.

"Do you remember that time he tried to take us on a surprise picnic? He was so proud of himself, and he wouldn't tell us a thing about it."

Mark's sardonic half-smile couldn't be repressed as he remembered.

"Didn't he put on this long show, and tell us to close our eyes?"

"Yes! He even threatened to blindfold us if we peeked."

"He was so quiet when we arrived that we thought he was attending to details, but really he was trying to figure out what to do because the dogs had gotten loose and eaten our whole lunch."

"He bore the blow with more grace than Nancy did."

"I forgot about that! I thought she was going to hunt those dogs down and serve them for lunch. She was furious!"

"But your silver-tongued father was able to talk her out of her rage, and she ended up eating with us in the kitchen."

Though Mark allowed himself a full smile at the memory, he felt the joy slipping away like a fleeting wisp. He could tell by the furrowing of his mother's worry line that her joy ebbed quickly away, too.

"Do you think we'll see him again?" he asked softly, his voice surprisingly flat.

"One day," she replied with a nod. "Perhaps not now as we would wish, but one day when Agumbra gives way to Peros we will see him. If only we could be patient for that time."

She had slipped into the glassy gaze he knew so well. She was seeing past the tangible into that which still remained unnamed to him. He had learned the songs of Rohirt by memory, but she seemed to see into their beating heart. His own heart broke with desire. This other place had haunted him his entire life, but he was no closer to knowing what or where it was. Perhaps she would tell him now. Maybe she would finally share with him the story he was destined to know. Taking a breath, he dared.

"Mother, where did you and Aiden come from? I mean, where was your home before you were married? You talk about doing some kind of work. What work? Was that where we were going before Hope was taken?"

The openness on her face snapped shut like the hasty closing of a book.

"I will tell you when you're older," she said, getting up and walking toward the laundry.

"How much older must I be!" he exclaimed, rising to his feet. The anger that simmered in his chest had laced his voice with an unintentional harshness he didn't like, but it couldn't be helped now. "I'm nearly a tradesman and a man by rite to everyone besides you. The truth can't be hidden forever. It's a part of me, I can feel it, yet every day you keep it from me. What can you not tell me?"

She stopped and sighed as she wearily measured him up. Mark was sure he saw fear in her assessment.

"You're correct. The truth is a part of you. However, the

truth will take you from me. It's selfish, but I cannot bear to lose you yet."

"Lose me? How will you lose me?"

"Trust me when I say it will. Things were different when we were going to go as a family. But now that Hope…"

She stopped and tried to rein in the grief flowing from her heart.

"If Hope were here, I would tell you and we would go there. I can't leave her though, not when she is nearby. Please Mark, grant me that."

"But when will you tell me? When is *old enough*? "

"You're old enough now," she said, sighing sadly. "You have been for a while. I've been coveting you, when I should have told you."

Nearing him, she ran her hands over his face. Her pale visage accented the angry scars running down her cheek. She had suffered and lost so much, but so had he. He had to know.

"They have taken so much from me," she began, still tracing his face. "My home. My husband. My daughter. But I have been left so much in you, my son. I would have abandoned hope long ago if not for you."

"I don't want to hurt you," he said, pointing to her scars, "But I am no longer a child. Please tell me."

She didn't answer. Instead she placed her head on his chest and his arms gladly held her. He had never realized how small she was. Her resolution had always made her seem bigger, but, as she trembled in his arms, he realized his steel-willed mother was human too.

"Eighteen. When you turn eighteen I will tell you everything," she finally said, quitting his arms to walk away.

"So long?" he asked, knowing the question was ungrateful even as he asked it.

"Yes, son. Unless Hope comes home before then. Be patient, it's only a handful of months."

"I'll try," he answered meekly.

"Thank you, Mark. Now could you be so kind as to get some more water for us? I'm afraid I used most of it for the wash."

She handed him the buckets, and he obediently made his way to the well, his mind a rush of activity. Everything he wanted to know would be revealed to him when Hope came home. That meant there was no time to lose. It was time to fetch his little sister. He didn't know how he would do it, but he had never been called undetermined. His mind began marching through endless possibilities—searching for the best way to attain all he desired.

Fifteen

"UNCLE JOHN!"

At the sound of that happy voice, a dual reaction fired in the pit of John's stomach. Part of him shuddered with delight that such a winning soul was so pleased to see him. He far from deserved her affection, and, when he was away, he could convince himself he didn't need it. But such callous thoughts disappeared whenever he heard her gleeful greeting at his return. The other, equally strong part, was annoyed; annoyed at his own delight and at her dogged perseverance to like him.

She had grown since he had been away. It didn't seem he had been gone long enough for her to change so much. At six, Hope was a slender, wisp of a girl with a big heart and an unguarded personality. John watched her run to him, all elbows and knees, and wondered if she was truly happy at Baymontiac with him. The answer was clear in those bright eyes. Despite all of Agumbra plotting against her, little Hope was happy. Even more incredible was that, despite himself, John had grown fond of the child — a reality that deeply irked him.

When Hope finally reached him, she clung to his leg with both her arms and both her legs. Giggling, she looked to him in anticipation. His leg moved of its own accord before his exasperated mind could stop it. Without willing it, he raised his leg high in the air with the child wrapped around it. Positively cackling with joy, Hope begged him to continue the tradition they had adopted years ago. He could only lift her a few more times before his leg cramped. She was growing so fast. Soon they wouldn't be able to play this game anymore. He was surprised how disappointed it made him feel.

Having let go of his leg, Hope reached for his hand but found his fist filled with a crumpled letter. When he realized he was still holding the letter, his demeanor darkened. That page of script had brought news of another girl in his life, one who had once been this small, but now had grown into a woman. He scowled at the thought of this woman. Scowling was easier than trying to piece together his confused feelings toward her. Usually he was able to force her from his mind altogether, but that wouldn't be possible anymore. He was going to have to face the demons of his past because they were coming to live with him again. The letter had told word of Rosemary. She was coming home at last.

DEAR ROSEMARY,

Forgive my negligence in writing! I was always so put off when my *friends would graduate, get married, and then never write me. It always felt as if they were forgetting all about the friends they left behind. Now that I am both a graduate and an old married woman, I can tell you I have not forgotten you! However, I find being the mistress of my own estate a daunting task, at times requiring every ounce of my mental faculties. Peter is, as always, a husband as encouraging as any wife could ask for. I have warned him now that we've been married for almost a year, he will soon cease to find my lack of skill endearing. He merely laughs and tells me he doesn't see himself being anything but madly in love with me. I, of course, can do nothing but concede, seeing as I am also madly in love with him.*

Enough of me. I wrote this to congratulate you! Soon, you will join the ranks of the 'those who have gone before'. Are you nervous? I know I was. The unknown seemed to simply hover near in its desire to overwhelm me. It still frightens me at times, but it's gotten easier. I believe I have found a routine, though it has taken longer than I expected.

Dear me, I began this hoping to encourage you, yet as I reread my words I fear I may have the opposite effect! Imagine me stumbling over my words. Impossible to fathom, right? You were always so patient with me though, and I don't know if I ever properly thanked you. Though you have such a gentle soul, it has been paired with an iron clad resolution; both things I needed in a friend as I changed from awkward teenager to awkward adult. You are so dear to me, friend, and I hope for nothing but good things for you as you prepare to step into a new stage in your life. Please continue to write me, though I understand if time eludes you. Goodness knows I have set the bar low enough! Much love to you, Rosemary, now and always.

Your friend, Elizabeth

Rose finished the letter with a smile before folding it neatly again. Though it had only been a year since the girl with dancing green eyes had graduated, Rose missed her friend terribly. Having remained reserved throughout her years at Verderva, Rose had become close only to Elizabeth. In her letter, Elizabeth had thanked Rose for being so patient, but the truth was Rose could never grow tired of such a caring girl.

Rose couldn't believe she had been in Verderva for five years. Somehow time had slipped by as she devoured books and became proficient in music. Her scarred hands had learned to dance across the void of an instrument and bring forth beautiful music. She imagined her hands were unlocking the sanctum of her soul that stored beautiful ideals to add to the greater song that thrummed beneath Agumbra's crust. She tried to dwell on these ideals rather than the truth she knew — there was darkness inside her.

Standing before the mirror, Rose pondered the stranger she found there. She had always been slight, but she remembered a child's round face looking back at her. The face of the stranger she now saw was the face of a woman; a woman with high cheekbones, set features, and eyes almost impenetrably dark. She studied that face, looking for similarities to her father. It took time, but the evidence of John Clifton was there in the hard line of her set jaw and in the furrowed brow that hid her dark eyes. She knew from Leonard that those hard lines could melt into easy smiles, but she couldn't find any of that softness hidden in herself. She wondered if their father had used all his goodness in Leonard, leaving her with the bitter dregs.

Involuntarily, her fingers crept to touch the strange woman's face. She had buried these thoughts of darkness during her school years, but she realized now that wretched thoughts ingrained during childhood never die. In that moment, looking at herself with no outward display to hide behind, she had to examine herself again. She had learned so much in these years, enough to know what kind of person she wanted to be, yet she was unsure if she had the character to attain it. Crawling up her throat, fear lodged at the back of her mouth and made swallowing a chore. Rooted at the base of her insecurities was one overriding fear that mocked her for being so terribly naive. For years she had hoped her father was more than the cold man he had become — that there was a heart capable of loving her buried somewhere in the yawning grave of his chest. Or at least of liking her. She wanted to believe she could belong to him. She wanted to believe she could deserve her true name.

When she returned home, would she prove herself to be the deceptive daughter of a deceptive man? Rose hoped for reconciliation with her father, but she feared she would wake up one day to finally understand the depravity of her father and know how like him she was. Tears of uncertainty appeared in the foreign woman's eyes, and Rose desperately wished to know what kind of person she was.

A knock at the door startled her. Wiping her eyes in haste, Rose composed herself in a nearby chair.

"Come in."

"I'm glad I caught you awake," Lady Diane said as she

entered. "I wanted to come and say a proper goodbye before tomorrow's rushed departure."

"Rushed and terribly early, I'm afraid," Rose replied, forcing lightness.

"Your journey is an extended one so I understand why your grooms preferred an early start."

"It's a shame that pragmatics is a flimsy support to lean upon when braving the early hours of dawn."

"I most heartily agree," the lady said with a laugh.

If Lady Diane sensed any of Rose's recent broodings, she didn't show it. Rose determined she would keep her inner turmoil to herself. She didn't want to ruin her last moments with Lady Diane by dwelling on dark thoughts. The elder of the women contemplatively paced around the room before speaking again.

"It's always bittersweet to me when it is time for a girl to go home. We have grown together, and they have all become extraordinarily dear to me as I watch them change from frightened little girls to ladies. And then, once we've cried with each other, laughed with each other, and changed with each other, they are women, and it's time for them to leave and find out who they really are."

Rose felt pressure building behind her eyes as the lady spoke. Her emotions threatened to overflow as Lady Diane continued.

"You have grown so much from the wounded little girl I first met. You have become a beautiful lady in every sense of the word. I will miss you terribly."

"I'm going to miss you too, Lady Diane."

"None of that now. You are a lady now; just like me. I hope you can simply call me Diane."

"I'm afraid that might be impossible. You will always be Lady Diane in my mind."

"Well then, you must permit me to call you Lady Rosemary."

"It's so foreign. I don't know if I could respond to it."

"Like all things, you will get used to it in time. You're fortunate, though. Rosemary is such a beautiful name, and Lady Rosemary sounds particularly regal. You are blessed your parents had such fine taste when they chose your name."

Her bitter musings still lingering near, Rose felt something crack inside of her at the mention of her name. She attempted to shove it all away again, but the mere act of raising her eyes was enough to release a gush of tears.

"Rosemary! Whatever is wrong?" Lady Diane exclaimed as she rushed to gather her in her arms.

Rose was unable to answer immediately. Her grief demanded a reprieve before giving an explanation. Lady Diane simply waited for the calm after the storm. Rose was afraid, even when the calm came, as she prepared to reveal what she had never before revealed to anyone.

"My name isn't Rosemary," she finally said.

"What do you mean? That's the name your father sent to us."

"Rosemary is the name I am known by, but it is my middle name; not my first."

"But why would your father only use your middle name? What is your first name?"

Though Rose had stopped crying, her answer stuck hard in her throat. It was as if the words were begging her not to speak and solidify their shame.

"According to Leonard, my mother only lived for a few hours after I was born. As she lay dying, she asked father to name me for her. She knew she was going to die, and she wanted to leave a part of herself there with him to ease the transition. My father agreed, unable to refuse his wife her final wish.

"Apparently my father did try to call me by her name for a time. Unfortunately, my mother's desire produced the opposite effect than she had hoped. Instead of bringing my father peace it increased his torment. He loved her so desperately, and her loss almost drove him mad. Then one day, finding he couldn't persist in the charade anymore, he stopped calling me by my true name."

She sat in silence, unsure if she wanted to finish or not. But Lady Diane drew her on with more questions.

"What did your father tell you?"

She laughed again. Not because anything was particularly amusing, but because if she didn't laugh then she was sure to cry again. She went in quiet pursuit of the right words, but the right words never came, so she went on without them.

"He was most eloquent on the matter when he was

inebriated. However, no matter how intoxicated he was, he always managed to remember to say the same thing.

"*'Do you know what your mother's name meant?'*" she said, imitating her father.

"He always made me say, *'What did it mean, father?'* and he threatened me if I refused.

"'Your mother's name meant good gift, and she was the best gift I had ever been given. You took her from me, and, rather than acknowledging that fact, I foolishly agreed to give you her name. You have yet to prove yourself to be a gift, let alone a good one. So I will not lie, nor will I desecrate my wife's memory. Until you prove yourself to be a good gift, you will not answer to her name. Rosemary was good enough for your grandmother, and it will be good enough for you.'"

Rose closed her eyes as she impersonated her father. The darkness somehow made recalling those hurtful words easier, as if she weren't really facing them if she couldn't see. She had thought that by talking about it she would begin to feel better, but she felt out of place, unworthy, dirty, guilty, and completely overwhelmed by all of it instead.

"What was your mother's name, Rosemary? Better yet, what is your name?"

The question was asked softly, but it was still potent enough to twist the corner of her mouth upwards in a painful grin.

"I am eighteen years old, yet I still haven't earned my name. I am not yet a *good gift.* For many years I was ignorant of what it even was. When Leonard returned from the war he told me one night in a whisper. He didn't dare but say it once, and even then, he didn't address me by it. So, though it may sound strange, I don't want to say it aloud until my father calls me by it. It is my self-proclaimed rite of passage."

Tears floating in her eyes, Rose grinned sheepishly at Lady Diane.

"Forgive me this display. I know I am naught but a silly girl," she said, attempting to joke and brushing her tears away.

But Rose had never seen a graver soul than the pensive woman who sat there looking at her. Lady Diane moved to sit in front of her. Laying a hand on Rose's scarred cheek, she reached with the other to hold one of Rose's scarred hands.

"You listen to me, Lady Clifton. You are a woman actively choosing to hope, and I think it is one of the most courageous things I've ever witnessed. You are beautiful, Lady Clifton, in both body and soul, and I am better for having known you. If you take nothing else from your time here, take this. You have been nothing but a good gift to our school. You always have been, and I foresee you continuing to be a good gift to the world as you go forth. I only hope your father comes to his senses soon to see what is obvious to everyone else."

Rose felt comfort radiating from the heartfelt words. She leaned her face into the hand against her cheek to better bask in the warmth of those words. But it couldn't last. She loved Lady Diane and had entrusted her with her most grotesque of secrets; however, those kinds words could not heal the wounds her father had made. Only he could bring those ragged edges together and suture them shut—a gesture she didn't expect him to make. She anticipated living in this manner indefinitely, but she had forgiven him, and it was her lot to wait for him to do the same.

The night inevitably gave way to dawn. Waking early, Rose was met by the Lady. They parted tearfully, but with no words. The elegance of the uncluttered silence between them was enough. She bade farewell to Verderva and watched as the roads transformed into those she remembered as a child. She saw children stopping to stare as her carriage went past. Their open admiration brought color to her cheeks. She may have been educated as a lady, but she felt a closer kinship to the gawking, mud-splattered children she now passed. She was a hoax; a stray dog dressed up on parade.

As they approached Baymontiac Estate, she steeled herself for meeting her father. In her mind, she practiced the right words to say, and tried to imagine what five year's worth of change had done to him. No matter how desperately she dreaded meeting him, Rose grasped the certainty of their encounter along with the certainty that she would never be ready to face it.

Upon arrival, she was met by a servant who informed her of her father's unavailability due to work. Disappointed by the lack of importance he had placed on her homecoming, she quickly summoned up what she hoped was a pleasant smile. When the servant's features didn't alter to return her kind expression, she felt her own smile wobble, then fall.

Quietly following the servant to her room, she was able to

form an impression of her new home. It was as large and opulent as she had expected! But when she compared it to Decedeo, she found this manor couldn't equal. She wondered if she was only romanticizing a childhood memory, but the more she saw, the more she was convinced that, though the house boasted all the right elements for a lovely home, it lacked the fine details that made coarse stone walls into safe confines. It was utilitarian, she decided. This was a building that sheltered a lord; Decedeo had been a retreat that housed a family.

She was shown into her room, and told what time supper would be served. Unsure what was expected of her, she assumed she was to simply bide her time until then. With a few hours to pass, she went in search of the dining room, hoping to find the most direct path to it for when dinner time came. In her wanderings, she didn't see another living soul, not in the halls, nor any of the rooms she checked. A conspicuous silence consumed the entire house, confirming her original impression of the place.

After a time she found the dining room, and somehow meandered her way back to her room in time to prepare for the evening meal. She wanted to look elegant the first time she saw her father, giving him nothing to criticize. A lady's maid arrived and helped transform the stranger in the mirror into a surprisingly stunning woman. Rose wished she shared the confidence the woman exuded. Rather, with trembling extremities, she dismissed the maid and steeled her nerves, once again, for the long walk to the dining room. Upon entering, she was shown to the table and seated with the help of a servant whose expression of awe at the sight of her was pleasing, while at the same time stirring timidity within her. Though she felt like an intruder in this skin, she hoped her father would be equally impressed.

She anxiously waited for his arrival. Trying not to fidget, she kept her head tall, even when she grew tired of the inactivity. Just when she thought she could stand it no more, a servant informed her she would be dining alone. Her disappointment, unhidden this time, only deepened more when he reported that her father had been called out on an urgent matter and would be gone indefinitely. She thanked the servant graciously, but her entire dinner was blurred with just contained tears.

This monotonous routine carried on for a week and a half. She spent her days alone familiarizing herself with the house. No matter how she wandered, she couldn't help thinking she was missing entire rooms. The few people she saw refused to look her in the eye, and their conversations ended abruptly when her presence was noticed. But she soon realized contact with people was a rarity. She spent hours in complete solitude searching for another living soul. When the house grew wearisome, she began to explore the gardens, which were so extensive that there were moments when she was sure she was lost. Soon, she intentionally tried to get lost simply for amusement. It worked for a time, but soon she was able to recognize her surroundings so quickly that the game became useless.

Every night, she returned from her ramblings with plenty of

time to prepare for dinner. Not knowing when her father would arrive home, she always prepared for dinner as if he would be attending. Thus far she had returned to her room every night disappointed...and more hurt than the night before. She was not ready to resign herself to this life of solitude, yet she felt closer to doing so with each growing disappointment.

Tonight, once again, she dressed as an elegant lady, yet she was trudging to the dining room in a gloomy spirit. It had been a disheartening day. She had started reading several times in the small library, only to quickly lose interest. She played a few measures on her instruments, but even they sounded lonely. Unable to bear their mournful sounds, she set those old friends aside. Though she never thought she would, she missed the prattle of her schoolmates. School never carried a silence like this. A silence that threatened to crush her as the days passed.

Suddenly, as abruptly as a slap to the face, the silence was shattered...by laughter. And not just any laughter, but the laughter of a child. Rose spun wildly looking for the source of the foreign sound. A girl of no more than six or seven flew around the corner and ducked into one of the nearby rooms. Rose immediately followed her. She couldn't stop herself. The child's giggles were the first bright spot she'd witnessed since her arrival. Once in the room, the culprit wasn't hard to locate. The girl was giggling incessantly, and the sound drew Rose to a nook in the corner. Pushing aside a chair, Rose got her first good look at the girl, who, in her surprise, stopped her merriment. She had obviously been expecting someone else. Rose's heart sank when the giggling stopped. But the girl's reticence was soon replaced by unashamed curiosity.

"Are you a princess?" the girl asked. Rose was taken aback.

"Excuse me?"

"Are you a princess? You're dressed like one."

"No, I'm not a princess. I am dressed for dinner," Rose replied with a laugh.

"That makes sense. You're beautiful like a princess, though. I don't eat with the grownups, they bring my food straight to my nursery. Nanny stays with me sometimes. Sometimes not though. Sometimes I eat with King Tykris. He has to eat on the floor, though, because he's a dog. But when Nanny isn't there, I put him on the table with me so we can eat together. Sometimes..."

The innocence of her childish ramblings was like eating a good meal after a long fast. Rose could have listened to that rapid prattle for hours and gone to bed satisfied. It didn't even matter what she was saying. What mattered was she was saying it, and she was saying it to her.

"Nanny has been acting strange all week. I haven't been allowed to go outside and play for so long. And it's been so nice! King Tykris and I look out the window and it makes us sad that we're stuck inside. So I ran away, and Nanny has to find me. I thought I had found a good place to hide, but you found me real quick. You must be good at hide-and-go-seek."

A bustling sound from a nearby hall signaled the approach of the discarded nanny. Rose sighed in frustration that their meeting would be over soon.

"Your nanny has arrived, and I'm afraid our time is over. Before you go, could I have the pleasure of knowing your name?"

"Of course! My name is Hope."

Time stood still. Rose felt her eyes dilate, and she grabbed for the support of a chair. It was obvious now. The child had Uncle Henry's eyes and cheekbones, but she had Aunt Anne's hair and coloring. This was Hope Poynter! At their last meeting the two of them were children. Hope had fallen asleep in her arms as they ran from the soldiers who would claim her nonetheless. Rose had expected her dreams to come back and haunt her, but never as a flesh and blood poltergeist. Thankful for the support of the chair she was holding onto, Rose felt her knees begin to give way.

"Are you okay, lady?"

Hope approached to check on her, and Rose desperately wanted to reach out and touch her face — that face she had kissed when it belonged to an infant. It felt too taboo, though, and she couldn't bring herself to do it.

"Yes. Sorry Hope. I'm fine. And please, call me Rose."

Her smile fading, Hope stepped away. Aching from her missed opportunity, Rose now wished she had capitalized on it.

"Are you Lady Rosemary?" the child asked, almost frightened.

"Yes," Rose admitted in a flat voice, preparing for the inevitable.

"I've been forbidden to talk to you."

The child had slowly been inching to the door when the nanny finally appeared, out of breath and looking cross. At her arrival, Hope scurried to hide behind her, and Rose's heart broke all over again. The nanny eyed Rose sharply, as if ascertaining how Rose had beguiled her young ward.

"Lady Rosemary," she said coldly, as she performed a stiff bow.

Rose responded as expected, and then the two of them were gone before she could take a last glance at Hope. Rose didn't feel lady-like and elegant anymore. Rather she felt like a tired child who only wants to go to sleep and, while sleeping, awaits a new and better day.

She didn't think she had the heart to suffer through another dinner alone. On the other hand she didn't want to go back to her room either. Both of those places were too large and imposing, and she felt too vulnerable as she sat in them alone. She wished for a small hiding place to tuck herself into until the world was a kinder place. She wanted to go somewhere where the laughter of children wasn't a foreign concept and silence was welcomed, but not imposed. Massaging her forehead in an attempt to relieve a growing headache, she stepped into the hall and looked both ways. One direction led to the dining room, the other to her room. What she really felt was tired...so very tired.

She couldn't do it. Her encounter with Hope had struck too close to home. She couldn't sit in that cold, empty room and pretend she was fine. She may look like a princess, but she wasn't going to dine in silence like one.

Hastily, she retreated to the unsatisfactory hideaway of her room.

Sixteen

$\mathcal{T}$HE WHISPERINGS IN TOWN MANAGED TO CEASE before he could make out the topic. Mark knew enough to know it concerned him, though. If anyone dared to meet his eye, it was with knowing glances. Many preferred to keep their eyes lowered while guiltily kicking the dirt. Mark played their game for only a few days before he opted to inquire with his most trusted source.

"Mark! It's been too long," Robbie said. "The boys and I have missed you. In fact, what'cha doing tonight?"

"I have yet to decide," Mark said, playing along. "Are you going to present a favorable option?"

"I believe so. The *Beauty* sails tonight, and would highly welcome your company. You have missed many adventures with the crew."

Mark smiled at the mention of the little boat they had built as children. It usually stayed upright and afloat…usually.

"Haven't you had enough punishment at the hands of that little boat? How long are you actually in it versus being capsized along with it?"

"Long enough," Robbie said with a smile. "Long enough to know we miss you."

"And would that have something to do with the fact I can get that thing turned right side up faster than anyone else?"

"Perhaps," Robbie answered with a playful grin.

"I'll think about it. Fair?"

"When the usual answer is, 'No', absolutely I'll accept it."

"Excellent. Now, seeing as it's been a while, are you busy because you're a new tradesman or because you've been spending a lot of time with a certain someone whose name *may* or *may not* start with an 'M'?" Mark asked.

"Maybe both," Robbie answered with another grin. He had grown tall, like Mark, and very handsome. Mark knew several of the girls favored his friend. Their attentions were in vain because Robbie only had eyes for one girl.

"MAYbe both? *May* I ask if Mae has been busy too then?" Mark asked.

"Maybe," he said, blushing fiercely, but still smiling.

"You two have been seeing each other for a long time. It's quite a walk from here to Baymontiac town and surely you're tired of traversing it. You're a tradesman now, so what's keeping you from talking to her father?" Mark teased.

"Nothing," Robbie said, pulling a slender ring from his pocket. "Nothing at all."

"In earnest? Congratulations, Robbie!"

"Thanks," Robbie said, tucking the ring away. "But I'm

assuming you didn't come here to hear the details of my romantic endeavors. What can I do for you?"

"I was coming here to ask you a favor."

"Name it."

"What's the news no one seems willing to share with me?"

"I don't know what you're talking about," Robbie said, trying to act nonchalant while lying through his teeth. He'd always been a terrible liar.

"Be honest, Robbie. You know exactly what I'm talking about, and you're only intensifying my interest," Mark said.

Robbie transitioned from carefree to serious so fast Mark actually had to blink to make sure he'd seen correctly.

"Are you sure you want to know?"

"Yes," Mark said, matching his friend's seriousness. "It won't stay secret forever, and I'd rather hear it from a friend."

Robbie remained uncertain, but Mark waited patiently, despite his anxiety to know.

"She's back, Mark," Robbie said quietly.

"I don't understand. Who's back?"

"Rose Clifton. She's back from school."

Rosemary Clifton. Her name caused a buzzing in Mark's ears and made it hard to concentrate. The next few minutes were hazy, but somehow he ended the conversation with Robbie and managed to stumble out the door. Before he was even cognizant of himself, Mark realized he was running. He didn't know where to, but at the speed he set, he was sure to arrive soon. He was in the woods outside of town when he finally stopped. His limbs still jittering with anxious energy, he began to pace in earnest.

After all these years, she'd come back. Emotions overwhelmed him as he paced back and forth. Long suppressed but deep seated rage threw off sleep to pursue the warpath. All the bitter pain he had been ignoring swelled over him, and the easiest way of escaping its tumult was to allow his rage to scream inside him. But when the echoes of the screams died away, he remembered the mercy and forgiveness he had always been taught, and questions began running through his mind. Maybe there was a reason she had never answered his letter. Maybe she could explain herself. Maybe she was innocent.

Or maybe she wasn't. Maybe she was exactly who he thought she was. Would his parents still ask him to forgive if they knew Hope was gone because of her? His anger toward her was so finely cultivated he didn't know if he wanted to give grace. To him, justice was first and foremost. Anything less felt like pardoning a crime.

Grace and anger raged against each other. Mark favored first one side, then the other, then back again. A path formed in the ground as he paced. Time passed and he was no closer to choosing a side than when he began. Sitting down, he put his head in his hands, exhausted. He knew he couldn't come to a clear answer until he talked to her. He had to know if he was ever going to make sense of the turmoil in his head. Somehow he would get a message to her and they would meet. Suddenly, he realized if he could trust her, then she could help him bring Hope home! But if he couldn't trust her, his closure to their friendship would remain. Either way, he needed to see her.

The first hurdle to overcome was Morgan. The healer was hyper vigilant, making access on or off the property without notice nigh unto impossible. A smile spread across Mark's face when he realized Robbie had provided the perfect alibi. That meant he had to move that night. Dread knotted his stomach but he quickly replaced it with steely resolution. So much the better. He doubted he could have endured waiting any longer anyway.

Mark had years of practice hiding his emotions. Years ago he'd discovered that if he pigeonholed his thoughts and separated himself from the present, he could act completely normal when he needed to. Numbness being normative now, he didn't doubt he could hide his true intentions. Vacancy settled over him as he walked home and prepared for the night.

"Robbie invited me to sail *Beauty* tonight. It's a moonlit venture, so I won't be back until late. I'll bunk down in the loft of the barn so I won't wake you when I return."

"That contraption hasn't sunk for good yet?" Morgan said from the corner as he worked on one of his whittling projects.

"We attempt to scuttle her for good with each voyage, but her will to live is indomitable," was Mark's equally dry response.

"Be sure to pack an extra set of clothes for after you submerge yourself," his mother called out to him

"Have faith, Anne. Maybe their deathtrap will finally stay afloat," Morgan said with a small grin.

"Your confidence is overwhelming," Mark said, remaining as

numb as possible. Both his mother and godfather seemed to notice something, and he worried his facade was falling. His mother drew near with a smile and a bag of edibles. Nodding his thanks, Mark began to turn away. She stopped him though, by a touch on the arm. He turned back to see her still smiling, yet examining him. Her eyes didn't sparkle much anymore. He hoped to change that soon.

"Enjoy and be safe, son. I love you."

"I love you, too," he said automatically before walking outside. The sun was slipping away beneath the horizon. Soon it would be time. However he felt a presence join him before he could leave. Morgan had quietly stepped up beside him and was watching the horizon with him.

"Are you well, Mark?" he asked after a time.

"Yes, sir. Do I not seem it?"

"You seem a little distracted. I understand though. Today is the anniversary."

Mark realized it had been exactly five years since the day Sir Richard had wrecked their lives. Four since Morgan had warned him against any rescue attempts at Baymontiac. He recognized the irony that played between the day and the activity planned for the night.

"Much has changed since that day, Mark. I've watched you grow, and I'm proud of you. I know your father would be too."

They were silent again, the wind blowing softly between them.

"I believe I have watched you become a man. As a man, you

are no longer in need of a mentor. I would like to make your transition to tradesman official within the next few days. You've become a good man, and you have my trust."

No more was said, but guilt crept into Mark's heart. He was planning to subvert the man he loved best, the man who was going to christen him a man in the stead of his father. Hanging his head, Mark took a deep breath. Morgan gave his shoulder an affable squeeze.

"Try not to get too roughed up. We can't have you looking poorly for the ceremony," he said before leaving Mark alone. Mark silently struggled to rein all the emotions Morgan's simple speech had riled. The sun was nearly set before he mastered it, but, when the numbness had returned, he set out.

The night was cool. Cooler than he'd expected. The trees raised their twisted hands toward the sky, grasping at the moon. The moon stayed high above, though. Its weak light creating crazed shadows upon the road. A great owl momentarily darkened the moon's soft light as it spread its mighty wings in search of some prey. It stayed aloft for a second before it tucked its wings and plummeted into the foliage. Straightaway an animal's shriek rent the night, but the cry was soon stifled. And still the moon shone on, leaving garish shadows with its light.

It took two hours of jogging with intermittent walking to journey to the Estate. He was sweating profusely and there was a stitch in his side he kept massaging. However, he had plenty of time to complete his mission.

Hoping to find Jack, he planned to go to the stables and

enlist his help. If Jack wasn't there, he thought he could find Rose's riding tack and slip a note into it. Since she was the only "lady" on the estate, her belongings should be easy to identify. He was eager to get away quickly. Every shifting shadow stretched his nerves tighter as he imagined men waiting to take him captive. Of necessity, every step was painfully slow. He jumped when he thought he saw something moving near a gazebo in the gardens. Halting his steps, Mark waited with his heart in his throat until he was positive no one was there. The lonely gazebo considered him, mocking Mark's strung out nerves. Mark, ready to be done with his errand, kept moving forward.

Fate smiled upon him. As he neared the estate he saw an open window with a light on inside. A slender silhouette was outlined in the window space. Mark hunkered down and studied it. He could tell it was a young woman. Warding off the chill by wrapping his arms around himself, he waited. If he was to follow through on this lead, he had to be sure. The woman sat in the window, and Mark became convinced it was her. After all these years, she still held her head the same way. She moved away, and after a time the light dimmed. Now was his chance.

Reaching into his pocket, he found the paper and pencil he'd pocketed before leaving home. Jotting a quick note on it, he tied the note to a rock, aimed, and threw it into her room. Backing into the shadows, Mark waited. It seemed like forever, crouched in the darkness with his nerves strung out. She didn't disappoint him, though. The slight silhouette appeared in the window again and began to look around. He waited a moment then whistled a bird call. The figure stiffened and turned toward the noise. Mark continued waiting. Then, soft and unsure, came a return whistle of the same bird. She remembered then. As children they had used those calls to signal each other. Though his note should suffice, he wasn't satisfied. He had waited so long to face her, and, notwithstanding the less than ideal situation, he could wait no more.

As gracefully as he could manage he stepped forward out of the deep shadows and into the flimsy light of the moon. By what little he could tell, five years had changed her, too. She moved with the same fluidity as his mother. No more nervous jerking this way and that, like a rabbit caught in a trap. He knew she couldn't see him properly either, but the way she regarded him in such focused silence told him she suspected who it was.

For a moment, they continued watching each other in the darkness. He didn't need to say anything; he only wanted her to see him. Just as he readied himself to retreat, she made a small movement. He tensed, expecting her to raise an alarm. But she didn't. She simply raised a hand, palm facing him. This simple sign of goodwill told him volumes. She was asking for the grace he had been trained to give. She wanted him to know she was sorry.

But something made it impossible for him to raise his own hand in the same gesture. The hard smoldering near his heart suddenly flared as he looked at her. He did not feel goodwill toward her, at least not tonight. Tomorrow may be different, but tonight she still had much to explain and his pain — the pain he had dammed away deep inside — burst forth and pulled him down in its undertow. The familiar rage kindled, and he clenched his hands into fists. He retreated into the darkness and was gone.

Seventeen

A COOL, BUT NOT UNFRIENDLY, BREEZE WAS BLOWING out of the woods causing the nearby trees to knock on her window. She had been too upset to answer the beckoning when she first returned to her room; however, the soft "tap-tapping" persisted until she could no longer ignore it. Freeing her hair from its constrictive prison, Rose allowed it to hang loose around her shoulders. When she opened her window, the wind rushed at her, twirling her hair persistently around her face until a smile grudgingly came to her lips. The sky was clear and the stars shone brightly in the inky dark. She gathered herself in her wrapper before assuming a resting spot in the window.

The evening was sweet in its simplicity, and she breathed deeply the fragrance of Agumbra's night. The concert of bullfrogs and crickets held her almost as comfortably as her wrapper, and shutting her eyes, she let the sound wash over her. Growing drowsy during her unnecessary vigil, she began to doze in the window seat, but a knock at the door jarred her from the sleep stealing over her. She almost fell out the window in her scramble toward consciousness. Reflexively, she bid the knocker to enter, even as she continued to blink the sleepy haze from her eyes.

Opening tentatively, the door revealed, to her surprise, her father. He had changed out of his formal dinner attire, but remained clothed in garments far nicer than anything he'd worn as overseer. He seemed slightly uncomfortable, as if five years hadn't been long enough for him to adjust to his new life. Or he was uncomfortable coming to see her. Both were likely.

It was hard to tell while he was in the shadows, but there could have been a touch of gray at his temples, and there were perhaps a few more lines around his eyes. Otherwise, five years seemed to have left him much the same. As she studied him, she realized, with a resurgence of her insecurities, that he and the stranger in the mirror shared more similarities than she had originally realized.

To her annoyance, she realized his impassive eyes were raking her from head to toe in their own examination. This is not how she had desired their first meeting to be. She had wanted to appear regal in, what Hope had called, her princess dress. Instead she was dressed for bed, windblown, and vulnerable. Despite her common appearance, she stood straighter — exuding the grace and poise she had been taught at school. That much she knew she could do.

"You didn't come to supper tonight," he finally said, breaking the silence between them.

"No. I wasn't feeling well," she said coolly.

You weren't going to be there anyway, was what she wanted to say. So many accusations wanted to fly out of her mouth, but she bit them back in an effort to give him a chance. He seemed to be struggling with what to say next, meaning he either had too much to say or not enough.

"You look so different."

The hot retorts she had just restrained reentered her mind with a vengeance. Only the sincere curiosity in his expression kept them from showing their ugly face. He wasn't making a slight on her current apparel. He was commenting on the physical changes she'd undergone. She softened.

"Five years is a long time."

"It is. A lot can change in five years."

He seemed to retreat into himself as if he had suddenly become lost in a forest of introspection. Unable to find himself, his eyes roamed and pleaded for direction. Caught off guard, Rose softened further.

"Did you need me for something, poppa?"

Finding himself with a start, he looked at her as if for the first time.

"I haven't been called 'poppa' in a long time."

She also wondered at her choice of words. After that awful night she'd made a transition to calling him "father" without even realizing she had done so. Her sudden switch back was an enigma even to her.

"No, I don't need anything," he said. "I was just expecting

you at supper. I had… Well, that is… I wanted to ask you about your time at school."

His lame finish told her it was her turn to talk. She chose her words carefully, not wanting to fuel either side of her prejudices toward him.

"I'm sorry I missed dinner. I assumed your business was still pressing, and you would be absent."

It felt like a fair response. In an effort to keep him from becoming defensive, she had taken extra care to avoid adding vice or sarcasm to her voice.

"Yes. I should be around more. I'm sorry you were left alone."

Rose tried to hide her surprise. She could not think of another instance when he had apologized to her. She wanted to believe in his sincerity, but their last interaction had seared itself indelibly in her mind. He'd played this weakness of hers before to cataclysmic results. Trying to discover any motive he may have, her mind spun in circles, yet she couldn't detect anything through the fog in her head. Defensively, she said the first thing that came to her mind.

"I saw Hope today."

Whatever he was going to say, wherever he was trying to take the conversation, whatever angle he was trying to play, was gone in an instant. The openness he had begun to reveal in his face snapped shut with the ferocity of an attack dog's jaws. He was blank, unmovable, and unreadable again.

"You did?"

His response was collected, calm, and cold all at once. Rose's heart fell hard. Why had she allowed her hopes to rise in the first place? Stupid, stupid heart.

"Yes. She was happy until I told her my name. Then she all but ran from me."

"I did what I thought was necessary."

Her head suddenly felt very heavy. She squeezed her eyes shut and grit her teeth but resisted the desire to press her face into her hands. She was determined to be strong while he was around. Hoping he would leave soon, she realized she was almost too heart sore to maintain the strength of her conviction.

"Father, I can't play these games tonight. I don't have the energy or the mental facilities to guess your intrigues. Perhaps tomorrow, but not tonight. For the past five years I have prayed for nothing but reconciliation between us. Perhaps I'm a fool to keep hoping all will be made right...that one day you'll love and want me. A fool to hope one day I will be to you a *good gift*, like my mother for whose death I bear the guilt. But, though I can't let that hope go, no matter how foolish, it will not come to pass tonight. So I beg you to leave. I will try again tomorrow, but I can't tonight."

Not waiting for his response, she turned to the safe harbor of her window seat. She looked at the stars without seeing them, her arms wrapped tight around herself. After a time she heard the door open, then shut, and his curt footsteps down the hall. She was alone again.

Thoughts ran wild and free in her mind, and she didn't even

care to try rallying them. Corralling those jagged thoughts into some semblance of order would only awaken her pain. So she let them run like truant children. When she awoke from her reverie, her knees were stiff from standing for so long. Sighing, she stepped to the window to close out the chilly night air. But, when her hand touched the pane, she couldn't follow through. It was silly, but the wind seemed to promise to carry the peace she'd felt earlier into her dreams. Her heavy heart begged her not to shut it out. She complied, and decided to sleep in her wrapper in hopes of warding off any chill.

Climbing into bed, Rose turned to put out the light burning beside her bed and found she didn't have the heart to do that either. The flame looked too bright and cheerful to deserve being snuffed. It reminded her of Hope and her carefree chatter. Settling into bed, Rose allowed her imagination to take her away. She imagined the flame to be Hope crackling in happy conversation. The breeze causing the Hope-flame to flicker was Aunt Anne caressing her daughter. Rose felt the breeze play across her face, and that became Uncle Henry giving her a kiss on the head good night. They had forgiven her betrayal, and told her they loved her. Mark was the glass that surrounded the small, but happy, flame. He sheltered the light, and winked at Rose with the conspiracy of a shared joke. Even Lady Diane was there as the down comforter that hugged her tight. It was a world better than even the dreams she would doubtless have.

When she was almost asleep, something flew through her window and startled her awake. Bolting upright, her eyes raked the half light of her room. There was a bump on the rug. Intrigued, she walked over and picked it up. It was a rock with a note tied to it.

Rock still in hand, she walked to the window and peered into the darkness. She didn't know what she was expecting to find. Maybe that's what made the nothingness outside so unnerving. Then the nothingness was broken by a single soft bird call. Stiffening, she looked toward its origin. It couldn't be him. For five years, she had waited for a word from him. Yet not a stroke, not a whisper, of communication had come. She nervously wet her lips to give the answer, again not knowing what to expect. Someone stepped from the shadows, and she could see it was a young man. The faint moonlight kept her from recognizing him with certainty, but everything seemed to fit.

Mark had come to see her.

A mixture of joy and fear caught in her throat and left her speechless. She merely lifted her hand to him, hoping he could tell it meant she was sorry for all her mistakes. He continued looking at her for a second then melted back into the shadows. After a few more moments, Rose let her hand drop to her side.

She turned her attention to the note wrapped around the rock. Untying it, she walked over to the light of her lamp. There she unfolded the rough paper, revealing its precious contents.

Meet me tomorrow at the gazebo. Come at midnight. Come alone. - Mark

Her thoughts were racing again, yet she tried to catch them this time. Mark wanted to meet. Her mind threw out a thousand ideas ranging from he wanted to run away with her to he was going to exact his revenge. The longer she thought, the wilder her ideas became. She contrived excuses to clear her name and pleas for grace. She was halfway through a particularly impassioned plea for mercy when she stopped herself. She had no idea what Mark wanted. All she could do was meet him and be completely honest with him. She would hide nothing, gloss over nothing, and excuse nothing. He deserved to hear it all clearly, and he could make a judgment from there. She would submit herself to whatever he decided.

Despite her racing thoughts, exhaustion fell over her and she stumbled to bed. The night was half gone, but it felt like she had lived three lifetimes in one day. She sought the confines of sleep with hopes of avoiding more meetings with ghosts from her past. Immediately she fell asleep and stayed asleep long after her lamp ceased giving light. When she finally did wake, the shadows were short, and the sun was high in the sky. Shocked that she had slept so long, Rose felt the press of panic. Her meeting with Mark was twelve hours away! There was much to do! She dressed quickly, favoring one of her simplest dresses, and stole down the hallway in hopes of escaping to the gardens unnoticed. Then she could explore the little gazebo and the grounds around it.

"Rosemary?"

She stopped in her tracks at the sound of that voice. Biting her lip, she turned to face her father.

"What are you doing?" he asked sternly, coming near.

246

"I missed breakfast and lunch so I was hoping to eat a late lunch outside, father," she said meekly, ready to submit to whatever his punishment was.

"I missed breakfast, too," he said, half to himself. "There's no need to look so guilty. You are welcome to all the food in the house and welcome to eat it whenever you like. You're the lady of the house."

"Yes, sir. Thank you, father," she answered, surprised at his leniency.

There was an awkward silence between them in which she waited for him to speak.

"Rosemary, I thought a lot about what you said last night. I'm not sorry for the decisions I've made, but I do regret some of the ways those decisions manifested themselves. I wish to make amends. I've talked to the nanny, and I'll talk to Hope tonight. If you would like to speak with Hope, you can for an hour in the afternoons, starting tomorrow. She shouldn't be afraid of you anymore."

Stunned, Rose was rendered speechless for a time.

"Thank you, father. That is an incredibly meaningful gift to me."

He remained impassive, but he nodded once to affirm he'd heard her. Taking that as a sign their talk was finished, she took a step toward the door.

"And Rosemary?" he called, almost as an afterthought.

"Yes, sir?"

"Could you call me poppa? At least every once in a while?"

Something knotted inside her. She couldn't tell if it was pleasure or pain.

"I can try...poppa."

He nodded again, and she fled. She spent the rest of the day puzzling over his strange actions and anticipating her meeting with Mark. More than anything else, she wanted reconciliation with these two men. She agonized between the two extremes presented before her. She was either on the verge of achieving whole relationships or blindly walking into another situation fraught with pain. Though these thoughts were wearying, they dominated her mind through the afternoon and evening.

Finally, the time came. She donned a dark dress she hoped would keep her concealed. As she stepped into the hall every noise seemed magnified a thousand fold. Her heart hammered in her throat, sure of discovery with each passing moment. Managing to escape outside without incident, her feet automatically carried her to the gazebo. Thankfully the moon was shining brighter than it had the night before when Mark stood outside her window. It lit the way to the gazebo and would enable recognizing Mark, too. She expected him to be waiting for her. But when he wasn't, she was bewildered and didn't know what to do. Sitting on the bench lining the inside of the gazebo, she settled in to wait for him and tried not to fidget.

At least half an hour passed before anything happened. Despite her keyed up nerves, she was beginning to doze and only caught the tail end of the bird call. She perked up, unsure if she'd heard it or imagined it. Thankfully, it came again. Wide awake this time, she answered back. Before long, Mark stepped into the gazebo with her.

Her breath caught in her throat. It was Mark, yet also the Uncle Henry from her memories. Tall and lanky, yet he moved with surprisingly sure movements, just like his father before him. But his face, though it was the same as Uncle Henry's, was serious and lacked his father's laugh lines. Rather, his expression was focused, almost intensely so, and right now it was trained on her. She wanted to squirm under that gaze, but she looked him in the eye instead. She could still see the semblance of the little boy she'd been best friends with, but he had changed so much; as had she. How much had the two of them changed? Had it been too much?

"It's been a long time, Rose," he whispered, still trying to avoid discovery.

She caught her breath again. Even his voice was the same as Uncle Henry's! Tears came to her eyes as she remembered.

"Yes, it's been a very long time," she said softly, hoping there was no one listening nearby.

Then they were quiet. There was so much she wanted to say to this man who had been her best childhood friend. She groped for the right words and hoped he was doing the same. She couldn't bear to think anger defined his silence.

"It's good to see you, Mark. So many times I wondered if I ever would again."

His eyebrow shot up in cold disbelief.

"I'm surprised you thought of me when school was keeping

you busy."

Something very akin to malice laced the inflection of his voice. It struck her like a physical blow.

"It couldn't keep me busy enough to keep me from thinking of you."

Shaking uncontrollably, she heard that the tears in her eyes had found their way to her voice. Mark softened some.

"We never talked after that night. I never heard your story."

"No," she said, trying to steady her voice.

"Well?" he said impatiently. "What happened?"

What had happened? Did she even know? That night was so shadowed in shame she couldn't remember the details anymore.

"Tell me what you know, and I'll fill in what's missing," she replied, taking a deep breath.

She could almost see him handpicking the right words as he appraised her.

"What I have been told was Hope was in a safe place. But then, even though Morgan told you not to, you told your father where she was. He, in turn, told the king, who rewarded the two of you with nobility. The king took Hope, and we haven't seen her since. What's missing?"

The question was said as a statement. It was an accusation, a dare, to answer back. To him, all the missing pieces had already been supplied. There was a deeper story that hadn't been told, but, looking into Mark's eyes, she knew, once again, she should have listened to Morgan and Nancy instead. She had been weak. She should have known better. Nothing could change these facts.

"I did tell my father where to find Hope. I did it against my better judgment, but I did it nonetheless," she said as her voice caught in a hitch. "Every day since that day, I wish I could take it back," she said, her voice disappearing into a whisper. She tried to meet his gaze, but found she couldn't lift her eyes that high. She heard him sigh in resignation.

"It appears we share that regret. At least we still have one thing in common."

If he had slapped her across the face, it couldn't have hurt as much as those bitter words. She still wasn't able to look up.

"Mark, I want your forgiveness more than anything in the world. What must I do to receive it?"

Her eyes had finally overrun with tears. It was as she had feared; he blamed her. The guilt she'd worn for years wasn't borrowed, but hers by right. Lady Diane had been right about so many things, but she had been wrong when it came to this.

"There is something you can do for me."

Her eyes found their way up to his at last. He was grave and guarded, but she dared herself a sliver of hope.

"What can I do?" she asked eagerly.

"You can return what you helped lose. You can bring me Hope."

Her mind immediately began to reel with the ten thousand things that could go wrong. It wasn't like they could just walk out and meet Mark. However, she remembered the long nights she had dreamed of a path of reconciliation. She had claimed she'd do anything, so if this was the price of her penance, then so be it.

"When and where should I bring her?"

Mark nodded in approval.

"Three days from now the two of you will meet me here again at midnight. From there I will take Hope, and your part will be finished."

Her heart sank.

"Where will you go?" she asked.

"Away," was his firm response.

"And if I wanted to go with you?"

His sure figure studied her unsure one for a time.

"We'll cross that bridge when it comes."

That was his final answer, and she could tell it would be no good to talk about it more now. She sighed. It would have to be enough for now.

"I will see you in three days," he said, turning to go.

"Wait! You're leaving already?" she cried in a heightened whisper, sounding desperate even to herself.

He turned back to her, his solemn countenance looking almost tired now as he stood in the moonlight.

"What else is there to say?" he asked, not unkindly.

"What has been said?" was her first response. They had been close once. He had once been all but a brother to her. Was there none of that affection left for the stranger in the mirror and this serious Henry to share together?

"I've missed you, Mark. I've missed you so much."

A few tears streaked down her already wet cheeks despite her efforts to hold them back. Mark stepped near to her. She had to look up to him now. She remembered how he had been so jealous when she had suddenly passed him in height. Uncle Henry had always said one day he would grow taller than her. That day had finally come, and she wished Uncle Henry was here to see his boy who looked just like him. She couldn't help it; her hand acted of its own accord, and she found her fingers were tracing his cheekbones. Blushing, she pulled away.

"I'm sorry. You look just like him, Mark. I miss him so much, and seeing you was like remembering a happier time."

"And you. You look so different."

"Is…is it a good different?"

"Yes," he said, tucking a strand of hair behind her ear. "Yes, it's a good different."

She smiled up at him, and she was elated when he half-smiled back.

"I miss him, too. I miss him every day," he said, his voice thick.

Instinctively she drew close to take his hand, something they had done as children to comfort each other, but he shook free and took a step back. Drawing in on herself, she took a step back as well, having realized her mistake too late. His side to her, Mark looked deep into the darkness around them.

"Three days, Rose. Three days, and I will come for Hope."

"And me?"

"I don't know. I think I'll be able to forgive you once you

bring Hope, but I can't before then," he said, his voice tight with emotion.

"I understand," she said meekly. "I will see you soon. I'll have Hope with me. You'll be amazed, Mark. She's so beautiful."

Mark closed his eyes, struggling within himself.

"I always knew she would be."

He turned away from her.

"Mark, wait," she pleaded.

He paused without turning.

"I am bound by honor, truth, and love."

She waited breathless for his response.

"Goodbye, Rose."

Then he was gone. Drawing a shuddering breath, she passed her hand over her eyes. His show of solidarity toward her by responding to the poem was too much to hope for, she knew that now. She didn't regret hoping, though. She shook her head. There was so much to do. A plan for spiriting Hope away must be contrived...and in only three days. Briskly, she began walking back toward the house with her mind racing at such high speed she didn't even notice when she came to the back door. Those thoughts would have to rest until morning; she was too tired for anything else that night.

Suddenly, as she was pulling the door open, a heavy hand pressed down hard over her mouth. She squirmed and tried to fight, but her assailant had wrapped his other arm around her middle and pinioned her arms to her side. Terror overwhelming her, she bucked and reeled as if her life depended on it. Yet, the harder she fought, the tighter the holds became. Her mouth and nose were covered by the large hand and what little air she had was being expelled as the squeezing around her middle cinched tighter and tighter. Nothing she did could stop the growing weakness she felt overtaking her. Finally, she succumbed to the darkness.

HER HEAD HURT unbearably. It felt like someone had bashed it in. That was all she knew. She didn't know what had happened or why. But oh, her head…

"I believe she's coming around, sir."

She felt gentle hands sit her up to make her comfortable. Opening her eyes, she saw that she was in the sitting room, and there was a strange man beside her. Then she saw the king standing nearby and smiling. She cringed. It had been years, but she recalled with startling clarity her intense dislike of him. As her head swam, her grimace deepened. He laughed.

"I see you have a long memory, pretty one. Don't worry, I just want to talk."

She only managed to stare at him with large, frightened eyes.

"My staff believes I am wasting my time. They think I should simply incarcerate you now and save my breath. But I think you are a smart girl. That's why I had Barinne bring you to me. He was overzealous though, and I apologize for your discomfort."

"What do you want?" she asked.

"Barinne tells me he saw your meeting with the Poynter boy tonight. He also tells me the boy was less than a gentleman to his old friend."

She colored in anger, but didn't say a word. She was beginning to feel nauseous and didn't want to open her mouth more than necessary.

"I don't see why you would be loyal to him. He was wrong to treat you like garbage. What have you done to him?"

"You don't know!" she yelled before it could be stopped.

"You're right. I don't know. But I do see. And do you want to know what I see? I see a scared little girl who has tried to be brave for a very long time. Yet, no matter how hard she tries, it never seems to be enough because no one will be on her side."

He had moved forward until he was kneeling before her. Taking her hand, he looked deep in her eyes. He wasn't frightening when he was close. He could have been a grandfather, her grandfather even, and he was saying the things she hadn't heard a man say to her in years.

"You're tired of being alone and brave, aren't you, Rose?"

She didn't trust herself to speak. She nodded instead, but the movement caused her to feel like she was falling. Her head had never felt so muddled before.

"I thought so. I could see it in your eyes. What I'm saying is we can help each other. I will be on your side. I will take care of you. Would you like that, Rose? For someone to take care of you?"

Almost reluctantly, she nodded again, tearing up this time.

"I thought so. And what better place to start than by getting revenge on the one who has hurt you tonight?"

"What are you saying?" she asked, pulling away. Her head hurt so much, and the strange muddiness of her thoughts interfered with understanding what he was saying. It felt like she should fight against his words, even though some of them seemed kind.

"I'm saying in three days you'll go meet young Marcus. He will come to you, and, when he least suspects it, I'll make him pay for hurting you. Then you'll be safe."

She couldn't think straight. Something felt terribly wrong, but she couldn't place it. Her stomach clenched as the nausea grew worse. Her head continued to pound. Now her ears were buzzing, too, and she could hear a commotion brewing outside the door.

"Stand down! I am still lord of this estate, and I say stand down!"

"I'm sorry, sir. But I can't!"

"You can, and you will! I have reason to believe my daughter is in there, and she's drugged! Move aside now, or you will be detained!"

Annoyed, the king stepped away from Rose.

"Let him in, Barinne, before he wakes everyone."

Barinne obeyed. No sooner had he opened the door a crack than it flew open with a vengeance. Rose's father stormed into the room looking angrier than she'd seen him in a long, long time. Seeing her, he took a step nearer, but then saw the king and stopped dead.

"My liege! What are you doing here?"

"Good evening, John," the king said, remaining calm.

With an effort, her father reined himself in.

"Good evening, sir. Pardon me, but what's going on? I was informed by members of the staff that Rosemary had been detained and drugged. They said nothing of you being here."

"That is because they didn't see me. I am here on business of a particularly sensitive nature."

"I see. What does the girl have to do with these plans? What has she done?"

"Oh, nothing. I've just been keeping an eye on her since she left to go to school. You see, I think she is the perfect one to help us finish the business dealing with our mutual friend."

"I see," her father clipped and then was quiet. Rose could hardly process what they were saying. She now had chills and bile was rising up the back of her throat. She felt hot, then cold, then hot again. Through it all her ears kept ringing and her head kept pounding. She felt as if she were dying.

"I know that this isn't the smoking room, but do you mind if I smoke?" the king asked in mock deference to her father.

Her father nodded his approval, and the two men kept talking as the king prepared his pipe. In her misery, Rose heard nothing they said. The king lit his pipe, inhaled, and then blew a thick stream of sweet smelling smoke. Too sweet, actually. Rose's throat clenching, she could not delay the inevitable. Leaning over the side of the chair, she vomited. In the throes of her heaving, she felt someone rubbing her back. As she finished, she began to gain clarity of mind. Sweet, sweet, clarity.

"There you go. That's it. Good. Good."

She saw her father beside her. She smiled at him, truly thankful.

"Thank you, poppa."

He merely nodded back, but she could tell he was pleased.

"Lord Clifton."

The king's voice was sharp and cold, severing the brief father and daughter moment. John Clifton turned away from his daughter to the king.

"Yes, my liege?"

"Can I count on you? Your daughter has already agreed."

Her father looked back to her, and appeared to be, for lack of a better term, crestfallen. She couldn't understand why, but she couldn't think on it for too long. Her memory was returning.

"No, I didn't. I did not agree, and I will not agree. I will be no part of anything that hurts the Poynters."

Her father's disappointment suddenly changed to triumph and hope. Though his expression baffled her, she only watched the king. He looked murderous. Quickly controlling his countenance, he put on his grandfather mask again. She knew the truth this time. He was a hungry wolf in sheep's clothing.

"Now Rose, you're ill and not thinking straight. Marcus deserves this."

Her legs were shaky, yet she managed to stand to her full height. She felt a wrath she thought could match his and took courage from it.

"You're right, he did hurt me terribly tonight. Yet, even if he didn't take me with him when he left, I would help him. I will always help him because that's what friends do. They forgive each other."

"But he isn't forgiving you, Rose. Just think…"

"No! I can't control him, but I can forgive him. I will stand beside him. That's where I'll be, no matter the lies a snake like you will tell."

All pretense was gone now, only rage was on the king's face.

"You will regret crossing me."

He rounded on her father.

"And what of you, Lord Clifton? What is your choice? Are you siding with me or will you choose this wretch and that pathetic, self-righteous Henry Poynter? Will you be like him? Weak? Foolish? Not to mention…"

Something inside of her snapped as he mocked her sweet Uncle Henry. The same man she loved and had seen reincarnated in his son that night. Her feet moved of their own accord as they carried her face to face to the big man, her hands automatically clenching in fury. She drew back and, with all the force she could muster, slapped the king, dragging her nails across his face and feeling his skin gather under them. There was blood on his cheek when he recoiled from the blow.

"You aren't even half the man Henry Poynter was! How dare you?"

The king looked at her, mask in place. He raised a finger to touch the wound she'd inflicted. He looked at the blood on his finger then looked at her again. Nodding slightly, he took a step back.

"No!" her father yelled. She turned just as something heavy struck her across the shoulders, forcing her to her knees. Another blow landed, and she fell to all fours. From there she was kicked onto her back and a melee of blows rained down on her. Curling into a ball, she covered her head. She cried out in pain as a crack sounded forth from her forearm. Still the blows fell. For an eternity. When they ceased, every part of her body throbbed with pain, and when she spit, it was bloody red.

"Lord Clifton, I believe your daughter to be too intrinsically flawed to be a lady. Instead she will be a servant at the castle. If she longs to be with filth, then she will be filth."

She tried to put weight on her arm to sit up and collapsed with a cry. Without a doubt it was broken.

"Your majesty…" her father began tentatively.

"Yes, Lord Clifton?" was the icy response.

The following silence frightened her. Surely he would speak of behalf of his only remaining family.

"Poppa, don't let him take me," she managed to say at last.

"Lord Clifton, it is time for you to choose a side. Either loyalty to me or loyalty to her. I warn you though, one is treason."

She watched her poppa through a haze of pain. The war was clear on his face, and her heart sank. If he was struggling like that there was only one answer he would give. She recalled the words they'd interchanged five long years ago.

"Do you hate me, father?"

"Sometimes. But not nearly as much as I hate myself."

She knew the choice he'd make.

"When will you leave with her?" her father asked, his voice and demeanor tortured.

"After we apprehend young Marcus for trespassing and deal with his crime accordingly."

Father and daughter regarded one another. She felt so broken lying on the floor beaten, bruised, and abandoned. She couldn't even take comfort in the wild pain she saw in his eyes. She only felt pity for him — pity he couldn't act on his own convictions. Tears dripped from her eyes as they silently said goodbye.

"Barinne, put her in the holding cell until we leave. Have a healer look at that arm."

Roughly, Barinne dragged her to her feet. Her body screamed in protest, but he pushed her onward. Casting one last look at her father, she saw no hope of rescue by him. Not now, not ever. She turned away from her father and walked down the long hallway with Barinne, who was yanking on her wrist all the while.

Eighteen

*S*OMETHING WAS WRONG WITH HER SON. THE PAST FEW days had found him in an increased state of agitation instead of his usual, staid composure. Several times she caught him clenching his hands repetitively as he concentrated on empty space. His usual search for employment seemed more like purposeless pacing, like a caged animal. And his eyes. Those gray eyes were so distant, as if he couldn't comprehend what was right before him. Anne hated, yet again, how much of an enigma her own son was to her.

He had gone sailing again the night before. Bless Robbie Hemming and his endeavors to include Mark, who having slept in the barn last night, had yet to greet Anne that morning. His late rising for the day was odd, too, since he generally was up before dawn completing chores before breakfast. Another symptom of his strange malady she supposed. Aiden entered and interrupted her musings. He looked so much like a true farmer that she couldn't help but smile as he bid her good morning.

"And what, may I ask, is so amusing?" he asked in mock anger.

"You. I never thought I'd see you domesticated. Yet here you are, an established village healer, coming in after a morning of early chores on the farm. And, dare I say, it's a good look for you."

"You're right," he said. "The greater mystery lies in how much I enjoy it. I have become complacent in my old age."

"You are getting old," she replied with a grin.

"Cheeky as ever," he said fondly. "Is Mark sleeping in? That's not like him."

"I'm unsure. I assumed he could use the extra rest after sailing last night."

"There's no point sleeping through breakfast when there's work to do. He knew this was a risk when he agreed to go last night. I'll go get him."

"You eat. I don't mind getting him."

Nodding his thanks, Aiden sat down to eat. She wiped her hands clean and made her way to the barn. Noticing the sun peeking over the trees, she could tell it promised to be a lovely day. Flooded with a simple happiness for it all, she whistled a bird's song back to it. She sighed. If only Mark would enjoy it too. She touched the scar on her shoulder, received from Richard's sword. That blow had been meant for Mark, and he had been too serious ever since then. Maybe rafting last night had lightened his recent slip into anxiety. She positioned herself at the foot of the ladder to the barn loft.

"Good morning! It's time for breakfast!"

She called out in a chipper, sing-song voice, expecting to hear groans from the loft in response. But no sound broke the silence above her. She called out again with the same results. A small flame of worry sparked in the back of her mind, but she hedged it in before it could grow. Surely there was a reasonable explanation for the silence. Placing her foot on the bottom rung of the ladder, she called out again — louder and more serious this time. Still there was nothing.

She started up the ladder, calling his name as she did. But no sound disturbed the loft. Breaching the top, the flame in her mind crackled into deeper substance. Mark wasn't there. Her mind whirred in place until she spotted a note nailed to a beam. She tried to keep her hand from trembling as she raised it to her eyes, but she found steadiness impossible.

"If you've found this, that means that I'm not back yet. Don't worry, I should be back soon. I'm bringing Hope home."

The small flame of worry burst into a wildfire inside her head. All she could hear was its mad cackling as it burned away all coherent thought. Her body was already moving, even as all logical thought turned to ash. She stumbled down the ladder and dashed wildly to the house. Bursting through the door, she saw only a shocked Aiden. But there was no Mark.

"Anne! What's happening? What's wrong?" Aiden exclaimed, almost knocking over the table in his haste to reach her.

"He's gone, Aiden! Mark's gone, and I fear he's done

something terribly reckless!" she yelled. Her voice sounded ragged even to her, but it couldn't be helped. The garish bonfire inside her was ravaging what self control she still had.

"What? Anne, calm down. Talk to me. What has Mark done?"

His steady voice gave her the faculties to hand him Mark's note. As the paper left her hand it seemed to take the strength from her legs. She half fell, half sat into a nearby chair. She watched as Aiden's eyes raked the note and then as the same fear she felt conquered his features.

"No! That fool!" he exclaimed under his breath. "Grab some cloaks and my sword. I'll get Armon ready."

Then he was gone, his years of training taking over. She tried to rise, but it was impossible. Taking several shaking breaths, she attempted to call her body to action. She had faced desperate situations countless times in the past, and her body had never failed her as it was failing her now. Frustration and fear brought tears to her eyes.

It was because this mattered more than anything ever had in the past. She had come to the aid of countless strangers, but this bond was deeper than all those combined. This was Mark. This was her son; her boy who looked like her lost husband, and who was the last family left to her. And now that there was a possibility of losing him, she found herself desperately afraid. So instead of moving, she sat and trembled.

Aiden whirled into the room, his motions quick and deliberate. When he saw her, his determined features collapsed into a look of pity. Kneeling in front of her, he gently took her hands in his. His hands were unpolished, dirt-stained, and eclipsed hers in their girth. Hers looked so small and helpless next to his, reminding her how out of control she truly was.

"I can't lose him, Aiden. He's all I have left, and I can't lose him. I'll die before that!" she declared with soft and terrified vehemence. Feeling a few stray tears slip down her cheeks, she brushed them away with annoyance. Aiden reclaimed her loosed hand and gave it a reassuring squeeze.

"Let's hope it doesn't come to that. Until then, we have to move. It's the only thing that can help him now."

"You're right," she said standing. She maintained clear thought for the first time since she'd found Mark's note. "I'm sorry, I've been wasting time. Forgive me, Aiden."

Her effort to hem in her feelings added a hint of steel in her voice. He smiled sadly, and touched her still wet cheek.

"Oh, Anne. My Anne. There's nothing to forgive. Just don't give up hope."

Raising her shining eyes, she gave him a weak smile. She wasn't giving up hope. She just couldn't shake a clinging fear things had already started going desperately wrong. Though she was trying to be brave, she felt her smile growing watery.

"I'll grab the cloaks, Aiden."

THEY RODE HARD to Baymontiac City. Armon did his best, but was unaccustomed to galloping, especially with two passengers instead of one. However, sensing their urgency, he pressed on valiantly. Anne whispered a blessing into the winded animal's ear when they arrived.

The ride had cleared her head, and, while her fear was still present, it wasn't consuming her anymore. She was thankful to find her warrior's skin still fit after all these years. Completely unknowledgeable of what would be waiting for her, but, having run through as many scenarios as possible, she was mentally prepared to face it.

She had assumed they would have to canvas the city for word of Mark. However, they soon noticed a general pull of the citizens toward the center of town. Anne and Aiden followed wordlessly. Each step filled her heart with a sickening dread. There were few things that drove humanity to the center of town like this, the most prominent being unimaginably morbid.

Her fears went unrelieved as they entered the square. Everyone's attention was centered on the gallows thrown together for today. There was someone there, with hands tied, listening as the crier read a list of their crimes. Anne was too far away to recognize who it was. Nevertheless, she began to breathe with rapid, shallow breaths that made her feel lightheaded. Aiden's strong hand was supporting her, while he used the other to push through the crowd. Together they came up to a tall pair of men who blocked their view of the gallows. Resolutely pushing through them, Anne let out a little cry.

It was Mark. He had been beaten, but she knew it was him. He looked into the crowd, fear and defiance fighting for dominance in his face. Her mothers heart squeezed wretchedly, but her warrior mind pushed the desperation back. She had prepared for every scenario, this one included. She needed to harden herself if she was going to go through with her plan. Realizing this, a cold calm flooded her senses. All the ruckus from the morning faded to sweet silence as she accepted what she needed to do. She looked at Aiden, whose face was flinty and calculating. It wasn't surprising to see his hand on his sword hilt. Grateful sadness mixed with her new resolve. She put her hand over his sword hand, silently asking it to stay where it was. He looked to her, a question in his eyes. Oh, how she loved this man! Having first raised and loved her, he had cared for her family as his own. His gruff demeanor couldn't hide such a love, but this sacrifice was hers to make. She gave him a light kiss on the cheek.

"I love you, Aiden," she whispered.

Realization dawned in his face, and he tried to take her hand. "Anne, no!"

He was too late. Stepping away from Aiden, Anne looked in time to see them preparing to place a bag over Mark's head.

"Reclaitute! Reclaitute!"

Her voice shattered the stillness. All eyes turned toward her, yet she continued to shout.

"Reclaitute! Reclaitute!"

The crowd, gasping in awe, made a path for her as she made her way to the gallows. She only had eyes for her son. Despite her efforts to harden herself for this moment, her heart broke when she saw Mark. One of his eyes was swollen shut, bruises mottled every inch of him, and he was sporting a bloody lip. She wanted to run to him and enfold him in her arms, but she knew she would probably never do that again. Instead, she focused on the job she needed to do.

"I willingly claim the ancient rite of Reclaitute. I wish to claim his guilt so my innocence can be transferred to him. May this rite, given to us by Deteen himself, not be denied to me."

She faced the platform where the nobles sat. John was there, his normally blank expression twisted in genuine surprise. But he was not the one standing to face her. That honor belonged to the king himself. She stiffened instinctively, and consciously restrained her hand from creeping to the scar on her face. A storm brewed in Sir Richard's eyes as she was once again standing between him and her son. He was furious. But there was something more in his expression — the fear of a man trapped by circumstances he couldn't control. He returned her unflinching gaze, daring her to stand down. She gladly refused. Instead, he broke the gaze, gave a shuddering breath, and began the ancient recitation of words.

"You wish to claim Reclaitute and bear his guilt, even as he bears your innocence?"

"I wish it."

"The rite of Reclaitute cannot be undone by any but the guilty, now made clean. You will be bound, as the guilty is bound, to fill the demands of the law. Do you wish it?"

"I wish it."

"Face the guilty one."

She turned to her son. He had been cut free, and was rubbing his swollen hands. Seeing his face...how his jaw was set in the stubborn line she knew so well...her desperate fear returned.

"Your guilt has been made claim to. Take her hand to validate her claim," Richard said.

She extended her hands to Mark. This was the one thing that could foil her plans. He had to allow her to take his guilt. If he chose not to accept her gift, then he was lost. She saw the struggle in his eyes, and could vicariously feel the war he was waging. She silently begged him to take her hands. He had been resolutely staring at her outstretched hands until he finally dared to look at her. She saw his deep, almost wild, fear. At seventeen, he still wanted to live his life. She agreed. She wanted it perhaps even more than he.

"Please, son," she mouthed to him. He saw and understood. Still he looked at her, unmoving as stone. Just when she thought the king would speak and proclaim Reclaitute denied, Mark reached his hands forward and grasped hers. Relief rushed through her. Squeezing her boy's hands reassuringly, she tried to communicate to him this was how it should be, but she could still see the demons of doubt dancing on the edge of his relief.

"Reclaitute," the king began reluctantly, "Has been accepted. Bring forth the knife."

Somewhere a commotion ensued as a knife was procured, but all she could see was Mark. All she could feel was her heart entwined with his, the flow of motherly love toward her child. She still remembered that love's intense beginning when she first felt him stirring within her womb. The depths that love had plumbed in the past seventeen years was truly astounding. Now the crier was speaking to the crowd, recounting the details of the anticipated transaction. While he bellowed and flustered, mother and son seized a few private moments. Tears shimmered in Mark's terrified eyes as he tried to speak.

"I'm sorry, mother."

"Shh," she said, wiping away his tears, "You did what you thought you had to. I am doing the same. Always remember this is what I wanted."

She paused. The warrior's hardness faded and raw emotion welled passionately in its place. There was so much she still wanted to tell him — things that mattered and things that didn't. She wanted to sing with him and laugh with him. There were still a million meaningless conversations she wanted to share with him as they greeted, lived, and then bade farewell to a long stretch of days. Most of all, she wanted to tell him of the destiny she had kept him from for so long. She had been afraid of losing him to it, but now, he was still lost. So many missed chances. So many missed words. But, retaining time only for a single farewell, she said the one thing she absolutely had to say before they were parted.

"I love you, Mark."

"I love you too, mother."

And then their moment was over. The crier turned to face

them, knife in hand to complete Reclaitute. Grasping their clasped hands, he separated them and turned them palms up. Brandishing the knife to the crowd, he made a pair of elaborate movements which cut both of their palms. She heard Mark hiss at the sudden pain, otherwise he was still. The crier covered one of his fingers in the blood from Mark's hand, then smeared it across her forehead in a horizontal line.

"The blood of the guilty is now yours to bear and to become. Behold, the guilty one!"

"The guilty one," the crowd chanted back.

The crier then dipped his thumb in her bloody palm and marked Mark's forehead with a vertical line.

"The blood of the innocent is now yours to bear and become. Behold, the innocent one!"

"The innocent one," chanted the crowd.

The deed now done, she legally bore the guilt of her son. Bidden by the king's nod, the executioner stepped forward and bound her hands. As he did, the crier led Mark down into the crowd. Aiden was there waiting for him. Mark would be well cared for when she was gone. Anne could see them, but had to look away, Aiden's grieving eyes having made her courage falter. Instead, she looked where the executioner was leading her, squared her shoulders, and walked with her head held high.

MARK WAS ABLE to watch them lead his mother away but no more. Nothing made sense, but if he looked away from that graceful figure they were leading away, all of Agumbra would implode.

He felt a firm, but gentle, hand on his shoulder turning him away. Roughly, Mark pushed it away. The hand returned again, still gentle, but firmer this time. When he tried to push it off again he found it wouldn't be budged.

"Not here, Mark. We've got to move."

Morgan's voice was like his hand, gentle but firm. His mother was gone now; no doubt being loaded into the cart that had brought him here. Suddenly feeling very agitated, Mark began moving with jerky, restless actions. In the name of the Great King himself, what had he done? He wanted to shout and tell everyone this wasn't right! He was the one who should be guilty and bound, not her! He'd made a terrible, terrible mistake! Just as he began to announce his wish to reverse Reclaitute, the hand on his shoulder lost all of its gentleness, and spun him around coarsely.

"Don't. You. Dare," Morgan growled with barely controlled passion. "She didn't give you back your life for you to throw it away again. If you want to dishonor her gift, then lay claim to your guilt again, but you'll have to go through me first. You may not appreciate all this means yet, but I do, and it will be over my dead body if you take that away from her."

Mark bowed his head. He had forgotten how heavy sorrow was, exhausting his strength. He felt himself being led away. All of his focus was purposed toward putting one foot in front of the other, but he kept going. He didn't recognize when Morgan inquired at an inn, or when he led him to a room, or when he sat him on a bed. He didn't respond when Morgan sat with him in silence, or when he patted his shoulder. He hardly noticed when his godfather slipped out of the room and left him alone. What he did notice was the sudden, deafening silence.

Mark ran his hands over his face and felt the filth there. He remembered feeling so dirty his first night at Morgan's. He'd thought then if he cleaned himself on the outside, then some of the dirt on the inside would be removed, too. He felt that way again. Walking to the wash basin and mirror to clean himself, Mark saw he was covered in dirt, sweat, and even some of the guard's spit. When he approached the mirror, he noticed his swollen and bruised face first and grimaced at the thought of cleaning it.

But when he looked again, he saw it — the vertical line of his mother's blood streaked across his forehead. He recalled what he had read on Reclaitute. The vertical line represented standing into new life; a new life given through the one whose blood had painted it. He looked down and saw the gash on his own palm. It yawned there like a great, ugly mouth, spitting forth his tainted blood. It was that blood that now stained his mother's brow in a horizontal line. The horizontal line representing life freely given over; a life struck down under its undeserved guilt. It was the sign of his mother's death warrant to be fulfilled tomorrow on his account.

Hanging his head, Mark wept bitterly.

Nineteen

ECALLING MARK'S BRUTALIZED FACE, ANNE WAS
surprised at how gently she was treated as they led her
into Baymontiac Estate. One of the soldiers looked to be only a
few years older than Mark. He seemed troubled, so she gave him
soft smiles and made sure to thank him. Her surprise continued
when she realized she was being led upwards in the estate, and
she wondered if prisoners were held in a tower. Regardless, she
kept her head high and marched wherever they were taking her.

They didn't lead her to a tower. Instead, she appeared to be
in the main living area, the part reserved strictly for the owners.
Confused as she was, she didn't allow her steps to falter. Not
even when they entered the main sitting room did she hold back.
Her hands were bound and bleeding, and she was windswept
from the wild ride here. But still she refused to hang her head or
lose her poise. She was Lady Anne Poynter of Decedeo Estate,
and she was going to act the part, even if she didn't look like a
lady right now.

"Ma'am. Can I see your hand please?"

The young soldier was holding supplies for doctoring wounds. He eyed her nervously, as if he half expected her to refuse treatment. Giving him a warm smile, she extended her hands. Though they were still tied, he inspected the gash as best he could. Then he cleaned it gently and began wrapping it. She could tell there was something he was struggling to say. When he finished binding her hand, he continued to hold it in his quest for words.

"I'm sorry," he finally whispered.

"There's no need. You did an excellent job with my hand."

"No, not that. You probably don't remember, but I was there the day we burned Decedeo. I...I was the one who held you back as they attacked Lord Henry. I was the one who watched as they did those horrible things to you and your family. It was my unit that took Hope. I thought the shame would fade with time, but it won't die. I don't know if I can communicate how deeply remorseful I am for my part in that day."

Trembling all over, he wouldn't look at her. She felt pity for this boy despite all his offenses. Clasping his hand, she ducked her face so he could see her.

"I forgive you, son. I only ask that you learn from these things. Will you take the things you've done and use them to become a good man? I know you can because I see your soft heart. You're a soldier of Deteen, but don't forget to live as a soldier of the Great King."

He had composed himself enough to look at her. She saw

new resolve under lingering uncertainty. Releasing her hand, he bowed low.

"Deteen is losing a very great lady tomorrow."

He straightened when the door swung open. He glanced her way one last time then left. She watched him go and then turned to see Sir Richard and John walking her direction. The king looked smug even with a fresh set of scratches down the side of his face. She couldn't help but think they matched the set on her own face — scars he had given her at their last meeting.

"It's been a long time, Anne. Farm life has aged you, but you remain a striking woman."

She bristled, yet remained calm. His eyes were as cold as ever, but she met them unflinchingly.

"The law of Reclaitute has lain dormant for many years. Most will not call upon it. It was very…noble of you."

It had been a long day. It had been her last day. She had no time to play games.

"What do you want with me?" she said, ice in her voice.

"That's what I like about you, Anne. Nothing shakes you. You have literally placed yourself in the maw of death, and you still stand there proud and defiant. But I've always liked you, despite your poor taste at times. You're like me. Neither of us came from nobility, yet we became powerful despite our backgrounds. That takes a strength I can appreciate."

"You haven't answered my question. What do you want with me?"

She was done with this banter. With nothing to lose now,

she would listen to this snake only as long as was absolutely necessary. She saw his eye twitch and was pleased to think she'd touched a nerve.

"I want to offer you your life back," he said, all business now. "You are too remarkable to die like this. There is much life left for you to live."

"Thank you, sire, but I must fulfill Reclaitute or my son will bear his guilt again. I'm afraid whatever deal you offer me, my answer must be no."

"What if I told you Reclaitute could be satisfied without either of your deaths? What is the point of being king if you don't have certain power?"

She stayed silent, refusing to give him anything else to draw on. His face remained stoic, but, as he stepped closer to her, she could feel how tense he was.

"You will come back with me to be my personal attendant. You won't be my slave, and you will have power in the palace. Your job won't be hard, you will just need to make sure you take care of me."

He ran his finger down her arm, and she shivered at the implication. When he noticed, his internal tension became nearly palpable.

"That's all I'm asking. Mark lives, you live, and I leave your family alone. We all win," he whispered.

She moved away from him, blind fury smoldering under the surface of her skin. She wished she could wash her arm of his filthy touch. Rage filled her voice, making it soft and deadly.

"I'm sorry, sire, but you didn't let me finish. Even if Reclaitute was satisfied without the cost of my life, I would still refuse. You're a twisted man, and I would, quite literally, rather die than be near you. No sire, I will keep my appointment with the executioner tomorrow. With Reclaitute satisfied in full there will be no secret power you can hold over my son. You've lost. You can't sway me in any way. I swear though, by all I hold sacred, if you touch me like that again I will fight you until my life and breath are taken from me."

Her voice was even and clear. There was no mistaking her words or their meaning. They flew true, struck deep, and shattered Richard's calm. He stood mere handbreadths in front of her and shook with wrath. She thought of the blue-eyed Gruilitian she had stood before a lifetime ago. He had also quaked with wrath at her refusal. When she remembered his recompense, her heart skipped a beat. Still, she refused to stand down.

Richard moved so quickly that, even if her hands had not been tied, she never could have blocked his next action. His hand found her throat, the impact stealing her breath. As his grip tightened, she felt panic well up inside her. Her neck lengthened and her feet left the ground as he lifted her. Her mind began to go blank. She couldn't even gasp owing to the iron vice of his hold around her neck. It seemed like forever before the grip suddenly loosed, and she collapsed to the ground. Instinctively, she sucked in a breath, but it was difficult since her windpipe had swelled almost shut. Coughing and wheezing, she inhaled air in long, panicked gasps. In a haze, she realized Richard was hovering over her.

"Since you seem to be determined to die, I thought I'd give you a taste what the noose will feel like tomorrow."

She still couldn't speak. It took all her sense to even process what he was saying.

"You think you're protecting Mark? You're a fool. You're merely delaying the inevitable. He's a boy who always manages to find trouble, and I have both patience and a vendetta. You haven't saved him. I will still see him hang. Your death is meaningless."

She thought she heard rapid footsteps leaving, but was unsure the sound was real. All she thought of was replenishing her lungs through her ravaged throat. Time stood still while she labored at managing her ragged gasps. With regulated breathing came situational awareness, alerting her she was no longer alone. Raising her eyes, she discovered John Clifton kneeling next to her.

"Would it help to sit up?" he asked.

Not trusting herself to speak yet, she nodded yes. Her breaths came easier once he had helped her up, and she was emboldened to try speaking.

"Thank you, John."

The words came in a guttural sound, ripped from the chasm of her wounded throat. But, it was progress, and that pleased her.

"You're welcome."

His features were as hard to read as ever, but she could sense deeper waters were stirring within him. She felt uncomfortable around him and was afraid she would say something less than complimentary. All the evidence pointed to him as the reason she hadn't seen her daughter in five years and, try as she may, it wasn't easy to forgive.

"I know I'm probably the last person you want to see right now," he said. "Yet, while I hold no great love for your family, I don't hate you the way I once did. What the king has done and will do to you doesn't sit well with me. I want to make amends, even if it's something small."

He gently helped her to her feet, and then, with greater care, loosed her bonds.

"I'll have to retie you once this is through, but I trust you won't do anything foolish."

She shook her head as she massaged her throat in confusion. At the door, he stopped with his hand on the knob. He looked at her again, a strange expression peaking through his unreadable features. Then he opened the door, extended his hand to the space she couldn't see, and nodded reassuringly. A small hand filled his, and he ushered a little girl into the room. The room quivering slightly, Anne's knees suddenly felt weak.

"Who's that, Uncle John?"

"Hope, this is my friend, Lady Anne. You don't remember, but she knows you very well. She hasn't been able to see you for a very long time. Since you were a baby, actually. She's going away on a long journey, and won't be coming back. She wanted to see you before she goes. It would make me very happy if you could be kind to her."

He knelt so they were eye to eye as he spoke to her daughter. Anne could tell Hope was partial to him. She saw everything there was to see about her little girl. Tears welled in her eyes as Hope cocked her head at John just like Mark used to do when he was that age. She was petite, though, unlike Mark. Mark looked just like Henry, but from what she could tell, Hope looked like her. Tears overflowed in Anne's eyes when Hope turned to her. She had Henry's beautiful eyes. Those soft, expressive eyes she had fallen in love with almost before she'd fallen in love with him.

Hope looked at her with simple curiosity. No distrust or animus, just curiosity. She still held John's hand, and he led her forward while standing still himself. He nodded his assent when she looked at him again for confirmation. Dropping his hand, Hope approached her mother with a sure and steady step. Anne fell to her knees and watched her child come near. Her bruised throat ached with all the emotion caught there and she gasped. Frightened by the sound, Hope faltered in her approach. Anne quickly swallowed her tears.

"I'm sorry if I scared you, Hope. Please keep coming. I'd like to see you up close," she said. Her voice was still raspy, but improving. The child actually seemed intrigued instead of frightened.

"What's wrong with your voice, Lady Anne?"

"My throat hurts, that's all. I'll be okay."

"Are you cold? Because you're shaking real bad, Lady Anne."

"No, I'm not cold, Hope dear. I am just very, very happy to see you. It's been so long now."

"Uncle John said you knew me as a baby. Was I a pretty baby?"

She laughed at her child's frankness.

"You were more than pretty. You were a beautiful baby. Why do you ask?"

"Lucy, the maid downstairs, just had a baby. I went down to see her, and everyone kept saying that Lucy had such a pretty baby. But when I saw him I thought he was kind of funny looking. Since you saw me as a baby, I wanted to know if I was pretty or funny looking."

"I see. That makes sense. No, you were a beautiful, precious baby. You are still beautiful and precious."

"I think you're really pretty, too, Lady Anne. I think when I grow up, I'd like to look like you."

Anne, nearly bursting with emotion, bit back a sob as the irony struck a chord within her. Her happy baby had grown into a happy child with no signs she was being mistreated. Still, Anne wanted to gather her close and never let go. She wanted to tell Hope she was her mother and that she had a brother and a godfather who already loved her. But as Anne listened to the cheerful child chatter, she realized how unfair that would be to Hope. She could offer nothing but disappointment. Hopefully, John would tell her one day. Seeing her daughter before facing death would have to be enough.

There was movement by the door as a guard stuck his head in and whispered something to John. John nodded and acted immediately. He came to them even as Anne cried out silently for more time.

"Hope, I'm afraid it's time to go. Can you say goodbye to Lady Anne?"

"Already, Uncle John? I want to stay longer. I like her."

"I'm afraid not. Say goodbye. You won't see her again."

Anne wept openly again. She held her arms out wide to her daughter. Hope understood and came near. Wrapping her arms around Hope, Anne thought for a wild moment about running away. But the moment passed, and she knew she couldn't, no matter how she desired it. Instead, she held onto Hope with all her might, and tenderly kissed the top of her head.

"I love you so much, Hope. I have always loved you. I am forever thankful I was able to see you before I leave tomorrow. Just remember, whatever happens, I love you very, very much."

Hope considered her. The little girl knew she was missing something, she just didn't know what. John called her, and she looked his way to affirm she'd heard him. In one last attempt to solve the mystery of this strange woman, she quickly looked back to Anne. When John called her again, she obeyed. She looked back, though, smiled, and waved.

"Goodbye, Lady Anne. I really liked meeting you."

Anne waved back, and then her daughter was gone. Blinking several times, she collected herself from the surreal world of belief and disbelief. She placed her face in her hands and drew long, shuddering breaths of both joy and sorrow. Conflicting emotions cascaded in her heart and mind creating a stunned numbness. Paradoxically, she wouldn't trade it for anything.

"I'm sorry I had to cut your meeting short. My men informed me the king is looking for me. If I don't go soon he'll seek me out. Needless to say, his rage would be murderous if he saw Hope with you."

Her heart was still too full for her to lift her eyes from the cradle of her hands. After a momentary silence, she felt John gently take them. Finally looking up, she saw he was holding a length of rope.

"I'm sorry," he said.

Nodding dumbly, Anne surrendered her hands to the paradox who was John Clifton. This was the kinder man Rose had always hoped, no matter what. Or perhaps, this was the man Rose had waited to see. Anne was seeing a glimmer of that man now. He used delicate motions she could hardly feel, and, when he finished, she took his hand between hers. She held it tight as she raised bright eyes to meet his.

"That was the most beautiful gift you could have ever given me. A simple thank you seems inadequate, yet it's all that I have. Thank you for the gift of my daughter, John. Thank you for caring for her."

He nodded once, but said nothing. His face was again unreadable as he led her to the door. She stopped him, needing to say more.

"Many days when Rose came to the house, I could tell you had been cruel to her. Never physically, but cruel nonetheless. There were days when I held her on my lap and wished with all my might she was my little girl, so I could love her the way she needed to be loved. John, if I'm perfectly honest, there were days I tried very hard not to hate you. I don't think that was ever Rose's struggle. She was afraid and hurt by you, yet she never hated you — not even the nights you were so cruel to her after Leonard died. She could somehow look past all your coarseness to see the man you must have been before. I never understood how she could. I encouraged her to keep loving you, even as I secretly wondered if the man she saw was make believe.

"I see now Rose was a wise little girl. Tonight, I caught a glimpse of what she has always seen, and I have never been more thankful to be wrong. John, there is more to you than the anger and bitterness you've allowed to control you. You may not know it, but I see the heart of a proper Kingsman in you. I guess the question is, will you choose to believe those old legends of Rohirt and allow their hope to change you? I hope so, because there is grace still left for you."

She could feel, rather than see, that she had stirred the deep waters of his soul again. Not wanting to ruin his thought processes, she waited patiently for his response. Only when he finally looked up did she realize how deeply troubled he was.

"I'm afraid there is no grace for me. I'm too far gone," he said bitterly.

"Nonsense. No one is too far gone. Rohirt is full of stories of men who were redeemed from darker paths than yours. Read them, and take heart! And when you take heart, teach my daughter to do the same."

Stubbornly, he continued to hang his head. She sighed, pitying this sad man.

"John, there is one final thing I must ask of you. Please be kind to Rose. She loves you so much. Don't allow your hate to destroy that."

Scoffing, he massaged his eyes.

"That girl is the reason I know I'm too far gone. I can't seem to stop hurting her. I can't help it. Even when I want to be kind to her, I'm cruel."

"It's your choice, John. No one else's. I encourage you to learn from your daughter, just as I have. If she can sing after all she's been through, so can you."

"I'm afraid she's done singing now," he said almost inaudibly.

Her blood froze in fear at his words.

"Rose is back?"

He didn't answer, but his formidable silence told her more than anything he could have said. The terrible fear she had felt for her son flooded her heart anew. This time it was for the child she had always wished was her own.

"Oh Jubion, help us! What have you done to her?"

He was quiet for a second before he answered. She watched the softness he had allowed into his face, freeze over, leaving nothing but a barren tundra behind. His eyes burned with a cold, slightly manic, light in the mask of his face.

"Never mind. It's none of your business," he said, his voice harsh. "I won't see you tomorrow. This is goodbye, Lady Anne."

"John, what have you done?" she insisted as the guard took her by the arm. He didn't answer and the guard began to pull her away. She resisted with vehemence. "No! Answer me, John Clifton! What have you done to your daughter?"

He met her eyes, and, though the light still burned, she also saw he was tortured with dark doubt. A shiver ran up her spine.

"I don't know," he whispered. "I don't know what I've done."

Twenty

MARK HOPED THIS WAS A DREAM. SURELY IT WAS TOO garish to be his reality. He was running uphill in a shifting darkness that seemed to be reaching forward, trying to grab him. He barely avoided the grasping tendrils of shadow. His lungs burned as he panted for air. There was no direction in this shadow land, no guiding light, only chaos, and an unexplainable urgency to keep running.

A pinprick of light pierced the distance, sending a white hot shaft of dawn straight through the hellish tangle of night into his chest. Though it was miniscule, he set his bearing on that lone star and pursued it with all he was. Notwithstanding the thorns and brambles that obstructed his path, he pushed on even as their tiny hands ripped his skin. The light never grew and there were times it was blocked out completely. In those moments, when he was again encased in darkness, he bore down in stubborn trust that conquering the next ridge would reveal his hope once more. He knew he couldn't carry on like this indefinitely. Surely there must be something more substantial than a pinprick of light in the always far off distance.

Then, just as he thought he could strive no more, the speck of light grew stronger, beckoning him onward, promising rest. Joyful tears trickled from his eyes, and his feet churned the twisted ground with renewed vigor. He felt hope rise as the light expanded its scope to more and more of his body. Having just dared to let it fill him, he noticed he was no longer alone in his mad dash. Creatures and demons were chasing him, trying to cut him off from the light he had pursued for so long. Worry niggled at the back of his mind, but no dark thought or shadowy creature was going to keep him from the light that was nigh unto consuming him.

The light had grown from a pinprick into a glorious sunrise that cracked open the horizon. He was almost there despite the obstacles, snaking chaos, and pursuing devils. Having won, Mark stretched his arms out wide to welcome the dawn he had persevered toward. That was when he felt the sting...like the bite of a vicious gnat behind his ear. Slapping at it, he found there was nothing to hit. He cast his eyes about and locked on a wispy, wraithlike creature seemingly made of smoke laced with the smoldering of dying embers. Its long and knobby fingers were steepled, and, though it was faceless, he could hear it cackling insanely. An icy chill ran through him as he imagined the only creature he had heard described like this. It was a Ghoul of Bordeema, the dreaded hellions the Stone Pygmies had unearthed in their forced excavation of Raboneetha. Their sole purpose was to wreak havoc, and seeing one meant something ominous was coming.

The sting behind his ear was burrowing into his skull like a maggot making its path through moldy bread. Pain began growing in his eye socket — deep bone pain. He worked his jaw to soothe it, but it was in vain. Whatever had infiltrated his head pushed onward to his brain with maddening consistency. The pain encompassed most of his head now, and he had become disoriented. His trembling legs carried him on a weaving path then failed. He fell forward...falling...falling...reaching toward his goal even as he struck the ground writhing. The sting had reached his brain and exploded into a dreadful fever that now had him seizing. Snaking tendrils of chaos finally caught him, squeezing him in their churlish grip and quelling his jerky spasms. As the bright horizon faded, the devilish hunters howled victoriously over their downed prey. Above their raucous din, he heard the malicious cackling of the faceless ghoul who, with its spiteful sting, was responsible for his collapse. When his pursuers laid their burning hands on him, the light winked out completely. The tendrils, with their tiny hands and long, sharp fingers, wrapped around his bleeding limbs and dragged him bodily back to the dark. Every effort to resist was ruthlessly punished, and it wasn't long before he felt his heart fail him. He had no resistance left, and he allowed the demons to drag him through the inky chaos. Only when he heard the sniggering of the ghoul did he feel any defiance. He could bear all the other taunts that came hurling at him, but the demented cackling of that deplorable spawn of the earth was more than his tormented mind could endure.

These joint forces of the dark readied themselves for killing him here in the deeps of madness. He could hear them sharpening the knife assigned to the deed. At the sound, passivity fell from him like an ill fitting cloak as fear surged through him with an enlivening jolt. His mind pulsed with one thought, newly birthed and filled with desperate desire. He didn't want to die! He wasn't ready yet!

But then the darkness shifted into a million contorted shadow faces whose sole purpose was to watch his existence ebb away with his lifeblood. Terror drove him deeply inward, where he searched his soul but found no song to bolster his courage.

All at once, behind all the hideous witnesses, burst forth a Song that shattered the blackness into shards of light. All the shadow creatures hissed as the Song drew closer. Mark himself could hardly stand before it. The melody was soft as a caress, yet as strong as iron. It was sad and joyous, meek and majestic, terrible and wonderful all at the same time. It wasn't the light he had pursued in his earlier dash, but it hailed from the same origin. In all that it was, it was unimaginably beautiful.

The Song drew near to Mark and never stopped. Rather, it entered his chest and resonated within him, singing its rich melody, and causing him to tremble under the weight of its majesty. It sang words of liberty and pardon from his death penalty. It sang words of hope and the life he could still live. War began raging within him. His young heart beat with yearning to accept the offer of life. But foreboding reminded him death was his cross to bear and no one else's. Above it all, Fear clamored. It caroused and wailed as it imagined the sting of the knife and the subsequent fading of his mind into death. The Song did not condemn Fear's voice, rather it pleaded with him to accept its gift. Despite the vibrant voices telling him not to, he subdued Fear by affirming the Song's request. As the Song rejoiced, sunlight overwhelmed him, his bonds fell away, and his condemnation dropped to the ground. He was free.

The light faded, and he saw he was now amidst the audience. There, on the platform for the condemned, stood the Song. It had taken the form of a woman who, to Mark's horror, wore his bonds. The notes of her chorus shimmered before the evil who was to slay her. He had never seen anything so pure and beautiful in his whole life. He'd made a mistake. Burning in the marrow of his bones was that one thought. He tried to speak, tried to move, tried to do anything, but it was too late. The knife flashed then the light and music fell from the woman like bright, sad tears. In anguish, he watched as the song woman faded softer and dimmer until her golden life glistened on the ground.

Then she was gone; completely exsanguinated. He realized everything was gone. Everything except for himself and the bright puddle of song before him. He knelt beside it, trembling from shock. Staring into the golden pool, he was sure he saw some of the notes that had filled him with hope not long ago. Though the Song woman was gone, maybe there was some of her hope left for him. Surely, out of all the notes composing her, there was enough to make a tune he could sing. He leaned forward and tried to scoop some of the puddle into his hands. But as soon as he touched it, the bright pool turned to dark goo that bubbled and writhed.

He screamed as the world turned on its head. He was plummeting madly into blackness, dreading more unknown horrors. Head over heels, this way and that, but always down. Abruptly he hit bottom with a thud. There he lay, stunned, and waited for his world to stop spinning. Finally the gyration stopped and he dared to stand and look around. He was standing, singled out, on a tall pedestal. A man who was dressed like the town crier stood above him eyeing him with disdain then raising his voice to an unbearable decibel and crying out, "My lord, let us hear the case against Marcus Poynter!"

Mark turned and saw the crier had spoken to a panel of men whose faces were hidden behind grotesque masks. In a chair elevated above them, sat their lord, his face hidden in shadow. Unspeakable dread drummed through Mark's heart when he saw the faceless lord.

"Marcus Poynter, do you know why you are here?" the lord boomed.

"Yes, sir," Mark barely managed to say.

"Speak so all can hear you!" the terrible voice said.

"Yes…yes, s-sir." Mark stammered, managing to fill the room with his voice.

"Then explain. Explain so we all can hear and know."

"I went after my sister, sir. I was caught and sentenced to death by the king."

"We do not find you guilty on this front. Rather, tell us, how is it you are still alive?"

The picture of the bright song woman fading away filled his mind's eye. He thought again of her pure and majestic beauty.

"Answer the court!"

"My mother enacted Reclaitute. She took my guilt as her own."

The masked jury stirred furiously. They muttered and jabbed angry fingers his way.

"Silence!" the lord commanded. Instantly he was obeyed. "Reclaitute must be accepted, must it not? Tell us, Marcus, did you accept Reclaitute?"

In awe he became aware of the pool of bright music lying before him. Wanting so desperately to right this wrong, he reached for it.

"Answer!"

"Yes, sir. I accepted Reclaitute."

His hands dipped into the pool, and it kept its golden hue.

"Tell us why. Why did you accept Reclaitute?"

Mark's throat burned with his shame, yet somehow his words came out.

"I was afraid, sir."

Rumbling, the pool shifted into a thick, dark substance.

"Coward! You sacrificed what you were supposed to protect on the altar of your own fear!"

The masked men hissed and rained curses on his head. Mark looked at his hands and saw they were stained by the peculiar substance from the pool. The pure gold had turned to an ugly red he recognized as blood. And not just any blood. It was his mother's blood! His hands were so thickly covered with her blood that excess drops dripped continuously from off his fingers and landed in condemning speckles at his feet.

"It is for this you are condemned! Unless you can find mercy with these men. What do you say? Does he receive mercy?"

In unison, the men peeled away their masks. Every single one of them bore Mark's face. Every single one of them was him.

"Guilty! No mercy! Guilty!" the jury of Marks cried. They clamored until the lord signaled them to stop. Then he shifted and moved into the light. Now he could see that the condemning lord was none other than his own father, Henry Poynter.

"Bring the weights!"

All was madness again. Mark was torn from the pedestal by countless hands, and something enormous was placed on his back. He stumbled, but some of the hands sustained him while others strapped the weights into place. When they were secure, he was released and almost subsequently crushed beneath the massive burden.

"The weight of your punishment is just! How long shall he wear it?" his father cried.

"For life! For life! For life!"

The jury of Marks' chanted his guilt over and over again. They would never stop chanting and Mark knew it. Only one noise broke the monotony of their chorus. It was cackling — the mad, evil cackling he had heard after being stung. Though he could barely turn under the weight of the mass, he managed to see the culprit. There was the Ghoul of Bordeema, the dirty hellion who had betrayed him. Mark wouldn't be here if it hadn't been for its actions. The Ghoul laughed as its features grew more clear. Its structure was sharper and more cruel than he remembered, but he recognized the face. He was looking at, what he believed to be the true face of Rosemary Clifton.

Now all his surroundings swirled in a wild cacophony of sound and color — a churning mess that offered no chance of finding bearings. Thus, he spun and spun and spun…

His eyes snapped open. The day was idling slowly toward dusk. He didn't know where he was or what was holding him so tight. He began flailing in panic, trying to free himself. All of his efforts were in vain. It was the tentacles from the shifting forest! They had found him again! A sob rose in his throat as he kicked and bucked wildly. So wild were his protestations he soon rolled to the floor. The hit jarring him into stillness, he saw the enemy that held his arms and legs in tangled knots — the bed sheets, wrapped around his limbs had become his captor. A sigh of relief escaped Mark's lips. It was a dream. It was only a dream.

Awake and feeling sane after his tumble, he untangled himself from the sheets with ease. Striding to the window, he peered out across the dying day. It would be night soon, just like his dream. His dream that had been more than a dream. He could still feel weight on him — the one his father had placed — though he stood straight and true. Mark had earned the weight by doing what his father would never have done. Mark had sacrificed his mother.

The room was suddenly too small. The walls were moving in, and he realized he couldn't slow his breathing. He had to move...to get out before the room stifled him. Even being on the second story of the inn didn't stop him from nimbly climbing over the window sill and down the side of the building. He started walking; it didn't really matter where, just as long as his legs were taking him somewhere. He walked down empty alleys and passed shops that were closing for the day. If the merchants called out to him, he didn't hear them. He was too busy sorting through his thoughts. He had to do something about the hanging tomorrow. He could reclaim Reclaitute, but he was afraid. Afraid of death, yes, but more afraid of Morgan. He would find out, he could find out anything if he wanted to. But reclaiming was the only option. Every idea he had was risky, and the pressure bore down like a burden of weight.

"Mark! Hey Mark, wait!"

He blinked a few times as he heard his name being called. Turning to seek the source, he saw Robbie and the boys from the town weaving through the crowd toward him. Despite the discomfort of stretching his bruised face, Mark couldn't help but match Robbie's smile. Reaching each other, the boys clasped hands.

"I didn't think we'd ever find you! What happened to your face? You look about as bad as Caleb did the time he decided to attack that low branch with his face."

Mark was smiling so wide his cheeks were starting to hurt. He hadn't realized how starved he had been for a friendly face until there was one in front of him. And not just one, there were several. In fact it was their whole group. They nodded to each other like brothers-in-arms.

"What are you doing here?" Mark finally said.

"Anthony saw Morgan and your mother ride out hot this morning. Intrigued, he began some inquiries. A traveler told us a boy had been caught trying to kidnap the ward of Baymontiac Estate, and he was going to hang. We put the pieces together from there. We came because we wanted to help bring you home…no matter the state you were in," Robbie said.

"Or if there was a fight to free you, we wanted to be a part of that as well," Caleb said with a smile.

"Either way, we wanted to come and help," Robbie continued. "We were happy, yet confused, when we saw no hanging had taken place today. We've been looking for you since. So what happened? I'm glad to see you're here, but how is it possible?"

Mark's smile faded. The boys sobered with him and leaned in close.

"My mother invoked Reclaitute," he whispered.

Their eyes widened and some of them shot glances toward

his hand. He decided to save them the trouble of spying and held up his hand so they could see the jagged wound there.

"But, that means…," Robbie said.

"She'll die tomorrow, and I'll be free," Mark finished bitterly.

They were all silent as the gravity of the news sunk in.

"So, what's the plan?" Caleb asked.

Mark stirred slightly in confusion.

"Plan? What do you mean?"

"I mean we're going to rescue her, right?"

All the boys nodded in agreement.

"But why? Why would you take that risk?"

It was Robbie's turn to look confused.

"Because you're our friend, and friends take care of one another."

Mark couldn't help it, his eyes started to tear up. He dropped his head in embarrassment and the boys, his friends, gave him a moment. When he did raise his head, his eyes still shone, but this time it was with a daredevil light.

"If I have your help, then I have an idea that may work."

Mark never went back to the inn where Morgan had left him. Instead he and the small band of boys stayed up and plotted into the night. He went to bed with a fever in his bones — certain their plan would work. It had to work. Success was the only option. His friends were going to help him save his mother. They would save her or die trying. Only the morning would reveal which it would be.

Twenty-one

SHUTTING THE DUNGEON DOOR, BARINNE PLUNGED Rose into a world of darkness. Panic surged in her chest as her eyes sought light but found none. She had never been afraid of the dark, but this was different. This darkness palpated every inch of her skin. She tried to calm down as it smothered close. She even attempted to raise her shaking voice in song, defying the inky black, but the few words she sang were murdered by the stifling dungeon soon after they were sung. Rose was left to tremble, alone and afraid.

Soon her legs weren't able to hold her. She half sat, half fell to her haunches. It was relieving that at least the floor was level in this chaos. Comfort was an impossibility though. Her body ached from Barinne's blows, and her broken arm screamed for attention. Gingerly, she felt along the break with her good hand; an effort that brought hot tears of pain to her eyes. She could feel a slight deformity, but the skin wasn't broken, and she could still move all of her fingers. She supposed she could count her small blessings, even if she was stuck in a dungeon. Her quick moment of thanksgiving was soon snuffed out as another jab of pain shuddered through her.

Bearing the pain as long as she could, she soon passed out again. In her next cognizant moment someone was shaking her. It wasn't a rough movement, but it was enough to aggravate her sore body. Whimpering softly, Rose curled around her broken arm in an effort to protect it. The shaking came again. And again, she resisted.

"Easy girl, easy. I'm not going to hurt you."

The voice, warm with compassion, wrapped around her bruised psyche like a splint. She hadn't heard a kind voice since she had met Hope. That had been an eternity ago it seemed, back before the little girl had known Rose's cursed name. The thought of Hope and her own name, both earned and unearned, was too much for Rose who, beginning to cry, curled tighter, despite the gentle voice. Whoever was there stopped shaking her and became silent. She didn't know if she wanted company in her shame or to be alone and buried by it. She was only certain that it hurt.

"It's okay. It's okay."

The voice was back. It dried her tears faster than the realization that the darkness had been kept at bay by a lantern's light. It was like music, its melody bringing back sweet memories. She remembered Decedeo Estate, sitting on Aunt Anne's lap while Mark play-acted the story Uncle Henry was telling. She gave a start. This couldn't be Uncle Henry, could it?

Her eyes sought the speaker, only to be disappointed. This man was burly with dark hair, the exact opposite of Uncle Henry. She laid her head back down on the cold stones, hating that she'd allowed her hopes to rise.

"I almost got you to smile. That has to count for something."

She raised her sad eyes to appraise the man again. His merry eyes twinkled kindly at her.

"I'd been told you'd been roughed up some. I'd like to take a look at that arm if you'll let me."

Nodding, she awkwardly sat up, resting her back against the wall. He took her arm with a healer's tenderness and as he palpated it, she bit back her screams. He nodded sagely.

"I'm not going to lie to you, this next part is going to be unpleasant. I need to set the bone so it can heal properly. It will hurt, but once it's in place it will start to feel better. Then I can splint it and put it in a sling. Do you think you're ready or should I wait a little bit?"

She shook her head, "No, let's do it now."

He nodded, then placed both of his hands on her arm. She turned her head, unable to watch. The pain flared as he maneuvered the bone into place, but it hurt less than she had expected. Still, her heart was racing by the time he finished.

"All right, now I'll splint it for you."

He'd been right. The pain was less now. Her arm was not nearly as sensitive as he worked on the splint. The healer seemed genuinely kind, and she breathed another silent word of thankfulness. Soon he was putting the final touches on her sling. He lingered close to her while he worked — so close that she was able to catch the smell off his shirt. He smelled of pine needles; a good clean aroma that soothed her. Tying the last knot, he sat back and gave her a smile. Pain continued to besiege her, in more than one way, but his kindness was like his lantern, relevant enough, despite its size, to push back the darkness. She returned his smile with sincerity.

"There we go," he said, his smile widening and his hand patting her shoulder reassuringly. "That's what I wanted to see."

Something about his smile and lilting voice sparked a memory. She grappled with impression as he gathered his things, including the lamp, and stood to go. She felt small sitting beneath his towering figure with only the specter of the pressing darkness before her. Trying to look brave, she peered at the yawning blackness behind him and faltered. He must have noticed because he suddenly looked unsure about leaving. Finally looking around the cell for the first time, his frown deepened. He looked her over again, this time slowly, meticulously.

"They never told me who you were or what you'd done."

His voice was flat, yet probing at the same time. She knew he was no spy, just a generous man who had taken care of her. He deserved an answer for his questions.

"My name is Rosemary Clifton."

In the dim light she saw his eyes go wide.

"Lady Rosemary? How are you here?"

306

She felt the sharp defiance in her chest sparkle in her eyes.

"The king finds himself ill-disposed toward any who refuse to play his deceptive intrigues."

A chill from the cold floor caused her to tremble, shaking loose some of her defiance. She waited for his response, though she was unable to look at him anymore. For all she expected, it wasn't to feel his coat around her shoulders. Looking up, she found he had come near and was adjusting the jacket. He seemed to have picked up the defiance that had broken off of her.

"I've had a feeling the king was not all we'd made him to be. There are many who feel the same. There's not much we can do; however, take heart in knowing you're not alone. Keep fighting Lady Rosemary. I think we're going to need more people like you soon."

When he smiled again, she finally caught the slip of memory she'd been struggling to grasp.

"I know you," she said. "You were the man from the town square who carried me out of the crowd when I was little. Then you gave me a sweet."

His eyes narrowed as he wrangled his own version of the memory into submission. Then his face lit with remembrance.

"That was you?" he asked, almost incredulous. "Incredible! You came to my thoughts many times after that day. I always berated myself for not staying longer to make sure you were taken care of."

He looked around again, concern etched on his kind face as

he pondered the black. Returning his gaze to her, he grasped her good shoulder.

"I'm sorry I can't do more," he said. Then he stood and walked back to the door.

"Sir? You forgot your lamp."

"I'll not have a lady call me *sir*. Adam is good enough for me. And I didn't forget it. A body needs more than grit to keep courage down here. I wish I could carry you to safety again, but I must again leave you before I know for certain that you will be unharmed. This is the little I can do, though. I didn't refill it before I came, so conserve the oil," he said, pausing with his hand on the door. "Good bye, Lady Rosemary. I hope we meet again in a happier place."

He signaled for her to blow the lantern's flame out, which she did. Then the door opened and shut, leaving her in darkness once more. She had no heart to sing. The final abandonment of her father had taken that from her. She didn't know if she would ever be willing to try again. However, Adam's coat, the memory of his smile, and the light he left behind were enough for her to survive on for now.

Time retained no meaning in the pit. There was no way of determining a schedule for eating or sleeping. With naught else to do, she mostly slept. When she felt her mind dulling, she fought the urge by playing little mind games. But it was to small avail, and soon she sought more productive occupation.

When she could bear it no more, she lit the lamp and explored her cell. The space was larger than she had expected.

She shuddered at the sight of manacles bolted to the far wall and the pile of moldy hay previous prisoners had used as a bed. That's all there was. Noticing the wall to the left of the door was free of obstacles, she blew out the lamp, placed it in the corner, and began to pace back and forth with her hand on the wall to guide her.

The pacing helped her enormously. Her beaten muscles had cramped while she was sitting in one place, but the walking brought new blood flow and relief. While moving, she could focus her thoughts with greater ease, so she sharpened her mind with memory games and repetition. She thought about her future some, yet she avoided thoughts of how she had ended up in a dungeon. She knew that thinking of Mark, the king, or her father would cause her to give up. No song or failing lantern could pull her from such an abyss if she allowed herself to go there. So she paced, hoping to put distance between herself and such thoughts.

Though her legs and feet were sore from the exertion, she forced herself to maintain her visionless trek a little bit longer before sitting on the cold, stone floor again. That was until she heard the sound of footsteps coming closer, which wasn't in and of itself strange since she was brought food and water every day. What was strange was the number of footsteps she heard. It sounded like several people were coming her way. Panic struck her as she assumed she would now be led away to her new life in the palace. All the thoughts she had been trying to avoid rose up from the dark abyss in her mind. They clenched her tight in their strong talons and tortured her with irrepressible desperation. If all those footsteps were coming for her, then the king's business was done. She gasped as a new thought assaulted her. Mark had been the object of the king's wrath. Something must have befallen him. The king's spite had yet to find borders, and she shuddered at the possible fate of her friend. She had let Mark down again, yet she hadn't even had the decency to feel shame. But she felt it now, in full force. She felt the shame of abandoning him without even trying to think of a way to escape. Hanging her head and crying softly, she prepared herself to take whatever was in store for her. Deserving no mercy, she expected none.

She heard keys fumbling in the lock. Drying her eyes as best she could, then standing tall, she faced the door. Believing she knew she deserved whatever came next didn't mean she would take it sniveling. She had been trained to be a lady after all. She would meet this challenge with the dignity her title demanded.

When the door opened, light radiated beyond and she saw the silhouettes of at least three, possibly four, people. Instinctively, she stiffened in preparation for being seized. However, only one of the figures stepped into the darkness with her. Whoever it was, the entire personage was graced with regal carriage, as if to defy the dishonor of this rank cell. Without warning, the door slammed shut, plunging the captives into darkness again.

Rose waited, unsure what to do next. She believed her fellow inmate ignorant of her presence because of the deep darkness. If

Rose wanted to, she could remain hidden. There were advantages to such a plan. The dark would shelter her if her fellow was a dangerous man. He would find her eventually; even darkness was only so deep. Unless she wanted to starve or forego all sleep she would have to make herself known.

Then everything changed. Her fellow inmate drew a sharp intake of breath, an inhale that Rose instinctively recognized as feminine. The woman held that breath for a long time, as if trying to master something to no avail. A shuddering cry escaped her and was followed by the sound of her knees hitting the stones. The worst part came next as she began to heave with racking sobs. Rose felt like an intruder in the midst of such dreadful pain. She wanted to preserve the privacy of the moment, but she knew she couldn't remain silent indefinitely. She listened to the gut-wrenching crying for a few more terrible seconds, before she could stand the sound no more. This wasn't just crying; it was a wailing that portrayed foundational loss. She spoke into the darkness, even as she prayed it wasn't the wrong choice.

"Ma'am?"

Rose's voice faltered from disuse and the sobs continued.

"Excuse me? Ma'am?" she said louder; firmer. Her voice broke through this time, and the woman made a gasping sound in surprise. The woman began scrambling madly to control herself, making awkward sobs that were more difficult to listen to than the wailing. The woman finally gathered herself enough to speak.

"H-Hello?" the woman said, her voice shaky and raspy, but carrying strength as well.

"Yes, ma'am. I just thought you should know that you're not alone here."

"How many more of you are there?"

"It's just me," Rose said, not even thinking to lie. Hearing the woman's voice instilled both confidence in and pity for its owner, and Rose felt her own fear slipping away.

"That's good to know," she said. There was a heavy silence between them. "I'm sorry you had to hear that."

Maybe it was because she had been alone for so long. Maybe it was because this woman carried the same sort of class Lady Diane had. Maybe it was because she was so hungry to hear another voice. Rose didn't know what it was, but she trusted this woman already.

"Ma'am? I've been down here by myself for a long time, and I think they're coming for me soon. When they do, I don't have much to look forward to. I know this is odd, but can I come and be near you?"

"Oh my dear, that's not odd at all. I could use someone near me as well."

"Thank you. Let me come to you."

Rose picked her way carefully to the voice, and as she did, she felt the pain of her solidarity fall away as she stood near this stranger.

"Are you hurt?" Rose asked.

"No, I'm fine. They didn't cut my hands free, and my throat

is sore, otherwise, I'm fine."

"Well, I can cut you free. We've got time."

"Thank you, dear, but the knots are well tied. I would prefer not to cut them when we have no light to see by."

"But you see, I do have a light."

"How did you get a light in here?"

"It was a gift from a friend," Rose said, reaching for the woman's hands. "Trust me."

Finding the set of bound hands, Rose was saddened to discover how swollen they were. The woman didn't resist being led forward, and Rose worked her hardest to repay that trust. It was more difficult than she thought with one hand holding the woman's and the other in a sling, but her pacing was now paying off. She reached the wall without incident and then turned toward the corner where the lantern sat. Her feet, following the well worn path, were soon rewarded with the "clink" of the lantern as her foot grazed it.

"I found it. Lighting it is a little awkward for me because my arm is broken. There's a wall here you can lean against if you want to sit."

"I'll be fine standing, but thank you."

Whoever this woman was, she had the manners of a lady. Her voice was gruff, yet kind, and Rose was growing fonder of her with each passing moment. She fumbled with the flint, her broken arm growling a warning as she moved it more than she should. Pressing through the pain, Rose was soon making sparks to light the wick. After a few minutes, the wick caught, and light grew in the darkness. She took note of the diminishing fuel supply, necessitating a quick job.

Leaving the lantern on the floor, she stood and faced her comrade. Both women froze. The light was only one small flame in the darkness, but, despite the shadows, Rose saw a possibility that sent trembles through her whole body. The woman felt it too; Rose saw it in her searching eyes. As she stepped forward, Rose's trembling grew worse. The woman was older, thinner, with more lines on her face, but the eyes were the same caverns of love Rose remembered so well. As she drew closer, Rose saw they were wide with disbelief and shimmering with unshed tears. The woman was close enough to touch now. The breath in Rose's lungs was desperate to escape even as it was trapped in her chest. Raising her still bound hands, the woman touched Rose's cheek with a finger.

"Rose? Is it really you?"

Twenty-two

ROSE EXHALED A SOB AND BURROWED HERSELF INTO Aunt Anne's waiting arms. Both women cried unashamedly. Resting her head on Aunt Anne's chest, Rose sobbed the harder when those arms held her close rather than repulsing her away. The kisses Aunt Anne bestowed on her head were undeserved, but Rose allowed herself this moment. She was in prison, she'd been beaten, torn down, and forgotten by all of Agumbra, but that embrace told her there was a remnant left to love her. Allowing that love to fill her hungry soul, Rose feasted on it before the crows came to steal it from her. In that moment, she was safe.

"Let me look at you," Aunt Anne said, as she tried to untangle their awkward embrace.

"How about we get those hands free first?" Rose said, ducking beneath her arms. "I don't know how much fuel is left, and I would hate to lose it before you are free."

"Ah yes, that matter. Well, as you begin, I am proud to say

you are not the only one with hidden resources."

She nodded down to her right foot. She was wearing leather travelling boots that came up past her ankle. They were well-loved and worn, yet anything but extraordinary. Realization dawned upon Rose when Aunt Anne nodded again. Slipping her hand inside the boot, Rose felt her fingers close over the handle of a knife. She withdrew it, and Aunt Anne's eyes sparkled mischievously.

"No one ever thinks to search a lady. We're supposedly above such heists."

Rose smiled back, happy to be a co-conspirator. The sharp, little knife made quick work of the ropes. Rose waited as Aunt Anne rubbed life back into her sore hands, then she handed the knife back. The older woman sheathed it, albeit clumsily due to her still swollen hands, grinning conspiratorially at Rose as she did. Rose was so happy she didn't think it was possible to contain her joy.

"All right. No more excuses. I want to take a good look at you before we have to put out the lantern."

She came forward, placed her hands on Rose's shoulders, and looked her over from head to toe. This was not the first appraisal Rose had been submitted to since being home. But, where she had been scrutinized by her father and Mark, Aunt Anne was looking at her with rapture, drinking in all the changes. It was the look of a mother who had given up her child for dead, yet was now looking at her alive and well. Rose almost allowed herself to partake in the same rapture, but reality came crashing down around her. Aunt Anne must not have heard the truth of her betrayal. If she had there would only be contempt in those eyes. Withdrawing instinctively, Rose felt guilt conquer her again. She suddenly wished the lantern would go out so the darkness could hide the sagging of her shoulders as the guilt settled there. Seeing the shift, Aunt Anne became troubled. She took Rose's hands, wincing when she noticed the scars there.

"You were always such a pretty child. I loved it when you were so involved with playing or learning you forgot all the sad things around you. Nothing could outshine you in those moments. But, even when you were sad, you were pretty. Now you're all grown up and beautiful, just as I always suspected you would be. It's a shame no one has been around to tell you as such. My only regret is I wasn't there to watch."

Rose hoped the flickering light disguised her blush. Part of it was embarrassment, part of it was pleasure; however, part of it was shame. Rose knew Aunt Anne would not say such things if she knew the truth, and she ducked her head.

"Please. Don't…"

Aunt Anne ignored her feeble protestations, and raised her face firmly with her hand.

"There is one thing, though. It's your eyes. You have such terribly sad eyes. It makes me ache when I imagine what they have seen to make them so. If you could forget all the sad things for a while, like you used to as a little girl, I believe you would be positively radiant."

"I'm afraid you may be a little more than biased, Aunt Anne.

317

There aren't many people who would find sadness beautiful, especially if it happens to be bruised, scarred, and broken."

Aunt Anne's expression grew troubled again.

"I have my suspicions who broke your arm."

"I think you'd be surprised."

"Really now? Who was it?"

"The king was the one who gave the order."

"The king! How could he have a vendetta against you?"

Rose sighed. It was time to begin the story of her shame.

"The king ambushed me a few days ago after I met with Mark. He wanted me to betray Mark. You see, Mark was going to get Hope and run away. I was going to bring Hope to him, but the king found me first. He'd overheard everything and he wanted my help."

"You didn't help him, did you? I know you didn't."

"No. Not this time at least. I said I would never help him again. That earned me no favors."

"And that's why he did this to you?"

"Not exactly. He didn't take it kindly when I left a set of scratches on his face."

"That's what that was from," Aunt Anne said, half to herself. "But why would you attack him?"

Rose shuffled her feet in embarrassment.

"He was saying some horrible things about Uncle Henry. I couldn't stop myself."

Aunt Anne was crying again. Rose, knowing herself to be unworthy of those tears, wished she would stop.

"My brave girl. You are as lovely on the inside as you are on the outside. Thank you, Rose."

"I said I didn't betray your family *this* time," Rose said as the lantern light flickered and died. *"Good,"* she thought to herself. *"I couldn't bear to see her face anymore."*

"What are you talking about? You never betrayed our family."

"I did once, and I'm afraid it made all the difference."

Rose spared no details. From Robbie's appearance to the bitter end was relayed with no attempt to acquit herself. Rose needed Aunt Anne to know how instrumental she had been in Hope's kidnapping. Her broken arm cradled to her chest and her face buried in her knees, Rose hid in the darkness. The black was her one shelter now that all she had ever hidden behind was exposed. Suddenly, Aunt Anne was sitting beside her in the darkness. Rose stiffened, ready to receive her dues.

"It's been five years since that day," Aunt Anne said. Rose felt pressure building behind her eyes and knew tears threatened to burst forth. She bit her lip in preparation for the angry words she expected to befall her. What she felt instead was an arm slipping itself around her shoulder.

"Has this been your burden since then? Oh, my poor Rose, you've carried it five years too long."

"What?" Rose exclaimed, unsure if she had heard the words right.

"You didn't betray us, Rose. I think you made a tough choice in a tricky situation, but I don't think you betrayed us."

"No! You don't understand! You don't understand!" Rose wailed into her knees as she rocked back and forth.

"Shh, Rose. Shh!" Aunt Anne soothed, but Rose couldn't stop. She had expected so many things in preparation for this moment. She'd expected anger, sadness, disbelief, accusations, and hatred. Never grace, though. Never forgiveness. This turn of events overwhelmed her, reducing her to uncontrollable sobs. Amidst her tears, she was vaguely aware of movement around her; however, she couldn't concentrate on it for long. Suddenly, she felt unyielding hands on her shoulders, giving her a little shake. It wasn't hard, but it was enough for her to come to her senses.

"Good girl. Now be still for me, okay?"

Rose obeyed. Aunt Anne's voice hadn't been harsh, but it carried calm authority that soothed her. She heard the sound of a key rattling in the lock. The door opened, revealing a solitary silhouette in the doorway. She couldn't see much since Aunt Anne had stood, placing herself between Rose and the interloper.

"Is everything all right? I heard a commotion," the silhouette said.

"I believe so," Aunt Anne said. "We just realized we knew each other. It was a little too much for her at the time, but we're fine now."

In the following pause, Rose saw the guard moving his head back and forth in a searching motion. Panic clutching her, Rose looked for the lantern so she could hide it. But it was already gone, no doubt spirited away by Aunt Anne. It would seem her surrogate aunt had thought of everything. The guard concluded his perusal of the cell.

"All right then. Well, I guess… What I mean to say is… You two need anything just get my attention and I'll come."

"Thank you. We shall."

He looked at them for a second more, and then was gone. Aunt Anne found her in the darkness, placed an arm around her again, but said nothing. Rose knew she needed to say something, yet also needed time to craft the words she wanted to say. Aunt Anne was ready to listen.

"How is it you can forgive me? Weren't you listening to what I was saying? You should be furious."

"What is there to be angry about? What is there to forgive? You were placed in an impossible situation. You did the best you could, and it didn't go the way you were led to believe it would. I know you, and I know you would never willfully betray us. So why should I punish you when you've no doubt punished yourself far more than needed?"

Aunt Anne shifted so that she was able to put both arms around Rose. Rose willingly tucked herself into that safe place.

"I love you, Rose girl. I hate that I haven't been around to tell you. Nothing has changed in that regard, and it never will."

"I still don't understand. When I met with Mark he wasn't able to forgive me."

There was a silence that was broken, after a time, by a deep sigh.

"I'm afraid Mark has been very foolish. He has hidden himself from me, but I've suspected he was letting something warp him in anger for many years now. It appears I was right. He's looking for someone to blame in his anger. Sadly, it seems to be you. Forgive him, Rose. Hopefully this second chance changes his heart."

"Second chance? What second chance?" Rose said, sitting up. Then she felt the bandage on the hand that pressed her shoulder, and her heart froze. "Aunt Anne, why are you here?"

"It's not important," Aunt Anne said as she attempted to tuck Rose back into her arms.

Rose refused to be cajoled like a child. Shaking free, she groped for the injured hand. Finding it, she ran her fingers over the homemade bandage. Her elder inadvertently hissed softly in pain.

"Aunt Anne," she began purposefully, "Why are you down here? What happened?"

"You were always the inquisitive one. It was hard to deter you once you had your mind set on something."

Rose was silent, revealing her determined intentions now. Her partner sighed.

"Mark was caught when he came to get Hope the other night. He was charged with trespassing and attempted kidnapping. The king sentenced him to death."

Rose gasped.

"They didn't... He isn't..."

"No. He's safe now. I claimed the right of Reclaitute."

Though Rose had suspected as much, when she discovered the bandage, it was still hard to hear, let alone fathom. She ran her finger across that precious palm over and over again.

"So that means that tomorrow…"

"Yes, tomorrow I will take his punishment as I now bear his guilt."

Rose was again thankful for the darkness because it hid the grotesque grief on her face. Shuddering under it, she inadvertently gripped the wounded hand. Aunt Anne gasped, and Rose gasped a sob of her own.

"I'm sorry! It's just… It doesn't seem fair. I just found you."

"I know. I was having similar thoughts. Let's not think that way. I knew what I was doing, and I'm happy to see it through. I've had a good life and now my son has a chance to do the same."

"Then why were you crying when you first came? It sounded…painful."

"I'm not afraid to die to tomorrow, but before I was brought here I was reminded of all I am leaving behind. Rose, I saw Hope, my very own Hope. She was beautiful, yet different than I had imagined her. She was kind and brave and happy. When I spoke to her it was almost like I could see the years laid before her in one long road. There's so much she's going to do and learn, and she's going to grow so much. I became excited with all the possibilities until I remembered I wasn't going to be there to see any of it. I won't be there for her first heartbreak or the moment she realizes what kind of person she wants to be.

None of it. And so, while I don't regret this decision because it saves my son, I was grieving the years that I will miss with all of my children. That means you too, Rose."

"Me? Really?"

"Yes. I saw your father right before I was brought here. He was the one who brought Hope to me. He made it sound like something awful had happened to you, but he wouldn't tell me what. I was frightened for what had become of you, and grieving because I would never know who you became. I'm thankful I've seen what kind of person you seem to be; however, I must ask you something. Why does your father believe you're done singing?"

Did he care? How could that even be possible since he was the one who was most determined to tramp the song out of her?

"I don't know," Rose said honestly. "In some ways I want to be. It hurts too much to keep trying." The bitter pain of her father's constant rejection clutched at her throat. Her heart was weak from trying and demanded reprieve. "It's safer not to hope."

"It may be *safer*, but what kind of life do you think it will take you toward? Your father was at this same crossroad once in his life, and he chose not to hope. And, when he did, he allowed bitterness and anger to shape the man he is today. The path back from that place is a long one; a truth I think your father is figuring out right now."

"I want to believe you, but I don't know how to believe my father can change, not anymore. I want to believe he can, yet I don't think it's possible for him to do so."

"It is possible! I saw the man you've always been able to see. I think the day is coming when everyone will see him. And regardless of him changing or not, even if he chooses to be bitter, your hope doesn't change. All those stories are real, Rose. Flesh and blood real. Disappointment and pain are a part of this journey, but the ending is the same. So sing for the day when it all will be made right because singing reminds us there is hope even in the moments we want to forget. You've always made me stronger by your constant choice to remember. It makes me want to remember, too. So please, I'm pleading with you. Don't stop singing."

Rose's heart was sore. She still didn't want to sing. The effort to drag the gentle lyrics into the light seemed too monumental of a task. And under the effort lay a hardness wishing to settle into her heart. As Aunt Anne's words rubbed against that unmalleable place in her soul, the soreness of the wound ignited. The gentle pleading and the wounds chafed against each other, birthing hot words in Rose's mind. Aunt Anne's were just the same words she'd heard over and over before, and they were starting to sound tired. She simply didn't want to keep trying anymore.

But then she felt the scrape of Reclaitute's bandage on her skin as Aunt Anne squeezed her hand. Rose was weary of the same lesson, but maybe it kept repeating itself because she needed to hear it over and over again. Perhaps this was just another step in the progression of who she would become. Aunt

Anne's words collided with the unmalleable hardness and somehow latched onto hand holds. With Aunt Anne's love and gentleness pressing against the hardness, Rose felt some yielding.

"Will you sing with me?" Rose asked tentatively. "It's easier when I'm not alone."

"Of course I will," Aunt Anne said, kissing the top of Rose's head.

They lifted their voices to create a golden melody, complete with silver harmony. Rose's voice shook at first, and the hardness in her held. But as her voice found its strength, the hardness shifted even more. Belief made it strong, and, though she was still heartsick, confused, and scared, their song lifted a veil through which she caught a glimpse of hope merely waiting to be fulfilled. The struggle had somehow made it more lovely than she ever remembered it being in her childhood.

"Aunt Anne," she said when they had finished, "Will you tell me Rohirt's stories? Like you did when I was little? That way I can remember them when you go?"

"It would be my pleasure."

Wrapping themselves in Adam's coat, Rose listened as the storyteller began her tale. She listened to story after story, each faithfully recorded by Rohirt the Bard. And, as she listened, she remembered. She remembered Jubion and the Great King who had reigned there. She remembered the magic he possessed and had given to those who became the Magic Folk. Remembering what Agumbra had once been renewed her longing to see, with her own eyes, its splendor restored. She again yearned for the day when the Great King's heir would return from the North to reestablish honor, truth, and beauty. She remembered and her remembrance sustained her.

She must have fallen asleep because the next thing she knew someone was shaking her.

"Wake up, Rose. I need you to stay calm; however, I believe they're coming for me."

Rose was immediately awake and straining her ears into the darkness. Sure enough, she heard the sounds of some sort of collaboration beyond the doorway. Despite what Aunt Anne had told her, she began to panic.

"None of that," her elder said, wrapping her arms around her. "Remember Rose, this is what I want. Don't give them any reason to hurt you anymore. If I'm to keep my courage I need to know you aren't being punished any further. Chin up now. Neither of us were born to it, but that didn't stop us from becoming ladies of Deteen. Let's show them what that looks like."

Rose clung to those brave words as they stood. Facing the door, she heard the sound of footsteps approach them. Aunt Anne must've heard them, too, because she pulled her into a fierce embrace.

"No matter what anyone tells you, don't forget who you are. You're a Kings maiden, my first daughter, and I have always loved you. Keep singing after I'm gone, Rose, and pray that Mark and Hope do the same."

The key was rattling in the lock and Rose felt her hot tears soak into Aunt Anne's shoulder.

"I love you so much, Aunt Anne. You are the only mother I've ever known."

The door opened then, cutting off their conversation. One of the three guards standing in the doorway approached. Raising his lantern high, he shone it in their faces.

"Anne Poynter?"

"That would be me."

Rose's eyes watered from the sudden light, yet she surveyed her companion now that she could see her. Aunt Anne was filthy, with her hair matted and ratty. There was a bruise on her throat, tear tracks were plain through the grime on her face, and her dress was ruined. But there was no mistaking she was a lady. Only a lady could appear regal in this pit. The guard noticed as well and adjusted his tone.

"Lady Anne, it's time."

"Very well," she said gravely. But, before she submitted to the guard, she gave Rose another hug. With her good arm, Rose squeezed her tightly.

"The corner."

It was so brief Rose second guessed whether or not she had heard it at all. She was unable to ask because Aunt Anne had silently extracted herself from the embrace, and faced the guard, who bound her hands when he saw they were free. She looked at Rose once. Rose thought she saw a trace of uncertainty in her eyes; like she was finally feeling the finality of it all. The expression was fleeting and Aunt Anne covered it with a small smile. Then, looking away from Rose, she allowed the guards to lead her out. The door shut and all was dark again. She heard the key locking the door and the footsteps leading Aunt Anne away. Rose's mind reeled with the meaning of the coded message so much that she didn't notice that she was alone again. There wasn't anything in the corner except...

Her eyes widened in possible comprehension. Fumbling to the back wall, she followed it to the corner. Kneeling, she groped in the darkness until her fingers grazed the lantern, which she was able to pull close. If there was any oil left it couldn't be much. She tried lighting it anyway. After several tries, the wick miraculously caught, dribbling a puddle of light onto the floor. The light was sad, dim, and wouldn't last long. On the outskirts of the light she saw something she didn't recognize. Pulling it near, she saw it was Aunt Anne's boots with the hidden knife still sheathed inside the soft material. She smiled just as the light spluttered, then died. Aunt Anne had always taken care of her.

As she fingered the supple leather, a new emotion filled her chest. Though foreign, it was easy to name. Wrath. Righteous wrath, if she had ever felt such a thing. This wasn't just. It couldn't be. Mark wasn't wrong in what he had done. His actions were foolish and rash, but not wrong. Because of this injustice, she would soon lose the only mother she had ever known.

Quaking with the newfound wrath, she thought of her years long wish to prevent horrendous acts against her loved ones. She had been powerless, but it wouldn't happen again. Not this day.

This travesty would not commence if there was any power in her being to stop it. She placed the boots on her feet, the cold knife sheathed inside stoking the fire within her. Unsure exactly what she was going to do, she kept moving to keep her nerve from failing her.

Grabbing the extinguished lantern, she groped through the darkness until she found the door. She had to move quickly! Too much time had been wasted already. Every second was a second closer to Aunt Anne's demise. She positioned herself to slip out the door and set her feet. Hefting the lantern in her good arm, she mentally calculated its weight and her own strength. Now! Now or never!

"Guard! Help! Oh please, help me!"

She was barely subduing true frenzy as she implemented her insane plan. She kept screaming, the shrill words frightening even herself, and she was soon rewarded with the sound of running steps.

"Hurry! I beg you, hurry!"

The keys were clanging madly, his hands doubtless shaking like windswept boughs. Her hand tightened as she babbled shrill, incoherent words. Surprisingly, she heard the latch give way through the pounding in her ears. The door rushed inward, followed quickly by the young guard who had answered her cries earlier. Breathing a prayer that begged for his forgiveness, she acted.

Hefting the lantern with all the might she could muster, Rose sent it crashing into the side of his head. He was tall, whereas she was petite and only had one good arm for awkwardly swinging her makeshift weapon. All her physical weaknesses worked toward his well-being as they probably saved his life. As it was, she hit him with enough force to send him reeling backwards, striking his head on the heavy door. He collapsed and was still. With trepidation, she approached him, afraid a corpse, not a man, lay at her feet. But, as she drew nearer, she sobbed in relief when she saw his chest rise and fall.

Her fervor began to ebb slightly now that her plan was completed. She had never thought it would work, and, now that it had, she didn't know what to do next. She began trembling all over and the knife in her boot began chafing against her ankle.

Aunt Anne.

She needed to keep moving regardless of her fears. She was the sad substitute for an avenging angel; however, she would have to do. Bending down, Rose calmed her nerves by putting her hand over the knife handle. She had no idea what she was doing or what difference she could make. But she did know, though this had to be the most ridiculous venture she had ever struck out on, it was the most righteous crusade she'd yet to wage. Taking a breath, she steeled her nerves. Then, she took off at a run.

"Please. Please don't let it be too late!" she whispered as the castle labyrinth swallowed her whole.

Twenty-three

*I*T HAD BEEN AN OVERWHELMING DAY FOR THE BOTH OF
them. Aiden, who felt tired in his bones, could only
imagine what Mark must be feeling. The guards hadn't been kind
to him during the night he spent in their custody. However,
physical pain was transient. Looking into Mark's eyes, Aiden
knew there were deeper agonies torturing his godson. Mark, who
was always trying to carry the world on his shoulders, blamed
himself for his mother's death sentence. Aiden hadn't said a
word to the boy on the subject because, in all honesty, he agreed
with Mark's assessment. He loved the boy as if he were his own,
but Anne was truly his. All the pain Aiden had experienced in his
life paled to what he felt as she had been led away. He wasn't
going to lose her. He hadn't lost her when she had been
captured by the Gruilitians. Surely he could manage another
rescue now. Making sure the boy was still sleeping, Aiden
blended into the bustle of the street to sort through his thoughts.

Refusing to watch his Anne die, Aiden walked for hours

trying to solve the problem before them. He knew he needed help if he was to remove her noose without earning himself one. Mark's assistance was out of the question. If that boy reclaimed Reclaitute, Anne would never forgive him. And, if he didn't lay claim to his guilt again, he was sure to do something equally foolhardy. No, Aiden needed more reliable help. But there was no help to be had. Too many variables were in play, and he couldn't sort them all out. Finally stopping, Aiden noticed it was getting on in the afternoon. Instead of solutions, all he had created was a pounding headache.

Early in his musings, an impossible idea had entered his mind. Yet, the longer he paced, the less impossible it sounded. It had been years since he had attempted such a feat. He didn't even know if he could interact with the power as he once had, or how much energy it would pull from him. He could be useless by the time he was done making his request. But it wasn't the fear of weakness that had kept him from this transcendent contact for so long. It was *them*. Those things…those monsters who would surely come…still sent a shiver down his spine. Not wanting to draw such a plague upon themselves as they considered options for rescuing Hope, he and Anne had decided to forego using the very avenue he was now considering. They had known they weren't strong enough to combat such evil. They still weren't. But he couldn't think about that now. All he could think about was Anne swinging below the gallows. In that moment his resolve hardened. He had to at least try.

Knowing he needed a quiet, secluded spot for undertaking

his insane plan, he started back toward the inn. Inquiring of the innkeeper, he learned that Mark hadn't been seen. He then proceeded to rent a second room. The innkeeper was more than happy to oblige and handed Aiden a key. Anxious to get started, Aiden took the key and walked toward his new room. There was no telling how long this would take, so he stopped briefly to check on Mark, who he found tangled in the sheets and moaning from what Aiden supposed was a nightmare. Half of his heart went out to the boy, even as the other half still thought him a fool. Of course, he had felt the same way toward Anne when she had been that age.

Anne…

Shutting the door, Aiden completed the walk to his new room. Time was too precious to waste so he locked the door behind him, removed his boots, and prepared his mind to begin. This had never been a strong gift of his in the first place, so he was going to have to relax himself. Everyone had different methods, but his favorite had always been to lay on his back with his arms folded across his stomach. His friends used to joke he was preparing for his own funeral when he would lay like that. He laughed a humorless laugh when he realized how appropriate that joke would be now if he did this wrong. Pushing these macabre thoughts aside, Aiden focused his energy and began.

Nothing happened at first. More time passed, and, though he was searching as hard as he could, the connection he sought still eluded him. He'd heard of cases where disuse had rendered some people unable to interact with the power at all, even when they begged. Aiden felt a nearly irrepressible panic rising in him. He had to remain calm. If he grew frantic he would never succeed. But frenzy grew as results continued to elude him. In desperation, he clamored with every reserve he could muster. Surprisingly, his efforts weren't in vain. When he felt a small presence in the corner of his mind, Aiden could have wept for joy.

It was the Magic! He was still able to ask for the Magic!

Remaining small, it warily began to search him out. The Magic was unsure of him and his indecorous behavior, thus he became as polite as possible. If it was going to let him pass, he needed to be perfectly respectful. As the Magic drew closer, the room began to fade. Soon he would slip into the Magic's realm; a place where sight wouldn't be his primary sense anymore. As the Magic accepted him, he felt his consciousness being pulled away. In his prime, his relationship with this enigma had been close as it could without being a wielder. Lacking formalities, he had been able to ask freely of the Magic. Now he knew the interaction between them was akin to acquaintances. Thankfully, it would be enough for his simple task.

Finding him acceptable, the Magic began its dance. Aiden waited until it was time, then joined his form with the formal movements. Part of him had been afraid he wouldn't remember the steps, but the movements returned to him easily. He fell into the dance as if he had never left. It was different now. More distanced, not nearly as strong as it had once been, but that didn't stop the familiar joy from filling him. It folded around him, in him, and through him, and he knew the time had come for him to make his request.

"Please, may I speak with the Elder?"

The Magic shifted as it accepted his request. Feeling his consciousness shift with it, Aiden finally realized how weak he really was. He had enough strength for a few minutes at most, but no more. It would have to do. Another presence became apparent to him, a desperately familiar presence.

"Aiden? Aiden Morgan? Is it really you?"

Memory after memory rolled over him at the sound of that voice.

"Ridge?"

"Many years have passed since I was referenced by that name. Most call me 'Elder' now."

"You're the Elder?"

"Yes, my old friend, I am the Elder."

Aiden was still trying to fathom this news when he felt a sudden stab of weakness course through him. Ridge's presence ebbed slightly, but the contact held. He knew Ridge had felt the tremor as well.

"Aiden, what's wrong?"

"I don't have much time. I need your help. The king is going to hang Anne tomorrow, and I can't stop it on my own."

"Wait, Anne Vircel? Your Anne? What happened?"

"I can't explain now. No. Time. Please come."

"Aiden…you know our general stance on going abroad."

Aiden understood why Ridge was so uncertain. He wanted

to rescue Anne, yet must also consider the safety of their people. Aiden knew how much he had already jeopardized in simply making this connection. *They* would sense the Magic, and then they would come. If they did, and he was alone, Aiden would be a man on borrowed time. That didn't matter. Not as much as saving Anne. Let those monsters come. Let them come and tear him limb from limb. As long as Anne was saved. He knew this was not an easy thing, possibly a very selfish thing, he was asking of his old comrade. But what else could he do? Whatever the decision, he hoped Ridge would make it quickly.

"I am bound by honor, truth, and love," Ridge said.

If he hadn't been so absorbed in keeping the connection he would have cried out in his elation.

"To stand with you and wait for Peros that was," he finished.

"We will come, Aiden. Hold on, we will come."

"Thank you, Ridge. And I'm so sorry if this puts your men in danger of...well, you know what."

"Never fear, old friend. Our defenses have improved since you left us. If you use the Magic to contact anyone at Haven, the energy pull is unrecognizable. You're not alone, Aiden. We're coming."

With the last of his strength slipping away, Aiden dredged up the energy for one final sentiment.

"Thank. You."

Then the Magic had spent all it could spend with the energy he had given it. Aiden found himself back in the inn, feeling more like a miserable old man than he ever had. His breathing was ragged, and he couldn't get his body to move. Whatever did move was achy or numb. He was completely spent, just as he feared he'd be. But, before he could despair, the Magic shifted in him again, and his vitality grew.

"Carry on, my friend. We're coming," Ridge's voice sounded in his head.

Standing on shaky legs, Aiden looked around. The sun had set in the quiet city. It had taken him hours to relay the message. Even with the strength Ridge had sent, all he wanted to do was sleep. He looked longingly at the bed, but shook such thoughts out of his head. There was work to do and not much time to do it. To start with, he needed Mark. It was time that boy knew the truth, about everything. Anne had kept her son's destiny hidden from him for too long.

But Mark wasn't in his room, neither had the innkeeper seen him. It didn't take long for Aiden to put the pieces together. Mark had slipped away, and that meant only one thing. He was going to do something stupid.

Aiden panicked as he hadn't panicked in years. He possessed nerves so steeled he could stand in the thick of a battle without his hands shaking. It was a characteristic that earned him the nickname, "Ready, Steady Aidey" as a young man. But now he had lost track of his godson. Whatever the boy was planning, and there was no doubt he was scheming, it was sure to interfere with the rescue mission he had just summoned. He pursued his quarry to no avail. The city was a maze, and he was determined to rifle through every nook of it. So he pushed on with his flagging strength, searching for the boy who would either solve or ruin everything.

His seeking didn't stop the horizon from coming aglow, though. Dawn was coming, whether they were ready or not.

ROBBIE'S CONSTANT NUDGES reminded Mark to try not to look suspicious. Mark didn't know how it could be helped. He was actively staging a revolt against a well-liked monarch. He looked around nervously even as he thought the word.

"Relax, Mark. People can tell you're nervous."

Robbie's voice cut through the noise in Mark's head, and made him snap back into reality. He was thankful for his friend who, though clearly nervous, too, kept his calm and encouraged Mark to do the same.

"I'm sorry. I really need to get this right."

"I know. But remember, we're here to help you."

The two boys continued threading their way through the growing crowd making their way to the center of the city. The crowd was larger today. Much larger. The news of Reclaitute had spread through the surrounding area like gangrene. Throngs of people had come to watch its fulfillment. With the last claiming outside the recollection of most, watching this hanging was almost like watching history. Mark's ears burned with shame as he thought about it.

On their scouting ventures last night, the group of boys

became aware of Mark's rise to macabre celebrity. Everyone was talking about *that boy* and *his brave mother*. Mark's cut and bruised face made him easily distinguishable, so the boys had taken measures to hide him. While some of the boys procured a hood, others helped Jason, the most artistic of them, form together a powder made of dirt and other things they wouldn't name. Jason then applied it to Mark's face hiding the bruises. It seemed to be working…for now.

The gallows stood, looming like a judge who presided over the guilty. With the crowd relatively scattered, Mark and Robbie were able to shoulder their way up close enough to watch the proceedings, yet far enough away to avoid recognition. Looking up to the gallows he had stood on just the day prior, Mark remembered his own death sentence. The memory of looking on a sea of impassive faces as he prepared to die made his knees quake even now as he prepared to execute an escape plan conceived in lunacy.

If this was going to work, he had to stop indulging his memories. To bolster his courage, he put his mind to work reviewing their plan. During their scouting the previous afternoon, they had found an abandoned building near the square. Sneaking in the back, they secured it and plotted their mission. After debating, Caleb jokingly mentioned lighting the structure on fire.

"It would be distracting," he said with a laugh.

But Mark took him seriously. A fire would certainly stall an execution. The more he thought about it the more he liked it. As he talked it out with the others, he gained more and more ideas of how they could make it work. When it was put to a vote, they all said, "Aye!"

Once it was dark, they set to work. A pile of kindling was built in the middle of the room, waiting to be lit when the signal was given. Another group worked on protective measures to contain the fire to the empty house. Caleb would sit with the kindling to make sure no one came and disturbed it. Jason would wait on the outskirts of the crowd in line of sight with Mark. When Mark gave him a signal, he would run back to the house to help Caleb. Once it was burning, they would run to the square and raise an alarm. All the other boys would be positioned in key places of the crowd. They would begin clambering about the fire, raising a panic. Then, while the crowd surged in response, Mark would rush onto the gallows and free his mother. Mark wanted to go alone, but Robbie insisted on going with him. Mark finally agreed, though begrudgingly.

Searching the crowd, Mark saw the faces of his friends. They were idling around, trying not to look at each other. Mark also saw Jason, who was watching him like a hawk. Wishing for no more blood on his stained hands, Mark prayed for their safety in this dangerous scheme they'd concocted. A hush fell over the crowd. The path that had claimed his mother the night before was returning her to them now.

Mark consciously slowed his breathing trying to calm his nerves. He could see his mother being led through the crowd. She was filthy. But looked unharmed. He let out a breath, not realizing he had unconsciously stopped breathing. His pulse quickened as she began her ascent up the gallows steps. Her eyes were trained on her feet, which he noticed were bare. And it seemed to him as if she were intentionally trying not to look into the crowd. Otherwise, she seemed at peace. He couldn't describe it in full, but he could tell she was prepared to die. And to die with grace. He felt terribly sad and hopeful all at the same time.

She had climbed all but three stairs to the platform when he snapped out of his reverie. His eyes peeled themselves away from her and found Jason. There he was, perched and waiting. Their eyes locked, and Mark deliberately removed his hood. Though momentary, it was enough. Jason was gone before Mark could blink.

Noticing the signal, Robbie began to shift his feet in anticipation. Mark noticed his friend's nervous fidgeting and it steadied his own nerves. He was ready to take action. Only the burly executioner stood beside his mother, but he was unarmed. A single guard at the foot of the stairs didn't worry him either. The crier was reading something from a long roll of parchment; however, instead of listening Mark looked at the king and John, both of whom sat stone-faced in a booth near the platform, watching. Mark smiled as he imagined those set faces twisting in surprise as they watched their prey fall through their grasp.

His smile faded when he finally heard what was being said. The official reading's closure was imminent. Upon its finish the noose would be placed around his mother's neck, completing the impossible. His nerves returned as he looked toward the house.

But there was nothing to see. No pillar of smoke disturbed the stark blue sky and no screams were heard. All was silent as the people stood waiting to watch death claim its prize.

Mark looked again to his mother, who watched the official as he read. Her serenity made her look so much like a martyr that Mark wanted to cry out. He turned again to look for his friends, and the bottom of his stomach gave way with what he saw.

Caleb was being held by the scruff of his shirt by a large, angry looking man. Both he and the man looked singed; however, Caleb was also sporting a bloody lip and black eye. The man was shaking him as he pointed to the crowd. Caleb was surly, a sure sign he wouldn't give up his accomplices. Another man appeared with Jason, who was roughed up similarly to Caleb. No smoke plume disturbed the skyline, though. Robbie gripped Mark's elbow, a gesture that somehow made the enormity of it all more tangible. To make matters worse, his eyes met with those of a man whose attention had been caught by the charred boys and their captors. That gaze communicated volumes during its brief moments. Then Morgan broke it and began trekking through the crowd toward him. Mark refused to be stopped. He had made up his mind last night. He was either going to rescue his mother or die trying. Morgan couldn't take that from him.

Shouldering his way through the crowd with Robbie dogging on his heels, Mark saw the bag had been placed over his mother's head, and the executioner was approaching with the noose.

Mark growled and began forcibly pushing people aside. Eyes turned toward him, but he didn't care as long as he escaped the guard's notice. He found a fist sized rock and scooped it up as he went. He was causing enough of a stir that the executioner paused, causing the guard at the foot of the stairs to turn toward Mark and reach for his sword. But it was too late for the guard. Mark swung the rock toward the side of his head, knocking him down. As he fell a cacophony of metal striking the stones of the street rang out.

"Now! Now, now, now!" Mark bellowed as he wrenched the guard's sword from its sheath. A woman was already screaming and the crowd surged in motion. More guards approached the gallows as they drew their swords. But Mark's friends were also on the move. Bellowing in return, they moved to cut off the guards. The panic Mark had wanted, began.

Mark wasted no time. Rushing up the stairs, sword raised high, he barreled toward the executioner. Morgan had taught him some basics of swordplay, but merely the basics. Mark was hoping since the executioner was unarmed, he would give up without much of a fight. No such luck. The hangman easily threw the noose around his mother's neck and pulled the knot tight. Eyeing the trapdoor lever, he smiled at Mark who ran toward the two of them screaming unintelligible words and swinging the sword wildly. The executioner easily sidestepped him and pushed him to the platform floor, the sword clattering out of his hand.

Rolling over, he saw the executioner coming for him, wicked joy in his eyes. Robbie was close on the executioner's heels, but the guard was too busy moving toward Mark to notice. Mark watched as his friend lowered his shoulder, ducked his head, and launched himself at the bigger man. The pair fell in a tangle of arms and legs near Mark. Robbie was desperately trying to land a punch, but the executioner, having recovered most of his senses, dodged the boy's blows and landed one of his own on Robbie's side. Mark's friend fell, clutching the injury.

The guard was struggling to his feet, but Mark had already risen to his own. Tackling the executioner, the two struggled on the ground until Mark, fierce with desperation, gained the upper hand. Though he rained angry blows on the man, there was no waning of the struggle. Instead, the guard surprised them both by grabbing Mark's wrist and twisting it harshly to the side. When Mark cried out in pain, the guard aimed a blow for his chin. Mark's head jerked backwards and he saw stars. Then, before he knew it, his arm was wrenched behind him and his face was slammed into the ground. His shoulder erupted in pain as the man pushed him down and pulled his arm back farther and farther.

Suddenly he heard a yell and the pressure was gone. Ignoring the pain in his arm, Mark turned in time to see Robbie and the executioner tumble off the platform. Jerking to his feet, Mark ran to see if he could help, but Robbie waved him back.

"Go Mark, go!"

Needing no other urging, Mark ran to his mother, who was

frantically trying to loosen the noose with her bound hands to no avail. He picked up the sword and aimed for the rope that held her fast to the gallows.

"Stop boy! Or I'll pull this lever!"

Mark ground to a halt. He recognized that cold voice. At times his nightmares still echoed with it. Turning, he saw the king, boasting a sickly, triumphant gleam in his eye. One hand held his sword leisurely, while the other held the trapdoor lever. Mark saw as well his friends had been overpowered by the guards, and the crowd was beginning to calm down. Morgan was nowhere to be seen. They had lost.

"Drop your sword, Sir Poynter."

Behind him, his mother groaned. She had probably been hoping it wasn't him this whole time.

"Unless you want to see her hang, drop your sword."

Mark obeyed. A line of blood kept dribbling into his eye making it hard to see, but he could see clear enough to know how this was going to end. Archers, their bows trained on the platform were positioned throughout the crowd. More guards were mounting the platform with their swords drawn.

"You never disappoint, young Marcus. Your mother and I discussed as much last night."

A small grunt arrested everyone's attention. Mark saw his mother still working on the noose. The king nodded to one of his men, who approached the Poynters. When Mark stood in his way, the man knocked him down. Mark fell hard, landing on the shoulder that had just been wrenched. He hissed in pain, yet he rolled over on it again when he heard a choking noise. The guard who had knocked him down was pulling the rope taut around his mother's neck, causing her to stretch out until she was standing on her tiptoes and choking. He made to rise, but a sword point resting on his chest prevented him.

"No more heroics today, I'm afraid. You weary me Marcus, almost as much as your father disgusted me."

Mark heaved in indignation.

"I must say, you have more spirit in you. I wearied of taunting your father. He never fought back. Though I guess it worked in his favor. It's kept him alive all these years. Trying to break him has been my pleasure and my challenge."

Mark's breath caught in his throat at the news. The crowd was still quieting its ruckus, making the king's words audible to Mark alone. Sir Richard savored it, speaking slow to draw out the moment.

"Yes, Marcus, your father is alive. I couldn't break him. I tried and failed for years. No matter. I am finished with your family. I sent word to the good Captain Shargon a few weeks back. He collected dear Henry then set sail for Cej. And don't worry," he said leaning in close to Mark, "He promised to make your father's death slow and painful."

Tears of rage welled in Mark's eyes.

"I hate you," Mark whispered with vehemence; the poison he'd nurtured all these years finally coming to light.

The king smiled as if Mark had given him a present. When he snapped his fingers, the guard released the rope strangling his mother. She collapsed to the platform's trap door with a set of great, heaving coughs. The king's sword kept Mark from rising, but he tried anyway, until he saw the king's malignant stare. It was the same stare Mark remembered from the last time the king had threatened to kill him.

"I'm tired of your family, Marcus. In fact, I hate all of you. Even that sweet sister of yours. So I'm going to get rid of you all. Your father I've already dealt with. I've taken a particular dislike to you, son, so I'm going to make you watch while your mother dies. Then I will kill you, right here, right now."

The other guard was removing the bag from his mother's head. She fought him feebly, still racked with ragged gasps for air. Once the bag was removed, Mark saw her face already turning blue. Pitifully, she reached out her hands toward her son.

"As for your sister," the king continued to whisper in his ear, "I'm going to make her my new project. I've given her a gentle childhood until now. That ends today. I'm going to hurt her. I'm going to warp her until there's nothing left but an angry wretch. And, once I've broken her, then I'll kill her. I'll prove that any hope, no matter how pure its beginnings, can be shown to be only an angry sham. And that, Marcus, will be the Poynter legacy."

Tears of anger slipped down Mark's face as he struggled to speak. The king pressed a foot heavily on his chest, expelling all the air there and cutting off Mark's words of protest. Sir Richard raised his hands to still the final rumblings of the crowd.

"My people, have I not been a good king to you? Was it not

I who drove the Allies away? Was it not I who brought peace and plenty to your homes? Have I not been just and fair to you? Are there any who have a quarrel with me?"

The king paused, as if to rein in a powerful emotion working inside him. Mark's hatred grew.

"It breaks my heart that such rebellion could be found here, in you, the people I love. But this boy has now twice broken the laws set forth for the protection of us all. I believe such willingness to set aside those laws is a sign of moral compromise. Dangerous moral compromise at that. He was cleared of all charges yesterday, but he stands again beneath the judgment of the law. He must die."

He let the words echo in the silent square before he continued.

"Sadly, Reclaitute has not been satisfied. This means his mother must die as well."

The crowd murmured, and he raised his hands.

"It grieves me as well, but I must perform the justice given to me by you when you made me king. Take heart and know that those who abide in the laws are safe as long as I am king. Beware to those who would break them, for I will protect my kingdom with the power given to me."

The king nodded to the guard, who pulled Mark's mother to her feet and adjusted the noose around her neck. The dignity she had possessed at first was gone now, leaving unfathomable sorrow. Casting her sad eyes over the crowd, she stopped suddenly. Her posture tensed as she honed in on one person.

When Mark followed her gaze, he saw an archer. But, as he looked closer, Mark noticed he wasn't dressed as a guardsman. His attire was different from anything Mark had ever seen before. And now that he looked even closer, he saw the archer's bow wasn't aimed at himself or his mother. It was aimed at the king.

The guard gripped the lever to the trapdoor, flexing to pull it, but he suddenly paused. Mark had been so preoccupied with the king, and now the mysterious archer, he hadn't noticed anything else. Now he noticed something new. Everyone on the platform did. The ground was shaking beneath them, and a rumbling was coming nearer. Noticing it as well, the crowd turned toward the noise.

Then all hell broke loose.

Twenty-four

ROSE RAN THE TWISTING CORRIDORS, THANKFUL FOR the time she had spent wandering them. Her destination was the stables. She knew attempting a mad gallop into town with only one good arm was perilous at best; however, it was a risk she must take to make up for lost time. The stables came into view, and she hoped no one would be there. Once inside though, she was startled by a stable boy about her age. Somehow, his frank appraisal of her made the decision to be honest with him an easy one. Besides, she was too desperate to employ any wiles.

"Please, I need your help! Something terrible is going to happen in the city, and I have to stop it! My father is Lord Clifton. Oh please, help me!"

He looked her over slowly, debating what to do.

"You're Rose, aren't you? I heard you were being sent away by the king."

"Yes. I will soon. What does that matter?"

"So, you're running away?"

She was taken aback for a moment.

"Honestly, I hadn't thought of it. I must get to the city."

"To stop Lady Anne's hanging?"

She could lie. She probably should lie. She just didn't think she had the faculties to pull it off. She nodded her head solemnly. He gazed back at her with equal solemnity.

"You don't remember me, do you?"

Pausing for the first time, she suddenly saw someone from her childhood standing in front of her.

"Jack?"

"Yes," he said, remaining serious. "Maybe you remember my brother, too? His name was Jonathan."

She closed her eyes, as if hoping that would shut out the pain. Jonathan, the groom who had been killed when the soldiers came for Hope. One of the many whose blood was on her hands. Jack still blamed his death on her. Her hope began to wane.

"I remember Jonathan. I remember him very well."

They regarded each other in silence for what seemed like an eternity. She tried to meet his eyes a few times, but his intense stare never faltered. He was going to turn her in, and Aunt Anne was going to die. This thought stirring her newfound wrath, she boldly looked up at him.

"Jack, I know what happened to your brother was my fault. Time has only served to make my guilt more acute. I wish I could bring Jonathan back. I wish I could trade places with him.

But I can't."

His dark eyes flashed in his pale face. Rose saw and allowed it to soften her tone.

"What I can do is stop another murder. Please, let me try to save her. I'll come back and go with the king if you think it a fair penance, but please at least let me go."

Her voice was firm, and, she hoped, eloquent. She could probably say more; however, there was no time to lose on winded speeches. His stare remained the same throughout it all. She met that stare this time in hopes she could communicate how desperate she was. She was nearing the end of her patience when his stare relented. Looking off into the distance, Jack spoke with measured words.

"I've waited years to say some things to you. It seems I must wait a little longer. Lady Anne was good to us, and, if you have the chance to save her, then it would be wrong for me to stop you."

He began preparing a horse. When he finished, he offered his hand and helped her into the saddle. Mounting as best she could, she took hold of the reins and began to ride out, but Jack grabbed the bridle before she could.

"Don't take this to mean I forgive you," he said darkly.

"I wasn't expecting you to," she answered with sincerity. "Thank you, Jack."

He nodded and then released the horse. Trotting outside, Rose adjusted to the animal moving beneath her. She took a breath to calm her nerves and then, on impulse, looked back.

Jack watched her go with his arms crossed. She wasn't going to let him down again. Working the horse into a gallop, she hurried toward the city.

The stallion, bursting with energy, took full advantage of the free rein she employed, and she struggled to keep her seat the whole way. Holding on with her legs and good arm until they ached from exertion, she galloped to the outskirts of the city before pulling back and slowing the mad run. Trotting to a hitching post, she gratefully slid to the ground. She was almost shaking too badly to tie up the horse.

The city was so still that, if she hadn't known better, she would have thought it was deserted. Briskly, she walked toward the square, feeling nervous about what she would find there. Upon arrival, she felt sweet relief when she realized there was still time. Aunt Anne had just climbed the stairs to the gallows, and the crier was unrolling his parchment to read. Looking around, Rose tried to think of a way to help her. Since nothing stood out to her, she decided to look elsewhere.

She darted back into the city, waiting for revelation to strike. In her hurry, she didn't watch where she was going and she stepped in the edge of a cow pie. Wrinkling her nose in disgust, she turned to wipe off her boot and was struck by inspiration. Just down the road a ways, a herd of cows was corralled in a wooden pen near a butcher's shop. A couple of farmers had probably brought them to sell and, wanting to watch the execution, penned them up for safekeeping. The pen faced the road and included a gate. If the road were blocked just behind the pen's gate, then the only direction of travel was straight toward the center of the city. Rose had her plan. All twenty of the bovine watched her with bored eyes.

First, she had to find a way to block the street. A wooden cart nearby looked big enough to do the job. She removed the blocks that kept it from rolling. With her hidden knife she cut the rope that had held it secure. And then she started pushing on it. The cart groaned, but didn't move. She wouldn't be stopped. The post it had been secured to looked sturdy, so she wedged herself between it and the cart with her back on the cart and her legs on the post. She then pushed with all her strength. The wood cut into her back mercilessly; nevertheless, she could bear it, especially when she felt the wheels begin moving. She pushed until she saw stars behind her closed eyes, and the rolling wheels gained momentum. In a final burst she pushed with all her might, giving a yell as she did. It was just enough. The cart started down the slight hill it was sitting on and didn't stop until it hit the building next to the cattle pen. The road was now successfully blocked. She gave a cry of triumph, but hers wasn't the only cry. A scream echoed from the square, followed quickly by the sound of a mob of people moving. She didn't have time to figure out what it was. She only hoped it was an event that enabled her to carry out her plan.

Struggling to open the pen door, she was prepared to jump out of the way to avoid being trampled. But, none of the cows moved. They stood there, completely disinclined to move at all. No matter what method she employed they merely stood, as if bored, staring inside the pen. She had to find a way to get them to run. Jogging quickly down the street, her eyes dashed madly to and fro, hoping for a means of help. The sounds from the square were present still, yet fainter than before. She cursed time and its persistent struggle against her. She ran on, passing an inn as she did. A strange sound was emanating from inside it — like someone was furiously beating the door to the accompaniment of pitiful sobs. She was intrigued; however, she had to keep moving. That was until she actually comprehended the words being said.

"Uncle John? Uncle John, where are you?!"

That was Hope. It had to be. Rose debated for only a second before she ran to the door. It was locked.

"Uncle John? Is that you? Let me out!"

The child was frantic, and Rose had a hard time making herself heard.

"Hope! Hope, I need you to listen. Please, listen to me!"

"Who are you?"

"Hope, it's Rose. Do you remember? We met a few days ago."

There was silence from behind the door, causing Rose to panic slightly.

"I remember you. You were dressed like a princess. Uncle John said it was okay to talk to you now."

Rose breathed a prayer of thanks.

"Good. Now Hope, what happened?"

"Uncle John left me here with Reuben. He told me

something bad was going to happen, and the king may be looking for me. Uncle John said I needed to hide from the king or something else bad was going to happen. Reuben stayed here until we smelled smoke. He saw some boys trying to start a fire and he left to go stop them. He locked me in here by myself. Then people were screaming and I'm scared. I want Uncle John! Can you open the door and take me to him?"

Several thoughts collided in Rose's head. She could break a window and get the child out; however, then it would be too late for Aunt Anne. Or she could leave Hope and trust her father would take care of the girl. She didn't want to trust her father, not in the slightest. Then she thought back to last night in the dark cell. Aunt Anne had believed in him, and she had asked her to do likewise. Rose found the courage to try one last time.

"Hope, listen to me. Uncle John is busy now, but he will come back for you. Right now you need to listen to what he told you. Hide somewhere and don't come out unless Uncle John, Reuben, or I call for you. Can you do that Hope? Can you be brave?"

"But I'm scared!"

"I am too. But we love you, and this is best for you. Be brave for me, Hope. Okay?"

Rose heard a sniff followed by a small, "Okay."

"Good girl. Now go hide."

Rose left before she was sidetracked again. She didn't know if she was making the right choice, but she couldn't linger on that now. Instead she followed the faint smell of smoke. She found its genesis in an old, abandoned house. Lazy smoke drifted around the remnants of a fire that had been hastily snuffed. Hurrying inside, Rose quickly found a stick with dull embers on the end still smoldering. She grabbed it and dashed back toward the cows.

She was fast losing her breath, but she pushed on with the glowing torch held aloft. Hearing complete silence from the direction of the square, she feared it was already too late. When arriving back at the cow pen, she saw that some of the cows had wandered out, but they remained passive. Hurrying, she stuck the torch into the hay covering the bottom of the pen. With her gasping breath she blew on the embers and coaxed forth a flame. The hay soon caught. Removing the stick, she piled more hay on the little fire. The hungry flame mounted higher.

"Go! Get out!" she bellowed while poking the hot stick into the cows' backsides. Rose watched their eyes roll in terror. Then the beasts began to move, the terror of the cows closest to the fire infecting them all. They bucked and pitched forward, trying to escape. They made their way out of the gate and then stampeded straight down the road toward the center of the city. Stamping out the flames, Rose ran after them, the tiny vanguard to the mighty force she'd unleashed.

Twenty-five

$\mathcal{M}$ ARK, INCREDULOUS, SURVEYED THE RAGING stampede as it snaked through the crowd. He didn't know where it had come from, and if he were perfectly frank, he really didn't care. The crowd scattered before the crazed bovine like dust in the wind. The gallows, hastily erected for the event, began to sway beneath the torrent of rushing men and beast. Chaos was king, and Mark needed to act before this anarchy stepped down from its throne.

The king, in shock as this new element was introduced, had forgotten to point his sword at Mark. Seeing his chance, Mark acted without thinking. With a roar, he grabbed the king's foot, twisted it, and pushed it underneath the owner. The king cried out in surprise, lost his balance, and fell hard in a clatter of armor. Ignoring the pain pulsing through his body, Mark stood and aimed a kick at the prone king's head. Clumsy due to the swaying platform, his aim was awkward and his contact poor, but it was enough. The king's head snapped to the side, then he lay there moaning, but still moving. Mark hadn't killed the cockroach who masqueraded as royalty.

Shame, was Mark's first angry thought. But he didn't go back to finish the job. As much as part of him wanted to, killing a prone man felt wrong. Instead, grabbing the downed sword, Mark ran toward his mother. He was soon brought to pause by the oddity of the scene before him. A man in light, leather armor and swirling gray cloak was fighting the guard, who had been standing ready to pull the trapdoor lever. The strange man was smaller than the guard, yet unimaginably quicker. There was a quiver of arrows on his back and a discarded bow at his feet, but otherwise he was unarmed. His lack of weapons didn't seem to slow him down any, and Mark could tell he would soon best the man. Finally, Mark noticed a barrage of arrows flying past him, as well as corresponding cries of pain. Who were these people?

He ran to his mother. At some point the guard had pulled the rope taut enough to make her dance on her tiptoes to avoid suffocation. Mark severed the rope with a single pass of his sword, and she collapsed at his feet, where he could hear her coughing over the deafening cacophony around them. With quaking fingers, he finally managed to loosen and remove the noose. It left a bruise edged with angry chafe lines around her neck. But the most frightening aspect was the glassiness of eyes when she opened them between coughing fits.

"Mother! Can you hear me?"

Her breathing was deep and ragged, but she was drawing enough air into her lungs that her eyes were becoming less glassy. She struggled to speak.

"Mark…"

Suddenly, there was a heavy hand on his shoulder turning him wildly around. Mark prepared for a fight; however, his fists were nonchalantly blocked by the strangely dressed warrior.

"We've got to move!" the strange warrior said.

This new man didn't seem much older than Mark. That is, except for his eyes, which were scanning the entire situation with the careless grace of a veteran. Only then did Mark realize how perilous their position had become. Trapped in the square, the cows were still running mad. The screams of the crowd stirred them into an even greater frenzy. The masses trying to get away, were being pushed this way and that by cows, guards who were trying to get to the platform, and each other. The onslaught upon the rickety gallows threatened to topple it at any moment. Especially if the seemingly endless parade of guards kept adding their bulk to it.

Mark saw they had to go, and they had to go now. The warrior was deftly cutting his mother's hands free. And somehow, despite all the madness around them, she only had eyes for Mark. Even more astounding was the unmistakable smile on her slightly blue lips. That smile emboldened him, stirring him into action.

"We've got to go!" his guardian shouted, picking his mother up and putting her across his shoulders.

"No!" came an angry baritone. Mark froze for an instant before he and his new companion turned to face it. The king, furious, was on his feet, pale anger emphasizing the scratch etched on his cheek. Mark wondered if there was anything that could incapacitate that perpetually vindictive ruler, who had found another sword, and was approaching the trio.

"Not again!" the king screamed at them. Mark looked for the sword he had dropped, found it, and hefted it in his inexperienced, unsteady hands. The king's cold, angry eyes glinted in pleasure as they bore down toward Mark. But then a commotion from behind drew the king's attention, and he turned away. The guards who had been protecting him from the rear were falling beneath the blows of a manic swordsman, who cut through them with skill and then, when he felled the last in his way, charged the king!

It was Morgan like Mark had never seen him before. His sword moved in an expertly timed, flashing dance, making him look more like a moving poem than a swordsman. He was intent on only one soul as he threw himself at the king, who recovered in time to block the blow. Morgan fought steadily on, planting himself as a human shield between the trio he would deliver and the antagonist who sought their destruction.

"Run, Mark! Go!" Morgan said.

"You heard him! Let's go!" the warrior beside Mark yelled before dashing to the edge of the platform. Mark hesitated a moment as he watched the swordsmen dance. He caught Morgan's eye, but Morgan motioned furiously for him to go before parrying another cut of the king's sword. A terrible sadness choked in Mark's chest, but he obeyed his mentor.

Hurrying, he joined his companion who was on the edge of the swaying platform.

"See that road?" the stranger said while he pointed across a sea of chaos. Mark nodded.

"See you there!" he said to Mark with a cheeky grin.

Then he lowered himself to the ground with Anne still on his shoulders. Mark was impressed, but focused again when he realized the rescuer was leaving without him. Lowering himself down, Mark muscled through the mess of humanity, trying desperately to keep his mother in view. His body cried out in pain as he was jostled back and forth, yet he pressed on with his desperate flight.

He didn't know how far they'd gotten. Maybe halfway, maybe half of that. It was impossible to tell. However far it was, it wasn't far enough. He was so focused on following the strange warrior he was completely blindsided. He didn't even see what ran into him, all he knew was that he was struck down by a colliding body, and he was on the ground among the rushing feet.

The push of humanity was so strong he struggled to rise. He was kicked by careless feet and his senses were overwhelmed by their pounding. He had to get up before he was trampled to death! With a roar, Mark managed to get to his hands and knees. He braced there for a time to gather his strength for another push. Then, leading with his shoulder, he pushed himself to his feet.

He was spinning in circles as he dodged a cow and the

people it pursued. He had completely lost his bearings and his mother was nowhere to be seen. Guards were mixed in with the crowd now and were heedlessly pushing their way through it. Mark had to move somewhere and hope he could find his way to the meeting point from there. Thankfully, the throng, propelling its way through the city as one massive entity thrust him toward an alley. Recognizing his opportunity, he shouldered his way through the people until he could slip out of their grip and into the stillness of the little roadway. That had been the easy part. Now for the hard part.

RICHARD HADN'T FOUGHT a man more skilled than himself in a long time. He was amazed when he recognized his adversary as the healer the Poynters had stayed with all these years. No matter how he tried, Richard couldn't get past the old man and had to watch helplessly as the Poynters slipped into the madness.

"No!" he shouted renewing the vigor in his attack. The healer, audacious from the victory, smiled about it, enraging the king all the more. As they locked swords and drew near one another, Richard was pleased to see the older man sweating heavily and breathing hard.

"Did they get away again, Your Majesty?"

Richard allowed fury to fill him as he pushed his opponent away. The healer was fast; he thought ahead with his strokes, and he was perfectly controlled in all his movements. But there were a few factors rendering this a fair fight. The older man looked

366

exhausted, like this fight was his last, and he was giving it all he had. He was slowing by the second, whereas Richard's strength grew as his anger grew. Both men knew they were only delaying the inevitable end.

When the inevitable came both were surprised. Richard managed to slip his sword past his opponent's viper fast blade, wounding him in the side. As the healer grasped his side, Richard landed a punch on his temple. The healer crumpled into perfect stillness, laying at the king's feet. Richard, spitting on him, turned to the crowd.

Wiping sweat from his eyes, Richard searched for his escaping prey. If he could help it, they weren't getting away again. He scanned and scanned, but he might as well have been looking for a grain of sand amidst the thousands of tumultuous feet that assaulted the ground. His already heightened wrath was rising toward a crescendo.

Then he saw them. Or at least some of them. The young warrior and Anne. Mark was nowhere to be seen. They were pushing through the crowd, Anne on his shoulders still. He looked away, searching for a bow and arrow. He found them easy enough, nocked an arrow, and then searched for the pair again. For a second he thought he had lost them, and he ground his teeth. But he found them again. The warrior had placed Anne on her feet, though she appeared wobbly. She was furiously yelling at her companion. Richard didn't care. All he cared about was they were standing still.

Pulling the bow taut, he took aim. The swaying of the

platform had slowed, making it easier to find a line. It took him just a second, but then he had his target sighted. He let the arrow fly.

ANNE TRIED TO support her own weight once Mark cut her down, but her legs weren't up to the task. She fell hard, striking her head on the trapdoor that, thankfully, had stayed shut. She felt the relief of the noose being removed from her neck, and she was racked with coughs she couldn't stop. Her empty lungs ached as she convulsed time and time again, trying to refill them. Through a blur, she could make out Mark standing over her, yet she couldn't communicate to him at all.

She closed her eyes and concentrated on calming her breathing. Shutting out the chaos raging heavily around her, she worked at reducing the ringing in her ears. Thankfully, it wasn't long before the madness around her became clearer and the ringing stopped. She dared to open her eyes.

It was like stepping into a dream. A young man of her people stood with Mark. It was in his eyes, the way he moved, and the way he didn't move. Around him was an aura she could sense was different than what she had grown accustomed to. Her people had come for them. She was going home.

The young man was cutting her hands free, but she turned her eyes on her son. He was looking over the crowd, calculating. The cacophony didn't seem to bother him as he stood solid as a rock on the swaying gallows. He looked so like Henry; however, she could see now what she supposed she'd always wanted to overlook. He was Henry's boy. He looked and acted like him, but, deeper than that, he was like her, for better or worse. The life she had loved, yet left, was the life that had called to him for years. This was never meant to be his home. He would thrive with her people. She smiled at him, happy to see him in his element.

"We've got to go!" called a voice that cut across her musings. Then she was being lifted and placed over a set of strong shoulders. As they turned to leave, she saw the king. He was towering in his rage, yet she felt no fear. Only resignation and some pity brushed her feelings as she tried to imagine how much hate had twisted him.

Then she saw Aiden. Pushing through the crowd, he had managed to mount the steps. His sword was drawn and the warrior light she'd seen so many times before burned in his eyes. But as he cut down the guards, she could tell he wasn't at full strength. He was still deadly graceful with his blade, a fact the guards found out too late. Then, as he charged the king, she saw the desperation in his eyes. Everyone, himself included, could tell he was flagging. He wasn't planning to win this fight. He was standing in the gap long enough for them to get away.

"Run Mark! Go!" her father yelled to them.

The warrior holding her wasted no time. He moved to the edge, waiting for Mark to join them. As the two spoke to each other, she watched the final dance of Aiden Morgan, memorizing every movement.

"Goodbye," she whispered.

Then she felt herself falling as the young man stepped off the platform. Mark again hesitated for a moment, but was soon behind them. She kept watching, hoping that if she never looked away she could will an unbreakable cord to keep him near. Her determination seemed to work at first. She watched as her son moved skillfully in the teeming humanity. She allowed herself some hope they may actually get away. But then Mark was gone, lost in the crowd. Yet she was still fleeing. Without him.

"Stop!" she cried as loud as she could. "Stop! Go back!"

But the soldier soldiered on. She began to struggle and he grunted at the exertion of keeping her on his shoulders. As long as she could go back and find her son, she didn't care if he dropped her. After a time, they found an oasis of stillness, and the young warrior put her down. Immediately, she tried to rush back.

"Let me go! Mark is gone!" she yelled, clawing at the strong arms that held her back as well as upright.

"You can't go back in there. Besides if we went in there we'd never find him."

"We can't leave him! I won't leave him!" she screamed in his face. The past two days had stripped her of her former self-awareness and restraint.

"Lady Anne, listen! A scout had eyes on him this whole time. They will see where he goes and tail him. We're not leaving without him! I promise. I am bound by honor, truth, and love."

She didn't want to trust someone she didn't know. She

wanted to do it herself, in her own strength. However, her body quaked with all the strength she didn't have and death surely awaited her in the swarming humanity. This was the way of the people and creed she loved. They would find Mark and bring him home. She had to believe that. Taking a painful breath, she looked into his eyes.

"To stand with you and wait…"

Feeling a horrific pressure crash into her side, Anne suddenly couldn't speak or hear. Frantically, the warrior's eyes darted from her side to her face and back again. She looked down as well and saw the shaft of an arrow, the head buried deep within her. Her hands, which had instinctively strayed to the wound, were covered in her sticky blood. Awareness that her heart was beating at a rushing rate registered in her mind. Each pulse cascaded her with blinding pain.

"And wait for Peros that was," she finally finished, wishing more than ever that day was now.

MARK HAD NO idea where he was. He didn't know where he was going or who he was looking for. He kept running, hoping an answer would find him. At least the people roaming the side streets were less panicked than those in the square. Most were either catching their breath or helping those who were hurt. As he ran, street scenes flashed passed him — vignettes of people his healer hands could help. But he moved on. He thought of his mentor, who had given him the gift of healing hands, and hoped they would meet again.

People noticed him as he ran passed. They pointed after him, anger in their eyes. That's when Mark remembered he was a fugitive, who had just escaped the noose. Mark found it easy to imagine being hunted down and turned in by one of them. Even more so now that people they loved had been hurt while attending his execution. Turning down a small side street, he did his best to get lost in its twists and turns. Nervous he was being followed, he repeatedly looked over his shoulder. He had pulled his hood up, but, after his fight on the gallows, he was more recognizable than ever.

Turning down another alley, Mark stopped dead as he stood face to face with a boy of six or seven. They eyed each other for a time, the boy looking at Mark as he would a snake. Mark didn't know what to do; the boy was blocking his path. Slowly, Mark raised a single finger to his lips, silently pleading for the boy to be silent as well. This surged the boy to action.

"Help! He's here! The bad man is here!"

The boy's cries cut through the air with surprising clarity. Mark cursed his luck and barreled past the boy. He could still hear the voice raised in alarm after turning the corner. Frantic, he looked for a hiding place, only to be disappointed. His breath was catching in his throat as his options dwindled. Turning down another alley, he saw there were two right turns. He passed the first, hoping to go down the second. But when he came around the corner, he saw it dead-ended with only the adornment of a locked door. Throwing himself against it desperately, he yelled and kicked and ran into it again and again until his good shoulder hurt as much as his injured one. But it was useless. Even his rage was no match for the heavy door. Doubling back, he ran to the road he had come from, hoping to bolt down the first right turn instead.

But a scene from a nightmare met him in the alley. The king was approaching with a bow and arrow in his hand. He looked at the road that promised escape while raising an eyebrow at Mark, daring him to try. But Mark was spent. He knew he had been bested and, if he was going to die, he was going to do it on his feet, not laying on his back under the king's heavy boot.

"You're not even going to try?" the king said. "I'm disappointed. It would have tested my skill with a bow again today."

Refusing to be goaded by this man, Mark silently stood his ground.

"Aren't you going to ask what I mean? No? Well then, I'll just tell you. An arrow of mine found your mother not too long ago. I was at a distance; however, it appeared to be fatal."

Mark tilted his head back, weak with resignation. At least he would join her soon and spare her the pain of losing both her children. Hating that their deaths came at the hands of this man, he glared at his adversary in declaration of his defiance and hatred.

"Yes," the king whispered. "That's what I like to see."

He nocked an arrow, pulled the bow tight, and leveled it at Mark. Baring his chest, Mark closed his eyes, ready as he was ever going to be to embrace his own death.

"Only one to go now," the king whispered.

Twenty-six

As soon as Mark attacked the guard at the foot of the stairs, the king had leapt to his feet and run to the gallows. His personal guard had followed him, leaving John alone in the booth. The bottom of his stomach churned as he watched the whole scene. Mark and another boy were fighting a man twice their size, but he knew it wouldn't last. The guards were quickly overpowering other boys who had scattered throughout the crowd and created disturbances, and the king was mounting the steps. John had successfully watched the beginning, glory, and quelling of a rebellion in a matter of minutes. He leaned forward, his elbows on his knees, chin in his hands, and watched.

He watched until he saw the executioner knock Mark to the ground. At that point he could bear it no more, so he dropped his face into his hands. His mind swirled as his better man burst free, demanding to be heard. The question, "Do you really hate the Poynters?" roared in his mind. John immediately answered with an emphatic, "yes". He thought back to the nobles who had abused and murdered his mother. He thought about how he had grown in his hatred of them until it was his life's driving force. Those nobles had been power hungry, selfish, and cruel to those weaker than themselves. Every noble had lived up to the same calloused standard. Having grown so used to hate, it was natural for John to hate Henry and his family.

Looking up, John saw the king standing with his foot on Mark's chest and addressing the crowd as if the victim were himself. As he saw the cruel and blatant hypocrisy before him, something finally clicked in John's mind. Now he understood that the king had wooed him by playing into his hatred and claiming he was a self-made man who also hated the entitled nobility. He understood now he had been lied to and had allowed himself to be deceived. With the dawn of enlightenment came a sudden despair as he realized the imposter king who now stood before his deceived people fit the mold John had created for the nobility he despised. Henry Poynter had always been fair and gracious with him. Even after he had attacked Rose. And Anne knew the part he played in her daughter's kidnapping, yet she had looked him in the eye and forgiven him. For years now he had hated and betrayed a good family, a family exemplifying what nobility should be. Now that family was going to die, and he had abetted in the deed. Shame filled the void his hate had so recently vacated.

Noise shattered the stillness of the moment. John sat bolt upright. A literal stampede was tearing a path through the completely packed square. John leaned out of the booth and tried to see all that was happening. People were running and screaming, and cows, terrified and confused, wheeled in circles. John caught sight of Morgan desperately pressing toward the gallows. Surprisingly, he was making progress, though the crowd pushed him back hard. Looking toward the platform, John saw Mark on his feet standing next to a strange warrior. The two freed Anne in time to face the king. But Morgan, finally having gained access, challenged the king. John watched their fantastic swordplay. And he watched as Morgan fell to the king's blade.

But the king wasn't done yet. John felt sick as he saw him begin searching the madness for something. John, the sickness rising, began searching too. He should have known that it wouldn't end with the healer falling. It was too easy. He spotted Lady Anne as she was being carried through the crowd, but Mark was nowhere to be seen. John watched, silently pleading with the pair to keep moving out of sight of the man who would have them dead. Instead, they stopped directly in view of the king.

"Keep going!" he yelled, surprising himself. They paid him no heed. John's gaze returned to the king, and he was horrified to see him aiming an arrow at the pair. The big man's face was grim and set, his intentions clear.

"NO!" John cried. It was the most honest thing he had uttered in years, but its novelty couldn't stop the heinous act. He watched as Lady Anne jerked with the impact of the arrow. She stood for a few seconds then collapsed into her companion's arms. The gray clad warrior hastily picked her up and moved out of John's line of sight. John's hands hurt from clenching the railing so hard, but if he loosened his grip his legs would fail, and he would collapse. Dumbly, he stared at the little patch of ground where Lady Anne had been standing.

A terrific crack brought his attention back to the gallows. It was threatening to collapse, yet the king stood still, searching the crowd. Making up his mind, the king started toward the steps and began to push his way to a road near John. The king walked like John had seen angry wolves walk when they are intent on a kill. In fact, his whole presence was, if not wolfish, animalistic and primal. There didn't seem to be anything human left.

John decided then what he needed to do. He had to get Hope away from this animal-man who was sure to destroy her as he had destroyed the rest of her family. He'd aided and abetted that man, done terrible things, and now his hands were drenched in the blood of good people, his own daughter included. He was going to try something new. He was going to try to do something good. Maybe goodness would clean some of the blood off his hands. He had to try.

ROSE CLIMBED ON a box to watch her handiwork in time to see the battle acted out on the gallows platform. She watched the carnage with grotesque fascination, unable to look away. She watched an arrow fly too straight and too true and watched its target fall. Her agonized cries were drowned out by the ruckus around her, the mayhem serving to elevate her sense of helplessness.

But, before she could give into the emotions threatening to overwhelm her, she saw the king bounding toward a road not far from her. When she realized the king was on the hunt, she also realized Mark's whereabouts were still unknown. And then she knew in her core the king was looking for him and planning to complete a double execution.

With her mind racing, Rose thought she could cut through some of the streets and find the king. She wasn't sure what she would do when she found him, but she knew it was her best chance of helping Mark.

What she hadn't realized was how convoluted the streets and alleys were. She started running down one road sure it would take her to the king. But instead, it cut here, there, and everywhere but never reached him. When she finally found the right street, she could tell by the way the people whispered and looked down the road that the king had already passed. Determined, she trusted her instinct, no matter how weak the lead. Everywhere she went she watched to see which way the people were staring and chose that direction. All the while hoping she was right, because she couldn't let Mark down this time.

After a few minutes of pursuit she heard the voice of a child raising an alarm. Perking up her ears, Rose listened, attempting to distinguish the direction that carried the child's voice. She hurried in that general direction. Though the roads twisted some, for once they led her where she wanted to go. Once there, she found a child, red-faced from yelling, and stopped him as he began to wander away.

"Which way did he go?" she asked breathlessly.

"The bad man? He went that way. But don't worry, the king went that way, too, when I told him."

Her blood froze. Each heartbeat became painful. She didn't know how it happened, but she was suddenly running again, this time in the direction the boy had pointed. It was happening all over again. Her friends were in grave danger, and, though she was desperately trying to intervene, she feared she was going to fail them again. She ran harder, though her vision blurring from the exertion. It couldn't happen again. It just couldn't!

Arriving at an alley that ended in a "T", she heard a voice she could never forget followed by the creak of a bow as it was pulled taut.

No! It couldn't end like this! Not at the end of some dirty, blind street. Ignoring her body's pleas for rest and safety, she ran forward as fast as she could. Her mind running at lightning speed, she did her best to block out all thoughts except the one that drove her forward. She had to save Mark this time, knowing full well what it meant for her.

"Only one to go now," came a voice, silky with triumph.

She burst into the "T" just as she heard the bow twang. Turning to her left in an attempt to provide a larger target, Rose had long enough to see the beginnings of surprise in the king's face. Then the impact came.

She felt the arrow as it bit deep into her left shoulder. Her forward momentum and the force of the arrow's piercing caused her to spin and crash into the outside wall of one of the buildings lining the alley. Her head struck the wall hard, yet somehow she still heard the meaty thud of her body hitting the ground. It was hard to hear anything anymore. Her head lolled to the side, sending a spike of pain through her skull. That pain travelled to her arm where the arrow sat as a garnish to her broken forearm. She hurt everywhere, and though she tried to stir up her remaining strength, her body responded sluggishly.

"No!" came a ferocious voice that cut through the fog. The king was striding toward her, livid and dangerous. Lolling her head to the side, Rose couldn't help but smile.

Mark was gone. She didn't know how he had gotten away, but he had disappeared completely. A tear trickled out of the corner of her eye, and, despite the pain, she said a prayer of thanks. She'd finally been able to stand in the gap after all these years. It didn't matter what happened to her because Mark was safe. Or at least she hoped he was. The thought of hoping in something made her think of little Hope. Such great evil pervaded their world, but little Hope Poynter remained beautiful and innocent. She was a flower in a garden of brambles and thorns. As Rose's mind grappled with consciousness, she thought that as long as she knew there were flowers like Hope in Agumbra, she could keep singing.

The shadow of the king loomed over her now. She tried to clearly see his face, but her eyes kept going in and out of focus.

From what she could tell, it was not unlikely he would end her life right there. The thought of an end to all her pain actually brought a measure of peace, and she smiled. The king saw and interpreted its meaning correctly, then his face darkened even more. Picking up his foot, he lowered it onto her shoulder right next to the arrow and pressed down as hard as he could. Involuntarily, a horrendous cry escaped her. She tried to move away from him, but she was pinned by his boot. Though she was reduced to whimpering, he didn't release his hold. Instead, he increased the pressure as he dropped to a knee and hovered over her.

"No, dear. I'm not going to let you die. That would be far too merciful."

With that, he broke the shaft of the arrow just above the wound. And, though he hadn't promised mercy, this final jolt of pain settled her into a merciful unconsciousness.

Twenty-seven

MARK WAS UNSURE WHAT HAD ACTUALLY HAPPENED. He heard the distinctive sound of running feet drawing closer and heard the creak of the bow. But strange noises above him ignited a growing curiosity that overpowered his fear.

Looking up, he saw a rope drop from over the top of the building he was standing against. As soon as it hit the ground one of the strange warriors came flying down the line. Whatever was happening, it wasn't happening fast enough because he heard the sound of the tense bow being released. This new noise drew his attention back to King Richard, even though he didn't want to look. He expected to see the arrow that would take his life but instead saw the bearer of the running feet. Or, better said, he saw the person's back. He watched the form jerk to the side and saw the arrow meant for him growing out of their shoulder.

Mark started to cry out, tried to catch a glimpse of their face, but the man descending from above was all of a sudden near him. The strange warrior performed a few quick movements and, before Mark knew it, he was in a loop of rope. Cinching the rope tight, the man gave a sharp whistle. Then, with uncanny speed, they were being hoisted up the wall. Mark heard an arrow clatter near them; however, soon they were over the lip of the building. Mark and the man he was fastened to clattered unceremoniously to the surface of the roof, and Mark's breath rushed out of him when the other man landed on him. Before he could even register his difficulty breathing, more warriors joined them, and they began swirling in a cloud of gray cloaks and clattering equipment. By the time he could breathe again, everything was put away and they were ready to go.

"Can you run, boy?"

The man was brusque, but the question didn't seem unkind.

"Y-yes sir."

"Good," the man said with a small smile. "We've got a bit of running to do before we're completely safe."

"Run? Where will we run? There's no road?"

"We don't need a road, lad."

Whistling, the man led the crew over the rooftops. Mark hesitated for a second, debating whether or not to go back and see who his rescuer had been. But since he was fast being left behind, he ran after the warriors who were racing ahead of him.

"Thank you, whoever you are. I'll not forget you."

THE STREETS CALMED and the cows corralled, John was able to

move quicker than he had earlier. As Lord of Baymontiac he would have drawn attention to himself whilst walking the streets; however, so much had happened that no one gave him a second glance. This served as an enablement for the task he must complete.

There were a few men in town whose loyalty he knew belonged to him and not the king. He was on his way to find one of those men now and to give him instructions concerning Hope. In the midst of the chaos, John had slipped back to the inn where she was hiding. The door had been locked, but it hadn't stood long against his desperate kicking. When he called her name, she had come scrambling from a hiding place under the stairs straight into his arms. His heart swelled as her trembling slowly ceased in his embrace. He realized then he loved this little girl. All these years he had tried to forget how to love; however, she was innocent, tenaciously looked past all his sins, and instead called him *Uncle*. He had failed miserably with his own daughter, yet as he held the daughter of the man he had, until recently, counted as a nemesis, he wondered if he could have a second chance.

He gathered the child into his arms, whispering soft assurances, and then trotted into the crazed streets. In that mess he was just another man carrying a child to safety. Quite simply, he followed the mess of humanity until he saw a chance to head for the woods.

Trotting for a spell, Hope still clinging to his neck, John established landmarks in his mind, making sure they were still alone. He continued for at least half a mile before he stopped and set his cargo down. He could tell she was still afraid, but her fear had waned significantly since he had carried her away from the inn. Now, she held his hand and looked around more curious. He marveled at her trust in him, while at the same time hoping he could deserve it.

He found a good hiding spot for her in a thicket of bushes and left her with very specific instructions. A man was going to come for her. She was to trust this man. She would know it was the right man because he would whistle a tune she would know. When she heard that whistle, then she would know it was safe. Otherwise she was not to move from that spot. Though she was frightened again, she nodded solemnly. John kissed her on the top of her head, then left before his willpower waned.

Hurrying, he now looked for the man who was the perfect choice to spirit Hope away. He trusted this man not to turn her over to the king. He'd had three sons before the war and was now alone and angry about it. Far north in Deteen, deep in the Hytines, the man had a sister. No one would look for Hope there, and she could grow up without fear of being taken. It was the best John could give her. His only worry was how much he was going to miss her small hand in his.

On his way to find this trusted friend, he passed a group of teenage boys. They were roughed up and looking around as if they suspected arrest at any moment. One of the boys met John's eye and held it for a few seconds. The boy looked familiar, but John didn't have time to figure out from where. He kept walking, only to hear fast approaching footsteps from behind.

"Robbie, don't!"

But John already felt a hand on his shoulder roughly turning him around. The boy was tall enough to look John straight in the eye. By the looks of it, this Robbie had been on the losing end of a fight. His face was a collection of already mottling bruises, cuts, and swelling. He held his jaw slightly crooked, like it was one step from being broken, one eye was completely swollen shut and the other looked well on its way there. Using that good eye, he glared at his elder.

"This is your fault, you know," the boy named Robbie said.

"You seem to have the wrong man," John said coldly as he stepped back. Robbie stepped forward, filling the empty space.

"If you're John Clifton, then no, I don't have the wrong man. You see, I've had years to think about the night Hope Poynter was taken. Everyone said Rose was to blame, yet the more I thought on it, the more it didn't fit. She loved that family too much. She was too timid to interact with me, let alone plot with the king. No, the way I figure it, you tricked her somehow. That makes all that happened today your fault."

"What are you getting at, boy? I'm in no mood for games," John growled. He could feel the old spite rising again.

"I didn't think your day would be complete until you knew how much of this," he said gesturing to the torn streets and crying people, "Was your fault. Congratulations."

"Get. Out. Of. My. Way," John spat dangerously, pushing

passed Robbie.

"This should put you in better spirits," the boy called after him. "We just saw Rose. As far as we could tell the king had killed her. She was thrown over his shoulder like she was no more than some animal he'd hunted down."

Everything seemed to grind to a halt inside of John. Rose had always been there, no matter the hardship, like a strong shoot whose roots forbade it from being pulled up and cast away. She couldn't be gone, not now when he had hoped to start anew. He rushed toward Robbie. Robbie retreated, his brutalized face obviously expecting an attack. John pushed past his defenses, grabbing his shirt, and pulling him near.

"Where is she? Where!" he said, fear lacing his voice. Robbie was confused, not expecting this outburst, then pointed to his right. John released him and ran. It didn't take him long to find what he sought. In the section of road leaving the city he found the king and a few of his guards. He also saw Morgan prone, bound, and sickly near one of the horses. He was alive, barely. Then he saw one guard standing beside a horse and securing Rose to the front of the saddle. She wasn't moving.

"What is happening here?" he said, coming near.

The king snapped to attention, looking to see who had spoken. When he saw John, his scowl dropped and he looked back down.

"I'm glad to see you, John. The Poynters escaped. I am preparing to find them. I could use your help."

"What are you doing with my daughter? Is she dead?" he

said, sounding far too unsettled to escape the king's interest.

"No, she's not dead. She took an arrow for the Poynter boy, allowing him to get away. She may wish for death when I am finished with her."

John tried to rein himself in, but it was harder than usual. His gratitude at hearing she was alive faded when he realized she was still in danger of the wolfish king.

"I'll take her back to the estate, sire, so she won't slow you down as you search for the Poynters."

The king, suspicion in his eyes, stepped up to look him over.

"I want you with me. Someone else will take the wretch," the king said coolly.

"That wretch is my daughter, and I want her," he growled back, his calm breaking.

The men continued to face each other, the tension growing between them.

"No. You're with me. Besides, the hussy is no longer your concern, remember? She's mine now. You gave her to me. That means I can do to her whatever I want."

These words brought horrific images to John's mind, causing something to snap in him.

"What if I want her back?"

"I'd say you were too late. I'd say she was mine to keep or discard as I see fit."

John understood he was a horrendous father. But that didn't mean he could watch this happen without putting up a fight. He aimed a blow at the king, who unfortunately had been expecting the punch. He easily dodged the wild swing and delivered one of his own to John's jaw. John wheeled, stumbled, and fell. He heard the sound of swords being drawn and felt one's point between his shoulders.

"Kill him," was the callous command.

John thought of Hope. She was alone in the woods waiting for someone who would never come. In all likelihood she would die, as would Rose. His heart twisted in anguish as he thought of the two girls he was unable to save. A rough hand grabbed the shoulder of his shirt, dragging him to his feet. Harshly spun around, he stood facing his executioner who was a boy not much older than Rose. The boy blocked the path to the woods while his fellows blocked the path into town. With escape impossible, John attempted to catch a final glance of his daughter. But the young soldier stepped sideways, blocking his line of sight. Enraged at being denied such a simple final request, John turned the fury of his gaze upon the boy. The boy met his gaze, and John realized he was attempting to communicate something. His eyes very purposefully flicked from John to the path to the woods, then back again.

"*Run*," he mouthed. Understanding, John nodded almost imperceptibly.

"Now!" the soldier bellowed as he deftly disarmed the guard nearest to him. John didn't wait to see more. Instead, he bolted for the woods. He heard footsteps pounding behind him and was spurred onwards.

"Let them go! I need you to search for the Poynter boy," the king called, "Run and rot, Clifton! I have all I need, and soon I'll have the Poynter girl whom you've been sheltering."

John slowed upon hearing the king's taunts; however, the footsteps pursuing him remained. John wheeled with a savage cry, prepared to do battle.

"Stop! It's me!"

John slowed in time to recognize the soldier who had saved his life. His hands were raised as a sign of peace.

"What do you want?" John asked gruffly.

"To come with you. Any man who takes a swing at the king is a man I want to side with. I've seen and done wretched things for him. I'm ready to begin redeeming myself. Lady Anne saw something in me I didn't see in myself, and I think she's done the same for you. What do you say? Can we fight as Kingsmen together?"

John studied the boy, feeling a fire grow in him as he did. He had never planned to wage a war against the king. Neither had he planned to do it in the name of a King he never thought he'd believe in. But his companion's eyes burned with righteous fire, and John felt purpose blossom in his chest for the first time in decades. He extended a hand to the boy, who took it gladly.

"John Clifton, deposed Lord of Baymontiac," he said in introduction.

"Mason of Mejan," the boy returned.

"Well, Mason of Mejan, I don't know what I'm going to do, but you're welcome to join me. Let's see what kind of rebellion we can begin."

John couldn't go home, but he didn't care. It meant he didn't need to send Hope away anymore. He could care for her while he labored to bring his own daughter home. Whatever happened after that they would handle as it came. For now, he knew exactly what needed to be done. The two men waded into the woods in order to retrieve the Hope they were bound to protect.

MARK BOUNDED OVER the rooftops with the strange company he found himself in. He counted four of them, but it was impossible to tell if they were men or women, young or old, because of their gray cloaks. So many questions rumbled inside of him, but he held them back as he tried to keep up instead.

Coming to the end of the rooftops, instead of slowing down, they kept running at full tilt. Mark wondered how they were going to get down. Suddenly, he saw the foremost take a running leap off the building, then the others all followed suit. Mark, ignoring the pain in his tortured body, mentally prepared to jump as well.

Leaping forward, Mark felt his stomach churn as he fell. He wasn't very high, ten to twelve feet, but it was enough to make his head swim. Upon landing, he threw himself into a roll to avoid injuring his legs. Sharp pain ripped through his shoulders and he moaned with pain. But he saw the others already on their feet, waving him forward. Thus he swiftly stumbled to his feet and joined them in the cover of the woods.

"Good jump, lad. Just a little farther and we can rest."

Mark simply followed. After running about a quarter of a mile more, they stopped. One of them trilled a bird call, which was answered from nearby. They followed the sound to a small clearing where more gray cloaked strangers knelt. But Mark had no eyes for them. Only for the figure they were kneeling by. Running forward and pushing them aside, he knelt next to his mother and lifted her head into his lap.

He had hoped the king's claims were a bluff intended to torment him before he died. Seeing the reality of those claims was paralyzing. Blood was everywhere, seeping through the hasty bandage on her side. Placing his hand over the wound, Mark attempted to staunch the bleeding, but the knowledge he had learned from Morgan told him there was nothing to be done. Her white face accented her teeth stained red from coughing up blood. Her breathing was shallow, almost imperceptible. Miraculously, at Mark's touch, she opened her eyes and smiled.

"My boy. You're okay."

He nodded his answer. His throat was too choked with tears to speak.

"Don't worry, Mark. I feel no pain. I'm ready to go."

"No! Please don't leave me alone," he begged.

"I'm not, son. These are my people, the people we were going to. They will care for you as they cared for me."

"I don't want them. I want you," he whispered, putting his forehead to hers.

"I don't want to leave you either. But trust me and go with them. You've always been meant to go with them."

Blood gurgled in her throat and her breathing slowed even more. Searching about with her eyes, she looked at the man who had talked to Mark on the rooftops. The man's vibrant, red beard almost masked his sorrow-filled face.

"Take care of my son, Scaina. Please."

Scaina nodded, touching two fingers to his forehead as he did. Her eyes drifted back to Mark. Those luminous orbs, always so full of life, love, and laughter were dusky with death. Mark felt something crucial to life tear inside of him.

"I'm so sorry, mother. Please forgive me."

"There's nothing to forgive," she barely rasped. Her body convulsed in its final throes of life. And Mark, sobbing, watched.

"I. Love. Y…"

Her body slipped away before she could finish, her last word escaping her lips as a final sigh. Mark, trembling, kissed her forehead.

"I love you, too."

Then he wept. Forgetting about the strangers around him, he rocked back and forth with her in his arms and wept. He had meant to save her. He was the one who was supposed to die. But she had died instead. And so he wept, and he wept.

After a time he felt a hand on his shoulder. Looking up he saw Scaina looking down at him with sorrow in his eyes. He gave Mark's shoulder a gentle squeeze and then began singing a melancholy tune. His fellows joined him in his forlorn song.

No more. No more.
Wander no more.

Dear, weary wanderer; wander no more.

You've sung the song all these years.
Faithful even through your tears.
Now lay rest, all your fears
You've sung a song all these years.

No more. No more.
Wander no more.
Dear, weary wanderer; wander no more.

You've sung to keep hope in sight.
Always looking to the light.
Now your faith is no more a fight.
You've sung to keep hope in sight

No more. No more.
Wander no more.
Dear, weary wanderer; wander no more.

You've left a legacy of grace.
So though we long to see your face
We'll sing the song in your place.
You've left a legacy of grace.

No more. No more.
Wander no more.
Dear, weary wanderer; wander no more.

Their voices melded into a sound so beautiful it made Mark ache with his sadness while simultaneously longing for the hope they sang of. He closed his eyes and allowed the melody to wash over him in waves. When they finished, their sweet music dissipated into the woods, making them richer.

"Come, Mark," Scaina said. "It's dangerous for us here."

Mark's mind rocked like a cart with its wheels stuck in a rut. This man was telling him they needed to leave this sorrowful place, yet he found himself unable to move. His mother's body was still warm, yet here were her people, and they wanted him to go with them. The mystery he had sought his entire life stood with extended hand, but he needed basic answers before taking it.

"I don't understand. All my life I have wondered who my mother's people were. Now, apparently, you're here and asking I trust you blindly." Mark shook his head. "No, I'm not moving until I know who you are. I must know that much at least."

Scaina looked at Mark in amusement.

"I thought it was obvious by now, Mark. We're Forest Watchers. Your mother was one and so are you."

Mark's head spun. Then it became very heavy. His eyes focused in and out on his mother's still face. He ran his finger over the scar on her cheek, remembering the story of the one on her side. It couldn't be true.

He'd heard stories about Forest Watchers his whole life. They weren't Magic Folk, but they were people who were able to access the Magic. They served the Great King as the guardians of the woods covering most of his realm. They were vanguards and warrior poets; legends who preserved the sacred songs.

"I still don't understand," he began. "My mother was a Forest Watcher? That can't be. I thought they were only a part of the stories."

"No, lad. We are very, very real."

"Well…I mean… Then, what about the rest of the stories? Are you the only ones or…?"

Smiling, Scaina knelt so he was eye to eye with Mark, placing his hand on his shoulder again as he did so.

"No, son. We aren't the only ones. Of course the stories are real. Every single one of them is real."

Twenty-eight

ROSE HAD BEEN THROWN ACROSS THE FRONT OF A horse like a prize after a hunt. Her arm hung down, the sling having been lost long ago, and the hyperextension of her arm not only aggravated the break, but also the wound in her shoulder. She hadn't imagined there could be pain of such magnitude, a fact she was unfortunately wiser of now.

Thankfully, never being fully conscious meant the only details of her circumstance she could gather were painful tidbits here and there. She didn't remember being taken down from the horse, and was surprised to wake in the dark cell again. Tears flooded her eyes when she realized she'd come full circle. But this time she was completely alone in the darkness, in horrendous pain, and hopeless to escape. She was frigid laying on the stone floor, so she closed her eyes, allowing the hot tears to run down the side of her face. If only she had some light, she could face all her harrowing tribulations and sing a song. But the darkness sat on her chest like a weight. Thus, instead of singing, she let the darkness overwhelm her senses again.

A light.

Arguing voices.

Gentle hands holding her.

When she woke again she was in a real bed in a light, airy room. She almost didn't dare to believe it, but it felt so real. She was warm, and her arm had been cared for. She entertained the thought that she had finally died and was free of harsh reality. Such thoughts were proven false when a man she recognized entered her room. Adam smiled, his teeth flashing through his beard.

"It's good to see you again, missy. I was worried for a bit."

She fought to speak despite her dry mouth.

"Where am I? How did I get here?"

"You're in the overseer's cottage right now. You were in that wretched cell, but I told the king himself you were to be moved elsewhere."

"It was you who was shouting?" she asked, still testing out her voice and struggling to remember.

"I did get rather heated. I'll admit that. But I think a heroine such as yourself deserves to have someone fight for her."

She couldn't think of what she had done to deserve such a title. She was slipping away again, but she fought it this time.

"I don't...I don't understand," she murmured.

"Don't try to now. Just sleep. Sleep and recover."

She obeyed him somewhat reluctantly, too overcome with fatigue to truly resist. She fell into a dreamless sleep that kindled the light of hope in her heart. Through the warm darkness weaved a melody that held her close. It was the sleep she had been waiting to have for many years.

Soft light was playing on the floor when she woke in the morning. A tray with food sat near her. She didn't know how long she had lain in bed, but her stomach rumbled loudly at the sight of the food. Slipping out of bed, on her unsteady legs, maneuvered herself to the tray. She ate heartily, the sunlight brightening her demeanor as well as the room.

The food gave her strength and with that strength came the dull pain from her shoulder. She ran her fingers over the wound and discovered a thick bandage there. It was sore to the touch, so she let it alone. Any movement was a chore.

She wondered about her status in this new arrangement, whether it be free or prisoner. Walking to the door, she opened it just a crack. Then suddenly it was fully opened by a snarling guard.

"You aren't to touch this door! Do you hear me?" he barked, pushing her back. She almost fell, regaining her balance just in time. He scoffed, then slammed the door shut. She heard a key turn, locking her in. Turning her attention toward the windows, she discovered crude bars covering them. She was still the king's prisoner. She had half hoped he had forgotten about her and would let her go free. But an unknown and no doubt horrific future awaited her still. She recalled the unbridled hate in the king's eyes as he had stood over her. She remembered. And she despaired of any mercy for her as long as she was in his hands.

But she also thought of Mark's escape. She'd abetted the deed and rejoiced she could do so. Her joy was dampened though, when she remembered the arrow that had struck Aunt Anne. Her sweet Aunt Anne! She had to have survived her grievous wound. Agumbra would be too dark of a place if she had been taken from it!

Biting her lip, Rose realized she had to think on something else. Just as she had decided to begin exploring the inside of her prison, there was the sound of braying horses and wild feet running in the yard outside her window.

"You two! Come help!" she heard a voice cry out. She could have been wrong, but it sounded like Jack's voice. Whoever it was, they were frantic enough to pull her guards from their posts. She went to the window and saw several horses running wildly on the lawn. Then she heard a soft tap behind her.

She whipped around in surprise of the sound. A man was at her other window, watching her intently. She let out a small yell, but the man placed a finger over his lips, begging for her silence. Looking over her shoulder at the running men and horses, she wondered briefly if they could even hear her if she screamed. But she saw a guard roughly handling a horse he'd caught and realized it was those men who wished ill for her. Whoever the man at the window was, he was probably her friend.

She looked back, prepared to move toward him but froze in recognition. He was merely looking at her, no malice or deceit on his face. In fact, she felt like she was truly seeing him for the first time. She hesitated for a second longer and then walked over to him. It was her father. In silence, the two regarded each other, the bars separating them. His eyes searched her over, stopped at her shoulder, arm, and then the bruises on her face. She was surprised to see him wince slightly.

"I can't stay long," he began. "Jack said he could only give me a few minutes."

"Wait, Jack who works in the stable?"

"Yes. Adam told me he'd been looking for a way to help after he heard how you'd been hurt."

Tears filling her eyes, Rose wondered if she had been forgiven at last. She shook her head, afraid this wasn't real. Weariness filled her as she thought of the prospect of playing her father's games again. Though she'd left Hope to him, she still didn't know if she had made the right choice or how much she could trust him. She opened her eyes, looking at him levelly.

"What are you doing? Can't you just unlock the front door?"

"I have been displaced."

Her interest caught, she involuntarily took a step forward.

"What do you mean?"

"The king did not appreciate my attempt to rescue you."

"You tried to save me?" she repeated, unsure she'd heard him correctly.

"I would have tried again, but he would have killed me and then there would have been nobody to take care of Hope."

She rushed forward at those words and took his hand.

"Hope is with you? Is she safe?"

"Yes. Hope is safe."

He was silent then, and she took the time to examine him again. Something had changed on a fundamental level. She couldn't identify exactly what had changed, but she could sense this was her poppa, not her angry father. At least, she wanted to believe it was her poppa. She wanted to believe that idea so badly. If only she could know for sure!

"What happened to you? Why are you here?"

She wasn't accusing him of anything. She just needed to know the nature of the man who was talking to her. She had suffered the fickle facets of his character, his deception and lack of love, too many times to suddenly trust him. He seemed to understand and gathered his words.

"I have finally understood that I've hated the wrong man for years. You were right all along. I want to make amends now. As long as I live, Hope will be safe from the king. I swear it.

"I can't save you today," he continued. "I'm a wanted man and need to travel faster than your condition would allow according to Adam. But I had to see you. I had to tell you how sorry I am. I've hurt you so much and an apology doesn't seem enough."

He reached through, running a finger down her jaw line. She wanted to lean into his hand and let it rest on her cheek. She wanted to feel safe when she was with him, but she didn't think she could. She gave a sigh.

"I want to believe you, but we've been here before. That night you took Hope, you said similar things. Then you betrayed me."

It hurt to say, nevertheless it had to be said. With surprise, she saw regret and guilt invade his countenance. He withdrew his hand and rested his forehead in it.

"I remember. The plan had always been to deceive you. I knew if I paid you any attention you would do what I asked. Something happened I hadn't expected though. I saw you for the first time since you were born. I was able to look past your appearance being so like your mother and all the hurt seeing her in you usually brought. And when I did that, you were so like her. She was the good that was able to soften all my hard edges, and I became a better man with her in my life. I'd lost all of that when she died, and I wanted to hurt you because I thought you'd taken it from me."

Though his face retained some of its normal stoicism, Rose could see it cracking on a fundamental level, allowing his authenticity to shine through. She felt her heart wring in her chest at the sight of his eyes shimmering with tears.

"But I was wrong. When I actually looked at you, I saw the same goodness that could make me a better man again. You did things the exact same way she did, and it all caught me off guard. You smiled at me, and I thought about trying to deserve it. I had wild thoughts of trying to make all those changes then, but I was a coward. I listened to the lies of the king and let him give me the power I'd always wanted. The better man slipped back into the shadows.

"I don't know how you did it, but you could always see him.

I'm tired of keeping him in the shadows. I want to be the man you could always see and the Kingsman Lady Poynter envisioned. I don't know how long it will take, but I needed you to know I'm going to try for your sake."

The noise outside was calming and his eyes flicked toward it.

"I have to be short. They'll be here to check on you soon. I can't save you today, but I won't stop trying. The king is going to hurt you, he told me so, but you can't give up hope. I will come for you."

"Okay, poppa. I'll try," she said, her own tears tracing their way down her cheeks. He nodded to her and then reached inside his shirt, pulling out a pendant on a silver chain. She had never seen it before, and she realized he probably never took it off. Studying it intensely in the morning sun, he kissed it, and then placed it into her hand.

"This was your mother's. It's been my prized possession for eighteen years now. Will you keep it safe for me? I'll ask for it back on the day you're free and safe."

She nodded again, unable to speak. He pensively enclosed her scarred hand in both of his.

"It's time you had something else of hers as well," he whispered.

Her heart hammered all of a sudden. So many impossible dreams had just happened, it seemed preposterous the most impossible of all could also find substance. In anticipation, she held her breath as he placed a hand against her cheek.

"Jane," he whispered, "My own Jane. You have always been

the best of gifts. I've been too foolish to see it. Forgive me, little Jane? Oh please, forgive me?"

An emotion beyond happiness, beyond joy, flooded her battered heart. She leaned into his hand, the hand that would strike her no more, and cried.

"You said my name," she whimpered. "Oh poppa, you said my name!"

"Yes," he said smiling. "Even though it's eighteen years late for starting."

"Can you say it again?" she begged, needing proof this wasn't a dream. He tilted her chin up, her puffy eyes looking into his, and the sincerity she saw there made his blue eyes radiant.

"Jane. You are my little Jane. You are your mother's daughter and my good gift. And if it's not too late, I would like to try to be a good poppa to you."

Words escaped her. Instead she came forward to lean her forehead into his. He couldn't get his arms through the bars so he had to put both his hands behind her head and lean into her. She didn't care. It was the most meaningful embrace she'd ever received. For the first time in her life she belonged totally and completely. His hands were warm and gentle. Looking at her own as they clutched the bars, she saw that time had softened the scars there, and though they were still visible, they dulled in the light of her poppa's smile.

Approaching footsteps sounded from nearby.

"I love you, poppa."

"I love you too, Jane. And remember, I will come for you."

The key rattled in the lock, and he gave her a kiss on the top of her head. Then he was gone. She stared dumbly at the place where he had just stood, happiness practically paralyzing her. She didn't turn when the door opened.

"She's still here," the guard said to his partner before slamming and locking it again. But she didn't mind this time. They could lock her in a prison. They could beat and bruise her body. They could degrade and dehumanize her. But she was free. That was a truth as real as the silver promise she clutched in her hand. Ever since she was a little girl, she had hoped in a kingdom that would displace the broken one she lived in now. Even when it had been distant, she had hoped in it. Now the reconciliation with her father bolstered her faith to unshakable grounds. She was loved and she had her true name. She was a King's Maiden, guardian of the hope she looked forward to, and nothing could take such a powerful song from her. Rather, she would defy the darkness with its strength as long as she drew breath.

The guards were hot and flustered, and their mood was not improved when they heard the prisoner's clear voice ring out in the morning air.

The Golden East. The Golden East.
Soon, soon the dawn is breaking.
And soon we all, from great to least
Our joy, no more forsaking.

MARK AND THE Watchers travelled hard for three days. They

moved as fast as was possible while carrying his mother's lifeless body. They had insisted on bringing her along with them so she could receive a proper burial once they reached Haven, the secret home of the Watchers.

He had so many questions. They ran recklessly through his head pressing the boundaries of his reason, leaving him wondering where to start in his quest for understanding. He was walking with legends! He had always believed the poems of Rohirt were real, but it was a completely new experience to watch his faith being replaced by sight. The longing he'd felt his entire life was finally gone, having found the port it had sought all these years. His wonder fought for dominance with his grief, which was renewed every time he glanced at his mother's body, though. They had wrapped her in their extra blankets and cloaks, so he didn't actually see her growing colder and less life like, but he could sense it somehow.

The Watchers spoke sparingly and, though he was with them in an intimate setting, he wasn't able to ask his questions. They were obviously nervous about being so far from Haven with a body slowing them down. They kept moving, resting sparingly and in silence. After the first few days had past, the novelty waned, leaving only the acute awareness of his mother's corpse.

Thinking of his mother made him think of his father, and Mark wept silently for him. His father had been alive all these brutal years. What had the years been like for him, Mark wondered in the dark. Had he been scared? Had he tried to escape? How cruel had Richard and his been to him? Had he lost his mind and forgotten about them? Yet none of it mattered anymore because the king had him sent away to be murdered all over again. Mark's sudden toss into orphanhood twisted painfully in his chest during the long nights. In those moments, Mark half wished his mystery savior had been too late to stop the king's arrow from piercing his heart.

He recovered quickly from his morbid thoughts, thankful for his salvation from death. There was so much work to be done. Hope was still alive. He didn't know where she was, but he knew the king meant to hurt her. Somehow he could save her, and they could finally be together.

Being alive also meant he could seek vengeance on all those who had wronged his family. The king topped that list. Mark allowed his hatred to germinate in his soul, and if he were honest, he cultivated it rather than trying to prevent it taking root. He wished he could go back in time and kill the man when he had been prone before him on the gallows platform. That man had regained his feet only to kill Morgan and his mother, and Mark could have stopped it all. That guilt would be his for the rest of his life, but, instead of shame, Mark felt mostly anger. He would make the king answer for the blood he had spilled and the lives he had ruined. With every passing second Mark's resolve hardened. He didn't care how long it took. He would have his vengeance.

The king hadn't acted alone, though. The puppets who had willingly abetted him in these dastardly plots would bow to

Mark's wrath as well. And that meant the Cliftons, too. They had made these atrocities possible, rending them as guilty as if they had committed the actual deeds themselves. John and Rosemary would be punished as well. Once the sun rose, he was ashamed of such thoughts. That didn't mean he could stop them from returning and growing.

The end of three days found them deep in the Hytines. The way was unmarked and convoluted and Mark quickly lost his bearings. He persevered in silence, too ashamed to complain in the presence of legends. The sun was beginning to set, and he wondered how far away they could be. They were approaching a waterfall that crashed down a craggy bluff and filled a small pool at the bottom. He wondered if they would stop there for the night, but the leader pushed on up the craggy bluff. Mark followed with a sigh. Soon they were walking on a trail that disappeared behind the rushing water.

Someone had been carrying torches in readiness or lighting, and they were quickly set ablaze and passed out. Mark held his aloft and followed the Watcher in front of him. They entered into a cave that quickly snaked in so many directions his head began to spin. Focused on following, he refused to think of the complete darkness that loomed just outside the light of his torch.

But then they turned a corner, and he saw a patch of light. As they traveled toward it, the Watchers' moods became less and less terse. As they drew closer, the torches were extinguished. The path grew wider and they no longer needed to walk single file, so Mark walked abreast with Scaina. Blinking, the two of them stepped into the sunlight.

Mark's breath caught, and he stood with his mouth agape. It was beautiful. Their houses had been built to intertwine with the forest making it almost impossible to tell where one began and the other ended. A river ran through it, sparkling in the light of the dying sun. In fact it all sparkled, almost as if this was the place where the sun went away to sleep until the next day. From what he could see, the settlement stretched for miles and miles. Mark couldn't tell how far it reached. This was the cradle where all the hopes he'd clung to were nursed. The wind rushed against him and he could feel, deep inside, that this was the place he had longed for his whole life. He trembled, nearly overwhelmed by the beauty he was seeing.

His comrade slapped him good naturedly on the back, looking at it with pride.

"Welcome to Haven, Mark. Welcome home."

Twenty-nine

HE WAS DREAMING AGAIN. HE COULD SENSE IT immediately. He was out of body, yet still able to twist and turn as he travelled across distance and time. Faster and faster he went until he couldn't tell where he ended and the madness began. Still the world spun.

The ethereal being he inhabited slowed even though his surroundings remained convoluted. Sometimes in these dreams he inhabited a body he could feel with his hands. This time he was only able to share the emotions of the man he occupied. The man was angry, furious even. Something this man had wanted had escaped from him. And this wasn't his only loss. He had lost something else, too. Something he'd previously possessed. At least one of them had been taken by someone who caused the man great fear. Someone who wasn't supposed to exist. Seeing this someone in the flesh meant his kind and their magic were real, and, if their magic was real, that meant they could overthrow him. It meant someone was more powerful than he. Realizing all these things, the man trembled.

Not all was lost to this inhabited man though. He had gained a pair of valuable prisoners. One would talk, both would suffer, and this gave him pleasure. Though not as much pleasure as the news he'd just received. He was going to learn the dark magic. With the dark magic subservient to him there were none who could stand in his way, not even the mysterious someone. The pleasure this prospect brought him mixed with his anger and fear creating an ugly trifecta, increasing his determination. He would not rest until he was the power of Agumbra. It didn't matter how many had to fall on his way to making his dream come true. And, no matter the foe, he knew he would win. He always won.

Foreboding sitting heavy on his chest, Leonard woke with a start. His sheets were soaked with sweat despite the cool breeze coming through the window. He ran his hands over his face, partly to wake up, partly to make sure he had completely returned to his body. He always did after these dreams, but when they were as vibrant as this one had been, he wondered if he had left part of himself in the nether world.

Getting out of bed as quietly as possible, Leonard walked to the window. As he stared north, he drank in the night. He didn't know why his consciousness insisted on connecting him to the king of Deteen through these awful dreams. It was hardly ever pleasant, and fewer times was it helpful. It only filled him with pain as he was forced to remember Deteen and all he had left and longed for there. If only he could wield the Magic better.

Maybe then he could protect his mind when he was sleeping.

A stirring behind him roused him from his thoughts. Asuwith was approaching with her heavy tread. He waited until she was beside him before looking to her. The moonlight reflected off her face, accenting her mammoth belly. Much to Asuwith's relief, their first child was due any day now. Watching his wife now, Leonard didn't feel the joy and panic he usually felt when he thought about his approaching fatherhood. The dream was still sticking too close to his skin.

"You dreamed again, didn't you?" she asked him.

"Yes."

"Was it bad?"

"Yes. Something happened in Deteen, and I fear it has made the king a far more determined foe. I wish the council would listen to me. I wish they would send a ship north so we could learn what is actually happening. These dreams leave me guessing while also filling me with deep dread."

She leaned into him, offering comfort. His hand found her rounded belly and was rewarded with a kick from their child. Jumping in unison, the couple laughed at their joint reaction. The mood lightened, but Leonard still couldn't shake himself free of the feelings that had come in the dream.

"You're making progress with the council, Leonard. With you at the helm we are destined to send ships north eventually."

"I know. It's just...," he said, looking north again.

"It's just what?" Asuwith asked.

"It's just, I hope it's not too late when we finally decide to go," he said, measuring his words. He shivered as the north wind blew against his damp skin. Drawing Asuwith close, he spoke again, "A season of midnight is headed for Deteen, and I can only pray she's strong enough to weather it until the dawn."

About the Author

A native of Springfield, IL, when J. E. Kestner isn't staring into space hoping for inspiration or preparing to hike the Appalachian Trail, she can be found staring into space hoping for inspiration or preparing to hike the Appalachian Trail.

Made in the USA
Lexington, KY
16 February 2018